Secondhand Sister

Secondhand Sister

Rhett DeVane

Secondhand Sister
© 2015 Rhett DeVane
All rights reserved

Date of first publication: October 3, 2015
Published by Writers4Higher
Tallahassee, Florida, USA

Cover design by Elizabeth Babski, Babski Creative Studios

ISBN: 978-0692528549

Library of Congress Control number: 2015952576

Printed in the United States of America

Dedication

In memory of my sweet sister Melody DeVane-Kight, who was by no means a secondhand sister.

I hope you feel the sisterly love up there, hon. And you'd best save me some chocolate.

To all of my earthly sisters-by-good-fortune, thank you for being in my life.

And to all of the people displaced and harmed by Hurricane Katrina. May time soften your wounds.

Acknowledgements

Rhett wishes to thank the following people:

My family, again. For my brother Jimmy DeVane, for suggesting the whole switched-at-birth idea. Good one, bro.

Denise Fletcher and the entire Fletcher gang, my heart-family, for their continued love and support.

The city of Chattahoochee, Florida, for being such a memorable hometown.

The Wild Women Writers critique authors—Donna Meredith, Peggy Kassees, Susan Womble, and Hannah Mahler.

Tallahassee Writers Association: a group of the most supportive fellow scribes on the planet. We have all taken turns talking each other down from the ledge. Writing is truly not a competition, more a good jog with others who share this wacky life.

Elizabeth Babski for her excellent graphic design and friendship.

Editor extraordinaire and friend Gina Edwards. I'm sure I make you laugh and shake your head, hon.

Adrian Fogelin for her expert advice and friendship. Also, the Fiction Among Friends Retreat compatriots. Love you all!

Law enforcement expert and friend Kathy Kennedy.

Medical/nursing information expert and friend Mary Menard, RN.

My coworkers for attending book functions and listening to me either whoop or whine. What an amazing group of people, also my friends!

My network of old and new friends, near and far.

My patients—bless your hearts, you have been there every step of this journey.

My readers. You are the reason I get to have this much fun.

And to this universe for allowing me to create. Being a writer means living with a host of characters yammering away inside my head. It is a blessing, most days.

At Twilight

When day is ending,
And night starts mending
The havoc and strife
That makes up one's life
When sweet dreams wipe away
The troubles of the day
This is the time that I like best
When everything is at rest.

When the sun goes down
And shadows creep around
To wrap a coat of darkness
Around cares and distress
When the whip-poor-will's call
Echo beyond the falls
This is the time I like best
When everything is at rest.

By the late Theresa Gibson DeVane

Chapter One

Fall 2006
Chattahoochee, Florida

A tiny brass bell jangled when Mary-Esther pushed open the glass door of the Borrowed Thyme Bakery and Eatery. As if it mattered when she entered anywhere.

She chose a bistro table next to the row of windows, plopped into a chair, and rubbed her burning eyes. Just to sit down, somewhere other than behind the wheel.

Two hundred and thirteen dollars left. Shouldn't waste a quarter. But the aroma of brewed coffee snared her, more than the smell of cooked bacon and warm cinnamon.

A man wearing a white chef's apron appeared by her table with a carafe. Thank the saints. "Coffee this morning?"

Mary-Esther met his eyes. The man blanched and his hand shook. Wow. Did she look as kicked-dog as she felt?

"Are you passing through?" He idled beside her table.

Passing through. Yep. Like I have a place to be. "On my way to a town near here. I . . . I've been on the road a bit." *Since my home got washed away in Hurricane Katrina,* she often added to explain her vagabond clothing and hair. "I must look a mess."

"Oh. No. Sorry." The man wiped one hand across the apron. "You remind me of someone I once knew."

She turned a chunky, white porcelain mug over in its saucer. "I'll take that coffee. As long as it's black, strong, and *not* decaf."

He poured. Steam curled. "Let me tend my pancakes before they burn and I'll be back to take your order. Menu's on the clip."

Mary-Esther took a sip—no cream, no sugar. She closed her eyes for a moment, savoring the flavor. Wasn't the chicory blend she craved, but better than fast food sludge. If they charged four bucks a cup, it was still worth it.

Even in their low-rent borough, her Nana Boudreau had insisted on decent coffee. Loss sucked at her. That last failed marriage, Nana Boudreau, and her mother.

Then her city, ground to mud.

Maybe the caffeine would ease the weariness. She couldn't remember a time in the past months when she hadn't felt bone-deep tired.

Mary-Esther watched the man scurry back to the griddle. Didn't seem like the short-order cook type. Words too precise, no Southern drawl. In a few minutes, he had delivered loaded plates to nearby diners, refilled mugs, and once again stood by her table, giving her that same odd stare. "Decided?" he asked.

Mary-Esther twirled a stray hank of auburn hair around one finger. Maybe she could stick to coffee. Shouldn't spend any more, but dear God, did this place ever smell good. "Give me an egg over easy and one piece of wheat toast."

"I make a mean Southern buttermilk biscuit. Sure you won't try one with your egg?"

The smile barely made it to her lips. "Sure."

He left again.

She picked at one torn cuticle until blood pearled at the edges. Suppose it fit in with what remained of her ragged, crap pile life.

Moments later, the man—Joe Fletcher, according to the embroidered script on his apron—slid a plate in front of her.

She stared at the dish. "That is the biggest biscuit I have ever seen."

"Cathead biscuit. Made the old-fashioned way. Recipe belonged to my late mother-in-law." Joe tipped his head toward a glass display shelf behind the cash register. "That was her favorite mixing bowl, up there." He then motioned to an oak sideboard. "Help yourself to the homemade jellies and honey. The tupelo's very good, a premium honey. Beekeeper is local. His tested out at ninety-eight percent pure. I was accustomed to buckwheat honey, up in New York."

He dashed back to the tiny kitchen, but Mary-Esther caught him studying her. Like he was trying to see through her skin. It probably looked dirty too. Other than spot cleaning in rest stop bathrooms, she hadn't had a decent bath since she left that last shelter in Alabama.

She hated to hurt his feelings, but walking the two feet to the sideboard would take more energy than she had. Sitting slumped, Mary-Esther Day Alford Fernandez Sloat slathered on butter and nipped pieces of the hot biscuit. Perfectly cooked, but her mouth tasted like delta mud. The runny egg yolk made her stomach roil. Crazy, starving yet too tired to eat. She wrapped the remaining biscuit in a napkin then pushed the plate aside.

Mary-Esther focused absently out the plate glass window facing West Washington Street—Chattahoochee's main business thoroughfare. It had taken her less than two minutes to drive from one city limit sign to the other. Except for the state mental hospital at the east end, it looked like every other small Florida Panhandle town she had passed through. Still, she preferred the secondary roads to the interstate.

No doubt, rows of cozy houses lined the other streets in this town. Houses with contented families going about mundane duties—watering flowers, chasing tow-headed toddlers, gossiping to neighbors over mugs of coffee or syrupy sweet tea. Same way in New Orleans, only the chicory coffee was stronger and most folks on her old street didn't budge until mid-day.

Did these people dream of escaping to somewhere, *any*where else? Didn't they know how lucky they were?

Mary-Esther cradled the mug. For a little over a year, since nature's fury had wiped the Louisiana and Mississippi coasts like a damp rag dragged across spilled gumbo, her home had been a sun-bleached blue Chevy van.

Fine for drug-crazed hippies, but not for a middle-aged woman with little money and less hope.

Chapter Two

A few miles east of Chattahoochee, Mary-Esther pulled into a weedy rest stop, double-checked the locks, and crawled onto the thin mattress in the back. In spite of the caffeine, she fell asleep. Six hours later, she jerked awake and drove the remaining twenty miles into Quincy.

A Saint Christopher medallion dangled from the rearview mirror. Patron saint of travelers. Mary-Esther sent up a rote prayer. *Carry me safely to my destined place.*

She pulled into a vertical parking slot on a paved cul-de-sac and turned the key. For a full minute, the engine bucked and shook, and finally died. The scent of scorched oil filtered into the cabin. The low sign off State Highway 90 had read: Gadsden County Sheriff's Department, W. A. Woodham Justice Center. Mary-Esther double-checked the address of the hospital listed in faded print on her birth certificate.

"Great. A dead end."

What was the point? Did she seriously believe evidence of her roots lay in the sandy North Florida soil? And if she did uncover some shred of truth, what then?

An aged Southern magnolia tree shaded a broad patch of grass near the parking lot. Even during the mild Deep South winters, the waxy, thick, green leaves would remain. Her favorite magnolia shaded Nana Boudreau's back yard, or it used to. Who knew what it looked like now? If it was as she had seen in the TV clips of her borough, the winds had probably shredded it into twisted knurls.

She sighed, pulled a diet soda and half of a bologna and cheese sandwich from a battered Styrofoam cooler, and shoulder-bumped the driver's side door until it opened with a loud groan. She walked a few feet and threw a frayed towel onto the ground in the tree's shade. *I can eat lunch in peace, if nothing else.* With all the patrol cars lined up, who would be dumb enough to bother her?

The solitude lasted for a short while before a deputy stepped from the building's double doors and walked toward a line of patrol vehicles. He opened the door of the third car, stared in her direction, then clicked it shut and sauntered toward her.

Oh, wonderful. Would he be another person prompting her to move along? All she asked was a few minutes. Cram a sandwich down, beneath this tree, then gone. *Like I was never here.*

"Afternoon, ma'am." He punctuated the greeting with a head dip.

Mary-Esther brushed the mayonnaise and breadcrumbs from the corners of her lips. "Afternoon, officer."

"Having yourself a picnic, I see."

People had such a penchant for stating the obvious. "Seemed as good a place as any."

"There are some benches off the backside of the building, if you'd rather not sit on the ground."

Heat rose to Mary-Esther's face. She was a genuine sucker for a man in a uniform, no matter if he had spare padding around his midsection and a fair share of wrinkles. And this one had one of those deep, chocolaty voices. "Thank you. I kind of like this spot, unless it's trespassing or something."

"Not at all." The officer, *J. Blount* from his gold-tinted nametag, looked up. "Yep. This is a fine old tree. Blooms the size of grapefruit, come late spring. Glad they didn't cut 'er down when they widened the parking lot."

Mary-Esther grappled for a conversation point. Exactly what did one talk about to a local deputy? Sergeant Blount squinted in the direction of the parked van. "Passing through, are you? Noticed your Louisiana plates."

Ah, the real reason for the polite chat. Was she a threat to order and harmony? "I was looking for something." She motioned with her head. "But I found the sheriff's department instead."

When he didn't offer a reply, Mary-Esther crumpled the plastic wrap and soiled napkin into a paper bag. "The Gadsden County Hospital. I was born here." She swiped a hand in the direction of the building. "At least, this is the address on my birth certificate."

"Yeah. Used to be on this spot. That was years back, though. Library shared our building for a while, but they moved out to a new location too. The hospital went up about two miles east of here, off Highway 90."

"Really?" She stood and shook the dried grass from the towel. "I'll head that way, then."

Sergeant Blount rocked back on his heels and bounced, his thumbs tucked beneath the wide, black leather belt holding his gun and an assortment of snap-on accessories. "It shut down a few months back. Money problems."

Mary-Esther's shoulders sagged. "Great."

"What're you looking for, exactly? Not trying to pry into your business, mind you. But I've lived in these parts all my life. Maybe I can point you in the right direction. If not, surely someone in the department can. C'mon inside with me."

Mary-Esther pinched her lips together and fought the press of tears. So many people had offered assistance since Hurricane Katrina. Well-meaning folks. Folks who arrived with truckloads of ice and food. Pats on the back and hugs. Staffing shelters for weeks past the storm. Trying their best to help her put her life back together.

Like that was possible.

She threw the towel and trash into the van and followed the officer into the building. Inside, a sixty-ish woman with tightly coiffured hair in an odd shade of orange looked up from a computer console.

"Sheila, this lady needs some help." Officer Blount nodded towards Mary-Esther, and she gave a brief rundown.

The woman tapped her chin with a manicured fingernail. "Don't know of any of the doctors who would still be around from then. Tell you who might be able to help, though. My Aunt LaJune. She was a nurse at Gadsden County Hospital back in the day. She's in the assisted living home about four blocks from here. Some days, Aunt Juney can't remember what she had for breakfast, but she can recall years ago like it was yesterday."

The woman scratched a name and address on a yellow sticky note and handed it to Mary-Esther. "Tell her Sheila sent you. Aunt Juney will talk your head off. I don't know if I'm helping or hindering by sending you there. Her mind wanders, so you'll have a time of it keeping her on track."

Mary-Esther tucked the slip of paper into her pocket. "I'm used to wandering."

Mary-Esther parked the van in a tight spot opposite a gold vintage Cadillac and contemplated going inside. Sewanee Springs. What a name for a retirement home. Bet there wasn't an actual spring for miles.

The facility's white-columned, faux Dixie mansion façade didn't fit with its true nature. Lanky, well-dressed plantation gentlemen smoking cigars and sipping mint juleps beside their hoop-skirted consorts would have been better suited to the setting than the scattering of elderly residents taking in the mid-afternoon breeze.

"What the heck." She turned the key and tugged it from the ignition. The engine wheezed twice then fell silent. It would probably leave the usual pools of fluids on the pavement.

A reception room with overstuffed chairs and mahogany tables continued the graceful old-folks-at-home theme. The bubble-haired woman behind a spotless desk glanced up and smiled. "Welcome to Sewanee Springs." Her voice oozed Deep South charm. "How may I help you?"

Hep yew? Did people really talk like that, all syrupy and slow? Sure, New Orleans *was* part of the South, but none of *her* people spoke exaggerated Southern. "I'm here to see LaJune Eldridge."

"Is Miz LaJune expecting you?" The woman's thin, penciled eyebrows arched.

"No, but I'd like to speak with her."

"I'm afraid I cannot give out her private information without her consent."

National security? Homeland protection? What? Mary-Esther mustered her best congenial attitude. Since the terrorist attacks on the Twin Towers in 2001, people didn't have tolerance for pushy strangers asking questions. Not even in a small town in the middle of Podunk.

"Could you perhaps be so kind as to phone her and ask her to meet me down here?"

The woman looked her up and down, her lips pursed.

"It's really important. I've come such a long way." Mary-Esther paused. Should she play the sympathy trump card? "I drove in from New Orleans, you see."

It worked. The woman's face morphed instantly from guarded to gracious. She patted her hand to her upper chest in a genteel gesture meant to convey either sympathetic shock or an attack of gas. "You poor dear! Did you go through that dreadful Hurricane Katrina?"

Mary-Esther almost smiled at the way the woman added extra syllables into dreadful. No need to fabricate the answer. "Yes. I did."

"My husband's second cousin lives in Biloxi, Mississippi. Or he used to. His home ended up flattened like a pancake, bless his heart. The foundation and some steps were all left standing. He and his family are staying up in Georgia with kinfolk."

"I know how he feels. I don't have a house to go back to either."

The woman picked up the phone and jabbed a series of numbers. She returned the headset to its base after a short conversation.

"Miz LaJune is in the activity room at the present. It's bingo day. I can't interrupt The Bingo, not for the President himself. But I did let our activities director know to send Miz LaJune down as soon as the last set of numbers is called." She glanced at the gilded wall clock to her right. "They should be finishing up in a few minutes."

The receptionist motioned to a spacious room off the main foyer. "If you'd like, you may wait in our parlor. Feel free to change the station on the TV, or there's usually a magazine or two lying around. There's coffee, iced tea and water on a table immediately down the hallway. Please, *do* help yourself."

Chapter Three

Never a cheerful early riser, Hattie Davis Lewis bumbled into the bright country kitchen to pour a cup of strong black coffee. Ugh. Monday. Again. How did that keep happening? One breath at a time and be thankful for it, her effervescent mother would have reminded her. Shammie, her aging Persian, head-butted her leg. Hattie dumped a handful of kibble into the cat's bowl.

Her husband Holston sat at the long oak table with their adopted daughter. Splatters of cereal smeared Sarah Chuntian's round face. Most of the butter from her toast hadn't made it past her lips. Every time Hattie looked at the child, her heart felt warm. She blessed the day they had rescued her from that crowded orphanage in China.

The toddler chattered happily to her father as he alternately perused the daily paper and glanced at the network news. Sure, the child was still in the dreaded terrible two's, but so far, they hadn't been horrible. Hattie managed to have more meltdowns than Sarah Chuntian Davis.

Hattie brushed by long enough to kiss both of them then withdrew for her sanctuary. They wouldn't miss her. She started the day as usual, in her late father's butt-worn rocking chair on the shady front porch of the family farmhouse. Several natural springs laced the Davis homestead three miles south of Chattahoochee, and the gentle hills gave the property a mountain retreat ambiance. The solid, wood-framed house, a home the family fondly referred to as "The Hill," stood atop a slight rise at the end of a long, sandy drive named Bonnie Lane.

The roof leaked in three places, outside breezes crept inside through small crevices, and termites had chewed holes in a few of the wall studs. Hattie had once managed to burn the kitchen to smut with an unattended grease pot. Still, the Davis house had remained standing through hail showers, lightning strikes, and any number of raging tropical storms and hurricanes. If a structure possessed a personality, the house her father built would be that of a kindly grandmother with a huge, pillowed bosom: a woman who hugged away hurt with fierce, protective love.

Above the inherited money and stocks, above the rolling acres of woodland Hattie shared with her older brother Bobby, the house shone as the most precious thing Dan and Tillie Davis had left their daughter. Though Hattie rambled following high school graduation and college, The Hill drew her back.

The last place on earth she'd planned to be was where she ended up, sitting on this porch nursing her morning cup of coffee.

As her late mother had often commented, "If you chase after a dream long enough, sometimes it'll catch up to you."

The family mutt licked the tip of Hattie's fingers and pushed his cold wet nose into her free hand. She scratched Spackle's favorite itchy spot across the bridge of his long snout, a wiry white thatch of hair marking the brownish-red fur.

"Spackle, patchwork-pooch," she cooed. "Who's Mama's good boy?"

Jake Witherspoon, Hattie's best friend and owner of the business connected to hers, had named the mixed-breed pup. The animal had joined the family during the renovation of Jake's family mansion, a time when most everything, moving or stationary, sported at least one smear of spackle or paint.

Hattie looked down Bonnie Lane. Though thick trees hid the houses farther down, Hattie sensed the comforting presence of her nearest neighbors. Her remaining sibling, Bobby, had moved to the land with his wife Leigh and son Josh, a couple of years back following their mother's death. The couple's cypress log home huddled in the forest on a separate driveway off the main lane. Old family friends occupied the other house, a modest ranch-style dwelling close to the state highway.

Hattie mentally tabbed through her day. Only one massage therapy client scheduled in the main street clinic in the early afternoon. Thank God. Though she dearly loved the profession, her left shoulder had begun to complain in the last few months. Some days, it hurt to reach overhead to shampoo her hair.

She slung one leg over the rocker arm and pushed with the big toe of her other foot until the chair pitched back and forth.

Her thoughts drifted to her adopted child's namesake, Hattie's older sister Sarah Davis.

The middle child. The lost baby. The one who didn't stick around long enough to enjoy sibling rivalry.

Odd, how often Sarah had crept into her mind lately.

On The Hill, no one said her sister's name. Sarah remained shrouded in mystery, a ghostly figure on the periphery of the Davis family.

Hattie recalled speaking directly to her mother Tillie about Sarah only once. Bobby had perpetrated some unforgivable act of brotherly meanness, and Hattie snuffled to her mother. "If my sissy was here, he wouldn't pick on me anymore!"

Her tone had been, no doubt, whiny and high-pitched.

"My big sissy would be pretty and she would protect me. She would squash Bobby Davis like a cockroach!"

The flash of pain that had flickered across her mother's features froze in Hattie's memory like a Polaroid snapshot. Hattie had cried bitterly, not so much over Bobby's infraction, but because of how she had somehow hurt her mother.

When their adopted baby arrived in the States, Hattie bestowed the name on her. Hattie enjoyed the feel of her sister's name on her lips.

But the Sarah she had never gotten a chance to know still haunted her thoughts.

Spackle nudged her hand and she ruffled the hair around his ears.

How would my sister be as an adult? Hattie swilled coffee and nestled into her favorite sisterly vision. Sarah—wispy and beautiful with fine, aristocratic features, a boon from Tillie's side of the family.

Hattie imagined them seeing each other every day, or speaking on the phone—long, lazy conversations about everything and nothing. Grumbling over the high price of gas and the irritating traits of beloved husbands.

They would shop for hours for shoes and sip mocha Frappuccino with mounds of chocolate-dusted whipped topping. When Hattie discovered a new author, Sarah would be the first person to share the latest novel. Her sister would return the borrowed book. And never dog-ear the pages.

There would be Thanksgiving and Christmas holidays, when they could take turns cooking the fabulous family meals, served on the heirloom Limoges china.

They'd occasionally squabble. Sisters do. Nothing important.

"Want a refill?" Holston's deep voice came from behind her.

Hattie's hand jerked involuntarily, nearly upending the half-full cup. "Um . . . sure."

Holston stepped onto the porch and poured a warm-up. Fragrant steam mingled with the morning mists sifting through her favorite tree, the magnolia her father had planted the year Hattie graduated from high school.

"You're thinking awfully hard for first thing." He leaned against one of the porch supports.

Holston was a transplanted New Yorker, or *Damn Yankee*, as her late Aunt Piddie Longman had pegged him. After he vacated a high-pressure Wall Street job to write, his highfaluting, social-climbing wife left him for her orthodontist. When Holston arrived in Chattahoochee in the late nineties to cover the hate-crime assault on her heart-deep friend Jake Witherspoon, the town had drawn Holston in.

Now, living on The Hill with a cherub-faced daughter, one mutt dog, and a fat cat, Hattie and Holston had settled into a union as comfortable as hole-pocked blue jeans. How in God's green earth had she lucked into such a man? Drop-dead, honey-hush gorgeous with thick, black hair tinged with gray at the temples. He had no idea the snake-charmer effect he had on people, especially women.

Hattie flushed with warmth, looking at her husband. Standing there with that smile teasing his lips. Wasn't pure luck and circumstance that had brought Holston into her life. No, that was due to Aunt Piddie, the ultimate matchmaker. Not that Holston needed any help.

"I am perfectly able to ponder deeply in the morning, thank you very much." Hattie slumped deeper into the rocking chair. "I *can* function before nine, you know."

"Right." Holston's lip lifted higher on one side, showing off a dimple. "By the way, Shammie acts like she doesn't feel well. She barely touched the food you put down."

"Probably another hairball." The aging Persian required more and more care in her kitty golden years. "I'll give her some of that gross medicine before I shower."

"Appreciate that. I really need my hands intact."

"She licks that God-awful paste right off my fingers."

Holston opened the screened door. "Oh, she takes it from me too. No problem. But she gets a little jubilant and bites down when she's done."

Chapter Four

Elvina Houston stabbed a red-hot painted nail at the computer. "You ain't gonna beat me, you hear."

It beeped. Sassed by a dang piece of technology.

Another day, another dollar as the supreme ruler of the Triple C Day Spa and Salon, and head of Chattahoochee's little-old-lady hotline. Heavy responsibilities.

After her best friend Piddie Longman passed away, Elvina had taken the wheel and the Triple C evolved into the social nucleus of Chattahoochee and several surrounding communities. Nothing slipped past the scrutiny of the day spa compatriots and their faithful clientele.

Mandy Andrews, head stylist, paused at the door to the reception room with a steaming mug of Earl Grey in hand. "Mornin', Elvina. How's Buster doing?"

"That dang cat is fine. The doc sewed his ear back on. Reckon I'm going to have to stop letting the little fool roam. It's not like he has any working male parts anymore. He only goes out womanizing as a consultant. There's a black and white Tomcat somewhere behind me that exists only to beat the tarnation out of poor Buster."

Elvina frowned at the monitor. Lord knows how she'd survive the transition to this century.

Give her a columned book, and she could color-code and move massage, manicure, and hair-stylist appointments around until the Second Coming of Christ. But learn the computer at her age? It would take a reservoir of green tea to ricochet her around the learning curve.

Mandy peered over Elvina's shoulder. "What do I have first thing?"

Elvina tapped a couple of keys, grumbled when she didn't reach the desired screen, tapped again. "Bertha Littleton is coming at nine for a color. Why you don't convince the woman to go gray is a mystery to me. No matter how much energy you put into it, I swannee, her hair looks more like a Halloween fright wig every year."

"I do the best I can working with what she has left, 'Vina. Bertha's happy. Suppose that's what counts most." Mandy took a loud swill of tea.

"She tries to do it herself between visits to you. And I'm here to testify, the color she comes up with doesn't occur in nature."

The click of the back entrance door sounded deep in the rear of the mansion. Elvina glanced up from the monitor. "Bound to be Evelyn. She's coming in to get a head start on the jackets she's making for the holidays."

Mandy checked the time on the ornate wall clock behind Elvina's desk. "Unreal."

Elvina nodded at the supreme seamstress when she stepped into the room.

"Mornin', glory!" Evelyn said in singsong. Shopping bags hung from both arms.

"Mornin', yourself. I don't recall ever seeing you vertical this time of the morning, Ev." Mandy flicked a conspiratorial wink toward Elvina.

"No time to sleep." Evelyn blew out a breath. "The holidays will be upon us before we know it. And chenille is *not* the easiest fabric to tame. It'll take me longer than that quilted satin I used last year. But . . . one must keep up with current fashion."

"What are you and Joe doing for Thanksgiving?" Mandy asked Evelyn.

"The usual." Evelyn shifted the bags. "Probably out to The Hill. Hattie has more space for the family. By the way Elvina, I do hope you'll come this year. Mandy, you and Bull too, if you'd like. Heaven knows, there'll be plenty of food to go around. We never know how many will show up. Hattie likes to take in folks who don't have anywhere to go. She's like Tillie was. Heart the size of Texas."

"Thanks for the invite, Evelyn," Mandy said. "Bull and I are considering taking a Caribbean cruise this year."

Elvina sniffed. "Floating around on a party-barge the size of a football field is no way to spend a family holiday, but suit yourself. As for me, I wouldn't pass up the meal on The Hill. It makes me not miss my dear friend Piddie so much." Her eyes burned. Time had passed since her best friend had died at age ninety-eight, but Elvina's grief knew no bounds.

Every morning before beginning her day, she visited the small flower memorial garden behind the mansion, the final resting place of Piddie's ashes. Or part of them, at least. The rest lay in Alabama, scattered across the plot of her departed husband. Leave it to Piddie Longman to have a vacation grave.

14

"To each her own," Mandy said. "I look forward to acres of food I don't have to fix myself. It'll be the first time in as long as I can remember that Bull and I went on a trip, other than to a dang fishing tournament or to a Bass Pro shop."

Evelyn turned to head back to her sewing workroom then spun around. The bags tethered on her arms banged against her body. "I almost forgot! The strangest thing happened to Joe."

Elvina leaned toward her. Second only to the Triple C, Joe's main street eatery claimed the award for town gossip. Biscuits and fresh coffee provided a big draw for community relations.

"Some lady came in for breakfast," Evelyn said. "Joe said she was the spitting image of Tillie. Really unsettled him."

"Did he find out where she was from? She staying around town?" Elvina asked.

"Joe didn't say," Evelyn said.

Elvina frowned. "Too bad she didn't stop by here. Joe, bless his heart, is not inquisitive enough for my liking."

Evelyn agreed. "He hates to meddle."

"You'd think after all those years spent coaching those mental patients up at the State Hospital, your husband would've gotten the hang of ferreting details. If you don't pry the lid off a person, you'll never see what's inside." Elvina snapped her head up and down for emphasis.

Mandy pulled a face. "Lord help, 'Vina. You sound more like Piddie every day."

The compliment flowed over Elvina like warm honey. "That, I consider high praise."

Mary-Esther waited in the cheerful Sewanee Springs parlor with its pillowy chairs and coordinating couches, widescreen plasma television, piano, and tasteful framed art. No matter how fancy the surroundings, facilities for the aged struck her as waiting rooms for the final boarding call. And they all had *that* smell.

Mary-Esther harbored an affinity for the elderly. Most appeared to share the same emotions keeping her company: fear, confusion, abandonment.

In the hall, two female residents pushed walkers. They paused long enough to give her the once-over then wheeled past.

Years back, she had worked as an aide in a nursing home. Draining job. Though she tried to leave the feelings behind her when she pushed from the facility's front door, the sum of their afflictions stuck to her

15

along with the scent of stale urine. Still, she tried her best to listen to them, to make them feel someone, anyone, cared.

That smell shoved her into the past and her mother's final months. Mary-Esther struggled to push down the melancholy. She'd had her fill of hospital rooms, brisk nurses, and abrupt physicians. Faced with their own inability to turn fate in a patient's favor, most preferred distance to empathy.

Yet, there had been times when she too had become frozen to her mother's scuffling efforts to live. Toward the end, Loretta Boudreau Day boiled in the soup of her septic kidneys. Mary-Esther prayed for The End.

Guilt waited to escort her through the funeral. Guilt remained her companion. It sat right here next to her now, breathing the stale Sewanee Springs air.

A shuffling noise sounded from the hall. A squat toad of a woman pushed a silk flower-decorated walker into the parlor and squinted at her through smudged glasses. LaJune Eldridge, no doubt. The family resemblance to Sheila, the dispatcher, was clear. LaJune's dyed hair glowed, the pink of county fair cotton candy. Why couldn't old women settle for plain white?

"You the one asking after me?" the woman inquired.

Mary-Esther stood, walked across the room, and offered her hand, careful to grasp LaJune's hand gently. Old joints and bones never appreciated a firm handshake. "Yes. I'm Mary-Esther Sloat. Thank you for seeing me."

LaJune motioned to the couch. "We'd best sit. My back hurts too bad to stand and pass the time. Too many years of lifting and tugging patients. I was a nurse, in my day." The old woman toddled to one of the long couches, backed into position, and locked the hand brakes on the walker before slowly lowering herself.

Mary-Esther chose a chair next to the old woman and sat.

"You bring my tomatoes?" LaJune's green eyes sought hers.

The question stalled Mary-Esther for a moment. "No, uh . . . no tomatoes. Your niece at the sheriff's office said you might be able to help me with something."

"Oh?"

"I'm looking for some of my relatives, if they still live in these parts."

LaJune pulled a hand-crocheted wrap across her lap and legs. "Are you cold? I am. It's like a deep freeze in here."

"No, I'm comfortable. Thank you."

16

"Back when I worked at the hospital, I wore the thinnest scrubs money could buy. The public spaces were okay, but the patients' rooms steamed like private saunas." The old woman chuckled. "Now here I am, complaining of the cold." She stopped, looked at Mary-Esther. "Why'd you say you were here?"

"My mother was married at one time, to a man named William Harvey Day. Does the name sound at all familiar?"

LaJune's white eyebrows knit together. "Day. Day. Lemmee see . . . used to be a family of Days lived out the Havana highway. Don't believe they're still around, though."

Mary-Esther took a deep breath and released it. How could she get answers when she didn't know what questions to ask? For the next few minutes, she related the story of her mother's final days. The details of the moment that doctor told her she couldn't save her mother spewed out: the sickly green shine of the fluorescent lights on wear-slickened carpet, the stained orange plastic chairs. No money. No insurance. No hope.

"I know all about that organ donation thing," LaJune said. "I may be old, but I still read my nursing journals." She drummed one finger on her leg. "Just because you're family, doesn't mean you're suitable."

"I started to doubt we were *even* related," Mary-Esther said. "Our blood types didn't match either."

"Still doesn't mean squat." LaJune leaned closer. "What made you suspect you weren't her daughter?"

"Don't know, exactly. Guess I always felt like Loretta and I were from different planets."

LaJune nodded. "Somewhat typical with a mother and daughter."

"I had a DNA test. Swabbed my cheek. Took hair from Loretta's brush."

LaJune let out a low whistle. "Bet that cost you a pretty penny."

"Two hundred dollars I didn't have. Begged and borrowed to scrape it together." Why was she confiding in this old woman? Had to talk to someone.

Mary-Esther stood and paced. "Loretta Boudreau Day left this earth believing she had passed on her genes. Or *did* she?" She stopped. The burst of energy spent itself. She sank back into the chair. "Wouldn't be the first time she lied to me."

Why bring all of this to the surface? The cardboard boxes in the van corralled all that remained of that life. Her treasured rock collection. And Loretta's ashes.

"Here's the thing, Mrs. Eldridge. I don't have a clue where to look . . ." Mary-Esther threaded her fingers through her hair. "I came to Quincy because, at least as far as my birth certificate states, I was born here on April 1, 1946. Seemed a logical place to start, at the time." Her shoulders curved forward. "I'm grasping at straws."

"April Fool's Day. What a delightful day to be born. Opens you up to all kinds of things, I'd think." The old woman leaned over and gave Mary-Esther's hand a pat. "Honey, I don't get many visitors. Most of my people have died off. My husband and I were never graced with children. Sheila drops by from time to time. She's a good girl. But for the most part, my days are long. Glad you landed here."

Small wonder LaJune had ended up in the nursing field. Her compassion felt genuine.

"And," LaJune continued, "call me by my first name. Mrs. Eldridge was my mother-in-law."

"You got it, LaJune." Seemed strange. Nana taught her respect for her elders. That included proper titles.

"I haven't ever been much on names, even when I was young like you. I confuse sounds, a defect I've lived with all my life." The old woman's lips curled up. "I've been to Boston, but never to Baltimore. Or is it the other way around?" Her brow crimped. "Both of them start with a B and they're both up north. Like now, I couldn't attest if you are Mary Evelyn or Maybelle. I know it starts with an *M*."

"Bet that's a problem for you."

"Only when I worked in Labor and Delivery. God knows, once you got past the boy/girl parts or skin color, those babies all looked alike." LaJune held up one finger. "Now, it was easier with adults. I could pick out something that stuck in my mind and after a few tries, I could get their names straight. But newborns? Hush!"

Mary-Esther dismissed a bizarre idea as swiftly as it formed. Nah, too much like the plot line of a daytime drama. "I appreciate your time, LaJune. I really do. Maybe if I stick around, I can swing back by and visit."

The old woman's eyes sparkled. "If you like The Bingo, you could come on a Tuesday or Thursday. Fellow who calls numbers is real good. We play for cheap dollar prizes, but we do have a high time."

"I'd like that."

LaJune touched her temple with a fingernail the shade of a ripe tangerine. "You know, I had an idea." She chuckled and winked. "That doesn't happen much anymore." She leaned toward Mary-Esther. "You

18

must go to the county courthouse, dear. It's only a hop, skip, and a jump from here. Right smack dab in the middle of town. Big brick building. Can't miss it. Check the records. Maybe you went home with the wrong family. Hospitals don't like to admit to it, but it happens."

"I don't know, LaJune. It makes more sense I was adopted." Or stolen.

"It won't hurt you to go and see, Mary Evelyn."

Mary-Esther smiled. "Suppose not."

"The one to talk to up there is Ruthie Longhorn, or is it Rhonda." The old woman pouched out her bottom lip. "Same difference, I suppose. Anyway, she's been back in the records department for years. Tell her I sent you and to give you anything you need. I nursed her grandbaby back, practically from the dead, years ago. She's beholding to me. Don't let her give you any of that new privacy crap, either. You might luck up on some kind of lead." LaJune pointed to her. "Report back to me. I do love a good mystery."

Mary-Esther stood, rested a hand on the old woman's stooped shoulder. "If I find out anything worth mentioning, you'll be the first person I tell." She offered a support hand, but LaJune waved it aside.

After three tries, LaJune stood. She unsnapped the lock levers from the walker's wheels. "Bring me some tomatoes next time, will you? Ones here taste like mush. They buy them from the store instead of a fruit stand or growing them in a garden. When they pick them green, they don't ripen correctly. Pretty on the outside. Not worth a toot on the inside." She pushed the walker toward the door, turning at the hall threshold to offer Mary-Esther a conspiratorial wink. "Kind of like some people. Present company excepted, naturally."

Chapter Five

Hattie stood in front of the master bathroom sink, studying the crowded shelves of the medicine cabinet. Just another in a string of mornings. At least it wasn't Monday. Tuesdays were tolerable. Since she made her own schedule, how could she really complain? But she still did—nursing a timeworn habit.

Growing up, she had claimed the bathroom in the back wing of the farmhouse. Inside its over-the-sink cabinet: toothpaste and brush, orthodontic retainer, aspirin, deodorant, Band-Aids, and a bottle of mercurochrome.

Now, with her and Holston well into their forties, the master bath cupboard looked like a well-stocked pharmacy: muscle rubs, headache tablets, eye drops, nose spray, cortisone cream, poison ivy wash, and a few prescription bottles.

"Why are you standing in here gazing into the Davis-Lewis drug repository?" Holston asked. His thick hair stuck out at strange, pillow-creased angles.

Hattie moaned. "Trying to find something, anything, to make my shoulder quit hurting."

"Isn't it about time you had it checked? You hug that ice pack more than me."

"I hate to admit defeat." She stretched her neck to one side and rubbed the crest of her shoulder. "You'd think, with me being a massage therapist, I could overcome nearly anything."

Holston gathered Hattie into his arms. "Your symptoms sound like mine when I had the rotator cuff issue a few years back."

She kneaded her left shoulder again, a gesture as automatic as blinking "I'll call the doctor's office. It's such a hassle. I have to get a referral, and then go for x-rays, maybe an MRI. Could be weeks before I can get in to see an orthopedist."

"Better get the process started." Holston stripped from the plaid Florida State lounge pants and cranked on the water. Hattie admired his backside. Keep the washboard abs, bulging biceps, and broad shoulders. Give her a pair of tight buns any day.

Holston caught her ogling. He gave a hip twitch before he stepped into the shower stall. Took her mind off her shoulder for a beat.

When she turned to shut the cabinet, Hattie spotted her mother's economy-sized blue jar of Vick's Vaporub— the ointment she and her brother had secretly referred to as "Tillie's Tub of Goo." The dang stuff lasted forever. She picked it up, unscrewed the metal lid. The pungent camphor scent reminded her of childhood, when a warmed mammy-cloth applied over her Vaporub slickened chest eased congestion.

She closed the jar. It would probably still be here after she was gone too.

When she first moved back to The Hill after her mother's death, Hattie resisted altering a thing. Each time she moved a knick-knack, she erased her parents' mark upon the home they had built, lived in, and loved. But gradually the house changed.

The master bathroom housed the final sentimental holdout. Her mother's intensely personal belongings mingled with Hattie's in the nooks and crannies.

Surveying the blend of her parents' possessions mixed with theirs, a feeling of comfort and peace enveloped her. The Davis family history provided the underlying tone, and new notes sang the melody.

A place for everything and everything in its place, her mother used to say.

"I'm going to walk down to Bobby and Leigh's and see if our child is ready to come home," Hattie called out to Holston's steam-shrouded outline.

Her daughter and Josh "Tank" Davis, her brother's chubby toddler, were inseparable. Many times, Leigh settled Sarah into the baby bed alongside her cousin.

"I'm heading up to my office at the Triple C as soon as I clean up," Holston called back over the sound of falling water. "Need to get busy on the final edit."

The front screened door banged shut behind her. Spackle lifted his head, barked, and joined Hattie for the short stroll. The dog offered a drive-by hand lick before loping ahead, his nose skimming the ground, tail erect. Somewhere in his mishmash gene pool survived the heart of a hunter.

Tipping her head back to feel the sun on her face, Hattie caught sight of a breeding pair of red-tailed hawks carving lazy arcs in the cerulean late October sky.

Hattie had once dreamed of relocating to North Carolina, had gone so far as to make several trips to consider mountainside property near Asheville. Since the move back to the Davis acreage, the desire had faded. How had she been so blind to the beauty of the North Florida woods? As hard as her father had tried to instill in his children his passionate love of the land, it took adulthood to set the hook.

Hattie smiled, remembering her father's favorite boast: "I know the name of *every* tree on this property."

The then-child Hattie had asked, "Who's that one right there?"

"That one?" He grinned. "Why, that's Earl."

"Whoa Nellie." Hattie's young eyes gazed across the treetops. "That's a gazillion names!" Her father was the smartest man Hattie knew.

Years later when she became a busy adult and her father's poor balance and endurance prevented long walks in his beloved magical forest, they had to use a secondhand golf cart to reach the one-acre fishpond. Even then, they still called out hello to the trees.

Hattie still loved the familiar jest.

In a few years, Sarah Chuntian would be old enough to play the tree game. As Hattie walked, she practiced, puffs of dust trailing her steps. "That one—Johnny Boy. The pine with the wide trunk next to the hollow log is Barney."

One of the hawks dove in front of Hattie and dropped behind a clump of broom sedge. Fascinated, she froze and watched the raptor's wings flap as it secured a kill. Spackle inched toward the brush. Hattie motioned him back.

In seconds, the hawk took flight. A rattlesnake dangled in the bird's clasped talons. Reflexive spasms curled its serpentine body, its head suspended on a thread of skin.

Hattie shuddered. Snakes served a purpose, but she held a deep-rooted, primal fear of the reptiles. Stephanie, friend and massage therapist for the Triple C, strongly believed in the appearance of certain totem animals: sentient helpmates and predictors of one's life path. What had Steph said about red-tailed hawks? Something about opening to new experiences and impending messages of grave importance. Hope that snake didn't add any kind of omen.

The downy hair at the base of Hattie's neck prickled.

"Lord help me," she whispered.

In the past, the unsettling sensation signaled major changes, not necessarily good ones. Hattie vibrated her head to dispel the growing dread.

"Get a grip! What do you think you are, psychic? More like psychotic."

Spackle snuffled the enticing scents of hawk and snake at the base of the broom sedge. He lifted his head in her direction and woofed once.

"I don't need anyone, not even you, agreeing with that last statement."

Mary-Esther's temples pulsed with the bloom of a tension headache. She gripped a stack of papers: the results of two days' worth of sifting through birth records. With Ruthie Longhorn's aid, the list of names narrowed to three babies besides her born the same week at Gadsden County Hospital. Two were Caucasian. Of the two, one was female. More encouraging, the similarity of the last names—Day and Davis.

Could it be possible? Apprehension and excitement churned in her stomach, adding to the drumbeat in her temples.

She noticed the white and green Gadsden County Sheriff's Office car parked behind the van as soon as she rounded the corner of the courthouse. "Crap. What now?" She looked up. No booming answer resounded from the heavens. Was there a saint for this? Nana Boudreau would've known.

Since the cruiser blocked her escape, Mary-Esther reluctantly approached the driver's side, ready to drag out her best manners. The tinted window lowered. Sergeant J. Blount's now familiar face appeared.

"Am I parked illegally or something?" She glanced toward the van. Like she could afford a ticket. Money disappeared, no matter how many bologna sandwiches she choked down. Plus the clunker of a van wasn't exactly fuel-efficient. Not by a coon-ass stretch.

"I was writing a note to stick underneath your wiper blade." He handed over a piece of paper.

"Your right rear tire is low," Mary-Esther read aloud.

When she looked up, Sergeant Blount grinned behind the mirrored sunglasses. Twin dimples punctuated his cheeks. Without the stern cop face, he was cute in a good-old-boy type of way. In spite of her headache, she found herself returning the smile like a rapt, nerdy schoolgirl.

"Looks like you might've picked up a nail," he said.

Great. That ought to suck half of her remaining cash. His smile snuffed some of the worry.

It wasn't only his regulation, brass-studded outfit, but the illusion of strength and authority that got to her. If her three failed marriages stood as proof, the combination often proved misleading.

Self-flagellation had become Mary-Esther's new favorite sport. It required no special equipment and was free of charge, one of the few indulgences she *could* afford.

She slipped the note into her jeans pocket. "Do you provide the same fine service for all of your citizens?"

"Only the ones I take a liking to." The officer's smile remained. "No offense, ma'am. I noticed your van and was stopping to see if you'd had any luck locating your people, when I saw the slack tire."

"Um . . . thanks."

"Have you?" he asked.

"Have I . . ."

"Found your people?"

Mary-Esther's neck prickled with heat. Star-struck *and* stupid. Might as well wear a *Take Me, Take Me Now!* sign. She waved the folded papers. "I have a possible lead in Chattahoochee."

"Still in my jurisdiction." Sergeant Blount fished in one of his front shirt pockets and handed her a business card. "Call me if you need help."

"Thanks." She glanced at the card and stuck it into her pocket alongside the note. "Since you know this town, who can fix my tire, cheap? The spare's balder than the other four."

"Brandon's Tire and Brake. About a quarter-mile west on Highway 90, on your way toward Chattahoochee. Left side of the highway. Milton's one of my distant cousins. Honest guy. Won't jerk you around."

She tucked a stray strand of hair back over one ear. "Well, umm . . . thanks again." Mary-Esther turned toward the van, paused, then spun back around. "Is there a place to camp around here?"

"Suppose you'd prefer it to be closer to Chattahoochee?"

"That would be a plus."

He tipped his head toward the west. "There's a federal campground a couple of miles north of Chattahoochee on Lake Seminole. Pretty spot. Take a right at the second stoplight once you get into town. You'll see the sign pointing to East Bank Campground not far after you cross the Florida/Georgia border. It's got clean bathrooms and showers, and full electric and water hook-ups."

Good. A federal campground. They cost half of the private ones. Mary-Esther inhaled and blew it out. The nagging thought of running out of money was not helping her head. "Now all I need is a job. Don't have one of them in mind too, do you?"

"Actually—" He pulled the writing pad and pen from his shirt pocket and scribbled a few lines. "Homeplace Restaurant. Southeast corner of the same intersection where I told you to turn. Mr. Bill's the owner." He tore off the top page and clicked the pen shut then slid both into their slots. "I was in there yesterday for a cup of coffee and a piece of pie. Noticed a *Help Wanted* sign in the window."

Mary-Esther accepted the offered paper. Another scrap for her growing Officer Blount collection. "Is there anything you *don't* know?"

"Math."

"Math?"

"Never was one for numbers." He chuckled and shifted the cruiser into gear. "I'll follow you to the tire shop, make sure you get there okay."

She grappled for her keys. "Thanks."

"Lead on, Miz Louisiana." The officer backed his car enough to allow her space to exit the parking spot.

"It's Mary-Esther!" she called out over the din of his engine. He idled there with his dark shades and a slight grin.

Dang.

Chapter Six

Through the tire shop's plate-glass window, Mary-Esther watched Officer J. Blount whip into traffic and accelerate toward Quincy. A gush of loss and longing overwhelmed her.

Stop! Now! She dug her fingernails into her palms until the skin blanched. The trick had helped her quit smoking years ago. It might curb romantic disasters too.

She fished two aspirins from her purse and took a few sips from a dented water fountain. Magazines curled with overuse sat on a veneered end table. The top two caught her eye.

"Nice. A ratty motorcycle magazine and a *Sports Illustrated* from last summer." Mary-Esther dug in the pile and picked up a torn copy of some hunting periodical. *Find the big bucks*, the headline read. Big bucks? She could use a few.

Mary-Esther threw the magazines down and slid into a seat beside a rack of chrome custom wheels. A small television blared the local news. She watched, trying to get interested.

In a few minutes, she saw a police cruiser pass by. Officer Blount? Mary-Esther sat up and leaned forward, watching until it was out of sight. She had no business starting up a romance. Not now, probably not ever.

She slumped back into the tacky black Naugahyde and picked at the scab of her marital history. As long as she steered clear of the raw center—the most brutal memories—she could worry the time-crisped edges. Her mind swept over the roster of men, at least the ones with a legal union. The others, she had long since quit trying to count and file.

She held up a finger. Ricky Lamar Alford. Husband number one. One year, two months.

Eighteen to her sixteen. They ran off to Las Vegas in Ricky's aqua blue Dodge Dart. So romantic, exhilarating. A ticket out of Loretta Day's cramped apartment and the endless stream of *uncles*.

Charismatic Ricky smooth-talked Mary-Esther out of her cotton panties, and the young virginal bride discovered she liked sex. Loved it. Craved it. So did Ricky, with any skirt that swished by. They drank and chain-smoked together, worked dead-end jobs to eke out a meager living. Drank some more. Until the night Ricky knocked her down and kicked her in the gut so hard she lost the barely-baby she carried.

And she never conceived again.

He or she would have been grown by now, maybe grandkids. *Don't go there!* She shook her head.

Mary-Esther held up another finger. Jesus Luis Fernandez. Husband number two. Five years, three months.

Fifty to her twenty-three. He came in for pancakes and coffee at the Waffle Hut where she waited tables and he left an hour later with his gullible server. "Everything good and kind, you can find with Jesus," he used to say.

Mary-Esther chuckled low. Wouldn't the religious fanatics have a field day over *that* statement?

Strangers often mistook the couple for father and daughter until the two of them lip-locked long enough to make others wish they would get a room. Under his paternal watch, Mary-Esther attended night classes and earned a G.E.D.

The only blip in the relationship: Jesus's possessiveness. Mary-Esther had no friends, only her husband. She had a home and plenty to eat, and it didn't matter. Jesus never struck her, only suffered abysmal sadness when she "disappointed" him. A heart attack snatched Jesus from her life when he was four months past fifty-five. He left a little money, enough for her to attend evening nursing assistant classes.

The long-faced tire shop owner interrupted the husband count to quote her a price on a cheap tire, then he disappeared through a stained wooden door. Mary-Esther fell back into her mental muckraking.

She had to give daisy-chaining husbands a rest when Nana got sick. Life really slid down the toilet after Nana Boudreau suffered her stroke. But Mary-Esther would do it all again—the caretaking, bathing, feeding. Her maternal grandmother had always been there for her.

Six months after Mary-Esther moved into Nana's cramped wooden frame house, Dear Loretta appeared on their doorstep, homeless and penniless, cast aside by the latest in a line of paramours. Mary-Esther struggled to extract a little peace, living in the same house with her mother. Again.

Then Nana died.

And Mary-Esther hooked up with the next loser.

She held up finger number three. John R. Sloat. Jazz musician. Forty-five to her thirty-three.

Mary-Esther accepted John R.'s bleary-eyed, boozy proposal following a marathon of Mardi Gras debauchery. Like most of her decisions, the marriage seemed like a good idea at the time. For the next twenty-plus years, she and John R. kept bad company.

If John R. could have satisfied his physical needs with the saxophone, his union with Mary-Esther would've been unnecessary.

She closed her eyes and could see him fingering the keys, his body swaying rhythmically. It wasn't too much of a stretch to say John R. made love to the instrument, and the audience became willing voyeurs. Mary-Esther envied the place he went when he attached himself to the sax. To be so totally lost in something.

She opened her eyes and took a deep breath. Her head felt swimmy. John R. still had that effect on her.

By the time her mother became ill, John R. was performing his instrumental magic for some other hapless woman and Mary-Esther was once again on her own. She moved back in to her grandmother's house, this time without the buffering influence of Nana Boudreau.

Her throat constricted when she thought of Loretta. Telling, that she called her *Loretta,* never Mom or Mama.

Love, longing. Anger, distaste. Was every woman's relationship with her mother as fraught with polar-opposite emotions?

Loretta's life had consisted of hopping from one man's bed to the next. Her mother drank too much and had no concept of money. The past and future didn't exist.

Only when her mother lay dying did Mary-Esther realize the number of traits they shared.

"To your credit, Loretta," she mumbled aloud, "you and Hurricane Katrina taught me: I can survive most anything."

Papers rustled. She looked up to see Milton watching her with his hangdog expression from behind the sales counter.

"Er . . . Miss. Your van's ready."

After Elvina Houston started a fresh pot of Morning Blend coffee in the Triple C's kitchen and checked the voicemail, she slipped from the back entrance and picked her way past the koi pond, butterfly garden, and birdfeeders to a small square flower patch. The daisies of late summer were gone, recently replaced with a thick carpet of lemon yellow and rust-colored mums. Such a pretty spot.

Jake had spent the better part of an afternoon working on it. Elvina's heart near to broke in two watching him out the back window. The leg that got so hurt when he was beaten up doesn't bend good, still. He stretched it out ahead of him and scooted along on his behind to plant every one of the mums.

"He's a good man, that Jake Witherspoon."

Elvina settled onto a cement bench and opened a bag of whole peanuts.

"Chip, chip, chip!" she called, searching the tall pines surrounding the clearing.

Gray squirrels in varying sizes scampered toward where Elvina waited, their pompom tails held high. Like rapt front-row fans at an Elvis concert, the animals lined up in a semicircle at her feet and settled onto their haunches. Six sets of round eyes studied her.

Elvina's gaze swept over the group. "Where's Elmer?"

One last rotund squirrel skittered down the pine to her right and queued up with the rest.

"Good of you to grace us with your presence, Elmer."

Elvina laughed. Give the rodent a tiny rifle and an Elmer Fudd hunting cap and he would look like a furry miniature of the cartoon character. The portly squirrel inched forward and reached a tentative paw to touch the tip of her shoe.

"Apology accepted, sir."

For the first few months when Elvina frequented the Piddie Davis Longman Memorial Garden, a single squirrel had braved her company for the price of a handout, long enough to snatch a peanut and haul butt to the closest tree. The squirrel grew steadily bolder as time went by. Soon it shared one end of the bench, contentedly chewing and chattering. At that early point, Elvina's emotions were raw. Human company would have been too much effort. Squirrel was fine.

Her therapist had strongly suggested the daily visit to the garden as a balm to her sore soul. When Piddie Longman was alive, a day never went by that the two didn't sit in her dear friend's tiny kitchen and ruminate over the town's residents, often speaking on the phone two or three times as well. Now, the daily one-sided conversations had become an integral part of Elvina's mornings, a last link to a woman who had once thrown her a lifeline. Too bad they didn't have phone service in the Great Beyond.

Elmer inched closer. Most folks thought squirrels all looked alike. Not so. Elvina could tell some of them apart.

That original gray-furred moocher, Gabriel—he had a star-shaped white clump of hair on his head—shared news of the mother lode with his cohorts. Depending on the morning, Elvina now had between four and eight visitors. The throng of squirrels she now regarded as fellow mourners brightened each day a bit more than the one before.

Elvina loosened the twist tie on the peanut bag. She'd have to raid the spare-change jar next to Buster's kitty treats and pick up a few bags next time she was in Lowe's. She doled out several whole peanuts and the group got down to business.

She thought about Piddie's final advice, left behind on an audiotape delivered by the lawyer after the memorial service. She had replayed it so often, she had it memorized.

"'Vina, go on and grieve. Cry and fall out and do whatever you need to do to get past it. Sadness bottled up will rise to the top later and spill over into your whole life. Miss me, 'Vina. That is tee-totally all right. Just don't go trying to crawl in the grave beside me."

She looked at the flower garden that contained part of Piddie's ashes. As good a place for a vacation grave as any. Or was the one in Alabama the getaway? Elvina harrumphed. Piddie never did anything the customary way.

"The Grim Reaper will come soon enough for you. In the meantime, do keep a watchful eye over the folks I've held dear on this earth."

Elvina dipped her chin down then up. She would, by God, look after the people she now considered family.

"We'll be together in the blink of an eye. I'll be right here on the Other Side, waiting for you with a nice cup of that God-awful tea you swear by, and I'll bet we will find a passel to talk about."

A wistful smile lifted Elvina's painted lips. Piddie had been so colorful, bigger than life. But Elvina had always been mousy and plain, unless it was a special occasion like New Year's at Dan and Tillie Davis' house on The Hill. Then she added a touch of snazzy.

Elvina glanced down. Wouldn't Piddie be surprised by how *she* dressed now? Eye-popping red frock with shoes to match. She'd chipped the bright polish on two nails last night trying to affix Buster's new rabies tag. Why did she bother? That cat could shed a collar faster than a politician lost tax money.

And wouldn't Piddie get a kick out of her hairdo? Piled up like her best friend used to wear it. Elvina shook her head. The chandelier earrings clinked like wind chimes, but the mass of curls barely trembled. Hair fixative products, a miracle. Without the benefit of an add-on, her coif would never reach the loft of Piddie Longman's 'do, but folks had noted the attempt. That was all that mattered.

"Morning, Piddie. Fine fall morning we got down here." Elvina's voice sent a jittery ripple through the squirrel line-up. She tossed out another round of peanuts.

"Lord, help. I thought cooler weather would never get here! That global warming business must be true. Mandy read a report somewhere, said it was on account of farting cows destroying the ozone layer or some-such, but I have my reservations."

Elvina looked straight up. "I know you don't concern yourself with such, up there in Glory. Thought I might mention it in case you want to put a bug in the Big Man's ear about cow gas and all this heat, that's all."

Elvina pitched peanuts to the barfly squirrel contingency.

"I'm uneasy, Piddie. Problem is, I can't put a finger on the reason to save my mortal soul."

Elmer joined her on the bench. He hunkered down and chinked a nutshell into papery confetti. Above her, a woodpecker jackhammered a pine.

"A changeling wind is blowing. I feel it clean to my bones."

Chapter Seven

Three miles south of Chattahoochee, Mary-Esther pulled onto Bonnie Lane. A petite woman with a red bandana tied around her head looked up from a flowerbed and squinted in her direction. Mary-Esther slowed the van. Her pulse raced.

Could this woman be her mother?

She checked the house number. Nope. Had to be another one farther down.

Mary-Esther continued up the drive, toward a white farmhouse with a porch full of rockers. Big block numbers over the front door. Correct address this time.

Cowardice had never been part of her make-up. Stupidity and blind hope, yes, but not cowardice. Mary-Esther swore under her breath.

What the heck. She should waltz up to the front door of the Davis family, ring the bell, and announce she might be their long-lost, mixed-at-birth, penniless and homeless relative.

Right.

Had to be a graceful way to make such a declaration. For sure, Hallmark didn't make a card for the occasion.

She slammed on the brakes, threw the shift lever into reverse, and backed to a wide spot where she could turn around. The bandana woman watched her pass by again, her hands propped on her hips.

Mary-Esther's foot trembled when she turned onto the highway and accelerated toward Chattahoochee. *Priorities*, she coached herself. She'd find the little restaurant, ask about the job, grab a sandwich, and head for the campground.

The scent of acrid sweat drifted from her body. Couldn't meet the family anyway, smelling like this, looking like the undead. A shower and some sleep would help.

Tomorrow, or soon, she could screw up her resolve.

The perfume of sautéed onions caught Mary-Esther off guard when she stepped into Bill's Homeplace Restaurant. Certain aromas flashed Mary-Esther to Nana Boudreau's kitchen. The fragrance from years of Cajun cooking had lingered even when Nana's ancient gas cook stove wasn't in use.

The contented feeling of being home washed over her, followed immediately by the realization home was no longer a place she could go.

A kind-faced woman rushed by. Her scratched silver nametag read *Julie*. "Seat yourself, hon. I'll be right with you."

Before Mary-Esther had a chance to answer, the server disappeared behind a scarred wooden swinging door. Mary-Esther chose a vacant booth next to a window facing the main thoroughfare.

A row of shiny booths lined two windowed walls and Formica tables formed various configurations in the middle of the long room.

Had to be a busy place. Other than the little bistro where she had the huge biscuit, there didn't seem to be many eateries in town. Did the locals tip well?

Julie the server appeared with eating utensils cocooned in a paper napkin. "What can I get you to drink, hon?" Even she studied Mary-Esther in an odd way.

"Water's fine. Thanks."

Julie pointed to the laminated one-page menu wedged between an aluminum napkin dispenser and a matched set of bubble-glass salt-and-pepper shakers. "Got most things on the menu, 'cept the buffet. That's only at lunch. We have fresh fried mullet today, choice of fries or cheese grits, special for $6.95."

Fatigue resonated in every joint. Mary-Esther mentally tallied what remained of her cash. If she stretched the bread and picked up a jar of peanut butter . . . "You fry in fresh grease?"

Julie winked. "You betcha. Best mullet you'll ever wrap your lips around."

"I'll take that with cheese grits."

Julie scribbled on an order pad. "Want me to have the cook throw a couple of fried onion rings on top? They're not Vidalia. A little too late in the season for them. Texas Sweets. Next best thing."

"Sure." If she was going to have indigestion later, might as well go all out.

The server shoved the pencil behind one ear and walked away.

The walls held pictures and country-themed memorabilia. Printed gingham valances topped the spotless windows. The linoleum floor shone. She had worked in far worse places.

The tourist joints in New Orleans would be the first to resurrect from the deluge, but what about places like this? Where the menus weren't fancy, the food was delicious and plentiful, and people knew you on sight. Most of the ones near her neighborhood no longer existed, if what she saw on the news could be trusted.

New Orleans would arise and shake its damaged wings to dry and heal in the salty marsh breezes. It always did.

Only she wouldn't be there to witness it.

For a few minutes, she watched cars pass by, never more than four or five at a time. Even at three a.m., New Orleans had more traffic.

When she turned her attention to the room, Mary-Esther caught the interested glances of several fellow diners. Hard not to feel paranoid when everywhere she went in this town, people watched her as if she was some lunatic serial killer.

Of the handful of dinner patrons, all appeared to be minding their own company, except one woman. Every time Mary-Esther glanced to the table where the old lady sat, she was met with eyebrow-raised scrutiny. Mary-Esther checked to make sure she had the buttons fastened on her shirt.

Back in the city, she might have called out "what *you* looking at?" Ill-advised here, especially if she wanted to land a job.

When Julie arrived with her water and a plate piled high with hot mullet, Mary-Esther ignored the old woman and dug in. She bit into the perfect blend of crunch, seasoning, and grease, and let out a throaty moan. Even at twice the price, the mullet would've been worth every cent. She chased the fish with a spoonful of cheese grits. Sharp cheddar hung in strings from her lips. The onion rings added a sweet gooey tang, with the same delicate crispy coating as the mullet.

She had surely died and lifted off.

Julie refilled the water glass before it was half-empty. No needful glance required. Mary-Esther ate in gluttonous bliss. Licked the sheen from her lips and fingers. So what if she looked like a cretin.

"May I ask you something?" Mary-Esther said when Julie produced the check a few minutes later.

"Sure, hon. If I don't have an answer, I can always make something up."

Humor and honesty. Mary-Esther immediately warmed to the server. "Noticed the 'Help Wanted' sign. What are you looking for?"

"Little of everything, really. One of our short-order cooks had to have surgery, and we're down a server. Mr. Bill will take either, but it would be nice to find someone who might be able to float."

"I'd like to apply."

Julie hesitated a beat too long. Gave Mary-Esther the once-over. "Mr. Bill does all the hiring. Won't be in this evening, but you can catch him first thing in the morning."

Mary-Esther wiped the grease from the corners of her lips, threw a couple of bills onto the table, and slid from the booth. "I'll come back for coffee in the morning. It'll save me from drinking my own."

The server motioned toward the checkout counter then led the way and took Mary-Esther's money.

A model of a '57 Chevy caught her eye on the way out. Mary-Esther stopped in the narrow foyer to check out the display. Husband number two had one like it, the real deal not a tiny metal replica. Only it was red, not turquoise.

"Elvina, you okay, hon?" Mary-Esther heard Julie ask the old woman who was still watching her. "You look like you just saw a ghost."

The East Bank Campground had everything Mary-Esther could ask for, and more. Only two other campers shared the deep shade on the banks of Lake Seminole, a deal at less than twenty dollars a night. She claimed a choice waterfront spot.

After getting set up, Mary-Esther took advantage of a long, hot shower. The soft, mineral-filled water poured over her aching body. She washed her hair three times. Whisked a week's worth of stubble from her underarms and legs. The steamy water beat down on her shoulders, a true luxury when most of her baths had consisted of swiping the important spots with a soapy rag.

Since the evening temperature had dropped into the fifties, she dried her hair with a compact blow dryer and slipped on a long-sleeved T-shirt and a pair of worn sweat pants.

Clean skin and fresh clothes went a long way.

She'd take comfort any way she could.

Next, she walked the grounds and found enough dry wood to start a small campfire in the metal fire ring by her site. Once she had the embers burning steadily, she untied a folded aluminum chair from the rack on top of the van and settled down to gaze into the flames. In ancient times, fire meant food, safety, and solace from the encroaching darkness. Funny, since she had so little, it didn't take much to fulfill the same needs.

It wasn't all bad, this fate-imposed poverty. Certainly, she had nothing anyone would care to steal. Freeing in a hobo-existence sort of fashion. No mortgage. No bills.

Mary-Esther heard a faint mewing noise and peered around in the darkness for its source. A low form hunkered down at the edge of the firelight circle. Raccoon? Possum? The shadow shifted and she discerned the outline of a small rounded head and two pointy ears.

"C'mere," she cooed in a soft voice. "C'mon. I won't hurt you."

Mary-Esther rose slowly and moved to the van, returning with a slice of bologna. The first pieces, she tossed into the darkness beyond the animal. It moved and knelt down to eat. Bit by bit, she coaxed it forward into the dim firelight. The kitten looked barely weaned.

"You're only a baby," Mary-Esther whispered.

Like the wicked-woods queen baiting Hansel and Gretel with gingerbread, Mary-Esther used snippets of bologna to draw the cat nearer. She extended a hand and stroked the soft fur between its ears. Startled at first, it regarded her with wary yellow eyes that matched the buttercream stripes across its skinny body. Mary-Esther settled back in the chair, careful not to make sudden movements. She held the last piece of bologna in her fingertips.

The kitten hesitated, studying her. Hunger overcame reticence and it stood and walked over to snatch the meat.

When the tabby finished eating, it glanced her way once before indulging in a long, drawn-out bathing ritual.

Mary-Esther understood. Being homeless was one thing. Being dirty was another. Just because you were one, you didn't necessarily have to be the other.

The kitten curled up in a clump of leaves and fell asleep.

When the embers died down, Mary-Esther banked the hot coals and retired to the van. The cold snap had eradicated the mosquitoes, so she left the back door slightly ajar to enjoy the fresh air. A bungee cord stretched between the door handle and a metal loop on the van's inner frame. Anyone trying to break in would make enough noise to awaken her. Didn't matter she was in the woods. City habits were hard to break.

With her stomach filled with mullet, her skin and hair scrubbed clean, and her soul warmed by the fire, Mary-Esther's spirit flew on the night winds to hover over the narrow corridors of the French Quarter.

In sleep, Mary-Esther found escape.

Tonight, she dreams of her grandmother's house. Everything rushes back: the scent of gumbo, Nana Boudreau's bosomy hugs, and the rays of the setting sun as it descends on a city with so much spirit it never sleeps.

The sensual low moan of a saxophone travels to greet her. She ambles along a narrow sidewalk and the aroma of night-blooming jasmine fills her nose. Sounds mute, but colors shine with neon intensity as she passes one favorite haunt after another.

She stands in the grass in front of her grandmother's house. The bushes stir with a slight land breeze. Inside, the solid shadow of Nana Boudreau shifts against the backdrop of yellow light.

Mary-Esther can't make her feet move. She settles cross-legged onto the grass, content to sit and watch. A little cat brushes up against one leg and she reaches to pet it. The kitten's purr grows and grows until Mary-Esther can no longer hear the night noises of her old street.

She slips into a peaceful, dreamless oblivion.

In the morning when Mary-Esther opened her eyes, the blonde tabby kitten regarded her with drowsy eyes, yawned, and curled beneath the covers next to her heart.

She named him Boudreau.

Chapter Eight

Hattie threw up one hand when she entered the therapy room at the Triple C Spa and Salon. "I know, I know. Don't say it. I'm in sad shape."

Stephanie Peters placed an herbal heating pad into a compact microwave and set the timer. "I can tell by the way you're bracing your left arm."

A healer seldom took the time to treat herself, but the shoulder had issued an ultimatum. Hattie's body showed the signs of age, though she didn't like to think about it. Wrinkles webbed her eyes, and she grew another chin hair every week. And those were just the surface issues.

She glanced around the space, similar to hers but with a different personality. A restful shade of pale blue covered the walls, and a thick, wheat-hued rug spread out beneath the electric lift therapy table. Soft, ambient music, a combination of harp and flute, emanated from a compact disc player.

Stephanie motioned toward the massage table, nodded, and closed the door on the way out.

Hattie knew the drill, and it didn't take long to strip naked and snuggle between the sheets. A sheepskin pad cushioned Stephanie's table. Warmth radiated from an electric heating blanket. The sheets smelled faintly of lavender. By the time she heard Stephanie's double tap, Hattie had nearly drifted to sleep.

"I'm going to start out on your feet, Hattie, while the heating pad warms up your back."

The weight of the herbal pack settled over Hattie's tender upper back and shoulders. "Umm . . ."

"Feels marvelous, doesn't it?" Stephanie's voice slipped into the gentle, even cadence of a healer.

Stephanie kneaded and pressed acupuncture points on Hattie's feet and ankles for several minutes before removing the herbal heating pad. "You are really tight, sister."

"Sorry I've brought you such a mess."

"Don't worry. I love a challenge."

Hattie concentrated on taking deep, even breaths. Some points around her shoulder blades referred lightning jolts of pain down to her elbow and fingers. When Stephanie depressed one spot, a memory appeared so vividly, Hattie jerked.

Her hands, those of a four-year-old girl, reach out for a stuffed bear. The bear is pink and wears a tulle skirt speckled with velvet hearts.

"Do you want a crumpet, Miz Sarah?" Hattie moves imaginary sweetbreads to a tiny china plate and pretend-pours steeped tea. Sarah is a name she heard her daddy say once when she listened at her parents' bedroom door.

"What'd you call that stupid bear?" Forced to play with her, Bobby sprawls in the chair beside the bear, whittling on a stick.

"Sarah."

His gaze flicks toward the end of the porch where their mother rocks, shelling peas. "Never, *ever* say that name."

"How come?"

Bobby leans over and whispers, "Just don't."

"But who *is* Sarah?" Her voice is loud.

Their mother's head pivots their way. Bobby's mouth falls open. Her mother jumps to her feet and runs inside the house.

"Now you did it, twerp. You made her cry."

Hattie stands, nearly toppling the table. When she steps toward the door, Bobby stops her. "Leave her alone."

"What did I do?"

"Sarah was our sister. And she *died*, okay?"

Tears seeped from Hattie's eyes and dampened the u-shaped pillow. She had witnessed emotional releases with her own massage clients but had never experienced it herself. By the time she rolled over for the final half-hour, she had managed to push down the sadness.

"Take your time getting up," Stephanie said. The door shut with a soft click.

Hattie rolled on her side, swung her legs over the edge of the table, and sat up. Her shoulder still throbbed, but her neck felt less tense. What was up with the stuff from early childhood?

Stephanie tapped on the door in a few minutes. "You decent?"

"Sure. Come on in."

Stephanie entered. "How's your body feel?"

"You did a fantastic job, but my shoulder still aches like I've been beaten up."

"I'm not supposed to diagnose—by law, you know—but I wouldn't be at all surprised if you didn't have a tendon or muscle tear. You don't have range of motion at all on the left side. The right side is busy trying to compensate."

"Welcome to the aging process, eh?" Her eyes stung. Tears, again?

"Maybe. Maybe not." Stephanie paused. "The body sends messages to us. The back is about support—the upper back being emotional support. The neck area corresponds to flexibility—stubbornness, the inability to see another point of view."

"Animal totems *and* mind/body connections. You are *so* cosmic." Hattie stepped over and gave her friend a one-armed hug.

"Bottom line: Hattie needs to take care of herself."

"If life will only cooperate."

When Hattie passed the reception desk, Elvina Houston waved her over. "Hey, gal. Did you enjoy your massage?"

"Yes. Only now I'm positive I have something major wrong with my shoulder." *And what about obsessing over my dead sister? That's nearly as worrisome.*

"Wait 'til you get to my age and you worry if you *don't* hurt. I'm so far over the hill, I'm back on level ground."

They laughed.

Elvina would never fill her aunt Piddie's bejeweled slippers, but she certainly gave it an earnest effort.

"I'm going to see a doctor soon, Elvina. I promise."

Elvina's phone chimed and she checked the incoming text message without missing a beat. "Have you heard anything about that *new* woman?"

"I know this town is small, but you don't really expect me to know each and every person."

"Figured someone might have mentioned her to you." Elvina's eyebrow crooked up.

"Why?" Hattie tilted her head.

Elvina wavered then she answered, "I've seen her with my own eyes. Joe has seen her too, couple of days ago when she first came through. Now it seems she's back, maybe to stay."

"It's not like we're overrun with people."

Elvina chewed on the tip of one nail before frowning and snapping her finger from her mouth. "I really have to stop that! I've had two touch-ups already this week. Being well-groomed is such a bother."

"You were saying . . . ?" Hattie prompted.

"Ah, yes." Elvina paused. "I don't really know how to tell you this, so I'll come right out with it. The woman I saw, and understand is now waitressing at Bill's, is the spitting image of your dear departed mother. A younger version, mind you. Late fifties, maybe. But the same face and smile. Even her hair—the part that's growing out from an unfortunate perm—is the color of Tillie's at that same age."

"Oh."

"Didn't mean to upset you, Hattie dear. I felt it my duty to let you know."

Maybe the hawk messenger was on target.

Chapter Nine

Mary-Esther rested in the folding chair with Boudreau purring in her lap. The sun dipped low on the horizon across Lake Seminole, reflecting brilliant streaks of scarlet and gold. A small campfire snickered in front of her, now an evening ritual.

With a minimal source of income and a place to return to at the end of a day of slinging platters of fried everything, Mary-Esther felt content. One day, she might live somewhere like this. She doubted she would ever make the kind of money to afford a view like the one she now enjoyed, but at least close to water.

The scent of moisture in the breeze rejuvenated her as no drug or alcoholic beverage ever could. Years ago, she and first loser husband Ricky had lived in Vegas for a time. Though the city teemed with ponds and fountains spewing arcs of water, the air was the life-sucking arid of the surrounding desert. Beyond the flashy strip and suburbs, the terrain blended into mile upon mile of flat, treeless monotony. Where were the moss-draped oaks and towering cypress trees? The scrim of algae and duckweed? She needed green, green, green.

Her swamp-rat skin had begged for moisture. Her cuticles cracked and her eyes felt raw. Her sinuses rebelled with frequent nosebleeds. Her hair stood out at odd angles and refused to be tamed by a brush or blow-torch.

"Get me out of this God-forsaken place," she had admonished her new husband after less than a month.

When that relationship tanked, she had never ventured to the desert again.

But Chattahoochee? Mary-Esther could see herself living here. The people were, for the most part amicable, though more than once she had caught them openly staring.

The wide Apalachicola River rushed southward in swirls past the Jim Woodruff Dam. When she had driven by the main landing, she spotted lines of people with cane fishing poles. A cement boat launch bustled with activity. Here, above the dam, Lake Seminole sprawled out in front of her. According to her creased map, it licked Gadsden and Jackson counties in Florida, before reaching its fingers into southern Georgia and the three rivers that gave it life.

Mary-Esther trained a flashlight on a small self-published book about the area, one she had found crammed beside the cash register at Bill's. In the river's heyday, paddlewheel steamboats and barges carried passengers and goods upstream. For years, the Corps of Engineers kept the Apalachicola bottom dredged of silt, forming wide sandbars with the cast-off, changing the river's course and biology. She had overhead a couple of diners discuss the war between the politicians and the environmentalists who fought to rescue the mighty, brown waterway.

A door slammed and she glanced up. Two days prior, a lone truck camper had pulled into a spot near the waterfront: a pick-up with a plywood slide-in. Mary-Esther took careful note of her new neighbor. In her section of New Orleans, lack of vigilance could get you robbed, or killed, or both.

The man looked to be in his late seventies. An aluminum johnboat tethered to a cypress stump bobbed in the shallow water in front of his site. He left early each morning and returned near dark, a line of fish dangling from his gnarled hands. At a makeshift cleaning table fashioned from scraps of board, he scaled and gutted the catch.

More than once, Mary-Esther had to call Boudreau away from the overflowing pile of fish guts in his trash bucket. Couldn't really blame the kitten. Raw fish innards had to taste better than Meow Mix. But if a gator decided to join the dinner party, a kitten might make a good appetizer.

The rumble of a car engine silenced the crickets. Mary-Esther craned her head to see who might be checking in; usually, the campers pulled in well before dark. A sheriff's car parked beside her van and an officer got out. Her heart beat wild when she recognized the man.

"Permission to enter your camp, Miz Louisiana?"

Mary-Esther noted the way he pronounced the state's name—*Lah-ooosee-ann-ner.* Cute.

Boudreau complained when she stood and settled him back onto the chair. "Permission granted. And I told you to call me Mary-Esther."

"Well, then, Mary-Esther it is." He sauntered toward her, his gun belt leather squeaking. "Seems I never properly introduced myself. Jeremiah Blount. Folks call me Jerry." He stuck out one hand.

She shook it. Strong and warm. The unsettling flare of interest sparked, again. "What brings you out to my homestead, Jerry?"

"You're just a hop from my zone, so I thought I'd ride up and make sure you found this place all right."

"Can't get much better directions than from a cop. It really is a nice campground. Thanks for telling me about it. I feel like I'm on vacation."

"And are you?"

Mary-Esther stuffed down her reticence. Why lie? Nothing gained. "Not really. Seeing as how this *is* home now," she motioned toward the van, "since mine got blown away by Katrina."

"I see. I'm so sorry." His eyes were kind. "Bad business, that hurricane."

"I'd offer you a place to sit, but—"

"I have a stool in the cruiser. I'll join you for a spell if you don't mind. Not much going on tonight in my part of the county, and it'll be good to pass a little time in pleasant company." He paused. "If I'm not interrupting anything."

Dear God. He was polite too. "Not like I have to clean house or mow the yard." She motioned to the leaf-strewn campsite.

"Got a Thermos of fresh coffee in the car. Like a cup?"

She nodded. "I even have an extra mug. Bring it on."

He returned with a small folding stool and poured two mugs of steaming coffee. "I have packets of creamer, if you'd like."

"I prefer mine black and strong. No milk, no sugar."

"What a woman!" Jerry held up his cup in a toast. He unfolded the aluminum and canvas stool and sat down.

"It's easier that way. The less you require, the better off you are."

His eyes twinkled in the firelight. "A person who doesn't come with a list of wants as long as the devil's arm. I've certainly died and made a bee-line to heaven."

Most men triggered Mary-Esther's alarms, but Jerry Blount transmitted no threat. It wasn't that she hated men, or had sworn off them. But after a few miserable times at bat, you decide the bench might be your best option.

They sipped in silence for a few minutes. The lull wasn't uncomfortable. Odd. Most of the time Mary-Esther reached to supply banal conversation.

"Heard you landed the job at Bill's," Jerry said.

"Have you to thank for that too. I dropped your name when I talked to the owner."

When Jerry leaned his head back and laughed, the sound rumbled from deep inside. "Good thing he likes me. I'd hate it if that had backfired on you."

Mary-Esther reached down and petted Boudreau's back. When she hit the tickle-spot near the base of his tail, his haunches raised.

Jerry's white smile flashed in the amber light. "Isn't that the funniest thing about a cat? Reminds me of those low-rider cars with the air shocks that jack up and down." He wiggled his fingers and the kitten ambled to him. Mary-Esther admired the way Jerry's strong hands rested on the kitten's fur. Those hands would feel so fine on the small of her back.

Mary-Esther dug her fingernails into her palm. Not a time or place for entanglements. Since Katrina, she imagined herself as a dandelion seed. Cast to the breeze, tumbling and spinning. She might light on the fertile soil beneath a stand of river birch. Or she could end up in the water, carried far downstream by the endless current.

She had no roots; nothing held her down, but little held her up.

Jerry refilled his cup. "Not meaning to pry, but have you had any luck finding those people you were looking for?"

Mary-Esther stared into the fire. "Haven't contacted them yet." It had been so long since she had a confidant. She had trusted LaJune, why not Jerry? "It's a long, sad story. Sure you want to hear it?" Her eyes met his. Their gazes locked for an instant before she looked down.

"Miz Mary-Esther, I can't think of a better way to pass a nice fall evening than sitting by a campfire with a pretty woman bending my ear." He reached over and topped off her cup. "I'm on duty until half past chicken-thirty. I can drop and run if I get a call, long as you don't take it personal if I have to leave in mid-sentence."

Chapter Ten

Bobby Davis plopped down onto a wooden rocking chair on his log home's broad front porch. Not long ago, he would've had a beer in his hand, one of the many it took to pass an evening.

Most of his twenties through forties and the first part of his fifties had floated by in an alcohol-drenched fog. When he finally pulled himself from the hellish pit, he looked around to a reality he barely recognized. His miserable first marriage had long since foundered, his job hung by a wisp, and he was at odds with his only sibling. His mother stood by him, even during the angriest parts of his addiction, but Bobby knew he had been a large part of the sadness of her later years.

The screen door screeched open. "Tell Daddy goodnight," Leigh said to the chunky toddler balanced on one hip.

"Bedtime?" Bobby asked, reaching for his son. He hugged the boy to his chest, kissed him on the top of his head. The kid was a real bruiser. His nickname *Tank* fit him.

Leigh held out her hands and his son leaned away from him, back into his mother's arms.

"He's wound up." Leigh propped the wiggling toddler on the opposite hip.

"Want me to take over?"

Leigh shook her head. "Nah. We're okay. I'll give him some juice and Goldfish crackers while I'm finishing up in the kitchen. Usually does the trick." She returned to the house.

Life tasted so sweet now. How had he pissed away so much time? Fifty-four, with a three-year-old and wife number two. At least he had another chance to get things right.

It had taken his mama's death and the fated meeting with a determined young woman who saw a glimmer of goodness flickering inside of him to shock Bobby into admitting his life swirled in the crapper. But good.

He pushed the rocker into a gentle back and forth.

Familiar noises sounded from the kitchen. Though he couldn't make out her words, he knew Leigh talked to Tank while she cooked.

Felt good not to worry about punching a time clock. For over thirty years, he had lived and breathed his career with the Florida Game and Freshwater Fish Commission. Bobby didn't want to be a part of that crazy, adrenalin-stoked game anymore. He dug into his past and resurrected his love for building with his hands, a talent nurtured early on by his daddy. This job wouldn't shoot you in the back, leave you bleeding out on some lonely country road.

I have a purpose. Two, actually. And soon, if God granted another great wish of his and Leigh's, he would have a third. Shoot, if not, it was fun to try.

In a few minutes, the screen door behind him screeched open. No matter how much he oiled the hinges, the door still protested under pressure. Such was the nature of wood.

"Want some company?" Leigh asked.

"Reason why we've got more than one rocker on this porch, I reckon." Bobby admired his wife's raven hair, blue-black in the gloaming light. "Tank asleep?"

Leigh settled onto the rocker beside him with a contented sigh. "Yep."

Good thing about his boy. After his nightly snack, he was out. "How was your day?"

"We got the flu vaccines in. Lots of folks coming by for shots. You need to get one too. I can give it to you so you won't feel a thing."

Bobby flinched. The idea of a needle piercing his skin stirred his stomach. He might have drunk himself into an early grave if he hadn't stopped. For sure, he wouldn't have been a junkie. "I'll ponder on it," he said.

Leigh boxed him playfully in the arm. "You amaze me, Bobby Davis. I've seen you reach down and grab a snake behind the head with your bare hands, yet you're squeamish about a little pinprick."

"I'll get one."

"See that you do. I've had mine. So has Tank. I don't want you dragging home sick as a dog some evening and the two of us having to take care of your sorry butt."

"I absolutely get no respect in my own home."

Leigh slung one leg over the arm of the rocker and dug her toes into his jeaned thigh. "You are so mistreated. I feel bad for you on a daily basis."

As the light faded in the thicket of pines and hardwoods surrounding the log home, crickets tuned up for the nightly serenade. Soon, a cacophony of peeper frogs sang from the boggy low land behind the house.

Bobby cherished the night music as much as his father had. At one point, his dad had installed an intercom between the fishpond deep in the woods and the master bedroom, and insisted on falling to sleep each night to the piped-in symphony. His mom called it "that gosh-darn racket."

"You finished up in the kitchen?" he asked Leigh.

"For the most part. Thanks again for washing the dinner dishes. My cake's cooling. I should be able to frost it before we turn in for the night."

"Let me know if you need me to taste it for you." Bobby winked. "I'd hate for it to leave this house without a proper quality test."

"Touch that cake and I'll starch your shorts, buddy."

"Oh, them's fighting words. You don't go messing with a man's under-drawers."

"Mister Davis, you don't go messing with a woman's contribution to the Fall Festival Cake Walk either. Got it?"

Bobby tweaked his wife on the cheek. "Loud and clear."

They rocked, silent for a moment before Leigh said, "You were sort of quiet over dinner. You okay?"

"How can you see right through me?"

Even in the low light, Bobby could sense his wife watching him. "I pay close attention to things that matter," she said.

Before he met her, no one approached Bobby for idle conversation. Hattie had avoided sparring with him as much as possible. Anger bubbled beneath his thin skin. Anything could send it spilling over the edge. Most of his molars had been flayed flat from clenching.

He looked over at Leigh. She didn't prod. Only waited.

For the first few months they dated, after Bobby committed to addiction recovery, he had spoken little about his feelings. Now he shared everything, no matter how insignificant, and he was learning to listen. Many nights after Tank drifted off to sleep, they talked deep into the evening until one or both grew too tired to continue.

If only he had met Leigh before all the wasted years. Could've been wife number one. Not two.

"I was thinking about how lucky I am," he said. "Can't imagine a single thing that would make my life more complete than what I have now, here with you and Tank." Leigh grasped his hand and planted a soft kiss across the knuckles. "And to live here, in this house . . . on The Hill near my sister—"

Leigh rocked a little, still holding his hand. Bobby gathered his thoughts.

"I can't help but wonder," he said. "If Sarah had lived, suppose she would've ended up out here close to Hattie and me?"

"Bet so. You have to figure, she would've grown up with Dan and Tillie as her parents too. Pretty good start."

"Good point."

Leigh fixed him with her intense eyes. "You miss Sarah, even though you never knew her."

The woman had a way of slicing through his mess. Hadn't he exorcised all of his demons? The deep unease told him one or two remained.

"We weren't allowed to talk about Sarah. Didn't *dare* mention her name. It was as if, when we stepped away from that little grave, all traces of her were stuffed in there with her." He took a breath, blew it out. "It's taken me a while to get used to Hattie naming her daughter Sarah . . . seems like we've stomped on a family taboo."

"Maybe it's time, Bobby." Leigh reached over and finger-combed his hair. "It's been my experience, when you bring something out into the light, you can see it for what it really is. Most of the time, it's not as threatening as it appears."

Bobby leaned and cupped her chin with one hand. He brushed her lips with his. "You ought to be on TV, woman."

"Keep your boots on, Buster! Mama's coming!" Elvina Houston bumbled her way through the hallway. Buster yowled outside. The last time he stayed out so late, he showed up punctured and bloody.

She clicked the lock open and shoved the heavy sliding glass door. "Dad-gum! The porch light is out again!"

Elvina flipped the switch once more to make certain. The new moon offered no illumination. From the pitch-black darkness, she heard the unmistakable sounds of a full-blown cat fight. She fumbled in the cabinet next to the door for a small flashlight. When she depressed the button, the bulb barely lit before it faded altogether.

"Well, Jumpin' Judas on a pogo stick!"

The cat screams escalated. Elvina gathered her chenille robe against the chill and grappled her way down the steps. In the daytime, she knew her back yard from memory, every bush, rock, and flowerbed. Recently, a roving marauder had visited her property, leaving random potholes where it had rooted around for whatever armadillos seek.

One minute, Elvina picked her way through the yard to rescue her wayward feline. The next, she lay crumpled on her side, her right ankle sending white-hot streaks of pain up her leg.

Piddie Longman would have called it an "O.S. Moment," the split second of clarity when a person realizes a regrettable error.

When Elvina could take a breath without crying out, she dug in the robe's pocket, flipped her cell phone on, and dialed 9-1-1.

Chapter Eleven

Mary-Esther pocketed her first paycheck. "I absolutely must get a haircut before animal control picks me up."

"You need to go see Mandy at the Triple C," Julie advised. "She's a wonder. If it wasn't for her, I'd have snatched mine out by the roots long ago."

Mary-Esther held a good stylist in high esteem. Even at her lowest point, when Loretta neared death, and joy and money were sucked from her life in equal measure, she still managed to scrape together enough for at least a decent cut. Katrina changed that.

After years of chemicals and coloring, her auburn hair crimped in unruly, frayed snarls. For the first time in years, Mary-Esther considered a short bob. Who had the time or energy to spend hours primping? Besides, the only mirrors in her life now were the fogged campground fixture, a compact she kept in the van, and the one hanging in the Homeplace ladies' room. That morning, she had almost succumbed to chopping her hair with a folding pocketknife. Instead, she had scraped it into an unkempt ponytail.

Mary-Esther flipped a couple of dollar pancakes. Perfect. Browned, not charred. "Is Mandy expensive?"

"Fifty bucks for a color and cut. Worth every penny. You'd pay twice that in Tallahassee. It's a good way to get to know the women in this town; that is, if you want to branch out from the handful of folks you've met here at Bill's. Most everyone goes to either Mandy or Wanda." Julie refilled two coffee carafes, her practiced hands working while she talked. "Wanda's a big draw for the black community. She does these weave creations that are nothing short of fantasy."

"Where is this place?"

"Corner of Bonita Street and Morgan Avenue. It's had a couple of owners since it belonged to Jake Witherspoon's parents, but everyone still calls it the Witherspoon Mansion. You remember Jake, the fellow who runs the Dragonfly Florist? He's addicted to our French dip sandwiches."

"Uh-huh." Mary-Esther shoveled the pancakes onto a warmed plate. Should know by now. No simple answers ever came from people in this town. They had to work the family history into everything.

Julie washed and dried her hands then flipped the towel over one shoulder. "Take the road beside our parking lot and it'll take you down Thrill Hill. Left at the stop sign. Triple C's a couple of blocks down."

Mary-Esther added two strips of bacon, a slice of orange. Had to pull double duty this morning. The new cook called in sick. Again. More likely hung over.

"Make sure you call first." Julie balanced a loaded platter on one hand, picked up a coffee carafe with the other. "Elvina Houston strong-arms the front desk. She doesn't cotton much to drop-ins."

That afternoon, Mary-Esther slowed the van in front of a sprawling, two-story house. Tucked between pines, dogwoods in red-leafed foliage, magnolias, and moss-draped live oaks, the mansion towered over the surrounding humble one-story homes like the town's ruling architectural monarch.

Mary-Esther followed the signs to a gravel-paved parking area and eased the dilapidated van into a tight spot between a gold Lincoln Towncar and a shiny late-model Buick. The van coughed and bucked before the engine died.

Mary-Esther took stock of herself. The scent of fried food wafted up from her clothing, and her shirt looked like she'd been in a grease war.

Oh yeah, I'll fit right in here.

She followed a slate path to a wide cement porch flanked with a row of Greek columns then entered the building through a massive pair of red doors. Upholstered high-back chairs and teak tables lined the walls of a spacious waiting room. A thick Oriental rug covered the polished wooden floor. In one corner, a rock fountain bubbled. Much fancier than the Sewanee Springs parlor.

Muffled conversations wafted from deeper in the house. Mary-Esther wandered into the adjoining room. An antique mahogany reception desk dominated one corner. The only other furnishings were an armoire and a wood and glass display case filled with a line of professional skin care products.

She glanced up to see several long, suspended poles displaying an array of garments. Some kind of specialized clothing store? The high-pitched wheeze of a sewing machine echoed from another room.

"Hello!" a voice called out from behind her. "Thought I heard the door. It's hard sometimes over the noise of the dryers." A short, perky woman with bouncy, brown hair walked past her and tapped on the computer keypad. "You must be Mary-Esther Sloat."

"Yes."

"Hope you didn't feel like you had been deserted. Most everyone from around here knows to come on back if no one's at the desk. But then," the woman gave her the up and down, "you're not from around *here*."

The woman's tone was friendly. Mary-Esther smiled. "No, I'm not."

"Usually Elvina Houston, our appointment specialist, is on duty. She would pitch a fit and fall in it, if she knew I had allowed a new patron to stand out here wondering what to do." The woman's brows knit together. "Unfortunately, Elvina met with a slight accident."

"Oh?" In New Orleans, the same declaration could mean someone had ended up in some muddy bayou. Gator bait.

"Elvina fell last night. Broken ankle. Had to have surgery, pins and all." The woman flicked her fingers through her bangs. "Where are my manners? I'm Mandy. Mandy Andrews." She stuck out one hand and Mary-Esther shook it.

So this was the famous local hair wizard. Mary-Esther had expected an older, wizened female with a strange-shaded beehive. Hard to tell her age. Late thirties? Mandy had that smooth, unlined skin, even around her eyes.

"Your appointment is with me in about . . ." Mandy consulted the wall clock. "Fifteen minutes or so. There's a fresh pot of coffee in the kitchen, next room over, if you'd like a cup."

Local protocol included coffee. No problem.

"There's creamer in the fridge, and sugar and fake sweeteners on the counter. Mugs are in the cabinet over the coffeemaker. Tea bags are in the glass jar by the sink, if you'd prefer. Help yourself, then join us back in the hair salon. No need to sit alone, and besides, you might miss something." Mandy flashed even, white teeth. "We don't ever *repeat* gossip, Mary-Esther. So you have to learn to listen closely the first time."

The stylist laughed as she turned to leave.

The place was loaded with antique gee-gaws. Mary-Esther didn't know a lot about such, but bet they were worth some bucks. Unbelievable, how folks in Chattahoochee assumed everyone trustworthy. Perhaps this was the way it was supposed to be, and once was, before everyone became so afraid.

Mary-Esther served herself a cup of coffee and took a long, appreciative sip. Not the cheap brand, for sure. If she ever settled down, her first purchase would be a new Cuisinart brewer and a coffee grinder. The heck with how much it would set her back.

She walked from the kitchen and paused at a mahogany archway leading to an elongated room. Mandy occupied one workstation and a red-haired woman Mary-Esther assumed to be Wanda commandeered the second. Three professional hair dryers whirred nearby, filled with seated patrons either perusing magazines or one-ear-outing the ongoing conversation. A few feet from the stylists, a blonde woman held court in a spacious nail care center in front of a humming exhaust fan.

Mandy glanced up through a fog of hair spray. "Don't be shy. C'mon in, hon."

Mary-Esther passed through the archway and settled into a tone-on-tone beige director's chair. Every female eye in the room studied her.

"Y'all, this is Mary-Esther Sloat. She's new in town. Works up at the Homeplace for Mr. Bill." Mandy motioned to each woman in turn with the pointed end of a rat-tail comb as she made introductions.

How would she recall all those names? She barely noted the regular patrons at Bill's, except the ones who took the time to call her by name. Or the decent tippers.

"You look familiar," one of the women under a dryer said in a too-loud voice. "You have people from around here?"

I don't know, do I? Mary-Esther pressed down a wave of dismay and formed a reply. "My family is . . . *was* . . . from New Orleans."

The women reacted as a group, nodding and clucking in sympathy.

"So," Mandy led off, "you're here following that dreadful Katrina."

"Not directly. I lived here and there for a bit."

Stylist Wanda Orenstein, a perky red-haired, green-eyed bundle of perpetual motion, spoke next. "It's as good a place as any to land, Mary-Esther. I've been all over, and I love it here."

Wanda's New Jersey accent caught Mary-Esther off-guard. Again, an assumption, that everyone in town would speak Deep-fried Southern.

Mandy's client, a young woman Mandy had introduced as local beauty queen and model Ladonna O'Donnell, held up a large, round hand mirror and studied the back of her new hairdo. "Looks real good, Mandy. Thanks!"

"When are you getting out of nursing school, Ladonna?" Melody the nail specialist looked up from the crabapple-colored polish she applied for her nail patron.

"This coming spring. Then I'll have to take board exams." The leggy blonde stood and shook the last of the hair snippets from her shoulders. "I dread that like having my nether hairs waxed. I never have been one much for those big tests."

Nether hairs? Mary-Esther stuffed a grin. *I need a translation book.*

Wanda peeled the Velcro neck strip apart and removed the plastic drape then patted Ladonna fondly on the back. "You'll do fine, hon. Anyone who can handle the rigors of beauty competitions and live to tell tale can do anything she sets her mind to."

The young woman gave the most exaggerated sigh Mary-Esther had ever witnessed. "This is *so* important to me. I don't want to blow it." She waved goodbye around the room. "Mandy, Mama said she'll pay when she comes in for her appointment later this week."

"Don't worry, sugar. I know where y'all live. It's not like you're some stranger just walked in off the street."

Was that comment aimed in her direction? *Get past it, Mary-Esther.* No need to dive into paranoia.

The women watched the ex-beauty queen turned nurse-wannabe sashay from the room. Every inch of her backside swayed.

Wanda used a broom to whisk sheared hair into a dustpan and dumped it into a waste container. "If Ladonna doesn't lose that wiggle, she'll cause more heart attacks than she helps prevent."

A titter of laughter rolled around the room.

"I bet her mama and daddy are relieved," commented a dark-haired woman seated in one of the side chairs. "Ladonna didn't have a sense of direction until she did that volunteer work over at Tallahassee Hospital."

"A woman can't rely on her good looks for her whole life. If she does, she's in for a rude surprise," Mandy said.

"I dunno," Wanda supplied. "It's worked for me for years."

Mandy cut her eyes at her coworker. "Humility certainly is one of your strong suits, Wanda Sue."

The tension eased from Mary-Esther's shoulders and back. The easy, familiar female banter offered a comfort she hadn't experienced in months.

Mandy patted the stylist's chair. "Okay, Miz Mary-Esther. Park your fanny. You're my next victim."

Mary-Esther slid into the vinyl seat and Mandy whipped the drape across her shoulders like a magician handling a cape.

"Don't worry. I'm in a passable mood this afternoon." The assuredness in Mandy's initial exploratory touches spoke of years of experience. "You want a cut too, right?"

Mary-Esther frowned at her own reflection in the mirror. "The ends are shot. Do what you can."

Mandy ran her fingers from Mary-Esther's scalp to the tips of her hair. "If you don't mind, I think we should go a tad below ear length. I'll shape it around your face for a little fullness. Maybe, some wispy bangs. A few layers. You really do have nice hair with a little natural wave. The *real* color isn't bad."

"Has to be heredity. If I'm not completely gray, or bald, after the last few months, it's a miracle." The irony of the statement caused her to pause. Heredity? How could she even venture a guess at her gene pool?

"I can use a couple of shades and put in some subtle streaking. The highlights will hide the bit of gray but look much better growing out. No roots to shine through."

"Do what you want. I'm ready to shave it to the scalp."

Wanda popped her gum. "Look at it this way, Mary-Esther. If you don't like the way it turns out, you can spit in her food. She's always ordering take-out from Bill's."

Mandy lobbed a damp white towel toward her coworker, but Wanda ducked in time and stuck out her tongue. No small wonder women hung out in hair salons. The stand-up humor was better than late-night TV improv.

A thin, older woman with shoulder-length brown hair bounced into the room holding a puffy crimson jacket in front of her like a banner. "What do y'all think of my new Teddy Bear Christmas sweater-jacket? It's part of a new line I'll have ready in time for the holidays."

The woman promenaded around the room and allowed the others to admire the piece. When she stopped in front of Mandy and her client, her skin paled.

"Mary-Esther, this is Evelyn Fletcher, our resident designer. I don't know if you noticed her handiwork when you first came in. Evelyn, this is Mary-Esther Sloat, new in town from Louisiana."

Mary-Esther tipped her head. Evelyn managed to squeak out a meager greeting.

After Evelyn left the room, Wanda raised her eyebrows and said, "Wonder what's gotten into her?"

Mandy shot a knowing glance Wanda's way. "Looked like she was about to faint."

Chapter Twelve

A nurse glanced over Hattie's intake form. "Do you have any metal in your body? Have you had any joint replacements? Do you have any pins, plates, screws, or staples?"

"No, no, and no," Hattie answered.

Thank goodness she didn't have any of *that* stuff. Aging provided enough little surprises. Wolf-like chin whiskers. Gas after every meal. Wiry gray hair sticking up from her scalp like mini horns. Even pimples.

The nurse's questions continued. "Have you ever had an MRI? Are you claustrophobic?"

"No, this will be the first. Not especially claustrophobic."

"Thank you, Mrs. Lewis. You'll go first to Radiology for an injection into the shoulder. Then you're scheduled an hour later for your contrast MRI at the Imaging Center two blocks down."

Sounded harmless enough. *Wait . . .* "Injection?"

"A contrast medium will be injected into the joint area to improve the image."

Nothing could be worse than the colonoscopy and the cancer surgery. Even those weren't horrible, especially since she hadn't died.

Hattie entered Radiology, filled out reams of forms, and a worker ushered her to the back. She stripped to her underwear and socks and donned one of the butt-flashing robes in a fetching shade of mint green.

"What's going on with your shoulder?" the radiologist asked.

She reclined on the padded vinyl table. "Don't really know. Hope it's not a tendon tear."

The doctor rotated Hattie's arm backward. She flinched and instinctively arched her upper back to relieve the pain.

"I'm going to take a quick positioning x-ray, Mrs. Lewis. Think you can handle this pose for a couple of minutes?"

Hattie bared her teeth. "I'm a tough farm girl."

With the digital x-ray image completed, the radiologist gently placed a heavy padded weight on her forearm, wiped the top of her shoulder with a cleaning solution, and applied a sterile drape. "You'll feel a pinch. Then a little pressure and a slight burning sensation. Keep very still."

Hattie took a slow, even breath, closed her eyes, and focused on maintaining the awkward position.

"There you go. Let me help you get up. Try to avoid moving this arm as much as possible. Is your driver here?"

Hattie shot him a questioning look. "Driver?"

"You must keep movement to a minimum. Didn't the person who confirmed your appointment inform you of this?"

"Nope. But I can drive fine with one arm. I've done it for the past few weeks."

"Can't allow that." The doctor's words came out in snips. "More you move, more the contrast medium liquid dissipates. The MRI image will suffer."

"I could call a cab, I suppose."

The doctor scowled and turned to his nurse. "We really need to address this issue. This isn't the first time there's been a breakdown in communication."

The nurse smiled. "I'm getting ready to leave. I can take her over. I don't mind."

"Still, that leaves me with a little problem," Hattie said. "My car will be *here.*"

The doctor scribbled on a logbook, bearing down so hard, Mary-Esther could hear the letters screech. "There's no one you can call?"

Hattie shook her head.

The doctor frowned. "They'll have to bring you *back* to your car after your MRI."

Best not to point out to Dr. Crab-cake that she'd still be driving home alone.

By the time the nurse deposited Hattie in front of the Imaging building, her shoulder throbbed with an insistent reggae beat.

More paperwork.

"Do you have any metal in your body?" the radiology technician asked when she showed Hattie to the dressing area.

"No metal. No staples. No plates in my head," Hattie rattled off before he could ask the same questions she had already answered.

"Are you claustrophobic?"

"I might be if y'all keep bringing it up." Hattie twisted her upper lip. The tech grinned. At least this one was in a decent mood.

Again she stripped, stowed her clothes and bag, and donned another, this time baby blue, butt-flash cotton robe. Her arm wouldn't move high enough to tie the neck or back closure, so she held it shut as best she could and padded across the hall behind yet another technician.

This is where having a big sister would've come in handy.

She reclined on the padded table as instructed and admired the pyramidal glass ceiling. Nice view. Easy to believe the master ship could beam her up. *No, no alien abductions. They do weird probing tests on humans.* Had to be worse than what she was about to go through.

"Here are some earplugs. It's a bit noisy. Do you need a blanket?"

"How long is the procedure? Five, ten minutes?"

The male technician shook his head. "More like forty, by the time I get the different aspects."

Hattie shivered. The MRI room temperature hovered in the sixties, to prevent fainting, no doubt. "Blanket would be good."

"Most people find it easier to close their eyes. I'll check in with you between increments. Remember, you must remain still. If you have to cough or anything, squeeze this bulb I'm putting in your hand. That way, I can pause and we don't have to start over. Okay?" He checked to make sure the earplugs were firmly seated then pulled a sheet around her arm, strapped her down, and layered a cotton blanket over her lower body. "Ready?"

"As I'll ever be."

The table slowly rose, then it slid down into the confining tube. Hattie shut her eyes a moment too late.

The top, inches from her face.

Like a coffin.

Daddy. Mama. Aunt Piddie. Baby Sarah. All, in a box like this.

Her chest constricted. *Cut it out, Hattie.*

For the next forty minutes, she pulled out every relaxation technique in her repertoire to fight the growing unease. She imagined sunning on a beach with a gentle sea breeze caressing her body, but the machine's clamor made it difficult to envision circling sea gulls—more like B-52s streaking overhead, dive-bombing close to her head.

She switched visions, projecting the face of a large, institutional-style clock. When the technician's voice announced the initiation of another series, she counted the minutes as the clock's secondhand made circles. One, two, three, three-and-a-half, four, five . . . Breathe.

You're safe. She imagined her big sister saying the words. *No, you don't have a bad, stinging, maddening itch on the side of your nose. Ignore it, sweetie.* Her panic subsided.

The final set lasted five minutes. Hattie emerged triumphant. As she dressed, Hattie chatted aloud to her imaginary big sister.

"Surreal experience, Sis. Let me tell you what it felt like. First, wrap yourself in a sheet so you can't move. Next, cram your body down into an oil drum with a fan blowing a gale across your head." She whipped the good arm in a circle. "Then, hire a bunch of raving hoodlums to bang hammers on the outside of the drum. Do this for at least a half-hour or more until your head explodes."

If anyone heard her, they'd lock her up for sure. Hattie peeked from behind the privacy drape. A woman seated in the waiting pen stared at her. Hattie offered a sheepish, sane-person grin. The lady went back to her *Southern Living* magazine.

Had Sarah been alive, she would have been here, laughing at the situation. They would have lunch afterwards, hit the mall for any sales. And she wouldn't have to drive alone back to Chattahoochee. With a limp arm.

But Sarah had been gone for years.

So why was her dead sister invading her thoughts so often lately? Hattie could pantomime and *if only* from here to Canada and back, and it wouldn't change history.

Hattie dropped the used robe into a bin and grabbed her purse. The waiting woman didn't glance up when she walked past. Probably too scared.

A pleasant young man shuttled Hattie the short distance to her parked car and dropped her off. After she noticed three drivers in a row one-arming while talking on their cell phones, and because she had no choice, Hattie risked driving.

Since she was only one block from the Tallahassee Hospital rehab unit, Hattie decided to visit a recent victim of fate. When she entered the semi-private hospital room, Hattie noted Elvina's leg, encased in a plastic, puffy, envelope sleeve and propped on a mound of pillows. The old woman motioned Hattie toward a vinyl visitor's chair and continued with her cell phone conversation.

"I've got to go, Angie. Hattie's here. I'll have my phone handy. Don't try to do it all. That job's not one you can learn in a day. It's a big help to Mandy and the girls having you there." Elvina snapped the cell phone shut. "That was Angelina Palazzolo. They broke down and called her to help at the front desk."

"That has to make you feel more at ease."

Elvina shifted positions and flinched. "She's managed to ride herd over her big family for years, and none of those kids turned out bad, so I reckon she can pinch-hit for me for a few weeks. She's not a computer whiz, but then neither am I. Yet."

"How are you feeling?"

"Fair to middlin'. They made me get up the second day after I got out of surgery. Prevents blood clots, you know. They have these nifty little pump jackets on my legs while I sleep or if I'm lying down for any length of time. I'll get a cast on soon."

"How long will you be here?"

Elvina's bony shoulders rose and fell. "Could be a while. I have to be able to do for myself, to a certain extent." Her eyes watered. "I don't know what's to become of me."

Hattie reached over and rested a hand over the old woman's thin, age-spotted arm. "You have lots of friends, Elvina. We'll work something out."

Elvina's expression brightened. "I am rich in that respect, for certain. Thanks to your late aunt, I have the inside scoop on most everyone. It pays to be nice to folks like us."

Hattie laughed. "You sound more like Aunt Piddie every day."

"*That* is a feather in my bonnet, for sure!"

"Jake and Shug are taking good care of your cat," Hattie said. "Buster will be spoiled rotten by the time you get home. When Jake lived out on The Hill, he hand fed Shammie canned tuna to bribe him into hanging out in his wing of the house."

Elvina made a growling noise. "If it wasn't for Buster and his philandering, I wouldn't be in this fix."

"Animals. Got to love 'em," Hattie said. "Jake talked with Bobby about converting your back porch into a Florida room. Bobby could install a cat door into the sliding glass door so Buster has a spot to enjoy the outdoors without facing the local bullies. It would give you a great place to hang out without worrying about mosquitoes toting you off." Hattie paused. "If you need a ramp to get to the side door, Bobby can build it too."

Elvina's eyes watered again. "I hate to be such a burden."

"Folks want to help, Elvina. Your job is to let them."

Elvina's roommate groaned behind the divider curtain, and they glanced in that direction.

"Poor old woman. She broke her hip. She's bad off. I'm surely glad I only messed up my ankle. Lord knows . . ." Elvina lowered her voice to a whisper. "A broken hip in one of us oldsters is the kiss of death sure as I'm sitting here."

"Should I call a nurse?"

"No. She moans and groans all the time. I think she's plumb out of this world. Never has anyone come by, either. It's the saddest thing. Having family, or friends like you, is beyond gold." Elvina's gaze focused across the room at a vague point, as if she looked into the past. "Did I ever tell you about when Piddie and I first met?"

Only about fifty times. Hattie braced herself to hear it again.

"I had recently moved into town from Miami. My dear husband Clyde had died and I was lost, lost, lost. The little house I live in now used to belong to Clyde's mama. It passed to me after he died."

She shifted position and continued, "I don't know what came over me, moving up here. Guess I didn't ever really cotton to Miami much. Clyde loved the weather down there, but not me. I like a little change of season, just not too cold for too long like way up north."

The ache in Hattie's shoulder subsided a little. She leaned forward and gave the older woman her full attention.

"I suffered one of my blue spells after I moved. Suppose all the changes I'd been through built up inside of me 'til I shut down. Depression is what I had, though back then, it didn't have that modern label. I didn't know a soul in town. I managed to pull myself together, but it was the hardest thing I'd ever done."

"How did Aunt Piddie figure in?" Hattie asked in a disguised attempt to keep the conversation on topic.

"She spotted me in the IGA, wandering up and down the aisles. I must've looked a sight. Skinny as a junkyard dog. Never could eat during one of my spells, so my weight would fall off pretty badly. Piddie marched right up to me, introduced herself, and went to talking a blue streak. By the time we hit the cash register, my buggy was full of stuff I didn't need, and I knew the dirt on half the town."

"Piddie could natter, that's for sure."

Elvina's thin lips curled into a wistful smile. "There wasn't a day that passed I didn't talk to her. I loved that little kitchen of hers more than any place on this earth. Piddie had a way of sensing when I was heading downhill. She would cook up some of those wonderful teacakes."

Hattie's mouth watered. Hot teacakes fresh from the oven. Her mom had cooked them too. Somewhere, Hattie still had the family recipe. Time to introduce the next generation to the joys of baking. Hattie imagined her daughter, flour dusting her hands, giggling with crystals of sugar wreathing her lips.

Elvina's voice broke Hattie's daydream. "I didn't grow up with much in the way of family. My daddy died before I was born and I never had any brothers or sisters. My mother was a cold woman, Hattie. And because I was born out of wedlock, her family disowned both of us. I have kin somewhere, I suppose. But I never met 'em. Wouldn't even know where to begin to look.

"Piddie told me as long as she drew a breath, I was not abandoned in this world. Said friends were God's way for making up for family. That's why I took it so hard when she passed. Oh, I do believe she'll be waiting on the other side for me. I *have* to believe."

"She will be, Elvina."

"That's why I've made a decision. Much as I loved Clyde, I don't want to be shipped off to Miami to be laid to rest when my time comes. I'll be cremated, like Piddie. Then I'm going to be sprinkled right alongside her at the Triple C."

Hattie blinked. What did one say to such?

Elvina slapped her hands on her lap. "I'm not ready to help her push up daisies yet. I got a good ten or fifteen years left in me, way I figure. I must move on with this healing business and get back to my obligations."

"Everyone will manage, Elvina. Take all the time you need."

"As soon as they let me out of this place, I'm hot-footing it home. Well, as much as I can with only *one* working foot." Elvina wagged her finger. "I can't begin to fathom the mess the Triple C will be in."

"Nice to know you're needed, isn't it?"

Elvina gave a definitive nod. "You're not just whistlin' Dixie."

What the heck did that old saying mean, anyway?

Elvina's intense gaze focused on Hattie. "Family is everything. No matter if it's your work people, your blood relatives, or your good friends you've made into family. Family is *everything*."

Chapter Thirteen

The extended column of thunderstorms rolling west across Lake Seminole sent a line of wind gusts whipping through the treetops. The temperature dropped. At first, Sergeant J. Blount assumed the loud rapping on the top of the cruiser's light bar to be hard rain. Then he noticed the bouncing silhouettes of hailstones popping off the hood.

He turned the cruiser north toward the Florida/Georgia border and accelerated. The only lights on the storm-darkened highway were his, slicing a path through the deluge. Small, detached limbs scudded across the blacktop, grabbing at his tires like skeletal arms.

Jerry took a sharp left and headed toward East Bank campground. Beneath his breath, he said a silent prayer for Mary-Esther's safety. The fact he cared about this particular woman's welfare unsettled him, but he shoved it aside. Just doing his job. Just looking out for a woman alone in a bad storm.

At the bottom of a steep hill, he veered left into the unpaved lane through the campsite. His high beams rested on the barren campsite.

What the heck?

No logs stacked by the fire ring. No evidence anyone had recently occupied the area.

Gone.

He took a pass through the rest of the campground. The drive back into Chattahoochee was slow, as if the tires slogged through heavy mud. It was his own fault for allowing the little Cajun woman to trigger his protective instinct. His mother said he tended to *let* stray cats and dogs follow him home.

He had a soft spot for needy things.

Jerry pushed through the front door of the Homeplace Restaurant. No fellow diners tonight.

Mr. Bill waved from the little office behind the cash register. "Evenin', Jerry. Bad night out."

"Nothing a hot cup of coffee won't help." Jerry shook the moisture from his jacket and draped it across the back of the booth. He eased into the seat and stared through the water-dappled window at the puddled reflections of the traffic light. Green. Yellow. Red. Repeat. A feminine hand placed a cup of steaming black coffee in front of him.

"Thank you." His voice sounded as deflated as his spirit.

"You look like you've gunned down your last friend, Officer Blount."

Jerry recognized the soft voice, glanced up. His heart stuttered.

"How about a piece of hot apple pie with a big scoop of vanilla ice cream?" Mary-Esther asked. "That lifts me when I'm in the dumps."

"Sure. Yeah." That was the best he could do?

Mary-Esther returned and slid a loaded dessert plate and fork beside his coffee mug. "Why are you out driving around? Surely no one in his, or her, right mind is out and about committing acts of larceny."

Jerry shrugged. The scent of warm sugar cinnamon blended with the coffee aroma. His mood improved. "Want to join me?"

Mary-Esther flipped a hand toward the empty room. "Why not? Not like it's a big tip night." She turned and disappeared into the kitchen.

When she returned, she carried a second mug and an insulated carafe and set it down between them. "Saves me a trip back to the kitchen."

"You're not at East Bank anymore."

One of Mary-Esther's brows lifted. "No. Rules say I can only stay there fourteen days in a row." She poured herself a cup.

"Thought you'd decided to leave town." He dug into the pie.

"Nope." She took a sip of coffee. "Had to go be a vagabond at a campground on Lake Talquin. I'll keep moving, long as I need to."

"You all right . . . out there?"

"Why wouldn't I be?"

He forced his gaze from her intense scrutiny. "Weather changes a lot this time of year. Getting cold soon."

"You're worried about me, aren't you, Officer Jerry?" She cocked her head to one side and studied him.

Women, and especially this one, made him feel as if he had rusty nail soup for brains. He slugged coffee to keep his throat from closing up. "Don't want anyone to freeze on my watch."

"I hope to be somewhere better soon. Mr. Bill has given me a couple of leads on some garage apartments. Imagine, I could move in off the streets and the local law enforcement wouldn't have to fret about me causing trouble."

"That never crossed my mind. Really, Mary-Esther—"

She reached over and brushed the tops of his knuckles lightly with her fingertips. A current zinged to his toes.

"I'm touched, Jerry. But I'll be okay."

"Some weather last night, eh?" Jake Witherspoon trundled to the front display window of the Dragonfly Florist. His cane-of-the-day, one of over two hundred at last count, sported decoupage orange, yellow, and red fall leaves on the shaft.

Hattie looked up from her appointment calendar. "Tell me about it. I thought the roof might blow off. It never fails. When Holston's out of town, we get a storm to end all storms. At least the electricity didn't go off. Before they reworked our lines, the lights went out if a dog peed on a power pole."

Jake shook his head. "Sister-girl, your language is *so* colorful sometimes."

"Took lessons from you, Jakey."

Separated by a decorative archway, Jake's store, the Dragonfly Florist, shared a common wall with Hattie's massage therapy room. Though Hattie's room wasn't nearly as spacious as Stephanie's at the Triple C, The Madhatter's Chocolate Shoppe and Massage Parlor nailed it for diversity.

Hattie inhaled the aroma of confections and freshly brewed gourmet coffee, blended with the scent of flowers. The combination pleased her.

A husband seeking atonement could purchase a bouquet of fresh-cut flowers, dark chocolate delicacies, and a gift certificate for an hour of relaxation massage. If that trio didn't get him out of the dog house, nothing short of jewelry could.

"You want Shug and me to come camp out while hubby is away? We could bring fondue and talk trash until the wee hours." The twin dimples deepened in his cheeks when he smiled.

"Appreciate the offer, but Sarah and I are big girls."

Hattie's best friend regarded her with a lifted eyebrow. "Something else eating at you, Sister-girl?"

"Probably nothing. Silly to mention."

Jake plucked a dead leaf from a mixed-plant basket on the front counter. "Every time I hear that *something* is probably *nothing*, I know it is more than likely *something*. Give."

"There's been a strange van driving by The Hill. Margie said it's pulled off the highway and turned around several times, sometimes in front of their house, sometimes a little farther up the lane."

"A delivery truck?"

"Don't know. Maybe. Our packages generally come by the post office or UPS. Occasionally, FedEx. Still, they would have left the box by the front door if I wasn't home."

"Have you seen this mystery van?"

"Not yet. But I'm keeping my eyes open. Usually, someone is on The Hill most of the time. We keep odd hours, so if someone's casing the area, it would be hard to pin down a time when all three houses are deserted."

"Maybe you should mention it to the county patrol officer, in case. He could drive by every now and then." Jake returned to one of three fall-themed floral centerpieces. First Baptist Women's Auxiliary luncheon, the work slip stated.

Hattie's cell phone rang and she stepped back into the privacy of her massage office to talk.

"Double doo-doo!" Hattie said when she returned to the Dragonfly Florist side of the business.

"Strong words, Sister-girl. Who crushed your Crayolas?"

"I have to go back to Tallahassee for another dang MRI."

"Did you not behave last time?" Jake pointed at her with a sprig of fern. "Bet you wiggled. I know I should've insisted on going with you."

Hattie stuck out her tongue. "I did fine, thank you very much. One of the nurses called and said they want a series of my neck. They didn't see any problems with my shoulder. But that is precisely where it hurts!"

"Nerve impingement," Jake stated.

"Let you shack up with a nurse, and all of a sudden you can diagnose the world."

Jake handed her a daisy. "You are positively foul when you're in constant pain. Good thing some of us can handle suffering."

True enough. If anyone had the right to grouse about pain, it was Jake Witherspoon. Since his abduction and assault, the small lines around his lips and deep circles beneath his eyes provided a constant reminder of the hate crime that had almost taken his life.

The worst scars didn't show.

She twirled the flower offering in her fingers. Such a sunny-faced bloom.

"I'm sorry. You're right." Hattie stuck the daisy behind one ear then reached over and hugged her friend with her good arm. "I hate the idea of another MRI. It took all I could do to get through the first one without absolutely crawling out of my skin."

68

"Can't they give you something in advance? Ask for the open-design machine. It's much less agonizing if you're edgy in tight spots."

"How can I take drugs and drive home?"

Jake reached over and cradled her chin in his palm. "Sister-girl, I can go with you."

"I couldn't—"

He dismissed her with a sweep of his hand. "It'll be fun. We can make it into a little outing, like old times. I'll get Jolene to cover the shop."

"But . . . Sarah. And with Holston out of town—"

"Leigh, I'm sure, will babysit for the little chinaberry. See? No obstacles. You really do need to get this thing taken care of. You're trying to keep up with your massage therapy patients, and you can barely move."

"Okay, okay. Deal. I'll phone the doctor and get them to call in something to relax me."

Jake grabbed a handful of daisies and expertly placed them into an arrangement. "As I recall from after your surgery, you're one of the most amusing people on the planet when you're on the dope."

Mary-Esther parked the van in a narrow driveway beside a wooden framed house off Satsuma Road. She checked the address. Had to be it, but where was the apartment? She turned off the key. The engine sputtered. She got out.

A thin, stooped elderly man tottered onto the side porch and waved her way. He descended two short steps as if each movement caused him great pain.

"Hi," she said as she stepped closer. "I'm Mary-Esther Sloat. Mr. Bill told me you—"

"I know who you are. Bill just called me. The place is in the back. Been empty for a couple of months. Could be musty. It'll need a good cleaning. I can't hold out to do it, and my wife neither . . . ." He stopped. "I'm Eustis Herring. Wife's Rose Herring."

"Pleased to meet you."

Mary-Esther trailed after the man, careful not to walk too fast as to pull ahead of him. Behind the house, a narrow, two-story structure leaned toward a large live oak tree as if it yearned to become part of the natural landscape. The open garage housed an old pick-up truck with at least two flat tires. A set of rickety stairs led up one side of the building to the second story.

"I can't make those steps." He handed her a scratched *Visit Florida!* key ring. "Look around to your content. Knock on my back door when you're done." He turned and wobbled toward the main house.

The stairs screeched and moaned as Mary-Esther ascended. Good thing she wasn't heavy. The key strained against the frozen lock mechanism, and she wiggled it to release the deadbolt. Two shoves and the door pushed open.

The scent of old dust tickled her nose. She sneezed twice. The efficiency wasn't fancy by any stretch. A brown couch and mismatched chair huddled in one corner. In the other stood a double bed with a small end table. A low-pile rug covered the painted wooden floor. No pictures claimed the walls, nothing to indicate the personality of the owners or the previous renter.

She squeezed into a single bathroom barely large enough to stand inside and shut the door. The tub and toilet were stained amber from years of mineral-tainted water.

A narrow galley-style kitchen held a deep porcelain sink, a compact electric stove, a small rust-pocked vintage refrigerator, and one countertop with a bank of cabinets overhead. She opened the doors to find an assortment of plates, bowls, cups, and glasses. Nothing matched. Drawers on either side of the sink held flatware and a handful of cooking utensils.

The door to the side of the kitchen led to a screened room. Mary-Esther clasped her hands together. It was like opening a plain brown wrapper to find magic. The oak's branches cradled the room on three sides, as close to standing in a tree house as she had ever been. Boudreau would love it.

Regardless of the amount of scrubbing needed to make the apartment livable, Mary-Esther vowed to move in as soon as she could give the dust bunnies and roaches notice. She locked the door behind her, creaked back down the stairs, and walked the few feet to the rear door of the Herring's house. The old man answered her knock.

"I'll take it, Mr. Herring."

"Rent's two hundred dollars, due no later than the fifth of each month. The utilities are on. They're on our line, so we'll have to see how much you use. If you go over fifty, I may have to up the rent to cover. It's not a big place, so it doesn't take much to run the lights and heat. No smoking. No loud parties." He jabbed a bony finger for emphasis. "We're peaceable people, and we don't abide trouble."

"I keep to myself, Mr. Herring." Mary-Esther pulled several twenty-dollar bills from her wallet and handed them over. "Do you have a contract for me to sign?"

"Word pledge is good enough for me." Eustis Herring extended a gaunt hand. "Give me a month's notice if you plan to leave."

Mary-Esther gently shook his hand. "Yes, sir. You got it."

She walked back to the van wearing a wide smile. She could move in right away. Easy, since she only had a few clothes and one box of belongings. Oh, and a folding chair and a cat. And some rocks. Don't forget the rocks.

Place to sleep. Place to cook. Place to shower. Roof overhead.

A couch. She had a couch!

Mary-Esther backed out and headed uptown to the Dollar Store for cleaning supplies, toilet paper, and necessities. Next, the grocery store. Then to the campground to retrieve Boudreau and her chair.

Mary-Esther hummed. Sometimes, you actually catch a break.

Chapter Fourteen

Hattie opened the fireplace damper. The night air crackled with the first chill of the season. Perfect! She piled up starter fire sticks, a handful of fat lighter wood—deadfall pine with seams of flammable resin—and several small oak splits. Then she settled onto a padded chair and propped her feet close to the hearth's warmth, sipped coffee. Sarah Chuntian played on a quilt, building her own little log stack with twigs.

Like her father, Hattie favored the fall. The hardwoods scattered amongst the evergreens showed off in gold, red, and orange; not the brilliant, drive-off-the-road magnificence of the Smoky Mountains farther north, but pleasing all the same. Fall was the time she most remembered her father, Dan Davis, affectionately known as Mr. D by his family and wide circle of friends.

As soon as the first frost drove the rattlesnakes into their winter hidey-holes, Mr. D took Hattie and Bobby on the long walk to check the fences along the periphery of the property. Hattie and her father would rest on the leaf-strewn ground and listen to the music of the woods. The only weapon he carried was a slingshot fashioned from a Y-shaped piece of oak and rubber tubing. They took turns firing acorns into the overhead branches.

Bobby was the one who loved guns. He lived to hunt. As soon as he was old enough to handle a shotgun, he stayed in the woods until darkness, cold, and hunger drove him to the house. Every hunting season, Dan allowed his son one deer kill off the property, plenty to fill the deep freezer with choice cuts of venison. Hunting had its place, her father emphasized. Without thinning their numbers, the whole lot would starve.

You kill it. You eat it. Her father's mantra.

Once when Hattie asked her father why he didn't like to hunt, he answered, "I don't know, Sugar. Reckon I lost the love of killing. One time, I had a big buck lined up in my sights. I was getting ready to squeeze the trigger when he turned and looked right at me with big, brown eyes. I couldn't shoot him."

Spring had been her mother's favorite time of year. Hattie's mother disliked the drab and dreary cold dampness of winter. It made her joints ache and her spirit sore. Where Hattie and her father energized, Tillie became morose and withdrawn, as if the plunging temperatures challenged her generally rosy outlook.

Hattie smiled. "You would've loved your grandmother," she said to Sarah Chuntian. "She adored springtime. She'd flit around this big old house, cleaning, deep-dusting, and singing until we wanted to choke her silent."

Sarah looked up, babbled some nonsense syllables. Shammie's ears perked up.

Funny, how families divided into similar camps. Bobby and Tillie chirped around in the morning in terminally high spirits. Both loved spring and warmth. Both could jabber on and on, without so much as a morning cup of tea.

In the a.m. hours, Hattie and her father growled like bears whose hibernation had been rudely interrupted. Neither made eye contact with another living thing for at least the first thirty minutes after awakening and bumped into walls, chairs, or anything else in their paths.

Hattie wrapped her hands around her cup and dove into the family memories like a deep bag of fine chocolates, savoring each one.

Thank the heavens for chocolate, and for coffee.

As she had since her teens, Hattie drank her favorite addiction hot and black. Back then, mornings on The Hill had followed a pattern. She could hear the family moving about. Her mom was first in the kitchen, humming some inane, chirpy, little song. In a few minutes, the scent of perked coffee sifted into Hattie's bedroom.

Next, the sound of her brother bounding through the kitchen. The back door slammed when he went out to feed the dogs.

Last, her dad. Hattie heard him mumbling replies to her mom. He'd appear at her bedroom door with blood-spotted pieces of toilet paper stuck to his clean-shaven face. The master of the house, come to evict his daughter from sweet sleep.

One flip of the light switch usually forced Hattie to moan and squint with one eye opened. Some mornings, her father snatched off her covers. As a last resort, he blared big band music, usually Glenn Miller, from a well-placed speaker by her bedroom door. Were other children similarly mistreated?

Hattie would bumble from bed into the bathroom then trail behind her father into the too-bright kitchen. No one spoke to the two grumps. Each person remained with his or her respective dive partner. Perky with perky, crabby with crabby.

What would the family dynamics have been if Sarah had survived? Maybe since Hattie was so much the copy of Dan Davis, the other daughter would've been a mirror of the effervescent Tillie.

It was a waste of time to speculate. Sarah Davis was a faded shadow, a mythical child who had never existed.

Hattie watched her own daughter Sarah playing with her pile of twigs. *This* child was no shadow.

Why did sitting in front of a fire cause her mind to skip from one random snippet of the past to the next? If Holston was home, she would ramble on and on, and he would listen. Or pretend to.

She stood, disturbed the coals with a poker, and added a large oak log. "Mama's getting pretty good at this one-arm thing, don't you think?" she asked Sarah.

The toddler picked up a piece of bark, studied it, and crammed it in one of her overall pockets. The little packrat. Each time Hattie did laundry, she found leaves, acorns, and rocks in pockets, and an occasional bird feather stuck inside the child's pillowcase.

Hattie turned her backside to the hearth. Warmth soaked through her jeans. The scent of burning wood triggered more thoughts of Mr. D, in his worn blue-plaid flannel jacket with a hole in one elbow.

"I learned how to build a fire from your grandfather. Wish you could've known him." She reached down and tousled Sarah's hair. "He would've eaten you up! 'C'mon Hattie-butt, let's you and me get a fire going,' he would say. Hattie-butt, that was his nickname for me, but don't share that with just anyone." Hattie moved onto the quilt beside her daughter and gathered her into her arms. "He would hold me close to keep me warm. He smelled like Old Spice."

Sarah hugged Hattie then pushed away. Hattie released her grasp and let the child return to her twigs.

"Daddy would pick up an ax and bang the sides of the lean-to where we kept the woodpile. Critters lived in there. Sometimes snakes. He'd chip a few splinters off a fat lighter stump, enough to get the fire started." Hattie plucked a twig from Sarah's mouth. Everything had to be tasted, obviously. "I loaded the smaller logs into the wheelbarrow. Daddy would carry an armful of the larger ones. 'Get some of this green wood,' he would say. 'Makes for a good, long-burning fire.'" Hattie pointed to one of the logs by the hearth. "You can tell the drier, seasoned wood by the cracks in the ends of the log. See?"

Shammie meowed. Sarah patted the Persian with one hand.

"If you use only the dry wood, you'll go through your whole supply in a blink. When you get your fire going, you add a couple of green timbers. They'll burn for hours."

Hattie's father knew everything worth knowing. And she'd teach her own daughter as much as possible. Life wasn't all about book learning.

The phone rang. Hattie jumped up and picked up the handset. "Hello?"

Dead air answered.

"Hello? Hell-lo!"

A disconnect click followed.

"Wrong number," she told Sarah.

She hoped.

Over the past few days, she had received a series of hang-up calls at various hours. Three times, the answering machine recorded the hiss of silence.

The phone rang again. This time, a familiar voice sounded on the other end. "What are my two favorite girls doing?"

Hattie released a relieved sigh and settled back onto a small ottoman. "Sitting in front of a roaring fire your daughter helped me build."

"Wish I was there. So, you've gotten a little of this crisp weather too?"

"Supposed to be in the thirties tonight. Maybe light frost. I moved the plants inside."

"I should've done that before I left. Especially with your shoulder."

"Miz Maggie helped me. And besides, it was eighty degrees when you left, hon."

Holston laughed. "Right."

"When do you think you'll be home?"

"I have one last meeting with my publisher tomorrow, and then I want to catch up with a couple of old friends. I've booked a flight on Wednesday, unless you need me to come sooner."

Hattie considered. "That's fine. I have to go over to Tallahassee tomorrow, but Jake's going with me."

"What's up?"

"They think the problem might be in my neck. I disagree. I know where it hurts, but I'll have the second MRI. That way, the orthopedist will have everything he needs next week when I go to the appointment."

"Sure you're okay?"

The concern in his voice touched her. Since her colon cancer surgery, Holston tuned into every nuance of her health.

"Positive. Sarah will be with Leigh, and you know Jake will hover over me like a mother hen."

"Anything else happening?"

Should she mention the van or the strange phone calls? No. Holston would worry, and he was miles away.

"Dull as dog dirt, here on The Hill."

They talked a couple of minutes. The house felt hollow after she hung up.

Sarah played at her feet, alternately staring at the snickering fire and taunting the cat with a pine needle. Though Shammie had been slower than Spackle to come around to the presence of a child in the house, she now adored Sarah and followed her around talking in short yowls.

Sarah babbled to the cat in a combination of gurgles and baby-talk. What did the two discuss? Baby food versus canned kitty tuna? Disposable diapers as opposed to a litter box?

The old farmhouse creaked, tiny moans and comments that served as its heartbeat. The walls wrapped around her and Sarah, a loving cloak.

Sarah rose, toddled toward the front door, and pointed to the knob. "Spua?"

Of course. How could Hattie forget the other four-legged member of the Davis-Lewis household? She opened the door and peered past the front door fixture's circle of light. "Spackle! Here boy!"

A noise like a huffing, galloping horse sounded from the darkness. The mutt-dog loped to the door, his tail held high.

"C'mon in out of the cold. Your baby sister misses you."

Spackle bounded inside. After a perfunctory cruise by the empty cat food bowl, he delivered a set of slobbery face-licks to Sarah. Shammie stepped aside to avoid the inevitable clubbing from the canine's tail. The cat gave an annoyed yowl.

Hattie reached down and tousled the Persian's ruff. "I know, Shammie. He has the manners of a cretin."

Chapter Fifteen

When Sergeant Jerry Blount pulled the cruiser into the narrow, rutted driveway beside the Herring's house, he spotted Mary-Esther Sloat sitting on the lower steps of the garage apartment, her face buried in her cupped hands. She glanced up and blotted her cheeks with one sleeve.

His chest constricted. God help him; he couldn't abide a woman's tears.

He shut off the engine, got out, and walked over to stand in front of her.

"Hi," she said in a weak voice.

"Looks like I've picked a bad time to pop by."

"Not really." Mary-Esther patted the stair beside her. "Join me if you like. Sorry, I don't have any chairs to offer."

He brushed a clump of dead oak leaves aside and sat. "Heard you rented this place. Wanted to stop by and see how you were settling in."

She offered a thin smile. "I'm as settled as a person with nothing *can* be."

The woman didn't sound like her usual upbeat self. Jerry's honed cop instinct kicked in. Body language spoke louder than her words. "How about your new landlord and lady? You okay with them?"

"Sure. Nice folks. She's a bit nosy." Mary-Esther tipped her head toward the back of the Herring's house. The curtains snapped closed.

"It's not like I'm exciting or anything. Television has to be much more entertaining than me."

Jerry shifted positions to alleviate the pressure from the wide service belt. "I'm glad you found a place, what with the weather taking a turn."

How could he ferret out her obvious distress without alerting her male-intruder alarm? Might as well take the Southern gentleman's approach. If he got his feelings stomped on, it wouldn't be the first time.

His mother often admonished him for being too much the nice guy and how it was going to cause him heartache.

"Anything wrong?" he asked.

"I think the old girl bit the bullet." Mary-Esther motioned to the van.

Good, something concrete he might be able to solve. "What's *she* doing?"

"Nothing, now. Made this tremendous banging noise like something had torn loose inside. Then she choked and died." Mary-Esther waved her hand through the air. "And there she sits."

"Sounds like you might have thrown a rod."

"I'd throw a spear, if I had one." She paused. "A rod. Sounds expensive."

Jerry noticed tears gathering at the corners of her eyes again. "Maybe. Maybe not. You recall, I have low friends in high places."

"Another of your third cousins fifty times removed?" Mary-Esther dabbed the moisture from her cheek with a fingertip.

"Something like that."

"At least I can walk to work from here."

"Might be able to help with that too, if you don't mind driving a wreck."

Her eyebrows shot up. "What? You're offering me a car?"

Jerry chuckled. "It runs, all I'll say. I use the county vehicle most of the time during the week. I have a vintage Mustang I fixed up for the other times. The pick-up, I bought secondhand to haul firewood, lumber, that kind of stuff. It's parked at my house not being driven. It would do me a favor if you'd run it a little. An engine tends to go down if you let it sit idle too long."

"That's kind, but—"

"Look, I can have the van towed to Quincy for next to nothing. I'll have Milton look it over, see what it'll take to get her running."

"The tire and brake guy?"

"Like a lot of folks around here, Milton has more than one job," Jerry said. "Tires and brakes are his specialty, but he does other repairs on the side for close friends and family."

Mary-Esther raked her hands through her auburn hair. "I hate this, feeling so dependent for everything! Seems like it's all I've done since before Katrina."

"Mary-Esther. . ." Jerry willed his voice to an even tone. "Everyone needs a hand, at one time or the other. This is *your* time."

Sometimes, people were a bit like spooked animals. They required a little reassurance and a gentle word. Folks called his eyes "doe-brown." Brown as homemade gravy and just as comforting, his grandma used to say. Maybe those eyes would help calm this little Cajun woman. Same way they had comforted his dying wife, or so he hoped.

"Grandma used to say a person's greatest challenge is to have grace," he said. "Grace to accept help. Grace to know when to give in and let go."

"Why is it, everyone around here tends to drag the wisdom of their ancestors into the mix?" she asked.

"Respect for our elders was beaten into us at an early age. Besides," he winked, "most of the time, they were right."

Elvina Houston chewed on the end of a pencil, intent on the Sudoku puzzle in her hands. Since they had moved her roommate, she didn't have the endless moaning for company. God as her witness, if she didn't get out of the rehab center soon and back into real life, she would lose what little mind she had left.

She heard a rap on the door and called out, "Come on in."

Evelyn and Joe Fletcher pushed through the door, all smiles.

Elvina chunked the puzzle book and pencil onto the wheeled, over-bed table. "Thank you, sweet Jesus! I prayed to Piddie this morning to send me someone to make the time pass by. Now here y'all are!"

Evelyn leaned down and gave Elvina a kiss on the cheek. "We'd have been over sooner, but I've been tied up, finishing my holiday line. I will never, *ever* sew on chenille again as long as I live and breathe. It's like trying to stitch up a rabid wildcat."

"You look good, Elvina." Joe gave Elvina a hug then set a basket of blooming African violets on the bedside table. "Jon sends his love, and Jake heard we were on the way over and insisted we bring you these."

"It throws me when someone calls Shug Presley by his real name. I hardly hear anyone call him Jon." Elvina admired the lush plant. "Aren't Jake and Shug the sweetest boys? I'll owe them for the rest of my born days for all they've done: keeping up my house, watching over Buster, watering my ferns. Why, do you know Shug asked permission to open my mail so he could make sure the bills were paid on time? I don't know how I could've gotten by without all the help I've gotten . . . from every-one."

"Jake's driven the Olds to work a few times, to keep the battery from going down," Joe said.

Elvina slapped her lap. "Bet that's a sight, Jake Witherspoon in my big ole boat of a car. He and Piddie tried to talk me into buying a newer model, something not so hard to park. Piddie used to say the Olds was so roomy, that when I died, I could be buried in it, laid full-out in the back seat. Y'all could be rid of my body and my car at the same time." She paused. "Only, I plan to be cremated. So I reckon one of y'all can borrow my Olds coffin."

They laughed.

"You know, Elvina. When Mama passed, I believed all of the joy had drained from my life. I am so blessed you are here to remind me to have fun." Evelyn settled onto one of the vinyl chairs. "We have something to discuss with you. Hear us out before you say anything."

Elvina leaned forward, plumped the stack of pillows behind her, and settled back. "Anytime someone tells me to *hear them out*, I worry."

"Joe and I would like for you to stay with us when you're released from rehab."

Elvina arched her brows. "Why in Sam Hill would I do such? I have a perfectly good house."

"Hold your horses before you say no." Evelyn held up a stop hand. "Joe and I have put a lot of thought into this. Mama's little apartment is sitting there vacant. Oh, I go in and clean it every few weeks, but it is do-ing no one any good. It's private and closes off from our end of the house. The bathroom has a chair-height toilet and grab bars everywhere. Plus the bath enclosure doesn't have a big lip to step over like a tub does, and we still have the shower seat Mama used."

"It's going to be challenging for you until your cast comes off," Joe added. "Our house has wide halls and ramps. Ev and I will make it a point not to intrude on your privacy, unless you need us."

Evelyn continued the pitch. "We can ride to work together. I know how much you miss the Triple C, and believe me, we miss you too. Not that Angelina isn't helping tremendously. She's just not *you*. I'll even bring the Olds over and we can alternate taking it to the spa."

"Hmm . . ." Elvina tapped one of her painted nails on her chin. "You'd have to get to work earlier, Evelyn."

"I will adjust." Evelyn glanced at Joe. "And another thing, Jake and Bobby have looked over your little house. I know Hattie said something to you about building a ramp for you to get into the side door, but Bobby wants to discuss some other renovations."

"Renovations?"

"Mainly the bathroom. None of us are trying to step in and run your life for you, Elvina. We're thinking ahead. Even when you get your cast off, you might not be as able-bodied."

Elvina sighed. "I so love to take a long, relaxing bath. I would hate giving up my old claw foot tub. I can put enough water in it to practically sink clean up to my neck."

"Here's the good part, Elvina," Joe said. "Bobby says they make an upright tub. You can walk in and sit down, close the door, then fill it with water. That way, you get to soak without worrying about taking a bad fall."

"All this sounds good, but expensive."

"We'll go easy on you," Joe said. "No rent at the Fletcher No-tell Hotel."

Elvina raised one eyebrow. "Kind of you."

"And," Evelyn added, "with Bobby doing the construction, it will be reasonable."

"Sounds like the decisions have been made for me," Elvina stated.

Joe, always the counselor, said, "It's your choice, Elvina. All of us would be pleased if you allowed us to ease you through this transition."

"That's what family is for," Evelyn said.

Chapter Sixteen

Jake Witherspoon used a credit-card-sized remote control to flip radio channels in Hattie's SUV. "This satellite radio is marvelous. I simply must have one."

"I got tired of commercials and deejays rattling on and on about nothing. This way, I can listen to what I want without all the garbage."

Jake consulted a laminated play list. "One whole station for disco and for rhythm and blues and Jeez-O-Pete, the Weather Channel! You can listen to old people's MTV in your car."

Hattie merged onto Interstate 10 East and accelerated. "I hate it when you call it that. The weather is important, Jakey."

"You are the queen of Weather Channel junkies, Sister-girl. Go ahead and admit it. It's constantly on at your house. You even know the names of most of the weather nerds."

"Whatever. It's my only flaw. It's not like I'm stealing from my grandmother to buy drugs, or something of the sort."

Two motorcycles zipped past, well beyond the speed limit. In seconds, they disappeared from view.

"Speaking of drugs, you haven't taken yours yet, have you?" Jake asked. "If so, you'd best pull Betty over and let me take the wheel. With your somewhat challenged sense of direction, combined with a sedative, we're likely to end up in Miami."

"No, I haven't taken it. What kind of a fruitcake do you think I am?" She glanced over to her friend. "Never mind. Don't answer that."

"I would never say such to you. I'm the only fruit in this relationship."

Hattie admired the way Jake didn't wait on others to comment on his homosexuality. He made enough snarky remarks to cover any occasion. Most people failed to realize his self-deprecating humor acknowledged their biases instead of agreeing with them.

"If you're the fruit, what does that make me?" Hattie grinned.

"White bread, Sister-girl. Married, straight, patriotic, win-one-for-the-allies, white bread. Probably Wonder Bread."

"You make me sound so ordinary." She accelerated to pass a caravan of motorhomes, probably bound for south Florida Mouse-land and that web of theme parks.

"Ah, but that's my point, and my compliment. In this day of everyone trying so hard to be different and odd, you are a breath of clean, country air. Besides, I like white bread. My most favorite comfort food in the whole wide world wouldn't be the same on whole grain."

"Fried egg sandwich," Hattie stated.

"Slathered with mayonnaise. Real mayo, not that no-fat, no-taste crap. With a middle that oozes out yellow yolk goo when you bite into it."

Hattie shuddered at the thought of oozing eggs. Give her scrambled any day. "Which reminds me, where do you want to do lunch? I can't take my medication on an empty stomach."

"There's a little eatery off Fifth Avenue that Shug and I lucked up on a couple of months ago—Bella, Bella. Fabulous! If you'd like to keep it light, they usually have a soup de jour. Shug had a crock of French onion, the best he'd ever had. And they make killer tiramisu."

"Sounds good. I prefer the little local places anyway."

"We might as well make a good day out of this. We can eat, do a little light shoe shopping until your sedatives kick in, and then go get you zapped." He studied the list of satellite radio channels.

When Hattie didn't reply, Jake asked, "Something else bugging you, Sister-girl?"

"Why?"

He switched to an R & B station. "You seem a smidge edgy lately."

Her best friend could read the subtleties of her moods. No use in trying to deny anything. She had been on Jake's radar screen since grade school. "I'm unsettled lately, Jakey. I don't even know why."

Three semi-tractor trucks flew by, rocking the SUV in their slip-streams.

"Gah! Sometimes I wish you had a heavier vehicle, Sister-girl. Those big trucks push little Betty around like she's pixie dust."

"You want to buy me a Hummer and pay for the gas, I will certainly oblige you by driving it."

"I'm not complaining, Hattie. It's just that I loathe feeling we're being swished off the highway." He flipped the satellite channel again, this time to light jazz. "A little tell-Jakey-your-worries background music. Now, you were saying?"

"I've had the strangest feelings lately. And little things have happened."

"Like?"

"There's an old van that keeps hovering around The Hill, for one. Margie's seen it a couple of times. For another, I've had a lot of hang-up calls at the house."

Jake frowned. "Have you called the police?"

"And told them what, that I'm paranoid?"

"Sister-girl, one can never be too careful."

She glanced from the road to her friend. "I know."

Before Jake's abduction and assault, Hattie never would've given a second thought to evil intent. Not in Chattahoochee! Between the hate crime and the recent downfall of a local respected attorney, the entire town had lost a good portion of its innocence.

"It's not only that. I've had the strangest sense of impending . . . ," she waved one hand through the air, ". . . something."

Jake tapped the dash in time with the music's percussion. "That's clear as mud."

"How can I explain when I don't understand it, myself? Something is building, like there's this thick cloud rolling in."

"You and the husband-of-the-century getting along okay?"

"No problem there."

"Delayed post-adoption, new-mommy syndrome?" Jake leaned toward her.

"Nope." Hattie dialed down the volume. "I'll admit motherhood is a challenge at times, but nothing the two of us can't handle. Maybe when she's a teenager, but not now. For the most part, Sarah's easy."

"Maybe it's this thing with your shoulder. You've never had much of a tolerance for pain. You can stub your toe and drama-queen yourself into a seizure."

She reached over and gave his arm a light sock. "You take that back! That is *so* not true."

"Right. I'll remember this conversation next time you go ballistic over a hangnail." Jake rubbed his bicep as if he had been sucker-punched.

"Oh, good grief. I didn't hit you that hard." Hattie snorted. "So I don't *do* pain. Okay. Anyway, I had this bizarre dream last night. It stayed with me all morning."

"You should come with a program, Sister-girl. Sometimes I find it hard to keep up with the way your mind fast-forwards to the next topic."

"Pay attention, then." She checked the light traffic around her then engaged the cruise control.

Jake turned his body to face her. "Undivided. You have me."

"In this dream, I was walking down the lane in front of the house and a hawk flew over. It was like what really happened a couple of days ago. Except, there was this baby crying somewhere close to the edge of the road. I went over to see where it was, and my mom was sitting behind the bush sobbing."

Jake whistled. "Deep."

"Then she held up three fingers."

"What happened then?"

"I woke up."

Jake flipped the satellite radio to disco. "I am *so* glad I'm not a shrink."

By the time the radiologist's assistant led Hattie back to the changing room, the mild sedative had kicked in, and she really would not have minded if they shoved her into the MRI machine and left for the day. Medication certainly had its place.

"The series will take about forty minutes, Mrs. Lewis."

Hattie offered a lopsided smile. "Okay, Mr. Radiation Person. Wake me up when it's over."

"It will be a little loud, so I'm going to put in some earplugs for you." He gently inserted the plugs then used a soft towel to cradle her head. A plastic device to hold her head and chin steady snapped into position. Next, he swaddled her securely in a sheet and spread a warm blanket over her legs and feet.

"That's cozy." Already a better experience than the last.

"Press the bulb in your hand if you need me to stop the scan. I'll be talking to you between sets. Ready?"

"Let 'er rip!"

The cushioned table entered the open-ended MRI machine. Hattie took one quick look and noticed the proximity to her face as before, but she could see the room in her peripheral vision. She closed her eyes. No need to risk freaking out.

"The first noises will last a few seconds. Then I will tell you when the first series starts."

The banging sounded, but the noise was muffled. Hattie took a deep breath and relaxed for the next half-hour. No clock face this time. No father, mother, sister-in-a-coffin thoughts.

"That's it. I'm bringing you out now," the radiologist's voice announced.

"Man, that was a piece of cake." Hattie's vision blurred and she had to blink to keep the room in focus.

Back in the changing room, Hattie dressed slowly, twice almost falling over. Jake met her in the waiting room.

"You look positively loaded, Sister-girl. How was it?"

"A beautiful experience. I think I saw God, Jakey. I really *did!*" Hattie's head lolled from side to side.

"That's nice, Sister-girl. I'll email the Pope. See if we can have it declared a miracle."

"I love you. Do you know that? Do you, Jakey?" She patted his cheeks with both hands.

"I am *so* glad you don't drink or take mind-altering drugs on a regular basis. You're a bit of a sap when you're under the influence."

Hattie batted her eyelids. "You love me anyway, don't you?"

"Madly, hon. Madly."

Chapter Seventeen

"Morning, Officer." Mary-Esther poured hot coffee into Jerry's mug. Around them, the Homeplace buzzed with the usual egg and grits crew.

He added two sugars and stirred. "Morning, yourself. How's the old truck working out?"

"Fantastic. I owe you."

"No debt between friends." He instantly chided himself. Would she take it as too familiar?

"That what we are, friends?"

"Yeah. Or I hope so. I am. I mean—" Jerry felt his cheeks flush.

"Relax, Jerry. It wasn't a loaded question." She took out her order pad and pen, smiled, then slipped the pad back into her pocket. "You want two eggs over easy, bacon, grits, two slices of wheat toast, strawberry jam, right?"

"I must be pretty predictable."

"Most folks are. Not a bad thing." Mary-Esther stuck the pen behind one ear. "Means you know what you like."

When she delivered his order a few minutes later, Jerry asked, "Do you have any plans for this evening?"

"You asking me out, Officer Blount?"

"No. Yes. Maybe." Heat crept once more from his neck to his face. "Um, the carnival. I thought you might like to go, or . . . meet me there or . . ."

Mary-Esther glanced toward the other morning diners before sliding into the booth opposite him. "Jerry, you really have to stop being cautious with me. First," she held up her index finger, "I promise I won't drop kick you into some muddy bayou." She held up another finger. "Second, I would take you up on it if I wasn't already going to be there working the Homeplace's booth."

Jerry couldn't get any words to form in his brain, so he busied himself salting and peppering his eggs and grits. Finally, he spoke. "I have to work it too. I'm leading the parade in the county car."

She reached over and tapped his sleeve with a fingertip. "Eww, touch you! I love it when the fire trucks and police cars blast their sirens. You probably don't throw beads and trinkets like the Mardi Gras Krewes. Still, I'm all in for a parade of any sort."

He picked up a fork then laid it down.

"Go ahead. Eat. Cold eggs are nasty," Mary-Esther said.

Jerry dug into the breakfast.

"For our booth, I'm making a huge pot of gumbo, my Nana Boudreau's recipe. I cooked some a couple of weeks back and Mr. Bill loved it. We may add it to the menu."

"Authentic Nawlin's food?" he asked around a bite of eggs. "Love Cajun cooking, myself. Went to New Orleans a few years back, me and some buddies from work. I ate until I nearly made myself sick."

"I'll have to make you some of my specialties sometime. The Herrings like my gumbo too, though I have to cut back a bit on the spices for them."

"You've made peace with your landlords?" Jerry asked.

"We never were at odds. Rose really is a sweetheart. She's not well, you know. Eustis tries to keep things up—clean, cook—but he's struggling. He's not healthy himself. It's times like old age when having children is a good thing. They don't have any, and nothing but a cousin from"—she waved a hand—"some little town near here."

"Eustis moved in with the railroad years ago. My grandpop knew him. I think they're originally from, maybe, Alabama."

Mary-Esther shook her head. "Mississippi."

"I stand corrected. You move to town and know more about someone in a few weeks than I know in a lifetime."

"I like to talk to people. They're interesting." She picked up the salt shaker, frowned, then used the end of a clean toothpick to jab clumps of crusted salt from the tiny holes in the lid as she continued, "Rose collects dolls. My Nana loved dolls too. Had them stuffed in every nook and cranny. Unfortunately, my dear mother Loretta got rid of most of them after I left home. The few that remained were probably ruined in Katrina." Sadness flashed across her face.

"Sounds like you're big friends with Mr. Eustis and Miz Rose."

"I've taken food over a few times, helped him with some light housekeeping. Nothing big."

"Sounds big to me."

She jumped up. "Be right back."

After refilling coffee mugs and making the anything-else-for-you-this-morning rounds, Mary-Esther returned. "Julie's whipping up the chili for the festival. One of the other cooks is making homemade chicken vegetable soup. Should go over big, since the weather has turned off cool."

Jerry coated a piece of toast with strawberry jam and bit in.

Mary-Esther leaned toward him. "You have a little . . . " She pointed to the border of her lower lip.

"Huh? Oh." Jerry wiped his mouth. "Thanks. Might not add to the authority of the uniform if I left here with a messy face."

"You working the festival after you lead the parade?"

"I'll be walking around looking official for a shift."

Mary-Esther winked. "Come by the booth and I'll give you a complimentary cup of gumbo."

Hattie stood in line for the carnival pony ride holding a wiggling Sarah. Leigh balanced Josh on one hip. Around them, excited children pointed out which pony they would choose. Hattie's gaze followed the lines of white lights laced between poles to supplement the streetlight's illumination. The area teemed with candied-apple-wielding kids and high-spirited adults.

The two-and-a-half-acre vacant green space in front of the Florida State Hospital had served as the fall carnival grounds for as long as Hattie could recall. That morning when she drove past, Hattie had seen volunteers constructing booths, drawing the circular cakewalk grid, and scattering autumnal decorations. Unlike the Madhatter's Festival on the banks of the Apalachicola River, slated for the third Saturday of each October, the smaller event attracted mainly locals. The Twin Cities Fall Carnival revolved around games, food, and community mingling.

Around her, children competed for best-costume prizes, rode the ponies, and tried their skills at the dart-throw and air rifle booths. Parents walked by, their plates piled high with chicken pilau cooked in black cast-iron pots. Others wolfed down hamburgers, hot dogs, and soup, and discussed Florida State and University of Florida football over cups of steaming coffee. Everyone watched out for the kids, regardless of family ties.

Hattie waved to Elvina Houston. Wrapped to her chin in a thick quilt, the old woman presided over the cakewalk from her wheelchair. An adjacent table strained with an array of cookies, brownies, and layered cakes. Contestants paid their fees and lined up in the number-sectioned circle waiting for Elvina to cue the compact disc player. Every few minutes, Elvina stopped the music then drew the winning number. Afterwards, the proud victor stood with wide eyes, surveying the table and pointing to the baked confection of choice. Hattie smiled, remembering the year she had won a fanciful chocolate cake in the shape of a cat.

The carnival was the same as others Hattie recalled from childhood. Members of the local Lion's Club flipped burgers and hotdogs over a massive wheeled grill. Fragrant steam rose and twisted in the night air. Announcements bounced from loudspeakers, paging misplaced parents or the start of raffle drawings. Laughter rang out. People called to each other through the din. The aroma of the charcoal fires blended with the scent of buttered popcorn and heated sugar from the cotton candy machine.

One of the tethered ponies whinnied. Hattie shifted Sarah to quiet the insistent throbbing in her left shoulder. "Too bad Bobby couldn't be here with you and Tank tonight," Hattie said to her sister-in-law.

"He's such a kid when it comes to this stuff," Leigh said. "But his cold is so horrible, he went to bed. He drank one of those awful concoctions your father swore on for coughs."

Hattie pulled a face. "One tablespoon honey, one tablespoon lemon juice, one tablespoon whiskey—heated and chugged down before you have a chance to gag." A momentary concern flickered through her mind: *Bobby. Alcohol.* Even if it was medicinal.

As if she had read Hattie's thoughts, Leigh said, "It's the only booze your brother will touch. Have to admit, it works."

"My theory is that it tastes so god-awful, you don't dare cough, just so you don't have to drink it again."

Leigh laughed. "Got to admire those old-time remedies."

"Right," Hattie said. "Let's see you take a dose of castor oil the next time you feel a little off. Or, how about a drop of kerosene on a sugar cube to cure chest congestion?"

"Am I ever thankful for modern medicine!" Leigh repositioned Josh's cap to protect his head from the brisk night air. "I thought Holston was going to be back in time for this. What happened?"

"Some snafu with his publicist. He had the choice of either coming home and flying back in a couple of days, or staying. Foolish to make two trips. He'll be in on Tuesday."

"I'd say you and Sarah could come bunk with us, but with Bobby hacking . . . I can bring Tank and stay at the farmhouse if you become uneasy."

"I'm perfectly fine." Hattie licked her thumb and wiped a smudge of hot chocolate from Sarah's chin. "But thanks. I know I can call if I get spooked. I have the most vicious watchdog this side of the Mason-Dixon line."

"This *is* the dog that, if given a treat, would let someone in and show them where you keep the family jewels."

Hattie flicked her eyes up, then down. "Spackle's good for barking. Suppose I wouldn't want an aggressive dog around the kids."

Hattie spotted Jake picking his way through the throng of revelers.

He stopped in front of them and motioned toward the food vendors with a tip of his head. "Sister-girl, you simply must visit the soup stand. The woman who looks like your mama is dishing up gumbo."

Leigh strained to catch a glimpse of the booth through the crowd. "Someone told me there's a lady working up at Bill's who resembles Tillie."

Jake flung a hand through the air. "Not only looks like, girlfriend. Is the spitting image of. As I live and die!"

"Everyone looks like *some*one, Jakey." Hattie waggled her head. "There are only so many combinations."

Hattie moved into position and helped the ride operator secure Sarah in the saddle. Leigh settled Josh onto the next pony in the tethered circle. As soon as the other four horses held their wiggling charges, the trainer clicked, signaling the lead pony. Hattie and Leigh walked alongside, each with one hand resting protectively on her child.

Every time Hattie passed Jake's position, he continued the conversation in snippets. "Won't hurt to check it out. . . . Aren't you the least bit curious? Everyone who knew Tillie is talking about this woman. . . . Really, Sister-girl, what can it hurt to *look*?"

The ride ended and they lifted their children from the saddles. Josh squealed disapproval.

Hattie pried a hank of the pony's mane from Sarah's sticky grasp. "All right, Jake. I'll go over there. I could use a cup of something warm anyway. I'd hate to stand there and gawk. That's plain rude."

Jake walked beside the two women until they reached the edge of the crowd. "I'll catch up with y'all later. I'm helping Mandy and Wanda judge the costume competition. Toodles!"

Hattie watched her friend melt into the throng. "That man lives to add drama to my life. As if I don't have enough already."

When she stepped to the front of the Homeplace soup line, Hattie spotted Julie, a familiar face. Another woman, wrapped in the restaurant's signature sunflower-print apron, bent over a steaming stockpot. Slim build, auburn hair pushed behind her ears. As if she sensed Hattie's scrutiny, the woman glanced up. Hattie's breath caught and held. The lady holding a long metal spoon was the double of her late mother, minus twenty years.

"Hattie. Good to see you and little Sarah." Julie tickled Sarah beneath the chin and a bubbly giggle rewarded the gesture. "You and your mama need to come see me at Bill's. Miz Tillie had Sunday lunch with us most every weekend after Mr. D passed." Julie stood with her hands propped on her hips. "We have chicken vegetable soup, beef chili with beans, chili without beans, and a heavenly Cajun seafood gumbo. What do you fancy this evening?"

Hattie finally found her voice. "The g . . . gumbo, please."

Chapter Eighteen

Forgoing the first man-toy Holston had purchased after he moved to The Hill, Hattie picked up a shovel and a set of hand tools. When Holston and her brother had bounced up the lane in Bobby's pick-up with the tricked-out John Deere lawn tractor lashed in the back, Hattie knew Holston had fully embraced Southern farm life. She gave wide berth to the machine with its multiple attachments and confounding dials, and preferred instead to load her weather-beaten wheelbarrow with bags of topsoil and mulch.

Hattie entertained herself by planning another accent flowerbed. As long as she favored her gimpy shoulder, the physical labor stretched her muscles in ways different from her profession. This morning, it also quieted the jumbled, niggling questions about the woman at the soup booth.

Took her mind off how much she missed Holston too.

Independence still pumped in her psyche, tempered by the growing interdependence of a sound union. Hattie had married late in life, well past forty. Where she could sometimes be guitar-string tight, Holston bumped along as if he had always lived in a big, needy farmhouse with a wife and baby. Hattie couldn't imagine her husband's former life: the high-powered, stinging stress of a Wall Street trader stuck in a loveless union with a status-clawing socialite.

And she had Jake. Thank goodness for her best friend. The day before, they had loaded Pearl—a small gray pick-up once belonging to Hattie, now Jake's—with an assortment of low shrubs and azaleas. The tender annuals would have to wait until after the last frost of spring. "It'll keep your monkey mind busy, Sister-girl," Jake had said. "Keep you from obsessing."

Hmmph. I don't obsess! Well, maybe a little. But who wouldn't, with the hawk omens and weirdo phone calls and—

Hattie stopped the mental chatter when she noticed the small, faded orange pick-up truck slow in front of Margie and John's house. The color reminded her of McDonald's special sauce.

The truck turned around in Margie's driveway then flipped a left onto the highway leading toward town. She dug the trowel into the soft dirt and disturbed a moist earthworm. Good thing she hadn't chopped the critter in half.

A few minutes later, she once again heard the faint buzz of an engine. This time, the same truck continued past the neighbor's and paused halfway between before executing a three-point turn and speeding away. Happily chewing an oak limb to sawdust, Spackle stopped to look up and woof.

Hattie leaned back on her tucked legs and wiped her forehead with the back of a gloved hand. "What the heck?"

Probably someone lost. Many of the drives off the main state road looked alike. Easy to make a wrong turn.

At least it wasn't a van.

She had settled the root ball of a Japanese elm into its new home when she saw the pick-up for the third time.

Inner alarms buzzed. She glanced over to the fenced sandbox where Sarah played. Spackle jerked to all fours, in full alert. This time, the truck came all the way up the hundred-yard lane, made a slow circle then aimed in the opposite direction.

"Hey! Stop!" Hattie stood and jogged toward the drive, waving her hands. "Hey, you! Stop!" Spackle dashed ahead, barking with his tail held high. The truck's brake lights flashed. It stopped and idled for a couple of seconds before the white back-up lights came on.

Hattie stood, dead still.

"Sometimes I have beans for brains."

Margie and John weren't home, nor were Bobby and Leigh. She glanced down at the narrow spade in her right hand. Like that was going to deter anyone.

Hattie took a deep breath and pushed the anxiety aside. No one was out to harm her or the baby. If she didn't convey vulnerability, everything would be okay. Her heart beat a rhythm in her ears.

The window lowered. The driver appeared to be female. Serial killers *could* be women, but the odds were in her favor.

"May I help you?" Hattie called out.

"I . . . I don't know."

That voice was vaguely familiar. Hattie stepped closer. "If you'll tell me whose house you're looking for, I can probably help."

"I'm trying to find Mr. and Mrs. Dan Davis."

For the first few months following her mother's death, Hattie had grown accustomed to old acquaintances appearing unannounced at her doorstep. Her father had been dead a number of years, but folks still looked up her mother. The visitors stopped as word of Tillie's death spread. This had to be one last straggler who had been on some other planet.

Hattie held up a hand to shield her eyes from the midday sun. "They used to live here. Both of them have passed away. I'm their daughter. Who are—"

"They're . . . dead?"

Hattie took a couple of steps forward. "Yeah. My dad about ten years ago. Mom, a little over a year."

"Oh." The voice sounded deflated.

When she neared the truck, the features of the driver came into clear focus. Hattie sucked in a breath. *That woman, the one from the soup booth.* She tucked the spade into her coveralls, shucked her gloves, and palmed the sweat from her hands.

"I'm Mary-Esther. I think—that is, it's possible—that I'm your sister."

Hattie had often heard the expression *so shocked, you could've knocked me over with a feather.* As flummoxed as she felt, a hummingbird tuft would have easily done the trick.

This is a lot to lay on you." Mary-Esther drank the last dregs of now-cold coffee and rested the empty cup on her lap. Her eyelids burned and her nose dripped its own version of sorrow. Never had been able to cry gracefully.

Hattie handed a tissue to Mary-Esther. "It makes my chest feel fluttery. Like I can't get enough air." She dabbed tears from her eyes. "To think, I grew up believing my sister had died."

"And your mother . . ." Mary-Esther thought of her own baby, or the promise of one, since she had been only a couple of months pregnant when Ricky Alford violently ended that bud of life. So long ago. "I can imagine the grief she felt."

"Mama was devastated," Hattie said. "Daddy too, though I think he handled it differently, probably by spoiling me rotten. My aunt Piddie was the one who talked to me about what happened, and only after I was in my late teens. Bobby *never* said Sarah's name. Mama would go to bed, sometimes for a couple of days at a time, before I was born." Hattie paused. "Guess having me helped her some, but she still had this sadness that didn't go away."

Sarah Chuntian slept on a pallet near the couch. One plump arm showed a smudge of garden soil her mother had missed in the quick wipe down. Hattie had to be a good person, to travel halfway around the world to give the baby a home. The kind of woman anyone would be proud to call a sister, Mary-Esther figured. The way Hattie spoke of her husband, he was golden too.

Guess making bad choices in men wasn't genetic.

"Oh." Hattie took a shuddery breath and put her hand over her heart. "It all makes me so very sad. You'll never know Mama, or Daddy, or Aunt Piddie." The sides of her lips turned up. "Stick around and you will no doubt hear stories about my daddy's colorful sister. Most of them are true."

For over an hour, words had poured from Mary-Esther in a garbled stream: her own patchwork life, the final harrowing hours of Loretta Day, and the winding path from New Orleans to Quincy and finally, Chattahoochee.

How foolish she must sound, like a fiction author conjuring up the plot line for a bestseller, or maybe some complete nutcase.

Hattie motioned toward Mary-Esther's mug. "Like a refill?"

"No. Thank you. I'll be up half the night as it is. I have the breakfast shift at Bill's. Five-thirty will come early."

Hattie's fingers twined together. "I have pictures . . . if you'd like."

Mary-Esther dipped her chin. Each time emotions surged, her throat threatened to close. She still couldn't believe she had worked up the nerve to drive out here. Again. Had Hattie not flagged her down, she might still be racing in the opposite direction.

Hattie hopped up and plundered in a cabinet by the fireplace, returning with two plastic storage bins. "I don't know where to start."

Why would this woman trust *her*? For sure, Mary-Esther would never invite a total stranger inside for coffee, much less give credence to a story like the one she'd just told. Lately, she had done a number of things far from her usual character. "Maybe, a picture of your parents?"

"Possibly, *our* parents?" Hattie snapped off one of the blue plastic lids and sifted through the photos. She handed over a time-faded eight-by-ten.

Mary-Esther stared at the portrait. The resemblance between the woman and herself was undeniable. Same slender nose, bow lips, and smiling eyes. The man looked like the kind of guy a child could count on. Not an *uncle*; there one day, gone the next.

Her hands trembled when she handed the picture back to Hattie. Tears trickled down her cheeks, regardless of her attempts to corral the emotions.

Hattie sniffled. She reached for the box of tissues with one hand and rested the other over Mary-Esther's. The touch, both familiar and foreign. "This is going to be a little strange for all of us," Hattie said in a soft voice.

"A little?" Mary-Esther choked out a muffled chuckle.

"One thing about this family, we persevere." Hattie gave Mary-Esther's hand a brief squeeze then let go.

Mary-Esther blotted her eyes. How could there possibly be any tears left inside of her? A wadded pile of tissues rested in her lap. She added another.

Were there any pictures of her old life left in Nana's house? Mary-Esther scraped her memory. Two cardboard boxes in the bottom of a hall closet. Those would be putty and mold by now. Only one other, framed on the mantle, if it had survived. Why hadn't she thought to grab any of them on her way out? She had taken time to pack those dang rocks.

Simple answer: She thought she'd come back. Something from her life would be intact. Joke's on you, the universe said.

Mary-Esther closed her eyes, breathed in, then out. She opened her eyes and studied her own hands, grasping the mug. Had her real mother had the same tapered fingers? "You said something about a brother?"

"Bobby. He lives down the lane with his wife Leigh and son Josh, except everyone calls the baby *Tank*. He's a chunk."

Mary-Esther glanced up. "Do you suppose . . . could I . . . meet him?"

Hattie's open expression shifted to something else—wary? "Sure. But not right away. He's not home right now. Bobby and his wife are over in Tallahassee at the doctor. He's had a cough for over two weeks. Can't seem to shake it. Leigh finally put her foot down."

Mary-Esther caught the nervous edge to Hattie's voice and how her gaze shifted to the side, the first time Hattie hadn't made direct eye contact. Years of mistrust had taught Mary-Esther, body language trumps words.

"Bobby's a typical *guy*," Hattie added with a slight lift of one shoulder.

"Too bad you have to go out of town to see a doctor. Must get old."

"There's a little walk-in clinic for minor stuff," Hattie said. The friendly demeanor resurfaced. "But when you're really sick, you need a primary care person who takes your insurance and can admit you to the hospital if you need it. Tallahassee's not far. Hit the interstate, and you can be there in a half-hour."

"I need to be going." Mary-Esther set down the mug and stood. "Thanks for the coffee."

Hattie jumped up and hugged her.

Resistant at first, Mary-Esther relaxed into the embrace. Hattie smelled of wood smoke mixed with some light, clean scent. *Well-scrubbed*, Nana Boudreau would've called it.

"I still can't believe this. It's so unreal!" Hattie pushed back and held her at arm's length. "I can't wait to tell Holston. And Jake and Shug, and the group at the Triple C, and who else . . . I'll call you . . ."

"No phone."

"Oh." Hattie rocked on her heels, stuck her hands in her jeans pockets. "So I'll come find you." She paused before adding, "I'm sure Bobby will jump at the chance to meet you as soon as he's not contagious." The downward tone told Mary-Esther not to expect any joy dances from "the brother."

Moments later, Mary-Esther pulled away from Bonnie Lane and drove for a mile before she eased the truck over to park on the side of the road.

She was Mary-Esther Day Alford Fernandez Sloat one minute.

Alone.

The next, she was someone else entirely.

Or was she?

A cloud gathered on her horizon: a horde of family, friends, and extended relations whose numbers she could only speculate.

And some who might not be as welcoming.

Chapter Nineteen

"You have *pneumonia?*" Hattie lowered Sarah into a playpen near the hearth and as far from her brother as possible.

Bobby and Leigh's log home oozed Southern woodsy comfort. Leigh's heirloom pieced quilts hung from wooden clamp stretchers on three walls. Newer crazy quilts made from irregular swatches draped across the chairs and back of the couch. In spite of the cozy room, Bobby shivered on the couch beneath layers of blankets.

Leigh slid a steaming mug of lemon herbal tea on the coffee table in front of her husband. "He's a pea-shade shy of being admitted to the hospital."

Hattie pursed her lips. "Be right back. Let me see if Miz Margie can keep Sarah."

A few minutes later when Hattie returned, her brother lifted his head and blinked rheumy eyes. "I'm not dead. Just feel like it." Bobby's words dissolved into a coughing spell. Leigh helped him sip the warm tea.

"Poor bubba." Hattie patted her brother's thinning hair. "I hate it you feel so horrid."

"They started him on strong antibiotics and an inhaler, plus an oral steroid," Leigh said. "If the congestion doesn't start breaking up in a couple of days, we're supposed to call the office. People are dropping like flies with this junk. Doctor said both hospitals are maxed."

Bobby moaned and cinched the covers around his neck.

"Chills again, babe?" Leigh's expression left no doubt of her feelings, the same soft-edged look Hattie had often seen passing between her parents.

Hattie laid the back of her hand across Bobby's flushed forehead. "You're burning up."

Leigh picked up the digital aural thermometer and stuck the fluted nozzle into his ear. In a few seconds, a series of beeps sounded. "One hundred and one, point two." She sighed. "Fever spikes in the evenings."

"Have you tried a lukewarm bath? Mom used to do that, or either an alcohol rub."

"Must have been in all of our mothers' handbooks. I'll stoke the fire and turn up the heat a bit, then I'll try that again. He shivered so hard last time, his teeth chattered."

"I can help you bathe him."

Bobby opened his eyes. "No, by God, you won't! I'll not have my sister bathing me. That's where I draw the line."

Hattie held her arms akimbo. "Not like I haven't seen it before, Bobby." How many times had she cleaned up his vomit and thrown his drunk butt into a shower? No need to bring that up now.

He struggled to rise. Listed to one side. Fell back onto the cushions.

Leigh's lips drew into a thin line. "I'll stick with wiping him down with alcohol. Help me sit him up."

This time, Bobby offered no resistance, verbal or otherwise. The two women peeled off his sweat-stale flannel pajama top. While Hattie supported him, Leigh used gauze pads to wipe his arms and trunk.

"My skin hurts." Bobby wrapped his arms around his midsection and trembled.

Leigh flinched. "I know, babe. I know. We've got to get your fever down." She gestured toward the back of the house. "Grab a clean pair of his pajamas off the dryer, will you? I should have thought of that before we started."

Once Hattie and Leigh managed to get the fresh top on him, they helped Bobby stand and removed his bottoms.

"Don't make me take off my drawers," Bobby whined. "Please, spare a man a bit of dignity."

"Like we're concerned with seeing the family jewels," Leigh said. "But okay. Let's at least wipe your legs down and get some fresh pajama bottoms on."

By the time they wrestled on the flannel pants and returned Bobby to his quilted cocoon, Leigh and Hattie were as winded as their patient. He slipped into a drugged sleep.

After a few minutes, Leigh took a second reading. "Seems to have helped. That and the Tylenol. Fever's down."

"Where's Tank?" Hattie asked in a low voice.

"Staying with my mom. I seem to do okay not catching something from Bobby, but let Josh get it, and the chances are good I'll get sick in record time. If I go down, we're all in trouble. Someone has to be the nurse."

"I could've kept Tank."

Leigh regarded her. "With your shoulder like it is, there's no way I would have even asked. Josh is a lot to lift, even with two good arms." She ran her fingers through her hair and released a breath. "Not that I don't love you stopping by, and certainly welcomed your help, but you'd best get out of the germs. I've wiped everything down with disinfectant so much my skin is chapped, but still . . ."

Hattie went to the kitchen to scrub and dry her hands. "If you need me, don't hesitate to call," she said when she reentered the room. "I can get Margie and John to watch Sarah, or I'll enlist Evelyn. Promise?"

"Don't worry. I will." Leigh walked Hattie toward the door. "Was there some reason you stopped by? I didn't even ask. I mean, other than checking on your brother?"

"It can wait. Can I get you anything from town?"

Leigh tapped her chin with one finger. "Maybe some more Gatorade. The original green kind. That and a little chamomile tea is about all I've been able to get him to drink."

A few minutes later, Hattie pulled onto Highway 269 and headed north toward town. "I know the perfect person to share my news with: my 'other sister,' Jake."

Sarah squealed approval from her car seat.

Hattie pulled the SUV to the curb in front of a white, wood-framed house. A warm feeling washed over her. Some of Hattie's fondest childhood memories revolved around her Aunt Piddie's home.

The two-bedroom, one-bath home resembled many bungalow-styled houses built in the late forties following World War II. Constructed in a time before air conditioning, it sported a deep porch across the front and a screened room in the back. A row of evergreen shrubs shaded the porch from the brain-simmering sun during the summer.

Sarah jabbered to herself. Kid chilled out in her car seat, no matter if the vehicle moved or not. Hattie took a moment to delight in the memories of her favorite female relative, outside of her mother.

Aunt Piddie and her best friend Elvina had spent many afternoons in those porch rockers, aluminum pans cupped in their laps, shelling peas or butterbeans while commenting on everyone who passed by. As a child,

Hattie had her own little pan and popped the peas from their hulls until her thumbs were sore and stained green around the nails. The child-sized rocking chair was still on the porch, freshly painted. Maybe her own daughter would sit there one day, learn that peas didn't come from a can or freezer bag.

Short-needle pine trees dotted the corner lot, looped with a maze of azaleas. In the spring, their hot-pink flowers transformed the yard into a magical place to play hide-and-go-seek with fairies, dragons, and knights on rearing white steeds. Now, the spindly shrubs bore only pointed green leaves.

In the sloping back yard beneath the broad limbs of a southern magnolia, Hattie had "baked" mud pies for a family of rag dolls. Bobby constructed a fort in a copse of trees and defied Hattie and her friends to cross the threshold.

Hattie closed her eyes and could see Aunt Piddie standing at the screened door, checking on her charges. In the fifties and early sixties, neighbors watched over each other, and children worried only about swatting mosquitoes or looking both ways before crossing the street.

Back then, no horrors lurked in the shadows. No one had to check an online predators' list to rest easy about the people on their block. Trick–or-treat candy didn't have to be x-rayed and scrutinized. And if you acted ugly at a friend's house, your parents knew the details before you got home.

She opened her eyes and glanced in the rearview mirror. Sarah watched her, contented in her car seat. "Different times then, baby doll." Hattie sighed. "Long before you were born, I used to dance in the living room to Motown singles Aunt Piddie played on this suitcase-style record player and we'd eat hot teacakes fresh from the oven."

Sarah gurgled a reply.

"I know. You met her before she went to heaven, but I wish she was still here to watch you grow up." She got out of the SUV then extracted the kid from her seat and balanced her on one hip. Her shoulder complained.

After Aunt Piddie died, Hattie had worried someone would raze the simple house to make way for a modern brick structure with little character.

Who could possibly love it and fill it with happiness as her aunt had once done?

Aunt Piddie knew that answer. She willed her house to the only son of one of her paint-by-numbers, thick-and-thin, life-long friends. Betsy

Witherspoon, for all of her money and uppity ways, had been an integral part of Aunt Piddie's circle.

Piddie was the first to fold Jake under her protective wings when he returned to town following his mother's death, and later came to his bedside to encourage him after his tangle with the hatred that might have crushed his spirit. Piddie had sensed something of herself in Jake: a flamboyant person who rose above pain, believed in the basic goodness of people, and shoved bad memories into the past.

Since Jake had played as many hours as Hattie in the deep yard, he had taken great pains to preserve the original plantings—many, antique varieties—and added complementary flowerbeds.

"You did good, Aunt Piddie," Hattie whispered. Nobody else could've loved the old place more.

Hattie extracted herself from the bittersweet past and carried Sarah onto the porch. She stopped to admire the refinished rocking chairs with their green gingham cushions. Pots of maidenhair and Boston fern hung from overhead hooks. The wooden floor planks shone with a fresh coat of dark green paint to match the new shutters.

No need to act like company and wait for permission. Hattie rapped on the door and stepped inside. "Haah-looo! Just me and Sarah!" She glanced around at the mounds of labeled cartons. Elvis, Shug's Pomeranian, scampered to the door, yapping. Hattie reached down and petted his head.

Jake trundled from the kitchen, wiping his hands on a red and white cloth. "Sister-girl. Good of you to stop by."

"What cha doing, Jakey? Cleaning closets?"

"Isn't this positively ghastly? Shug brought all of this down from the attic last night. It appears somewhat orderly now. But wait until he gets home and starts digging in. Give it five minutes, tops, and it will look like someone got sick and threw up Christmas." He tickled Sarah beneath the chin.

Hattie situated the baby into a playpen Jake kept for such drop-in occasions.

"Christmas?" Hattie's eyebrows flicked upward. "A tad early, don't you think? We just got past Halloween."

"Not if you live with Jon *Shug* Presley. You know how the man is all about Christmas. He's blasted so far over the top this year, by the time he finishes, you will be able to practically wipe your behind with tinsel, and you won't be able to look anywhere, and I mean *anywhere*, without being visually accosted by some jolly elf or a pig in a Santa hat or choirs of singing angels." He stopped to huff out a breath. "You get the idea."

Jake flipped the cloth in the direction of two large bags. "That's not all. On the excuse of replacing one of his little fake trees that looked overly ratty, the man went shopping and came back with three more. That brings the artificial tree tally up to," he stuffed the cloth in one pocket and ticked off a finger count, "nine! One is designed to hang upside down from the ceiling. And get this, another has a fuchsia Lava light trunk. That, I can't *wait* to behold."

Hattie laughed.

"This year, Shug's threatened to cover the entire front yard with those gosh-awful inflatable snow-globe things and maybe a Burl Ives snowman figurine. Those dang things constantly hum on account of the air machines that keep them blown up. It'll keep people up at night." Jake jabbed the air with one finger. "It will send someone who is teetering on the edge to murder his nagging wife." More jabbing. "It will look like the invasion of the Pod People!"

Hattie didn't comment. When Jake wound up, it was best to step back and let the curve balls whiz past. Sarah followed Jake's gestures and giggled every time he launched into a fresh tirade.

"I've warned Shug, this house may not handle all those electronics. He says he'll pay to have it rewired." Jake tilted his head back and rested one hand on his forehead. "I may have to leave town until after the New Year."

"I hear Tahiti is lovely this time of year."

Jake shoved aside a canister overflowing with tinsel and motioned her to follow. "C'mon back to the kitchen. It's the only place in this house with a bare spot." Elvis trailed behind them, his tufted tail wagging.

Good thing about the small house: she could sit in the kitchen and still watch Sarah playing in the adjacent room.

The aroma of cinnamon wafted from the galley-style kitchen. Some of the best Southern dishes in town had once been prepared in the cramped space with one metal countertop, a sink, and a gas stove. Jake and Shug had updated the appliances, replaced the cracked linoleum with ceramic tile, and painted the yellowed walls, but the original flavor of the room remained. Piddie's Formica-topped metal table, surrounded by four red and white vinyl-upholstered chairs, was the only furniture.

"What smells so good?" Hattie asked, her nose lifted.

"I had this wave of nostalgia. I made teacakes." When he grinned, the twin dimples showed. "Piddie's recipe."

Hattie's mouth watered. "Oh."

"Sit." Jake poured Hattie a cup of strong black coffee and slid it onto the table. "They're almost ready to pop from the oven. And yes, sweet love, you may have one or two or three."

"That's the signature scent of this house. I didn't realize it until now."

Jake smiled. "I have to appease the previous owner's spirit every now and then."

The timer bell tinged and Jake extracted a cookie sheet from the oven with a pair of silicone mitts. He scooped several teacakes onto a plate and set it on the table. "Don't be shy, Sister-girl. I'll be offended." Elvis stood on his back legs, begging. Jake broke off a chunk of teacake, blew on it for a couple of seconds, and handed it down.

Hattie bit into a still-warm cake and almost swooned, overwhelmed by the combination of taste and scent. "Ohmygah!" She closed her eyes. "I haven't had one of these in years."

Jake watched as she chewed. "Bliss looks good on you." He bit into a teacake. "These are to die for, even if I do say so myself." He dabbed crumbs from his lips with the tip of one finger. "To what do I owe the pleasure of you and the little chinaberry's company this time of the evening?"

Hattie broke of a piece of her cake and delivered it to Sarah. "I'm dropping her by Joe and Ev's after I leave here," she said when she returned to her seat. "Holston will be home in a couple of hours, and I decided to take Ev up on her offer to babysit."

"Ah, a little romantic tryst in the making."

"I thought it might be nice to have the evening all to ourselves. And you know how Evelyn loves children. I feel sorry for her sometimes. Byron lives too far away for her to spend time with their two grandsons, and who knows when Karen will have children, if ever. I think she has to wait a little while after her chemo to get pregnant. When Ev gets to spend time around Josh or Sarah, it's like she comes alive."

"Between that and sewing, she's quit redecorating and—thank you, our beloved Savior, for favors great and small—*cooking*." Jake faked a bow to the heavens.

"Seriously."

It was a fact. Evelyn Longman Fletcher—unlike her mother, Piddie—did not have a natural affinity for cooking. Fortunately, Joe had developed his culinary skills following retirement, and the gourmet kitchen had a true chef at the helm.

Hattie checked on Sarah. Happy kid. Surrounded by toys, with slobbery teacake clumped around her lips. Maybe Bobby would eat a teacake with his Gatorade, if she took some back.

"You decided to add to your evening by visiting your best girlfriend in the world?" Jake winked.

"You act like I never stop by."

Jake cocked his head. "Sister-girl, don't be defensive. Since you've been all disgustingly happily married to the hunk-of-the-century, we seldom have our long girlish chats." His mouth turned down for a beat before it resumed its customary upward curve. "Not that I'm not deliriously pleased for you . . . and me. I am in the throes of conjoined bliss too." He handed a chewy bone to Elvis.

"I'm sorry, Jakey. I never in a million years meant to make you feel like you don't matter to me."

Jake hopped up and wrapped his arms around her. "Sister-girl, we're all good, you and me. We could be apart for decades and still be best-est heart-friends. Now seriously, is there something bothering you?"

Hattie took another teacake. "Am I that transparent?"

"To me, you are."

"I have something really incredible to tell you."

Jake pilfered her teacake with an evil grin, took a bite, and then leaned forward. Crumbs littered the corners of his mouth.

"Jakey, I have a sister!"

Elvis stopped chewing his bone and looked up at her.

"Oh, sweet girl. Of course you *had* a sister." Jake put down the half-eaten cake and slid the plate toward her with a sad smile. "I'm sure you still think of Sarah. A lot of people get a little depressed around the holidays. What with Mr. D and Miz Tillie and Piddie gone, you're sure to feel melancholy. Look at all of us who love you . . . me, Shug, Elvina, Evelyn and Joe, Bobby and Leigh, Holston and Sarah Chuntian."

"No, no. I mean . . . I *have* a sister."

"Lost me." He made an air-circle with one finger. "Orbiting Uranus."

"You were the one who pointed her out. The lady at the fall festival. The one dishing up soup? Her name is Mary-Esther, and there's a pretty good possibility she is my long-lost sister."

The Felix-the-Cat wall clock ticked, its golf-ball-sized eyes swishing in time with a swinging, black-plastic tail. Elvis watched them.

Jake pinched off another small bite of teacake and handed it down to the dog. "Sister-girl, you have been watching *waaaay* too many daytime dramas."

Chapter Twenty

Mary-Esther swung a small Styrofoam cooler into the back of Jerry's truck and slid into the passenger side. "Do you realize this is our first official date?"

"Guess that makes me a skinflint. Should be taking you out for a nice meal," Jerry Blount said. "Instead, here I am, dragging you to Mule Days."

"For one, I'm not hard to please. Until recently, I'd been living out of the back of a van. For another, I'm the one who wanted to go to this shindig. You were nice enough to offer company."

Jerry backed from the driveway. The curtains parted slightly, Rose watching the action. "What's in the cooler?" he asked.

"Ham and cheese sandwiches and potato salad. Julie threw in a couple of slices of her famous lemon pound cake. Some soft drinks. In case we get hungry and thirsty."

"Aren't you the considerate one? But they have food booths at Mule Days. I should've mentioned it."

Mary-Esther flipped one hand. "We can eat them on the way back. How far is this place? Must be miles."

"It's about an hour from here. We had to leave early or else face a tremendous traffic jam."

"In Calvary, Georgia? I've never heard of the place. Can't be many people living there."

Jerry smiled. "These little festivals draw in folks for miles. You'll see. Plus, we wouldn't want to miss the parade."

"Parade?"

"Mules."

Mary-Esther's eyebrow lifted. "I see. Hey, we only have Jazz Fest in New Orleans with world-renowned musicians. What do I know from mules?"

His lips twitched. "This must seem like a foolish thing to you."

"Stop, Jerry. I mean it. You can be so infuriatingly *nice* sometimes."

"You'd rather I be mean?" He glanced over and winked.

Mary-Esther regarded him. "I didn't say that." Without the crisp, pleated uniform, he looked like one of many flannel-shirted farm boys. Still, an aura of authority clung to him like a used dryer sheet. She reached over and slipped her hand into his. He pulled her closer. His masculine scent wrapped around her, making her head swimmy.

Jerry grinned. "That's the beauty of an older pick-up truck with a bench seat. A woman can nestle right up under a man, if she's a mind to."

"Bet you've had lots of women in this middle spot over time." She noticed his features harden. Had she crossed some line?

"Only the one." Jerry stared straight ahead.

He turned onto a narrow county road and headed north into Georgia. They rode in uncomfortable silence for a few minutes before Mary-Esther spoke. "I seem to have offended you somehow. If I did, I'm sorry. I . . ."

The muscles of his jaw flinched. She scooted back to her side of the seat and snapped the safety belt. For several miles of tobacco barns and barren, harvested cotton fields, they rode in silence.

Finally, Jerry spoke. "I was married. For many years."

"So you're one of those walking wounded men who got left and never got over it?"

"Maureen died. Breast cancer."

Mary-Esther closed her eyes and clenched her teeth. It wasn't the first time she had blundered to a wrong conclusion. "Oh . . ."

"It's just—" His voice grew so low, she strained to hear. "You're the first since her."

She allowed silence to fill the space for a few moments.

"Jerry, I can't say I know how it feels to lose someone you've been committed to for years. My marriages weren't stellar. I lost one husband to youthful stupidity, one to heart failure, and one to . . . I suppose, lack of trust. But I did lose my Nana Boudreau. She's the only person who ever loved me unconditionally. Then my mother died of kidney failure." She paused. "Loretta and I had finally reached a truce. Quit fighting over every little thing. I think we might have done all right, if . . ."

"*If.*" He huffed. "Loaded little word, isn't it?"

The traffic on the county highway increased. By the time they were two miles south of Calvary, the line had slowed to a bumper-to-bumper crawl. Mary-Esther fiddled with the radio dial as stations faded in and out.

"You weren't kidding about folks coming from all over. I haven't seen this many pick-up trucks in one place in, well, ever."

Jerry patted the seat beside him. "Why don't we do a restart on this date?"

She unfastened her seat belt, slid over, and attached the middle safety belt.

Jerry slipped his right arm over her shoulders and steered with his left hand. "You're bound to get a kick out of this." His voice resumed its usual good humor. "There's a contest for tobacco spitting, handcrafted stuff, loads of funnel cakes, and fried bloomin' onions and gator tail. Lordy, how I love those fried onions! They make cane syrup in big vats the old-fashioned way. Good stuff. I'm always entertained when I come to Mule Days, but then, with you from New Orleans—"

"Don't be so quick to judge. I've eaten gator."

He glanced away from the road and regarded her with an astonished expression. "You don't say."

"Hello? I'm from a city below sea level, up to its armpits in swamp water. And I've sucked down more mudbugs than I care to count."

"Juice in the heads of those crawdads is nothing short of heaven." Jerry chuckled. "Oh yeah, don't look all shocked. I've eaten my share of those mudbugs myself."

Jerry followed the procession into a large open field where local deputies motioned vehicles into grassy parking slots. He turned off the ignition and grinned. "C'mon, Cajun gal. Much as you said you love a parade, this is one you don't want to miss."

"I don't think that mule with the white star on his nose was necessarily the prettiest. Who's to say?" Mary-Esther pulled a hot snippet from a deep-fried bloomin' onion and dipped it into a cup of ranch dressing. She would probably enjoy the worst case of indigestion she had ever had, but for now, the grease slid down easy. "And the one that got *most ugly* looked like the others. How does one judge these things, anyway?"

Jerry pulled an onion section from the opposite side. "Must be some type of score card. I've never known anyone to call for a recount."

"Not like the mules care."

Mary-Esther noticed the faint sheen of grease around his lips and blushed over the images prancing through her mind like spring-frisky colts. She swiped her mouth with the back of her hand, frowned at the oil slick on her skin, and reached into her back jeans pocket for a wad of paper napkins.

"Anything worth eating makes a mess." Jerry winked.

Mary-Esther stopped wiping her fingers and studied him. That winking business was going to get him into trouble. "I am not *even* going to touch that remark. Can't believe you're so good at flirting. Who would have ever guessed?"

"Suppose it's like riding a bicycle. A man never forgets how. He only gets a bit rusty."

She offered the dregs of the onion to him before dumping the flimsy paper plate into an oil drum turned garbage can. "I've had enough health food. Let's go see how many non-essential things we can buy. Other than my rocks, I have absolutely no character in my apartment."

Near dark, Jerry pulled the truck into the driveway beside his mustang and shut off the engine. The Herring's back curtains parted then closed shut. Nice to know someone cared enough to keep track of her comings and goings.

"I totally forgot to ask you," Mary-Esther said. "Have you had a report on my van yet? I feel kind of guilty keeping this truck so long."

Jerry hopped out and allowed her to slide out from the driver's side. "I talked to my cousin yesterday, matter of fact. Didn't want to spoil our date." He reached for the cooler and tucked it beneath one arm. "Engine's shot. He's looking to find a rebuilt one to drop in."

She walked alongside him toward the stairway leading to her apartment. "An engine? Sounds expensive." Mary-Esther could barely make out his features in the dim light shining down from the crest of the stairs.

"I helped him build his barn. He owes me a big favor, so he'll cut you some slack on the labor charge. Besides, a rebuilt engine won't set you back as bad as a new vehicle. By the time Milton gets finished, your van will purr like a kitten."

"Give me some ballpark idea of money, okay? I'll pull as many extra shifts as Bill will let me."

"I imagine it'll be about eighteen hundred dollars by the time he does everything."

Mary-Esther's spirit wilted. The amount would deplete the remainder of her meager savings, and then some. Shouldn't have spent anything at the festival. Oh, well. As her mother used to say when she hit another of her "lows": *life is a big shit sandwich and every day you take another bite.* Loretta Boudreau Day, the eternal optimist.

They stood at the bottom of the stairs, facing each other. Reminded Mary-Esther of adolescence, when the awkward front door scenario was both feared and anticipated.

"Would you like to come up?" she asked.

"Mary-Esther, I don't think . . . that is, I don't know if I can—"

She reached up and kissed him lightly on the cheek. "I'm not inviting you to sleep over. I'm not even asking you to pet heavily on the couch. It probably wouldn't withstand the action, anyway."

Mary-Esther tapped the cooler with one finger. "I have two really good ham sandwiches that are going to be wasted, not to mention my famous kick-butt red potato salad. And Julie's cake." She grabbed the cooler from his arm, turned, and started up the steps, calling over her shoulder. "I'm offering a quick meal on paper plates and some mundane conversation on the porch. Nothing more. Nothing less."

Could she be the same woman who generally bedded a man—heck, even married him—before she knew how he liked his coffee? The one who had no clue how to take things slow, unless she counted the time it took her to figure out how to extricate herself from a hopeless entanglement?

When Mary-Esther reached halfway on the complaining stairway, she heard the sound of Jerry's steps behind her. Her pulse stammered.

"Where should I turn?" Holston asked. He negotiated the swirling traffic on Tallahassee's Capital Circle.

"Take a left at the light." Hattie motioned to the next intersection. "The Orthopedic Center is past Capital Regional Hospital on the left. You'll see a big sign."

"You want to take in a movie after your appointment?"

"That might be fun. We can grab a paper and discuss it over lunch. This feels so strange, being without Sarah. I appreciate you wanting to come. It's nothing massive today."

"I wanted to be with my wife." Holston reached one hand over and held hers. "I feel like I haven't seen you in weeks."

Hattie laced her fingers in his. Nice, how they fit together.

The Orthopedic Center waiting room brimmed with people in various stages of healing. Wheelchairs, walkers, canes, and braces abounded. Lines formed at three sliding glass check-in stations. Worse than Walmart during the holiday rush.

"There's always a book of forms to fill out." Hattie plopped down in an upholstered chair next to her husband. "Good thing we came early."

A few minutes after she turned in the extensive health history, a nurse called her name.

"Should I come back with you?" Holston asked.

"I'm okay by myself. When else will you get to enjoy a six-month-old copy of *Field and Stream?*"

"I'm sure, if I search, there'll be a mangled *Sports Illustrated* swimsuit issue." Holston's left eyebrow flicked up then down.

Hattie stuck out her tongue at him and followed the nurse into the inner office maze.

"Please remove your clothes from the waist up and put on the gown. Dr. Henry will be with you shortly." The nurse exited and closed the door.

Hattie picked up the gown, pale yellow cotton with blue trim. Who picked out the material for these things? The cloth should be a fun print, something in keeping with the office's purpose. Maybe line drawings of feet, legs, shoulders, and hands, with ribbons of gauze twirling between.

The doctor completed his exam. "You have a classic case of frozen shoulder. I've studied your MRIs, and there's no tear in the rotator cuff tendons or the muscles, and no impingements in the neck."

"And I had this whole thing diagnosed."

"Step over to the monitor." The doctor pointed to the digital image of her shoulder. "This is the tendon attachment of the muscle you mentioned. It looks healthy."

"Then, why does it hurt so badly?"

"We're not really certain why this occurs. Sometimes, it is from an accident or a blow to the shoulder girdle area. I see it so often in Caucasian women, usually around your age, that I call it *white girl shoulder.*"

Hattie sniffed. "One more thing to attribute to aging." At least it wasn't the *Big C*, when a doctor started comparing the problem to the size and shape of some fruit.

"Age factors into a number of things, unfortunately. We become less flexible, lose muscle mass. I'm your same age. Consider myself to be in good shape, work out—all that. Couple of weeks ago, I pulled a muscle in my back getting out of my car. I moaned and groaned for a few days until it finally got better."

"I take it this shoulder thing doesn't require surgery?"

"No surgery. At one time, doctors prescribed aggressive physical therapy. Not so much, now." He handed her a couple of information printouts. "We use prednisone therapy first with a few gentle exercises. The idea is to reduce the body's inflammatory response in the area."

Hattie scowled. "Prednisone. For how long?"

"A week."

"Thank God." Last time she had to take that longer than a few days, she went crazy as a March hare, couldn't sleep, and tried to eat everything within a two-mile radius.

"You deserve to get some relief. This usually kick-starts the healing process." The doctor scribbled onto a prescription pad then tore off the top sheet and handed it over. "I'll see you in six weeks. If you are not on the upswing by then, we can discuss other options."

Six weeks. A lot could change in that time.

When Hattie returned to the waiting room, Holston asked, "What did he say?"

"He said I'm an aging white woman."

"Huh?"

Hattie laughed at his confused expression and turned toward the door. "C'mon. I'll explain over a massive plate of hot wings."

Hattie mentally reviewed Mary-Esther's visit as she led the way to the car. Jake's response had surely dampened her initial *new-sister!* enthusiasm. His words stung: *You're too trusting, Sister-girl. You believe everyone has honest motives. What if this woman is some kind of con? You'll get your little feelings crushed, or worse.*

Would Holston react in the same way? Was that why she hadn't shared this with him yet? Hattie stuffed the niggling doubts. She'd tell him over lunch.

Holston caught up to her and grabbed her hand. "What happened to your pre-Thanksgiving fast?"

"Can't fathom you'd ask a woman tormented by 'white girl shoulder' to deny herself one little pleasure. I'm having curly fries too."

Chapter Twenty-one

Mary-Esther noticed the odd pair of midmorning diners as soon as they chose a corner booth: the lanky, sharply dressed owner of the florist shop a block down West Washington and the old woman who periodically came in to have a cup of tea and stare at her. The woman struggled to sit down then the man folded the walker and leaned it against the end of the table.

Mary-Esther palmed the moisture from her hands onto her apron and walked to their booth. "Good morning. What can I get you to drink?"

The man spoke first. "I'll have a tall glass of unsweetened iced tea."

"Hot water for me. I have my own green tea bag. I prefer it over black tea. Antioxidants." She bobbed her head once to drive her point home.

From the old woman's sullen expression, Mary-Esther figured she might need more than antioxidants. Reminded her of a grade school teacher she once had. Sour, full of reasons why Mary-Esther was far from perfect.

After Mary-Esther delivered the beverages, she pulled out a pad and pencil.

"We didn't come in to eat," the man said. "We'd like a few minutes of your time."

"Huh?"

"We purposely picked a time when you might not be as busy. Please . . ." The woman motioned to a spot next to her. The pruned expression morphed to something a bit less threatening but still stern.

Mary-Esther shrugged and slid onto the edge of the booth seat.

"I know we've seen each other but never been properly introduced. I'm Jake Witherspoon. I own the Dragonfly Florist."

"And I'm Elvina Houston. I'm the business coordinator for the Triple C Day Spa and Salon."

Mary-Esther blinked, lifted her shoulders up, then down.

Jake flashed a smile. Unlike the woman, his eyes echoed kindness. "This may seem a little strange, so I'll dive to the point. What, exactly, are your intentions regarding Hattie?"

"Intentions?" Mary-Esther tucked one strand of loose hair behind her ear. "I don't follow."

"I've been Hattie's best friend, well, practically since birth," Jake stated. "I love her better than my blood kin, and I'll do anything to protect her from harm."

Elvina added, "Hattie's aunt, Piddie Davis Longman, was *my* best friend. I consider myself part of their family."

Mary-Esther crossed her arms over her chest and regarded the two. "So, you're here to what, interrogate me?" One thing about living in a small, close-knit community: you can count on your contemporaries to come to your rescue, even if you aren't drowning.

Jake flipped one hand dismissively. "Interrogate is such a strong word." He paused. "Hattie told me about your visit to The Hill and this claim to be her blood kin."

"I didn't *claim* anything." Heat crawled up Mary-Esther's neck and warmed her cheeks.

Elvina rested a hand over Jake's, reminding Mary-Esther of one tag-team runner passing the baton to the next.

"Perhaps we're coming across as a bit harsh, dear. What Jake is trying to say is that Hattie has been through quite a lot in the past few years, what with losing her last parent, and then that awful cancer. She's so sensitive."

Elvina stopped to drop a tea bag into the steaming cup of water. "The one thing Hattie has always longed for is her older sister. You see, no one talked about Sarah after she died. It hurt Miz Tillie too much. It's like Sarah was this big hole in Hattie's life."

Mary-Esther took a deep breath and tried not to sound defensive. "If that's the case, I would think you both would be happy about me showing up."

Elvina dipped her tea bag up and down in the hot water then said, "We would be eternally delighted *if* what you are proposing is true."

"But," Jake added, "please, please, please don't set Hattie up for a fall."

A three-time plea? Had a lot of emotion behind it. Mary-Esther tightened her arms. The heck with playing nice. "Seems to me, you're under the impression I'm some gold-digging grifter who's blown into town to wreak havoc." She leaned forward and lowered her voice. "Hattie's not the only one who's had a bad couple of years. Now, if you'll excuse me, I have others to attend to."

Jake reached over to Mary-Esther when she swiveled to stand. "Look, Elvina and I aren't Attila the Hun's advance henchmen. All we want is some assurance you're not going to hurt Hattie or any of the Davis family."

"And how can I do that . . . *assure* you?"

"A DNA test," Elvina answered.

Mary-Esther felt her brows crimp together. She'd have a permanent wrinkle if she wasn't careful.

"Elvina and I will pay for it," Jake said. "All we need is a bit of your spit on a swab. If you are a Davis, you'll know for sure. And so will we."

"If not," Elvina added, "you mustn't lead Hattie down a road that will cause her great suffering."

Mary-Esther stood and smoothed her apron. "Order the kit."

"We apologize if anything we've said has offended you," Jake said. "Not our intent."

Mary-Esther looked first at Jake, then at Elvina, and couldn't help but smile. "Hattie doesn't have to worry about hiring henchmen."

Mary-Esther reached the walkway of Sewanee Springs Assisted Living.

"Hey, gal. Over here!" LaJune called from the first white wicker seat.

Mary-Esther sent mental gratitude toward the heavens. No need to deal with the Southern belle watchdog at the front desk. "I'm surprised to find you on the porch this afternoon, LaJune."

The senior patted the cushioned chair beside hers. "I was pleased as punch when you phoned to say you were stopping by. Figured I'd pass the time out here 'til you arrived. Not many more days like this one due us, what with November here. Funny thing about the weather this time of year." She looked up, scanning the blue, cloudless sky. "It's like a moody child. Can't decide between being one way or the opposite. We'll have a couple of days when the north air whips down and nearly brings a frost to the pumpkins, then the next spell will turn off mild." She leveled her head and faced Mary-Esther. "I try to get out and get a little fresh oxygen when it's like today. Not good for a person to breathe nothing but bottled-up air."

Today was obviously a day when all of the brain cells engaged. Good deal. No lectures on garden vegetables.

"I have a little screened room where I live, and I spend as much time out there as possible." She handed LaJune a small, plastic container. "Brought you something."

LaJune's green eyes lit up and she popped open the lid. "Cookies! Did you make these yourself?"

"Baked them yesterday, especially for you. It's my Nana Boudreau's recipe. She called them Christmas Crescents, but I like them any time of the year. They're anise shortbread with powdered sugar." Mary-Esther frowned. "Although, I completely forgot to ask if you are okay eating sweets."

"I don't have a sugar problem. Lots of these old folks here do. Not me. No, ma'am. I get a touch of the gout in my big toe if I eat a lot of ham on account of the salt, but sweet things don't bother me. Still, I *will* sneak a bite of ham from time to time. If I get the gout, I suffer past it. Got to take the good with the bad in this life." The old woman winked. "Not a thing wrong with me except old age, Marilyn."

"Mary-Esther," she gently corrected. In the handful of times she had been back to visit the old woman, Mary-Esther had been tagged with various names starting with an *M*. Some she had never heard.

"What brings you over to my neck of the woods today? You didn't say when you called." LaJune bit into a cookie. Powdered sugar rimmed her lips.

"To see you, for one." Mary-Esther tipped her head toward the pickup. "And I'm returning the truck I've been driving, and rescuing my van. It had to have a new engine."

"I wondered why you were in that one you're driving. Thought you'd gotten the car fever and traded."

"Nope." If car fever bit her butt, she'd certainly *not* switch a battered van for an equally battered pick-up.

"An engine." LaJune's lips formed an *O*. "My, isn't that going to cost you a pretty penny?"

"About two thousand. But I'm lucky. The man who did the work cut me a little slack on the labor."

"Do you need some money, sugar? I've got plenty," LaJune said in a lowered voice. Mary-Esther glanced at the elderly man at the other end of the porch. Appeared to be asleep.

"Oh, no, LaJune." She patted the old woman's hand. "Kind of you to offer. I have a little savings." No use mentioning those savings added up

117

to less than two hundred dollars or that she'd have to string the engine payment out for months. "Maybe you shouldn't advertise you have money to spare. There are people who might take advantage."

"You're not *just anyone*, Matilda." LaJune offered a toothy grin. Cookie goo speckled her gums. "Would you like to stay and eat supper? I can tell them to set you a place."

"I would love to, but some other time. I'm having dinner with someone."

LaJune leaned over and asked, "Is it a young man?" One white brow arched.

"He's a friend, the one who let me borrow the truck."

"He from here? Maybe I know his people. What's his name?"

"Jerry Blount. He's a sergeant for the Gadsden County Sheriff's Department."

"Blount. Jerry Blount." LaJune tapped her chin with a finger. "Bet that's Harold Blount's boy. He ought to be in his late fifties or more by now. Law feller. That him?"

"Probably. I haven't met his relatives." Yet, wasn't that the next step? Mary-Esther's mouth went dry.

"If it's him, that's the saddest story about his daddy. He shot hisself when Jerry was a teenager. Don't think his mama remarried. The boy turned out all right. I figured he went into law enforcement on account of his daddy doing what he done." Her shoulders rose and fell. "Who's to say? Speaking of relatives, you ever find yours?"

"I think so." Mary-Esther absorbed the tidbit about Jerry's life. It made her feel closer to him, somehow—shared pain. "All things seem to point to them, anyway."

"It's always a good thing to have people." LaJune tapped the plastic container. "Fetch us a cup of coffee and we'll see if the rest of these here cookies are fitting to eat."

Mary-Esther parked the truck behind the white and green police cruiser and studied the house and yard. If the outside of the modest brick house was any indication, Jerry Blount was an organized guy. The grass grew thick and healthy, the hedges were clipped in even lines, and the driveway was swept clean of debris.

The front door opened before she reached the porch and Jerry appeared, waving her inside. "You didn't have any problems finding the place?" he asked, holding the door ajar.

"Your pointer about looking for the squad car was brilliant." She stepped into an uncluttered living room. A lemony scent welcomed her. Probably dusting cleaner. Jerry didn't seem the type to burn fragranced candles.

"Let me take your purse and sweater. I'll set them on the guest room dresser." He stepped down a narrow hallway and called back over his shoulder, "Make yourself t' home. There's beer in the fridge, also sweet tea, water, and soft drinks."

Mary-Esther glanced around the room. A few feminine touches belied the former presence of a woman: crocheted doilies, family pictures in decorative frames. Not a shrine to his dead wife, but not a typical single-guy lair. Touching, that Jerry hadn't tried to erase all traces of her.

She found her way to a galley-style kitchen and located a chilled bottle of beer. On the counter, a large cutting board held an assortment of salad vegetables. Otherwise, sparse and neat.

Jerry reappeared. "Didn't think to ask what you liked to drink. Guess I should've picked up a bottle of wine. I have rum if you'd like a mixed drink. I usually have a lite beer, though not tonight since I have to work later."

"Beer's fine. Thanks. When would you like to go pick up the van?"

"I have the keys. We can collect it most anytime. Already paid Milton. Hope you don't mind. His shop closes at five."

"Thanks, Jerry. That was nice of you." She stepped over and kissed him lightly on the cheek. "Guess I can make payments to you."

His face flushed slightly. Mary-Esther smiled. *A man who blushes. I'm so in trouble.* "Appreciate you making me dinner. You didn't have to do this."

"Used to cook all the time back when . . ." He stopped. "Hard to get all excited about cooking for one person."

"What are we having?"

"Figured you weren't a vegetarian, since you eat gator tail and ham sandwiches." His mood visibly improved. "I happen to make the most wicked steak this side of the dirt. My secret Blount-family marinade makes the meat so tender, it practically chews itself." He clapped his hands together once. "That, and a salad and some garlic bread. Okay with you?"

"Sounds fantastic." Mary-Esther's mouth watered. "I haven't had a decent steak in so long I can't even recall. Can I help?"

"If you want, you could cut up the salad. Everything's been washed. I'm running a bit behind schedule." He removed a shallow baking dish from the refrigerator. Two thick steaks rested in a puddle of dark sauce. "I slept longer than usual, and then Mama called 'cause her outside spigot sprung a leak. I just now got home and showered."

They worked together. Mary-Esther noted how comfortable she had become with this man, in such a short time. She pushed the feelings aside. If she dwelt on it, she would become too afraid to breathe.

Mary-Esther bit into a sliver of seasoned porterhouse and moaned. "This is the best steak I have ever tasted."

Jerry beamed. "Do I know how to impress a lady, or what?" He sawed off a hunk of meat and chewed. "So, how's the search for your kinfolk coming along?"

"It has become so convoluted, Jerry. Sure you want to know?"

He doused his salad with ranch dressing. "I have all night. Well, at least until I have to dress for work. By the way, if you aren't in a rush to get back to the 'hooch, you could stick around and I'll follow you back to your neck of the woods. I'll be going over there after check-in." He tucked into the salad. "I'd like to know you got home safely with the new engine. Those back county roads are awfully dark and deserted. If you had trouble, you'd be at the mercy of a passerby. You really should consider getting a cell phone."

"Maybe I'll do that with part of my next paycheck. After I throw some cash your way for getting my van out of hock."

"Back to the convoluted family story. I'm all ears." He cupped a hand behind one ear and grinned.

There were those dimples again! "Do you know the Davis family at all?"

"That'd be the ones out the Greensboro Highway, about three miles south of town?" he asked.

"Yes."

"Dan Davis used to run a fix-it shop uptown Chattahoochee for years. Good man. His wife was a teacher at the high school, from what I recall. I know Bobby. He is, or *was*, a Game and Fish officer." He paused, took a sip of tea. "Hattie, I don't know personally—just things I've heard. Some of the officers see her for massage therapy. When you tote around a heavy gun belt, your back starts to complain."

He sawed another hunk of meat, speared it.

Hearty appetite. Is that true of everything? Mary Esther forced her mind back on track. "I may be part of their family."

He glanced up from his plate. "How's that?"

120

Mary-Esther recounted the sum of evidence. Jerry whistled under his breath. "That's some story. I thought things like that only happened on TV or in the movies. Have you talked to any of them yet?"

"Only Hattie." She popped a cherry tomato into her mouth. Flavor exploded on her tongue. Homegrown. Somebody cared enough to plant a late crop. Boy, would LaJune approve.

"How'd that go?" he asked.

"She's ready to join hands and buy matching big sister-little sister outfits." Mary-Esther felt a smile tempt her lips. "It's not Hattie who's been an issue."

"Bobby?" He harrumphed.

Mary-Esther opened her mouth to tell him she hadn't met the infamous Bobby Davis then changed her mind. Any information gathered in advance would help.

"That guy used to be junkyard-dog mean at one point. I could see where he might raise a little fuss. Although, from what I hear, he's been on the wagon for the past few years."

She knew all about nasty drunks. For sure. "Do you make it your job to learn everything about everyone?" She used a hunk of garlic bread to mop up steak juice. The heck with impressive manners.

"I know Bobby from his days in law enforcement. Didn't much like dealing with him, but I had to sometimes." Jerry lifted one shoulder and let it fall. "Besides, being nosy gets to be a habit when you're in this business. I happen to care about folks. Plus, when I know people, I can find someone willing to help *me* out with information."

"Good. Put that to use and help me, will you? Hattie may be ready to gather me into the family, no questions asked, but everyone else around here treats me like a freak sideshow."

He paused, his steak knife in mid-air. "Like who?"

"Jake Witherspoon and Elvina Houston paid me a little visit a couple of days ago."

Jerry threw his head back and laughed. "That surprises me not at all." He wiped meat juice from his lips.

"Enlighten me, then." She pointed her fork in his direction and made tiny circles with the tines. "Explain why half of Chattahoochee looks at me like I've ushered in a herd of rats carrying the Black Plague. Like they're ready to circle the wagons and hide the babies and little old ladies."

He gave a little chuckle. "That's a bit strong."

"No it's not. I won't delude myself into thinking I'm such a dish, everyone comes into the Homeplace to gawk at me, but there it is."

"I come for the pie and coffee."

She jabbed him in the arm with a finger.

"You could get arrested for molesting an officer of the law, ma'am."

"I thought that only applied when you were in uniform."

She noticed his faint grin. He winked. They stared at each other for a moment, until she looked down.

Jerry cleared his throat then said, "You asked about Jake and Elvina. Jake's the only son of Colonel and Betsy Witherspoon. The Triple C Spa used to be his parents' place. Everyone still calls it the Witherspoon Mansion. Short version: Jake left town after Daddy died. Mother pissed away a fortune. Jake returned for the funeral and had next to nothing once he sold the mansion and paid off Mama's debt. Still, he managed to buy the florist shop and move into the back of it."

Jerry stabbed a tomato. Juice and seeds spewed into a pool of dressing. "Enter Hattie Davis. Her mama died—her dad had passed several years before—and Hattie returned home. Met back up with Jake. Jake falls victim to a hate crime, nearly dies. Hattie ends up moving back to The Hill and marrying this writer fellow who came to town to write about the hate crime. Holston bought the Witherspoon Mansion after the original buyers decided to sell."

"Talk about drama." Mary-Esther bit into a hunk of garlic bread.

"It was pretty hairy around here for a bit. FDLE and the FBI crawling around. Reporters camped out at East Bank. Total media hullabaloo." He shook his head. "Somewhere in there, Bobby meets a local woman, and makes nice with his sister. He lives out there on the property now, in a log home he built himself."

Mary-Esther's head spun. It was like hearing a synopsis of the World Book Encyclopedia. And "makes nice with his sister," what was that about?

"Now, on to Elvina Houston," Jerry said. "She's a piece of work. Knows dirt on the majority of Gadsden and Jackson counties. When I'm researching a case, one of the first people I turn to is Elvina. Woman has her finger smack dab on the pulse of things. She inherited the honor from a woman named Piddie. That was Hattie's aunt; Dan Davis was Piddie's much younger brother."

Jerry smiled. The skin around his eyes crinkled. *Is that cute or what.*

"Piddie was the most original woman I have ever met in all my years of law enforcement," he continued. "She had this hairdo that added a good foot to her height, and she stuffed flowers and all sort of things in it for decoration. She had a saying for any situation. One of the most honest, kindest, and funniest people who ever existed.

"When Piddie died—at dang near a hundred, I think—she passed the baton on to her best friend Elvina. Elvina is like a little banty rooster. Get her feathers ruffled, she'll come after you with spurs flying. And I guarantee you, you won't get the better end of it."

Mary-Esther's chest constricted. "I should have never come here."

"But you did. Didn't you?" He reached over and ran the tip of one finger down the side of her face. "Don't you think you owe it to yourself, and to everyone involved, to see it through?"

Her gaze dropped to her plate to avoid the warmth shining in his brown eyes.

Jerry polished off the last bite of his porterhouse. "As to the other kin, let's see. There's Joe and Evelyn Fletcher. Evelyn is Piddie's daughter." He pinched his eyes shut for a beat. "I can still call up the fishy aftertaste of one of her casseroles I tried at a church social over there." He whistled low. "If you happen to get invited to any family functions in the future, try to find out if any of the dishes came from her kitchen. No, take that back. Find out if *she* made them. Joe's a fine cook. He owns the Borrowed Thyme Bakery and Eatery on West Washington. Best cathead biscuits you'll ever put in your mouth."

"I've had the biscuits. First time I passed through town."

Hindsight brought things into focus for Mary-Esther. Was *every*one part of that family?

Jerry stood and returned shortly with two dessert plates. "Mama sent the pie. Can't take credit for that." He snapped his fingers. "Dang. I forgot the ice cream."

"I'm good." She dug in. Flakey crust. Gooey apples inside. The right combination of tart and sweet.

He sat down. "Joe used to be a psychiatrist up at the mental hospital before he retired. Evelyn sews. I know ladies in Quincy who wouldn't dream of going to a party without commissioning Evelyn. She's even made dresses for the first lady of Florida."

"Amazing, the stories behind people."

"That's how it is," Jerry said. "Folks think because someone is from a rural area, they're dull. Let me assure you. Not the case."

This time when Mary-Esther stepped into the sheriff's office with Jerry, LaJune's red-haired niece didn't greet them. Instead, a young man with a severe buzz-cut acknowledged Jerry and tipped his head once toward Mary-Esther.

Jerry stepped to the metal security door separating the reception area from the rest of the sheriff's office. A latch clicked and he opened the door. "You can come on back with me."

Mary-Esther followed him down a polished tile hallway.

"If you wouldn't mind waiting, I'll only be a few minutes." He nodded to a small room with a desk and two chairs. Was this where they interrogated people? "After the shift check-on, we can go." She listened to the squeak of his shoes on the polished tile.

Mary-Esther took a seat in the cramped room and watched other officers file past. Some nodded. Others gave her an inquisitive glance. A few minutes later, the process reversed. The ebb and flow of a law enforcement tide.

Jerry walked in. "You ready to roll?" There it was again. The uniform. The broad shoulders. All that leather. The authority. Wow.

"Sure." Mary-Esther swallowed. "It's kind of fun to see the inside of this place. To think, I was born in this very building."

Jerry looked around as if he was peering into the past. Every movement he made elicited a creaky remark from the various accessories clipped to his belt. Mary-Esther found the sound alluring. She imagined herself as the femme fatale who asked the gunslinger if he ever took off his gun then tried her best to provide such an opportunity.

"There's a ladies' room down the hall on the right, in case you need to visit before we leave," he said.

As Mary-Esther aged, she couldn't pass a restroom. Yet another thing that came with the territory. She reminded herself of a dog on a walk, how it would pee a few drops on every bush and blade of grass.

The man knew a thing or two about older women.

Outside, they stood beside his car like two teenagers stealing the last few minutes of freedom before their parents intervened.

"Eww . . . can I sit in the squad car?" Mary-Esther asked.

"If you'd like. Suit yourself." He opened the passenger door and she crawled in.

"Oh, thank God. I had this fear you'd make me sit in the cage in the back."

Jerry slid behind the wheel and buckled in. "Only if you act up and don't do what the nice officer asks you to do." His grin flashed.

Mary-Esther tilted her head and one corner of her lips lifted. "Who would think a law man would have such a sense of humor?"

"There are a lot of things folks don't know about me."

Oh yes. She could only imagine.

The radio chattered. The dispatcher spoke to different units. Mumbo jumbo and numbers. Ten this, ten that.

"Why all the code talk?" Mary-Esther asked. "Why can't you say *someone's shooting someone. Go to John Doe's house on Main Street*, or something."

"If we did, we wouldn't sound nearly so important and mysterious."

"I see." She trilled her fingers across the dashboard then mentally chided herself for acting like such a kid. "Where are you going tonight?"

"The county is broken up into zones to make it easier to manage the available officers. I'm over in zone four tonight. That's Chattahoochee and surrounding areas."

"Do you ride around and look for bad guys?"

Jerry chuckled. "Guess so, in a sense. Dispatch contacts us when a call comes in. Units in the area respond. As a sergeant, I supervise, but I answer calls and back up other units too."

"If there's nothing happening, it must be pretty dull."

Jerry cranked the cruiser. "It does make the time go by faster when folks are up to no good."

Mary-Esther studied the equipment and fought the urge to hit the switch for the siren and lights. "Wish I could go with you. That would be such a kick."

"They had a ride-along program a few years ago. Citizens could sign a form and accompany an officer for a shift."

She clasped her hands together and giggled. "I'd *love* that."

"They discontinued the program. Liability issues. We have auxiliaries who periodically accompany us, men and women who're attending the police academy."

"I'd have to sign up for law enforcement training to ride with you?"

"That, or break the law. In which case, you'd be comfortably ensconced in the cage in the back." When he smiled, Mary-Esther noticed those faint dimple parentheses beside his lips. One of those guys who grew more attractive by the second.

"I'll pass. I've never had so much as a speeding ticket. Oh, I lied about my age to get married when I was young and rash. And I'll admit to driving when I really shouldn't have, years ago. I've never committed a felony or anything."

"Nice to know, Mary-Esther." He locked eyes with her for a long moment.

Heat passed through Mary-Esther. She'd never kissed a man in a police car. Would that be a crime?

The radio crackled, causing them to jump. "Code Blue. 110 Satsuma Street, Chattahoochee."

"Code Blue?" She asked.

"EMS call-out. Means someone dialed nine-eleven. The call transferred to them, so it must be some type of medical emergency. Our radios scan the channels, and we hear the call-outs for fire, EMS, and for the different units."

The realization hit.

Mary-Esther's jaw dropped open. "Oh, my God, Jerry. That's the Herring's address."

Chapter Twenty-two

Hattie suspected something as soon as she stepped into Bobby's house. Elvina occupied one end of the leather couch, her casted leg propped on an ottoman. Jake sat in the matching chair, and Bobby rested in the recliner. Their stalled conversation hung in the air. The three looked like kids caught leering at their dad's porn magazines.

"Why do I get the feeling I'm being set up?" Hattie removed her sweatshirt jacket and hung it on one of a series of wooden hooks.

Jake pulled a face. "Now, Sister-girl. Don't go all dramatic."

Hattie's gaze rested on Bobby. "I dang near broke my neck rushing down here when you called, dear brother. Thought something bad had happened."

Bobby coughed. "It'll take a week or two to get all the crud from my lungs, but I'm hovering few feet back from death's door."

"And Elvina. Glad to see you up and around." Hattie flashed a smile in the old woman's direction. Elvina didn't return the gesture, only nodded.

"Coffee's on, if you'd like a cup." Jake motioned toward the kitchen.

"Must be heavy to round up the posse this late in the day," Hattie said.

"Sister-girl, stop looking for boogers behind every bush. Come with me and get a cup of coffee, then we'll tell you why we're here. Oh, and no worries, the coffee is decaf." Jake grabbed his mug and cane and shuffled to the kitchen for a refill. Hattie followed.

When they returned, Hattie settled into a wooden rocking chair by the hearth and cradled the hot mug. "Okay, who's going to tell me the reason for this little powwow?"

Jake glanced from Bobby to Elvina, waiting to see if anyone would take the lead. "Let's don't all jump at once." When the other two remained silent, Jake took a seat and continued, "We're here because we're concerned about this *alleged* sister."

"Ah…" Hattie looked to her brother. "So you've heard. I came to tell you right after I found out, but you were so sick, I didn't think it was the right time."

"No worries," Bobby said. "Half of Chattahoochee has called me. The other half has stopped Leigh on the street."

"One thing about this town," Hattie said, shaking her head, "no need to concern yourself about running your own life. Someone will always be there to prime the pump."

Jake set his coffee cup down and leaned forward. "Sister-girl, we all know how sensitive you are."

"I've heard you're one step shy of carving that Cajun's initials on our family tree," Bobby said. His voice had a slightly mean edge. Hadn't heard that since he'd sobered up.

"Okay, wise guy. Have you even *met* her?"

"Nope. Don't need to," Bobby said.

Wow. Not the least bit curious? Not buying it, buddy. "You go to the Homeplace all the time."

"Been sick, and busy. Besides, it's not that important . . . to me."

What a load of chicken poop. Unless her brother crawled in a hole, he'd bump into three-quarters of the residents in less than a week. That tiny muscle beside his left eye jittered like it always did when his words and the truth didn't match.

Hattie shifted her eyes from her brother's twitchy face and looked toward the others.

"How do you know the woman isn't some kind of scam artist?" Elvina jabbed her finger for emphasis. "She could be anyone."

"Has she shown you solid proof?" Bobby asked.

Hattie held up one hand. "If you'll slow down enough for me to get a word in edgewise. First of all, *she* has a name—Mary-Esther. In answer to your question, no proof, other than a birth certificate from the same hospital where Sarah was born . . . and died."

"Hundreds of people were born over there," Jake said. "It was the place most women went to around here, if they didn't have a home birth."

"Yes, but don't you think it's too much of a coincidence? Mary-Esther has the same birth date as Sarah, not to mention she looks exactly like Mama."

128

Elvina sniffed. "Well, there's that. She does bear a striking resemblance."

Bobby popped a cough drop in his mouth then said, "Hattie, all of us know how you love to pick up strays." The scent of menthol wafted Hattie's way.

"This woman could be setting you—all of us—up for a hard fall." Elvina shook a finger in her direction. "If she contacts a lawyer and proves her case, she'll weasel her way into part of your parents' land."

Hattie frowned. "Are you really all sitting here trying to tell me that someone who never even *heard* of Chattahoochee, much less the Davis family, all the way clean from Louisiana, for God's sake . . . what? Read Mama's obituary from a couple of years back, did the research, then went to a boatload of bother to look us up?" She stopped to suck in a breath. "If our last name was Rockefeller or Vanderbilt, I might entertain the idea. But the Davises of Gadsden County? Come on. Get real."

Jake cocked his head. "It does sound a tad far-fetched when you lay it out."

"Still, Hattie," Bobby interjected, "*I* need to see proof."

"That's why Jake and I asked that Sloat woman to consent to a DNA test," Elvina added.

Hattie's mouth gaped open. "You what?"

Bobby held up his hands. "If she really is a Davis, we'll know for certain. I sure ain't budging on this." He coughed. Phlegm rattled in his chest. Another breeze of menthol wafted her way.

Hattie took a sip of coffee, considering. "I happen to believe Mary-Esther. It's a feeling, deep inside. Mama and Daddy would be disappointed if they looked down and saw us not treating their middle child with kindness and respect."

"Good Lord, Hattie. You're such a sap," Bobby said.

Elvina repositioned her foot on the pillowed ottoman. "If she *is* your sister, you know we'll do whatever it takes to blend her into the fold." Elvina shot a warning glance toward Bobby. "If she isn't, then it's best to know now, before you get too attached."

Jake looked at Hattie, his gaze soft. "The truth will win out, Sister-girl. It always does."

Hattie rocked back and forth. Somehow, the gentle pitching of a rocking chair had always soothed her. Kept her from wanting to lash out at her brother.

Bobby reached over to a small wooden table beside the recliner and held a plastic envelope toward her. "Cheek swab, Hattie. I've already done one. As soon as we take this by to Mary-Esther, we'll send it off to the lab."

By the time Sergeant Jerry Blount arrived at the Herring's home and parked, an ambulance idled by the side entrance, its emergency lights turned off. He noted a Chattahoochee Police Department cruiser. Not a good sign. If someone required fast transport to Tallahassee, the ambulance would have been long gone. The absence of frantic activity pointed to one of two scenarios: the call-out had been unnecessary and the person was all right, or the person was beyond help and did not need the services of the paramedics. Given the age and frail health of Mr. and Mrs. Herring, the later was more feasible.

He glanced in his rearview mirror. Mary-Esther pulled the van in behind the cruiser and jumped out. Jerry caught up with her at the side entrance and held the unlocked door open.

Rose sat at the kitchen table, a confused expression on her weathered face. In the back of the house, Jerry heard the muffled conversations of what he assumed to be the paramedics and the local officer on duty. Jerry knew the drill. If a death had occurred, the call would go out for the coroner. After the death was officially confirmed and recorded, the funeral home would be contacted. Eustis Herring would leave on a gurney, but not one bound for the hospital forty miles away.

Jerry glanced at Mary-Esther then slipped from the kitchen toward the rear of the house.

Mary-Esther knelt in front of the old woman and spoke with a soft voice. "Rose, honey. What happened?"

"Eustis has taken ill. He complained he couldn't catch his breath, and he was sick on his stomach." She motioned toward the tiny kitchen. "I felt better this afternoon and decided to do a little baking. Eustis loves my sour cream pound cake. I think he had four pieces."

The old woman smiled. "That's what he fell in love with me for, so he claims." Her expression flipped to a frown. "He had me put in a call to the emergency people. I think it was carrying things too far, doing that. All he has is a sour stomach. Nothing a little antacid won't cure. He insisted, though. Now those nice folks—a lady and a man—are back there checking him over. I hated we made them come out in the cold for such." She shook a bony finger. "Men aren't cut out for any kind of discomfort, you know. It's why the Good Lord made it so a woman would carry a baby."

A uniformed officer entered the side door, followed by a second man. They disappeared down the hall. Rose followed them with her gaze. "Eustis must be really carrying on, needing such a crowd of folks."

Jerry returned to the kitchen. He looked Mary-Esther's way. The grim set of his lips spoke of the events unfolding down the hall.

"You must be the Blount boy," Rose said when Jerry pulled up a chair next to hers. "Mary-Esther has said such good things about you."

Rose looked to Mary-Esther. "He's handsome in that green uniform. I always did like the looks of a man in a uniform."

"Miz Rose," Jerry said. "I'm afraid I have some bad news."

"Eustis isn't insisting on going on over to Tallahassee Hospital, is he? I need to put a stop to this nonsense before it goes any further. He can be such a bother when he's not feeling well." She pushed away from the table and started to rise.

Jerry rested a hand on the old woman's shoulder. "No, Miz Rose. Please, sit back down." He blew out a long breath. "Mr. Eustis has passed on. I am so sorry."

Rose's eyebrows crimped together. "What do you mean, telling me such?"

"Ma'am, I would not say this if it wasn't true. Your husband has passed on." His voice conveyed a blend of authority and empathy.

Rose's face blanched. Her lower lip quivered.

"What do we do, now?" Mary-Esther asked Jerry. She smoothed the white curl that had worked its way from Rose's hairpins.

"We need the name of the funeral home you wish for us to contact, Miz Rose," Jerry said.

"Funeral home?" Rose blinked and squared her shoulders. "We'll use the Burn's boy when the day comes, but why would you need him?"

"Will you stay with her?" Jerry asked Mary-Esther. He stood and left the kitchen again.

Within minutes, the clang of metal and rolling wheels sounded in the entrance way. A suited man with a compassionate expression walked into the kitchen. People in the business of death must sleep fully clothed. How else could they be ready to drop and run at a moment's notice? Mary-Esther envisioned a funeral home much like a fire station, with rows of tasteful black suits hanging in readiness, along with spit-shined black shoes.

"Joe . . . Joe Burns?" Rose took the funeral director's extended hand. "What are you doing here at this time of night?"

"Miz Rose. I am so sorry about Mr. Eustis. You may rest assured, I will personally oversee all the details."

"Now this has gone far enough!" Rose's voice grew shrill. "Eustis has pulled some pranks on me over the years, but this one beats them all."

The gurney made the turn with its cargo. Rose stood and lunged for the edge of the wheeled bed with a speed unexpected in someone her age and level of disability. "Eustis, this is absurd. Get yourself up from there and stop this foolishness!"

Before any of the attendants could react, Rose grabbed the sheet and flung it back to reveal her husband's lifeless body. She stood motionless for a second then reached out and touched his face. Rose jerked her hand back as if it had encountered searing heat rather than the cooling stillness of death.

Mary-Esther circled an arm across the old woman's shoulders and gently guided her away from the gurney. "Let's sit down, Rose. I'm not going to leave you. I will be right here."

Chapter Twenty-three

Mary-Esther marveled at the management of death in a small town. By mid-morning of the next day, local cooks arrived with their contributions: fried chicken, chicken 'n' dumplings, beef stew, bowls of cooked, farm-raised vegetables, cold cuts, layered cakes, pies, and endless casseroles smothered with melted cheddar cheese. Other townsfolk brought paper towels and napkins, disposable utensils, hot and cold cups, coffee supplies, jugs of iced tea, and soft drinks.

Mary-Esther submerged her hands in a sink filled with bubbly warm water. Bits of ham and waterlogged flecks of lettuce clung to her skin. She looked up when she heard someone enter the kitchen.

"Where would you like this?" Hattie stood at the kitchen threshold, a foil-wrapped container in her hands. "It's a hash brown casserole."

Mary-Esther motioned with a tip of her head toward the countertop beside her. "Anywhere over here. Make a spot."

Hattie shifted two glass dishes and set down the casserole.

Mary-Esther rinsed the suds from her hands and dried them on a paper towel. "Nice of you to bring food, Hattie. I didn't realize you knew Eustis."

"Everyone knows everyone in this town. Mr. Eustis was just always *here*, you know. Like a number of people Mom and Daddy knew, so many of that generation are leaving us."

Mary-Esther stretched to find words, any words. Fatigue threatened to drop her.

"How's Miz Rose holding up?" Hattie asked.

"Reality is beginning to sink in. I spent the night on the couch, and she was up and down all night. I wished I had something to help her sleep. The strongest thing I had to offer was aspirin."

"I can speak to Doc Ricks and see if he can prescribe a mild sedative. I'm sure Rose is a patient there. Everyone in town has gone to the clinic at one time or another, even if they have a doctor in Tallahassee or Marianna. I'll stop by there after I leave here."

Mary-Esther tucked a sprig of hair behind one ear. "That would be great. I hadn't even thought of that."

"How could you? You haven't been in town long enough to know the ins and outs."

Mary-Esther's gaze roamed around the small kitchen. "Can you believe all this food? We helped each other out in my neighborhood in New Orleans, but nothing like this."

"It's something people *can* do. And it really helps. After Daddy and Mama died, it was so nice to not have to think about making something to eat. Not that any of us had much of an appetite."

Mary-Esther looked at the line of casseroles. "I'll have to help Rose get these dishes back to the rightful owners."

"The cook usually puts a piece of tape with the family name somewhere on the dish." Hattie picked up several of the containers and looked at the bottoms. "That or it's printed in permanent marker directly on the outside. Makes it easy for the bereaved family to send thank you cards too."

Mary-Esther closed her eyes for a second. One more thing to do.

"Got some paper and a pen?" Hattie said.

Mary-Esther rummaged in a jumbled drawer beside the stove and extracted a pencil and yellow note pad. "I'm learning my way around Rose's house pretty fast."

"Since I know most of the folks, I'll check the labels and tell you the first name of the cook. That way, Miz Rose can send out cards later."

"I may have to do that too. She's shut down. I helped her bathe this morning. She's like a little orphaned child."

"Everyone figured Miz Rose would be the first to go. She's been sickly for so long. Mr. Eustis took such care of her. Who would guess he'd be the first?"

Mary-Esther wobbled.

"You really need to get some rest. Why don't you go on to your apartment? Sarah is with my sister-in-law, and I'll be happy to stay. I can make this list too. Don't worry."

"You sure?"

"Absolutely. Elvina is probably on her way, regardless of her leg. I would put money on it. She prides herself on her funeral food." Hattie paused, a faint smile lifting her lips. "Aunt Piddie used to kid Elvina about how many funerals she attended. Said Elvina counted them as so-cial functions and had more black outfits than most funeral directors."

Mary-Esther offered a shaky smile. Hattie held out her hand. "Give me the apron and get your butt out of here. This is your maybe-sister speaking."

Before she could stop herself, Mary-Esther gave Hattie a hug. Hattie wrapped her arms around Mary-Esther and rocked her side-to-side. Nana Boudreau used to do the same. Loretta never did.

Mary-Esther pulled back.

"Now go." Hattie tied on the apron and motioned toward the back door with her head.

Mary-Esther trudged up the stairs to her apartment, barely aware of the clear blue, late-autumn skies overhead or the freshening breeze. She pulled off her shoes, piled the pants and shirt on the floor, and flopped into bed in just her underwear. Boudreau demanded a few pats before circling and curling up beside her.

She fell asleep with his purr-vibrating, warm body next to her heart.

At the Triple C, Elvina Houston appeared at the arched doorway to the stylists' room, her aluminum walker leading the way. The usual din of conversation and laughter muted, as if the death of Eustis Herring had cast a somber pall. Two dryers ran, and Mandy and Wanda worked steadily.

"Sure is good to see you up and moving around, Elvina," Wanda commented. "I know you were tired of that wheelchair."

Elvina tapped her way into the room and lowered herself into a chair. "As soon as I get my balance back to my satisfaction, I'm kicking this metal contraption to the curb too. I'll be even better when I can use a cane. That, plus I'm looking forward to moving back into my house."

"Things aren't going well at Joe and Evelyn's?" Mandy talked around a hairpin clamped between her front teeth.

Wanda aimed the pointed end of a rat-tail comb in Mandy's direction. "You missed your calling, hon."

Mandy swung her head toward Wanda's workstation. "What'd I do?"

"You should've been a ventriloquist. Never ceases to amaze me how you can carry on a conversation with stuff hanging out of your mouth. I didn't even see your lips move."

Mandy plucked the hairpin from her mouth and grinned. "I've had lots of practice."

"I came back here to let you know Mary-Esther called," Elvina said. "She's bringing Rose Herring by around eleven for a wash and set."

Mandy made a clicking noise with her tongue. "That poor, poor woman. I can't imagine losing someone after . . . how long had they been married?"

"Sixty years, plus. I remember the anniversary party we had for them at the church. Can't honestly recall if it was last year or the year before." Elvina repositioned her cast.

"Your foot bothering you?" Mandy asked.

"Not so much anymore. A little toward the end of a day." Elvina frowned. "It itches like all get out. If I could reach the skin, I do believe I'd scratch it raw as a plucked chicken."

"You could do like I did when I had mine on a couple of years back," Mandy said. "I took a coat hanger and straightened it out so I could jab it underneath."

Wanda flinched. "Sounds painful."

"Nope. It was close to bliss. Anyone who's ever had to endure a cast knows what I mean."

"Sounds a good way to court infection, you ask me." Elvina smoothed the wrinkles from her skirt. "To answer your earlier question, Mandy, things couldn't be better at Joe and Evelyn's. They've treated me like the Queen of Sheba. I want to be back in my own home, is all. Plus, Buster misses me."

Mandy took a long, appraising look at her patron's completed style. "You want me to spray it, Miz Beatrice?"

"Lightly, please. I don't like it so stiff."

Mandy misted Beatrice Whigham's hair as if she wielded fairy dust. "There you go." She detached the drape and spun the chair around to face the mirror to allow a better view of the completed style.

Beatrice reached up and patted the sides as she turned her head from side to side. "Exactly what I had in mind. You always do such a fine job."

"My pleasure." Mandy beamed.

Elvina leaned forward to stand, but Mandy motioned her down. "I'll check her out, 'Vina."

"Thank you, sugar." Elvina settled back.

Mandy returned after a few minutes and used a whisk broom and dustpan to collect the snippets of hair at the base of her chair. "Seems to me, from what I've been hearing, Mary-Esther is really helping out at the Herring's."

Elvina narrowed her eyes. "I may have to change my opinion of her."

136

"Well, well. Elvina Houston. What am I hearing? You're seriously going to cut that poor woman some slack?" Mandy stood with her hands propped on her hips.

Elvina held up one finger. "I like to be certain before I welcome a stranger in with open arms. In this day and time, it's only prudent. I have to admit, Mary-Esther's behavior of late has impressed me. She's stayed with Rose every minute when she wasn't working at Bill's, and she's made sure someone would take a shift when she couldn't be around."

Wanda motioned her roller-studded client to the last free dryer. "Pretty admirable, considering she's only lived here, what, a month or two?"

"Hattie told me Mary-Esther's tried her best to get Rose to eat," Elvina said. "Even cooked her some of her grandmother's recipes."

"Cajun food? Might be a bit harsh. Her gumbo is really good, but it's a smidge spicy," Mandy said.

Elvina drummed her temple with one finger. "It was some kind of potato and chicken soup, from what Hattie described. Rose must have liked it. Hattie said she ate a bowl full. Other than a little dab of scrambled eggs, it's the only thing Rose has touched since Eustis passed."

The distinctive whoosh of the front double doors sounded. "I'll bet that's them." Elvina pulled up on the walker and tapped her way into the other room.

After Rose settled into Mandy's chair, Elvina motioned Mary-Esther back into the front room. "We need to talk." Elvina pointed to one of the little-used reception room chairs.

Mary-Esther sat down, her face drawn and weary. Elvina felt a rush of compassion. When she managed a comfortable position on the chair next to Mary-Esther, she looked directly into the younger woman's eyes. "Seems I owe you an apology."

"For what?"

"I might have misjudged you. You have to understand, Mary-Esther. We look out for one another here. The Davises, Joe and Evelyn, even Holston, though he's a Yankee; they are like my family. When Piddie passed, God rest her soul, I swore a vow I would look after them."

"That's admirable, but—"

Elvina held up a stop-hand. "When you came barreling into town, claiming kinship, my hackles shot straight up. Jake's much the same way. We were trying to protect them from anyone intent on stirring up trouble." She paused. "I've seen a glimmer of Tillie Davis in you these past few days. You have that same selflessness Tillie had."

Mary-Esther picked at one of her cuticles. "I wish I could've known her."

"I am sorry for that, if indeed you turn out to be Tillie's daughter." Elvina reached over and patted Mary-Esther's hand.

Mary-Esther glanced toward the door leading into the hair salon. "Elvina, there's something I have been worrying about, pertaining to Rose."

Elvina leaned in. She truly lived for good insider information. "You can tell me, honey."

"This man and woman have come to the house since Eustis died. The only thing Rose will tell me is they are relatives of her husband's."

"Odd. No one has ever shown up to help them out before."

"This is the part that concerns me." Mary-Esther lowered her voice. "Rose had me search in the little fireproof safe in her closet for some paperwork. I came across this document. I know I shouldn't have read it, but I did. Thought it might be what she was looking for, the paid-in-full funeral arrangements she and Eustis had made a couple of years back. But it was some kind of legal trust, and the trustee was listed as a Jonathan Watson.

"Later, when I convinced Rose to lie down and rest, she started babbling about some cousin urging her to sell the house and move into an assisted living facility. Might not be a bad idea. It's not really for me to say. But I got an uneasy feeling about it. I've seen how relatives come crawling like rats drawn to cheese after a death in a family."

Mary-Esther picked at the torn cuticle until a bead of blood appeared. "Frankly, I'm afraid for Rose."

Chapter Twenty-four

"**What's to become** of my lovely dolls?" Rose asked. She stood at the entrance to the kitchen wearing nothing but a thin cotton nightgown, feet bare. Her white hair stuck out in unruly tufts.

Mary-Esther looked up from the book in her hands. "Oh, Rose. You're going to catch a chill!"

Rose shuffled over and slumped into one of the chairs next to the kitchen table. "Whenever I look around, all I see are their sweet faces staring back at me."

Mary-Esther jumped up, returning shortly with a pair of slippers and a thick robe. She urged the old woman to stand long enough to don the robe then helped her put the slippers on, one foot at a time. "Would you like some breakfast? I can cook eggs, soft-scrambled like you enjoy them. I have a pot of coffee on."

"I'm not hungry." Rose smiled vacantly. "The coffee might feel good."

"I'll bring you a cup. You need to try to eat a little. I'll fix those eggs."

Rose sighed. "If you insist."

A week had passed since Rose laid her husband to rest. Most of the food had been either eaten or thrown away, and the containers rescued by the same women who brought them. An addressed stack of thank you cards rested in a teetering pile on the kitchen counter, finished with the help of Elvina and Hattie. As soon as someone came to stay with Rose, Mary-Esther could leave for the post office then work.

"Why are you worrying about your dolls, Rose?" Mary-Esther poured a cup of coffee and added sugar and cream.

"I hate to think of them with no home. You will take them, won't you?" The old woman's rheumy eyes sought hers.

"Your dolls need to stay right where they are. If I took them away, you would miss them."

Rose grabbed Mary-Esther's hand when she set the coffee in front of her. Her weak grasp, delicate as rice paper. "Promise me! Promise me, the dolls won't be thrown out when I'm gone!"

"I will, if *you* will try to eat a little breakfast." Mary-Esther busied herself at the stove.

The old woman's head bobbed up and down. A calm expression spread across her face. "I know you will take good care of my babies."

"Yes, Rose. I'll take care of your babies." Shortly, Mary-Esther scraped the cooked eggs onto a plate and added a piece of buttered toast. "Now you must hold up your end of the bargain."

A couple of days later, Mary-Esther stood on the Herring's back step, barely in range for the cordless phone. She dialed the number scribbled on a scrap of paper.

"Elvina? Mary-Esther." She cupped her hand over the mouthpiece and lowered her voice. "You asked me to phone if I saw that Jonathan man again. He's here, and he has that woman with him, I'm guessing his wife. They're in the living room talking to Rose. I can't hear what they're saying, but Rose looks bewildered. They think I'm the maid or something. I'm not sure what I need to do, if anything."

She heard Elvina snort. "Stall them until I get there."

"You can drive?"

"I still have one good foot. All I need. I'm not up to long distances yet, but I've been taking short hops around town. It takes me longer to get in and out with a cast and walker. Do *not* let them leave!"

"What—?"

"Use your God-given brain, child. You'll come up with something."

Dead air signaled Elvina's disconnect. Mary-Esther slipped back into the kitchen and returned the phone to the charger base.

How would she keep them here? Her gaze roamed around the room and rested on a plastic-wrapped sour cream pound cake. She grinned. No Southern hostess would allow drop-in guests to leave without a cup of coffee and a slice of something home-baked. No conniving rat of a relative hell-bent on ripping off a little old lady would reject the hospitality, either.

She loaded a silver tray with cups, sugar and creamer, spoons, a coffee carafe, and three saucers holding generous slabs of cake. When she entered the living room, Jonathan Watson was perched on the couch, his hand cradled over Rose's. His accomplice idled in a nearby chair, a bored-stiff expression waxed on her painted face.

Jonathan reminded Mary-Esther of an evangelistic tent preacher with his puffy, stiff hair and pale blue leisure suit. His female partner provided the perfect complement in a tailored, gray wool skirt and jacket with matching pumps and handbag. What hairspray he spared shellacked her curled bouffant. Her lips, outlined a quarter inch beyond their natural borders, shone deep coral. *Never trust a woman who paints her lips twice their real size,* Nana Boudreau had warned. Judging by the overblown set on this woman, Mary-Esther wouldn't count on a word that oozed from them.

"I thought you and your guests might like a piece of pound cake and some coffee." Mary-Esther used her best servant voice, added in as much drawl as she could muster. "The cake is homemade and fresh. One of the neighbors brought it by earlier this morning."

"Well, now. Isn't that nice?" Jonathan said, releasing Rose's hand to accept a plate.

The woman appeared animated for the first time since they had arrived. She dug into the cake as if it was Fat Tuesday and she was giving up sweets for Lent.

"Rose, honey," Jonathan said between bites, "we really must resolve this issue. The sooner, the better." His vermin eyes glanced to where Mary-Esther stood. *Dismissed,* his manner said, *you are dismissed!*

Mary-Esther swallowed a curt remark and stepped back into the kitchen.

In a few minutes, the doorbell rang.

"I'll get it!" Mary-Esther called as she scuttled to the door.

Elvina Houston waited on the front porch, a paper bag in one hand. "Good morning," she said with a quick wink. "I'm Elvina Houston. Is Rose up for visitors this afternoon?"

"Oh, *yes.*" Thanks to every saint! Back up had arrived.

Elvina stepped inside, careful to position the walker.

"May I take your wrap?" Mary-Esther maintained the maid ruse.

Elvina handed her coat over with a knowing look.

"Oh, my. Had I known you had company, I would not have dropped by unannounced." Elvina toddled the walker across the room and paused in front of the seated threesome.

Relief washed across Rose's features. "Oh, it's no trouble at all. These are cousins of Eustis's—Jonathan and Sue Ellen Watson from Chipley."

She looked from the couple and back to Elvina. "And this is a dear friend of mine, Elvina Houston."

Jonathan stood and offered his hand. "Pleased. Our Rose has spoken of you often. Sue Ellen and I were just passing through, you see."

Our Rose? Mary-Esther steamed.

Elvina handed the paper bag to Rose. "I brought you some of that green tea I told you about the other day. It's good for the immune system and most everything ailing you. Those Asian people have used it for centuries."

Rose accepted the bag with a slight nod.

"Mind if I sit down?" Elvina chose a seat before anyone could offer an objection. She motioned toward Mary-Esther who hovered by the kitchen entrance. "Young woman, would you kindly bring me a glass of water, no ice?"

Mary-Esther dashed to retrieve the drink. She heard Elvina speak in a loud voice. "So, what brings y'all to Chattahoochee?"

Mary-Esther delivered the water with a slight curtsy. Elvina shot her a warning look. *Okay, a little over the top.* Mary-Esther slipped back into the kitchen and positioned herself so she could see and hear the exchange in the next room.

Jonathan motioned toward his wife. "Sue Ellen has friends a few miles this side of Sneads. We were so close, we figured we'd stop and see if Cousin Rose needed anything while we were nearby."

Needed anything? Mary-Esther clamped her arms across her chest. Like someone to pinch everything Rose owns and cast her to the curb?

"Wasn't that considerate of you?" Elvina's lips drew into a strained smile. "It's so lovely to have family who care about one's well-being. Don't you think? We *do* worry *so* about Rose. What's to become of her?"

Jonathan snatched the bait. "Sue Ellen and I were talking with Our Dear Rose about that, Miz Elvina. Eustis put me in charge of everything, so I'm trying my best to guide Miz Rose though this difficult time."

"Put you in charge, you say?" Elvina said.

His chest puffed up. "I'm the trustee of the estate for Mr. and Mrs. Herring. It is an awesome responsibility I don't take lightly. Not at all."

"You speak like a man who knows business, Mr. Watson. Are you?" Elvina leaned forward, clearly savoring the game. Mary-Esther covered her mouth to avoid snickering. One thing she'd say about Elvina Houston, the woman was *good.*

Sue Ellen chimed in, "Jonathan is the executive sales director of the Chipley Tractor and Heavy Equipment Company."

"Oh my." Elvina rested a hand over her heart. "You must be so very proud."

He glanced down, a pious expression on his face. "I've done nicely. Even if I do say so, myself."

Mary-Esther wanted to make a gagging noise. She held back.

Elvina took a sip of water. "What are you recommending to Our Dear Rose, if you don't mind me asking? It is *so* good to hear a real businessman's opinion on things."

Rose watched the exchange without comment. Mary-Esther stuffed the urge to run into the room and throttle the pompous idiot and his poodle-haired wife. So often, people treated the elderly this way, talking about them as if they weren't in the room. Really!

Jonathan Watson leaned toward Elvina. "You might be able to help us out here, Miz Elvina—you being such a good, caring friend of hers and all." His voice assumed a conspiratorial tone. "Sue Ellen and I are willing to dedicate our time to help Our Rose sell this drafty old house and relocate to a proper facility. Her failing health is such a concern, and we simply can't bear to have her living here all alone." His beady eyes flitted around the room. "Anything could happen."

"A nursing home? You're talking about a nursing home?" Elvina shifted her gaze to Rose. "Is that what you want, dear?"

Mary-Esther wanted to hug Elvina Houston.

Rose studied her clasped hands resting on her lap. "I'd rather stay in our home."

Silence cloaked the room. Mary-Esther peeked farther around the corner for a better view. The grand finale had to be close.

Elvina reminded Mary-Esther of an alley cat toying with a mouse. The creature might escape a few times as the tomcat released and pounced again. Finally, when the mouse tired, the bored feline would cease the game with a swift bite. Mary-Esther had watched certain Southern women do the same, the end kill cushioned with soft words and a coy smile.

"As I understand the law, Mr. Watson—and believe me, I *do* understand the law—" Elvina's expression hardened. "A trust is a legal instrument that only comes into play when the said parties are deceased. When Eustis passed, according to Florida law, his entire estate rolled to his wife. Rose is still very much alive."

Elvina's eyes glittered. "Rose is taken care of. *Well* taken care of. The lady who rents from her lives a few steps away in the garage apartment. We *all* watch out for Rose. Someone comes by to take her to church if and when she's able. Someone brings her food. We take turns riding her uptown to shop. Rose is not an invalid as you implied. She is sound of mind and perfectly capable of making her own decisions. I don't know if you do things the same way over there in Chipley—" Elvina pronounced the town's name with a sneer "—but this is *our* way in Chattahoochee."

Sue Ellen's skin paled behind the shellac of make-up, and Jonathan teetered on the edge of the couch. Mary-Esther clapped her hands together without sound.

Elvina's next words came out slowly, one at a time, heavy with intent. "I have many friends in law enforcement, and more than a handful are judges. Elder endangerment is a subject none of them take lightly. If I am out of line in assuming you don't have Rose's best interests at heart, I *do* apologize." Elvina offered a saccharine smile.

Sue Ellen stood and stuffed her purse beneath one arm. "Let's go, Jonathan."

He frowned. "But—"

Sue Ellen spat out the last word through bared teeth. "Now."

Mary-Esther scurried toward the door to show the couple out, but they departed without her aid.

The door slammed shut. Elvina chuckled. "Good riddance to bad rubbish."

Rose dabbed tears from her eyes with a linen handkerchief. "Thank you, Elvina. I don't know what I would've done if you hadn't stopped by. Some of the things they said sounded reasonable. Maybe I should consider—"

"Psshaw!" Elvina dismissed the notion with a sweep of one thin hand. "If the time comes for you to relocate, and it could, it will be *your* decision to make and not someone else's, hear?"

Rose reached over and held Elvina's hand. "You must be my guardian angel."

"Shoot. I only came by to bring you some tea." She shot a quick wink Mary-Esther's way. "And I could surely use a piece of that cake."

Chapter Twenty-five

Hattie pulled the SUV into a leaf-strewn clearing and allowed her passenger to take in the view.

"This is about the prettiest place I have ever been," Mary-Esther said.

"Daddy built the dam at a spot where three springs converged. Even in the worst drought, this pond stays at a consistent level."

Hattie loved the small valley. Tall hardwoods circled the pond, their autumn leaves reflected in the rippling surface. At the crest of one hill, a wooden, screened gazebo stood with a series of stairs and decks descending the slope to the water's edge. Parallel to the steps, a waterfall cascaded over river boulders. Clearly manmade, but beautiful. And the sound! She rolled down her window to hear the water sluicing through the rocks.

"C'mon. Let's go sit for a bit." They got out. Hattie led the way to the gazebo and motioned Mary-Esther toward a row of rocking chairs. "I come down here when I need to find a little peace. Daddy loved this pond. Mama too. But especially Daddy."

"Nice."

Hattie pointed to a rusty lean-to shelter on the opposite side of the pond. "Daddy built that. Looks awful, but neither Bobby nor I had the heart to tear it down. Used to be, you had to descend a steep set of dirt steps to get to the water. They washed out every time we had a hard rain, as did the road on that side of the embankment; one reason we chose this side for the gazebo. Back then, you were doing good to go half-way down the hill in a four-wheel drive truck without getting stuck up to the axles in clay."

"Are there fish in there?" Mary-Esther asked.

"Catfish. Big ones. Fun to catch too."

Mary-Esther's nose crinkled. "I didn't much like catfish back home. They tasted kind of . . . muddy."

"A lot of wild catfish do. They're scavengers. Not the same with the channel cats in here. They don't have to eat junk off the bottom. We feed them commercial floating food. The meat is white and clean, similar to grouper." Hattie's expression softened. "Mama and Daddy loved to entertain. Nothing fancy. He would catch up a big mess of catfish, and we'd invite folks out. He had this frying contraption he made himself. He'd dip strips of catfish fillets in beer batter and deep fry them. Man, were they ever good. Not greasy at all.

"Mama cooked the French fries inside while he handled the fish outside. That way, it all came out hot at the same time and the house didn't smell too stinky. As soon as he finished the fish and put the doughboys on to cook, he would signal her to start the fries. They did it for so many years, they had the timing perfect." Hattie snapped her fingers.

Mary-Esther's crossed arms released their grip across her chest and her face relaxed.

"We'll have to do that, soon," Hattie said. "Bring Miz Rose if she's feeling well enough."

"She'd like that."

"How is she?" Hattie asked.

"Better, since those awful relatives left her alone."

"Ah, yes." Hattie nodded. "I heard." They rocked for a moment before she added, "You could invite a *friend*, if you'd like."

"I don't know how your brother would feel about that."

"Bobby will get over himself, eventually." Hattie swiveled to face Mary-Esther. "It takes him a while to warm up to new people. Used to think being in law enforcement all those years made him that way. He had to be suspicious of everyone, to a point." She turned back to face the pond. The rockers creaked.

"Lately, I've come to accept; that's just Bobby. He and I didn't get along too famously for years. Things are much better since he stopped crawling into a bottle to find his comfort."

"I'm well aware of how alcohol affects people," Mary-Esther said. "My mother drank on and off for years. I was raised, for the most part, by Nana Boudreau."

"I never will understand the hold it has on some people. I mean, I have a beer from time to time, or a glass of merlot. Not that I've never overindulged. In college, I pitched my share of keg party drunks. The older I got, the less I wanted it." Hattie stopped and took a deep breath. "On the other hand, you rarely saw Bobby without a drink in his hand. When his first wife bailed, he sank into it deeper and deeper."

"Seems your brother expects me to show up one day with a herd of attorneys in tow, ready to snatch land and money." Mary-Esther stopped rocking and looked at Hattie. "That isn't my intention. You must believe me."

"I do. Bobby will come around."

"I can see where you both might consider me a big threat *if* I prove to be the missing sister." Mary-Esther took a deep breath then exhaled. "I don't have the energy or the desire to threaten anyone."

A great white egret sailed overhead and landed with a graceful swoop at the water's edge. They watched in easy silence as it stepped with spindly legs through the muck, eyed its prey, and jabbed into the shallow water. The sun glinted from the wiggling minnow dangling at the tip of the sharp beak before the bird flipped back its head and swallowed with one swift movement.

"It's like watching Wild Kingdom," Mary-Esther said. "I used to love that show."

"Me too. With what's his name?" Hattie tapped her temple.

"Marlon Perkins," they said in unison after a couple of seconds.

Mary-Esther tipped her head back and laughed. "I can remember that, yet I have a tough time recalling what I had for breakfast. So many of the kids nowadays have no clue who he was. More and more, I realize I'm the old fart now."

Hattie asked after a few minutes, "What was she like, your . . . mom?"

"I know." Mary-Esther thrummed her fingers on the rocker arm. "I can't really decide what to call Loretta either."

"She's still your mother. She did raise you, after all."

"Like I said, that credit goes to Nana. After Loretta's husband left—the man I used to think of as my father—my mother fell apart. She started staying out all hours, partying. I don't think she was ready to have the responsibility of a kid. You see, one way Tillie Davis and Loretta Day were fundamentally different: their ages. Loretta was fifteen when she got knocked up. The wedding was a shade shy of being held at the end of Nana's butcher knife."

Mary-Esther drew her legs up and wrapped her arms around her knees. "Nana told me that Loretta and my father met when he was stationed in Pensacola. He was twenty-one. Loretta Boudreau could've passed for the same. He and his Navy buddies spent a wild weekend in the French Quarter. He met Loretta. Fell for her, I suppose, or maybe it was only lust. She met him on several occasions whenever he came back into town. Loretta was a wild child. Even with Nana trying to ride herd over her, she was hell-bent on her own selfish passions.

"It wasn't until she turned up pregnant that he realized how young she really was. I think Nana threatened him because of Loretta's age. How she found out who he was is still a mystery to me. Nana never said, but I suspect it was one of her many *eyes and ears*—the folks she knew in every walk of life down in the Quarter."

Mary-Esther stopped to take in a deep breath and blow it out. "He wasn't ready to be a father any more than Loretta was ready to give up her party life. After a bit, he skipped out. We never heard from him again. His family certainly didn't want anything to do with Loretta and her demon spawn. I wouldn't have a clue as to how to go about finding them either. All these years later, what's the point? I'm not *that* child."

Mary-Esther offered a bemused smile. "How I ended up swaddled next to the baby everybody thought was Sarah Davis is another little twist of cruel fate. He and Loretta came for an ill-timed visit to my father's family when she was pretty far along. Again, not a forward-thinking gal. She went into labor. The rest is history. Except, the baby she ended up dragging back to Pensacola, and eventually home to New Orleans after he ditched us, was not their biological kin." She paused. "And the Davis family went through . . . a horrible loss."

Hattie watched Mary-Esther's movements. Little gestures: the way she twisted the corner of her mouth to one side when she pondered, her musical laugh, the softness around her eyes. So many things echoed Tillie Davis. Hattie didn't need confirmation of blood ties. She *knew*.

"Loretta didn't move back in with Nana at first," Mary-Esther said. "She had a way of locating men to shack up with. I probably lived all over New Orleans and most of the surrounding parishes by the time I was a toddler. One day, Nana showed up where we were staying and took me home with her. I lived with Nana off and on after that. Loretta would sober up, vowing to have changed, and Nana would allow me to go back with her. It wasn't that Nana didn't want me. She never made me feel unloved. She believed the best place for a child was with her mother. Nana had an unwavering love for Loretta and held faith she could make something of herself."

Mary-Esther paused, staring at the pond. "Loretta and I would move in with whatever flim-flam man she was seeing at the time. Things would bump along okay for a bit. I remember this one fellow, Charlie, who was kind of nice. I used to see him from time to time, even years later, but he died a few years ago.

"Nana always came for me when I finally had enough—can't even tell you how many times—and I'd go live in her little wooden house. I was happiest when I was with Nana."

Mary-Esther's gaze grew distant. Hattie pulled up what little she knew of New Orleans, tried to gather the feel of the place Mary-Esther had called home. Hattie had visited once during her junior year of college. The only lingering impression wrapped around sugary beignets with chicory coffee and French Quarter streets awash with drunken Mardi Gras revelers. And the smell of stale urine.

"Nana had this way of making me feel as if I was the smartest and prettiest little girl on earth. I used to make up songs and sing for her," Mary-Esther continued. "I'm tone deaf as a bull gator. To hear Nana tell it, I was bound for Broadway."

Hattie smiled. "You must've gotten closer to your mother toward the end. I remember you said you were living together before . . ."

Mary-Esther's eyes watered. "When I moved back home to help take care of Nana during those final days, I had pretty much scraped the bottom myself. My last marriage, if you would even qualify it as such, had hit the skids and I had no other place to go. Nana needed me. Then Mama showed up, destitute as usual, and Nana took her in. Again. I was furious at first. Now I had two women to watch over! Somehow Loretta pulled herself together and we took care of Nana as best we could.

"Strange, how good comes from bad. Nana said it often worked out that way." Mary-Esther's voice faltered. She cleared her throat. "Loretta and I got to the point we could stay in the same room without sniping and spitting fire. I don't know if Loretta grew up, finally, or if I did. Suspect it was a bit of both. The last year of her life, we became more tolerant of each other."

Hattie closed her eyes. The slow rhythm of the rocker eased the tension from her neck. For the first time in weeks, her troublesome shoulder did not throb in time with her heartbeat. One thing Holston had taught her, you learn more when you shut up and listen.

Mary-Esther rocked back and forth, matching Hattie's pace.

"Loretta got sick, and we were swept up in this nightmare of hospitals, doctors, and no money. It wasn't until the very end, after I was ready to give her a kidney to help her live, that I suspected she wasn't my biological mother."

"Did she know?"

"No. I ordered the DNA test after she died." Mary-Esther stopped rocking. "Even if I had known earlier, I would not have told her. No way."

Mary-Esther turned to Hattie. Tears glistened in her eyes. "Losing Nana. Losing Loretta. Losing my home. It's shown me something I didn't know before. I had a life in New Orleans. I had a family. Regardless of how screwed-up, it all *belonged* to me. I didn't come here to try to steal the past from you. I only wanted to find out who I am, or I should say, who I *might* have been."

"We should know for sure in a few days."

"What then, Hattie? What if I'm just some woman, not your sister? All this you've been doing—the picture albums, the stories, the walks in these beautiful woods—what if you've been wasting your time? And even if I turn out to be blood-related, I can't possibly be who you want me to be, can I?"

Hattie rocked, the creak of the wooden deck joints keeping time as the chair moved. "If you *are* my sister, I'll be the most thrilled woman alive." She stopped abruptly and faced Mary-Esther. "If not, I haven't wasted time if you turn out to like me enough to remain my friend."

Mary-Esther slept in fitful snippets, vacillating between cold enough to wrap in the comforter and hot enough to strip to the sheet. Boudreau tolerated the nocturnal calisthenics for a while but finally relocated to the terrycloth robe Mary-Esther had cast onto the floor.

Tonight, the dream starts in the usual fashion; Mary-Esther stands at the bottom of the front steps, looking up to Nana's time-faded red door. She ascends and lets herself into the unlocked house. The blended scents of Cajun spices and warm sugar pour over her. She continues down the hallway, much longer in the dream than it had been in reality.

Mary-Esther notices the hem of Nana Boudreau's long skirt floating inches from the worn tile floor. Nana hums. She chops okra, peppers, and onions. Every part of her grandmother sways: hands flying, rear swishing, toes tapping, bosoms bouncing. Mary-Esther calls out. Nana doesn't appear to hear at first then turns to where her granddaughter waits at the kitchen threshold. Nana's hand summons Mary-Esther in and she moves closer to linger in Nana's shadow, drinking in the essence of her grandmother.

Nana leans down. The cleavage between her pendulous breasts reminds Mary-Esther of the deep curb crevices that gush with water during a Louisiana summer rain. Nana Boudreau lifts a delicate gold chain circling her padded neck. The amulet, a small, gold cross with a single diamond at the center, dangles on its tether.

Nana's eyes grow large and round. She swings the cross in the air toward Mary-Esther. Back and forth. Back and forth.

What Nana, what? I don't understand.

The house, the kitchen, and Nana disappear. Only the image of the diamond-studded cross remains.

Mary-Esther jerked awake, her heart fluttering.

Please, Please, Nana. Don't leave me. You're all I have.

Boudreau meowed close-by. He jumped onto the bed and curled up in his customary position next to her heart.

Mary-Esther slipped into a dreamless sleep.

Chapter Twenty-six

Mary-Esther heard a crash, a thud. She threw aside the kitchen broom and rushed toward the back of Rose's house. A fall often proved an elderly person's worst nemesis, often initiating a deadly cascade of events. In a small bedroom, Rose's *doll house*, she found the old woman perched on a low stool amidst a toppled mound of dolls and cardboard boxes.

"Rose? What . . . ?"

Rose glanced up. She held a porcelain replica of *Gone with the Wind*'s Scarlet O'Hara. "You're quite pale, Mary-Esther dear."

"Because you scared the beejezus out of me. I thought you might have taken a spill."

Mary-Esther scanned the room. The shelves where the prized doll collection once stood were bare. Dust motes danced in the air. "I thought you were taking a nap. What are you doing?"

The old woman smoothed the doll's green velvet skirt. "Sorting and packing."

A flush of anger stung Mary-Esther's skin. Had the no-account relatives been back while she was at work and convinced the old woman to relocate? "Are you moving out?"

One of Rose's white eyebrows shot up. "Oh no. *I'm* not moving, but my baby dolls are."

Mary-Esther lowered down to sit cross-legged next to the old woman. "I don't follow you."

"I'm packing up my babies. You promised to take good care of them." Her red-rimmed eyes watered. "You promised!"

"And I will, Rose. But don't you want to have them displayed so you can see them?"

"You must take them out of this house immediately. The only one I will keep here is the rag doll on my bed. Little Lucy has been with me since I was a child. Don't believe I could get a decent night's sleep without my Lucy. The rest you must take away from here. I'll not have that Watson woman defile them with her stingy, piggy little hands. Do you hear?"

"I don't think they'll annoy you anymore. Elvina pretty much sent them running. They haven't been here, have they?"

"No. I don't believe so."

Mary-Esther relaxed. The vultures weren't circling. Just Rose's fear.

"If you don't help me get these dolls stored in a safe place, I'll have to find someone who will." Rose pursed her lips.

Mary-Esther held up both hands. "All right, Rose. I'll go to the Dollar Store and buy some plastic stacking bins to seal out moisture. As damp as it can get sometimes in my apartment, I would hate if they mildewed."

"Go then. Hurry. Pick up some tissue paper too. We'll tuck them in, snug as bugs in a rug."

She left Rose smiling, singing little ditties as she hugged one doll after the other. One thing Mary-Esther had learned about dealing with seniors was that she had to choose her battles. As long as Rose's desires didn't harm her health or put her in immediate danger, Mary-Esther would play along.

"I sure hope I'm lucky enough to find someone to put up with my crazy stuff when I get to be her age," Mary-Esther said to no one. She cranked the van.

"That's a weight off my mind." Rose looked around the empty shelves, her hands propped on her thin hips.

The dolls had been counted, swaddled in protective tissue paper and plastic bubble-wrap, and layered in labeled bins with lists of each doll's name and origin. *Where can I store them?* Mary-Esther visualized her cramped apartment. Maybe she could stack them two high, throw tablecloths over the tops, and use them as bedside tables.

Rose regarded Mary-Esther. "Have you seen your young man recently?"

"Jerry? Um . . . yes. He stops by Bill's for coffee every evening when he's on patrol."

"You've taken a shine to him, haven't you?"

Mary-Esther smiled. "Jerry's a good man. He kind of grows on you."

"Best watch out." Rose shook her finger. "That's the way I feel about my Eustis. Cupid will be shooting an arrow into your heart."

Troubling. The last couple of days, Rose refused to refer to Eustis in the past tense. Dementia or self-preservation? Did it really matter?

"I don't know, Rose. I haven't had such a lucky run with men."

"You mustn't give up, dear. If you chase after love, it will hide from you. But if you let it settle down next to you real easy-like, it will stay and be yours forever."

Mary-Esther fought the urge to roll her eyes like a petulant teenager. "I'd like to believe that."

Rose turned her head toward the window. "Is that rain I hear?"

"Sounds like it. It's supposed to shower then turn cold. The weather surely varies. One day it's fifty and the next, eighty."

"Never boring, this time of year. Not like summer, when it's so hot and humid you could melt your shoe soles on the sidewalks. The heat wears me out, anymore. Used to be, it didn't much bother me. Suppose that comes with age, not doing well with extremes."

"I prefer fall and winter, myself."

"Let's go onto the porch and listen to the rain." Rose's voice changed pitch, like a child's.

They sat side-by-side on the front porch swing, gently swaying forward and back. The rusty chains sang out. The old woman shivered and wrapped her arms around her chest.

"We should go inside, Rose. The temperature is beginning to drop."

Rose's lips turned down. "Then we wouldn't be able to watch the rain."

Mary-Esther stood and walked inside, returning with a soft pink wrap. She draped the coverlet across the old woman's shoulders. How frail Rose felt, as if her bones were turning to spun sugar.

"I thank you." Rose smiled. The old woman's gaze returned to the steady, soft drizzle misting the fall foliage. "This year, I do believe the trees are as pretty as I have ever seen them."

Mary-Esther agreed. "I was out at the Davis land a couple of days ago, and the woods were breathtaking. I never realized this part of the South had such great colors in the fall."

"We have all the trees they do farther north in the Smoky Mountains, for the most part. It takes a year with the perfect combination of cool nights and a little bit of rain, though not too much, to help us have a fall such as the one this year. Some years, the leaves turn brown and fall off."

"Guess I never paid it much attention, living in the city." Mary-Esther reached over and repositioned the wrap that had slipped from the old woman's shoulders.

154

"City's good for a lot of things," Rose stated. "I've been to two or three in my time. Eustis is more the traveler. That's where all those dolls came from. He buys one for me wherever he goes. Doesn't have to be a special occasion like a birthday or anniversary. He brings them because he wants to please me. The best gifts are that way, given 'just because.'"

The old woman turned to face Mary-Esther. "I want you to know, I have grown quite fond of you, dear. You've been so good to me, especially with Eustis away. He told me, if we could've had a daughter, she would've been like you."

Mary-Esther's throat constricted.

"But you see, I *do* think of you as my daughter." Rose took Mary-Esther's hand. A faint, gentle current of warmth passed between them. "And so does my Eustis."

Rose looked back toward the twin, yellow-flocked hickory trees flanking the street. "I do believe, when I take my leave, I'm going to fly right to heaven through those two golden trees."

Mary-Esther stood on the paved landing at the Apalachicola River and received instructions from Jerry.

"It's easy, Mary-E. All I want you to do is hold onto the bow rope and walk alongside as I back up. When I'm far enough in, the boat will elevate off the trailer. Then, I will pull away. Your job is to hang onto the rope. Once I'm clear, you can start to pull her in a little at a time." He pointed to a spot downriver. "Best to drag her clear of the cement landing so the bottom doesn't get scratched up, and you're out of the way. That place has soft sand; you can beach her so you don't have to hang on so hard. The current along the bank isn't strong."

Mary-Esther saluted. "Got it."

After Jerry parked the truck and trailer, he loped down the bank, helped Mary-Esther to board, pushed the boat away from shore, and jumped on. For the next few minutes, Mary-Esther watched as he used the power-tilt to lower the outboard motor, cranked it, did a quick check of the dials and radio, and aimed the bow downriver.

"Impressive."

Jerry smiled. "What?"

"You and this marine thing. I took you more for the hunter/land type."

"I grew up on the waterways around here. Nearly every weekend and sometimes during the week after school, my buddies and I either came over here or to the Ochlocknee River. I've never been one for saltwater fishing, but I could live on a river."

Mary-Esther admired the cabin cruiser. Not as fancy as some of the boats she had watched coming and going from the Port of New Orleans, but sturdy and adequate. "I noticed the name on her side, *Junkyard Dog*. Suppose there's a story behind that too."

"There's a story behind everything in this part of the South. If not, we invent one." He flashed a grin. "Found the hull in a junk yard. Paid next to nothing for it. Loaded it onto a flatbed trailer and dragged it home to Mama's. I worked on it, off and on, for a couple of years as I had time and money. The most expensive thing on her is the motor. Had to save up for that." As he talked, he flipped switches and checked some kind of digital monitor. "Her name pays homage to her origins. A junk-yard dog may be mutt-ugly, but it's mean and tenacious, and will protect its territory until death."

Willows and an occasional stand of color-popping hardwoods dotted the banks of the wide river.

"Hard to believe we're out here, and it's November," Mary-Esther remarked.

"I've taken the boat out in January. You never can tell when a patch of fair weather will hit. The beauty of being here during the week is we practically have it to ourselves." He glanced away from the river and gave her a nod. "I'm glad you could come along."

"Me too. Bill was happy to let me off. I've worked a lot of extra hours, paying off the van repairs. Besides, it's easier on them when it's a weekday."

"How's Miz Rose doing?"

"She's perked up these last few days. She's still very sad. No way can a person lose someone they've been married to for so many years and bounce back. If that is even possible." Mary-Esther paused. "Though, she often refers to Eustis as if he's still here, maybe away on one of his trips. She slips back and forth between realties." She spotted an alligator sunning on a bank. Even the critters were enjoying the unseasonable weather. "Elvina Houston stopped by and picked up Rose for an outing a few days ago. She's had other friends visit too. I try to be available when I'm not at work."

Jerry pulled his cap snug and clipped a narrow elastic tether to his collar. "Let's open her up a bit. I need to run the motor a little faster for a while. I've not had her out in a couple of months. Hang on." Jerry throttled up. The engine labored for a few minutes. Jerry adjusted the tilt of the motor, and the boat leveled off and skimmed easily down the wide brown river.

"Used to be a lot of barges on the Apalachicola." Jerry raised his voice to overcome the sound of the motor and wind. "At one time, there were paddlewheel steamboats too."

"We going to fish today?"

Jerry shook his head. "Fish won't bite much when the wind's from the east like it is today. Figured we could joyride. I want to show you one of the prettiest sights around these parts."

The river remained broad with long, slow curves. At several points, Mary-Esther noted series of granite jetties.

"Corps of Engineers has kept the river dredged for barge traffic." Jerry slowed the engine and motioned toward the jetties. "And the river's course has been altered. Unfortunately, that's affected the natural balance of things over the years. An environmental group's working to get legislation passed to stop the dredging so the river can return more to its natural course."

Jerry pointed to a wide sandbar. "When they dredge, the bottom sand is thrown to the side. At one time, you could walk along and find Native American pot shards and the occasional arrowhead. I still have a box of them somewhere at my mama's. A lot of people use these sandbars to hang out and ski, and picnic. When I was a teenager, my buddies and I used to camp out overnight."

"Sounds like fun, but weren't you scared?"

Jerry chuckled. "Only of an occasional skunk or thieving raccoon. Or of being toted off by the bloodthirsty mosquitoes. Those were simpler times. We didn't worry about the two-legged animals that preyed on kids, or deadbeats running drugs."

The hum of the outboard and warmth of the sun filtering in the cabin windows lulled Mary-Esther. She closed her eyes and inhaled deeply of the river's scent, a blend of fishiness and wet earth. "I've missed this."

"You used to boat in New Orleans?"

"You kidding?" Mary-Esther gave an incredulous harrumph. "We were lucky to own a car that ran, much less a boat. No, I miss the smell of water. This is a little different than the salt marsh, but still . . ."

"I love it too. Almost as much as the smell of the deep woods." He pushed the throttle, and they rode in silence. In a few minutes, they were miles downriver, and Jerry pointed ahead. "When we make the next bend, you'll see something spectacular."

As if some giant hand had pushed the land into a ridge, the riverbanks went from low to over two hundred feet on either side.

"Wow!"

Jerry throttled back and they idled along. "If you look up to that crest, you can make out a wooden fence on the overlook. There's a piece of Nature Conservancy property with a great hiking trail that comes out right over the bluffs."

Mary-Esther craned her neck to see the top of the cliffs. "What is this place?"

"The Apalachicola River Bluffs. We call it the Garden of Eden. You might not know this, but this area is part of the foothills of the Appalachian Mountains."

Jerry steered the boat to within inches of the bank and pointed to a small stream of clear water pouring into the muddy river. "That's a natural spring. Sweetest water you'll ever taste." He cut the engine and walked to the bow. After jumping onto a small spit of dirt, he held the bow rope and motioned for her to follow.

He secured the line to a root, took her hand, and led her to the source of the water, a small trickle flowing from inside the limestone rock.

"Is it safe to drink?" she asked.

"I read somewhere that there's no spring water on Earth pure enough to drink. That all of it has been tainted. I've swilled this water for years, and I've never gotten ill."

He cupped his hands, allowed the small stream to fill them, and drank. Mary-Esther followed.

"Got to die of something," she said. Water dribbled from her chin.

Jerry stepped forward and took her wet face in his hands. The kiss was soft and gentle at first, before morphing into something deeper. When he pulled away, Mary-Esther wobbled.

"About time, Officer Blount." She initiated the contact this time, and he offered no resistance.

After she changed from her river-dampened jeans, Mary-Esther scurried down the stairs and dashed to Rose's house like a young girl after her first date, brimming with giddy excitement.

She and Loretta had never enjoyed the kind of relationship that encouraged sharing heartfelt secrets. Nana Boudreau had been the first person Mary-Esther raced to when she was a grappling preteen. In the short time she had known her, Rose Herring filled a space long vacant.

"Rose, guess what!" Mary-Esther called out as she closed the back door. "He finally kissed me! Can you believe it?"

She dashed into the dimly lit living room. The television blared. Mary-Esther grabbed the remote and lowered the volume. "There. No need to have to yell. I had the most amazing time. We had a picnic on this wide sandbar and talked about everything."

Rose's silence caused her to pause. "How can you sleep through me telling you about the most flipping wonderful day I've had in forever?"

She peered through the blue flicker from the television, then reached down and turned on the reading lamp next to the recliner. The old woman's head slumped forward.

Rose's chest was still.

Mary-Esther probed the side of Rose's neck for a pulse. The papery skin felt cool to the touch. She knelt in front of the chair. Tears fogged her vision. She gently smoothed a lock of white hair away from the old woman's face. "Oh, Rose . . ."

When she could trust her voice enough to speak, Mary-Esther picked up the phone and dialed.

Chapter Twenty-seven

The next few days blurred together.

Joseph Burns immediately stepped in and followed Rose's detailed prearrangements. To Mary-Esther, the visitation played like a surreal re-run of Eustis's final time. Except for the tattered rag doll in the coffin. Rose had made that clear. Little Lucy had to be with her. Flanked with wire stands of fresh flowers, the coffin rested in the same corner of the Herring's small living room.

Friends came and went, bearing gifts of food. Once again, the kitchen filled with casseroles, cakes, pies, platters of fried chicken, ham, and cooked vegetables. Who could possibly eat all of that food? The only person who didn't come was Elvina Houston. From all reports, Elvina was bedridden with a horrible case of laryngitis, one of the few times anyone could recall her being unable to speak.

Strangely, people treated Mary-Esther as the long-lost and honored daughter of Eustis and Rose Herring. In the days following the simple arrangements, she heard story after story of the lives of her deceased landlords. The snippets only added to her grief.

Mary-Esther cried.

She wept for everything and everyone she had ever lost, as if the collective sadness had broken from a secret, wax-sealed spot. Each night, when she finally rested her head on her pillow, tears flowed. Great, shaking sobs. Several times, she cried so hard she rushed to the bathroom and lost whatever small amount of food she had managed to eat.

Every night, Mary-Esther dreamed of Nana. Different variations, same theme.

Tonight, she appears in front of the wooden house in New Orleans, anticipating the joyful reunion. Once inside, she walks directly to the kitchen.

Nana stands in front of the stove. Mary-Esther rushes in, anxious for one of her grandmother's smothering hugs, but Nana motions for her to sit. Mary-Esther opens her mouth to speak, to tell Nana about her new life, about losing Rose, about Jerry. Nana holds one finger to her lips. Then she points to the cross on its chain.

Nana, I don't understand.

The dream faded and Mary-Esther awoke. The ghost aroma of gumbo lingered in the air of her darkened apartment. She tossed the covers aside and got up. Boudreau complained.

Peaceful sleep never came after the dream.

A moving van pulled into the back yard one evening, six days after the funeral. Mary-Esther heard the low rumble of its engine and peered from Rose's kitchen window. She had wrapped and frozen most of the food—what she hadn't given away. The floors shone, and all of the soiled clothing and linens were washed and stored.

She met the Watsons at the back door.

"We certainly didn't expect to find *you* here," Sue Ellen Watson said in a frosty tone.

"I was cleaning up." Mary-Esther stood aside. The Watsons pushed through the door, followed by two muscular, young white men.

"That's nice," Sue Ellen said, offering a saccharine smile. "But your services are no longer required."

Jonathan Watson motioned the workers toward the back of the house. "Start in the bedrooms and work forward. Sue Ellen and I will pack up the dishes later. I'll be back shortly to show you what to leave in place. A house shows better with a few pieces of furniture."

"You're taking Rose's stuff?"

"My dear," Sue Ellen answered, "We are the legal heirs of this house and all of Cousin Eustis and Rose's belongings." She looked around, her lip curled as if she stood in a rat-infested trash heap. "We need to get this place sold as soon as possible."

"I suppose that means you want me out of the apartment too?"

Sue Ellen's smile appeared so phony. Mary-Esther wished she could slap it from those collagen-puffed lips. "You must understand our position. We simply don't have the luxury of time. I'm afraid you'll have to find other accommodations."

Mary-Esther propped her hands on her hips. "Just like that?"

"Well . . . ," Sue Ellen drawled the word out to three times its length, "it *is* our understanding you lived in a van before you imposed on the kindness of our dear Eustis and Rose."

"Imposed? I paid rent! I have a contract!" She didn't, but this bubble-haired witch didn't need to know.

"You *had* a contract, with Eustis and Rose," Jonathan interjected. "We are the rightful owners now."

Sue Ellen's expression reminded Mary-Esther of a plaster Mardi Gras mask: huge, with plump curlicue lips, and just as false.

"Nothing personal, dear. We have business to conduct. A couple of days should be adequate time for you." Sue Ellen looked toward her husband. "I'm going to see about renting a hotel room in this God-forsaken town. I simply can*not* start on this dreadful chore until tomorrow."

"Yes, my love. I'll give the movers instructions. Call me on the cell, and I'll have them drop me off at the hotel of your liking."

Sue Ellen heaved a sigh so prolonged, Mary-Esther figured she had superhuman lungs. "Must I take care of everything?" She turned for the door. "Don't you dare let them touch any of those dolls, Jonathan. I want to pack them myself. Some of them are antiques."

With barely a nod in Mary-Esther's direction, Sue Ellen spun on her designer heels and walked away, a cloud of sinus-clogging perfume in her wake.

Mary-Esther's mind raced. *Rose's dolls!* "Suppose I'd best start packing, myself." She shucked the soiled apron and folded it on the counter. "It won't take me long. I don't have much."

Jonathan Watson's face shifted to a veneer of condescending compassion. "I regret the short notice. Really, I do. It can't be helped."

If only she could vomit on demand, have it land on his shiny loafers.

As soon as Mary-Esther was out of sight of the back porch light's pool of illumination, she broke into a run. The first things she loaded into the back of the van were four plastic bins containing Rose's doll collection. She added clothing, a few Mule Days' mementos, her rocks, and a carrying cage corralling an aggravated Boudreau.

The urn containing Loretta sat on the front passenger seat. No need to fasten her seatbelt.

Except for a few soft drinks, sandwich meat, and condiments packed in a Styrofoam cooler, she left the food. The leftover shrimp spread would be perfectly ripe in a few days.

"Let that butt-lip witch clean it out." She slammed the refrigerator door. "Heaven help she screws up her thirty-dollar French manicure."

Too much. The entire day had been over the top. First her "brother" stopping by to meet her, officially. What a disaster. Now this. Maybe the whole find your roots thing had been another of her stupid, impulsive mistakes.

Mary-Esther grabbed a stack of unopened mail from the kitchen counter, took one long look back at the small space that had been her haven for a time, and locked the door.

The keys, she shoved under the mat.

Mary-Esther's life moved like a crab—sideways instead of in a straight line. One step in any direction. Two steps in another.

Here you are again, dearie, she told herself. *Sitting in the van in a space barely big enough for yourself and the cat.*

Back in the same camping spot by Lake Seminole, with the sun setting over the water.

As if the past few months had never happened.

The only testaments to change were the cherished dolls entrusted to her care. What would happen when that Watson harpy discovered their absence?

"We'll have to figure out something, won't we?" she said to Boudreau, pulling a soft drink from the cooler. Coffee would be preferable, but she didn't have the energy to crank up the propane camp stove or build a fire. She poured out a handful of kitty kibble and watched Boudreau eat.

Mary-Esther's body ached as if someone had crept in and beaten her to mush. To think she had slept in here for months after the hurricane. The thin padding serving as a mattress did little to cushion her back, and the previous night's Nana dream had been particularly vivid and unsettling. What was up with that cross pendant?

Frigid air crept in from every crack around the doors. Definitely, she would have to find a place to live. Not only for her, but for Boudreau. When she jostled one of the cardboard boxes, an official-looking letter fell from mail she had cast into a pile. Mary-Esther pulled a blanket around her shoulders and opened it.

"It's from the FEMA people," she told Boudreau. He purred and butted his head against her arm. "Says I need to contact them about Nana's house."

"Did you check the mail yesterday?" Hattie rinsed out her coffee mug and loaded it into the dishwasher. "I totally forgot when I came in from the grocery store."

Holston and daughter Sarah shared in their morning ritual of mutual devotion over bowls of oatmeal.

"No, I didn't. Sorry. Suppose I take it for granted that you always do it." He wiped a clot of apple cinnamon oatmeal from Sarah's chin.

"Not like anything earth-shattering comes in, anyway. Mostly bills and junk mail. I'll get Spackle to go with." She delivered drive-by kisses to them. "Back in a few."

Hattie stepped from the front porch and pulled her sweatshirt hood up. "No small wonder people stay sick this time of year. Hot, then cold."

Spackle bounded toward her, sniffed and licked the tips of her fingers, and fell into step. "C'mon. Let's go get the mail. The walk will do us both good. You're beginning to put on a little pudge, boy-dog of mine." He answered with a quick *woof.*

Her shoulder ached, but not as much as it once had. As long as she didn't lug a heavy purse and didn't try to move her arm behind her back, the joint didn't complain.

Halfway down the lane, Hattie noticed a red-tailed hawk perched on the upper limb of a spindly pine. It watched her and Spackle with golden-eyed interest.

"Don't tell me. Not another life-altering message," she said aloud. "Really, can't you go find another clueless human to torment?"

The hawk's wings ruffled once, then it continued to peer as she and the dog passed. Hattie glanced back when they were a few feet farther down the lane. The hawk had disappeared.

"Why can't I have an animal totem that portends a lottery win?"

Spackle sprinted to the mailbox and plopped down next to the post. Finally, the canine had learned not to dash across the highway.

She plucked the stack from inside the box and read the return address on the top envelope. "Jeez-O-Pete! It's the DNA test results!"

Spackle barked in reply. Hattie trotted up the dirt lane to her brother's house, knocked twice, and let herself in. "Bobby! Leigh! Hey, where are y'all?"

Her brother shuffled into the living room, a cup of coffee in hand. Leigh appeared behind him with Tank propped on her hip.

"You're getting too heavy for your mama to tote." Leigh put the toddler down. He dug into a basket of toy trains and trucks.

"What in the world has you so fired up?" Bobby asked. "Hardly ever see you this alive before ten."

Hattie waved the envelope in the air. "I'm pretty sure this is the test results."

Bobby made a circular motion with one hand. "Don't just stand there, open the dadgum thing. We can settle this once and for all."

"I can't." She handed the letter to him. "You do it."

Bobby stared at the envelope in his hand as if it contained a viper. "I don't know—"

Leigh snatched the letter. "Oh for heaven's sake. I'll open it." She peeled back the glued flap and unfolded the paper.

"What?" Hattie jiggled from one foot to the other. "What does it say?"

Leigh looked first at Hattie, then at Bobby. "The DNA proves a positive sibling match with Mary-Esther Sloat. Looks like you two have a sister."

"I knew it!" Hattie whooped and bear-hugged both of them then clasped her hands together. "Wait until Jake and Elvina hear. I have to run tell Holston!" She jerked. "I have to let Mary-Esther know. Jeez, wish she had a phone. Why doesn't she have a stupid phone? I have to find her right now!" She paused, folded the letter and slipped it back into the envelope. "No, maybe not. I should let myself settle for a day. Yeah, that's a plan."

"All of this, and you're not going to jump in the car and head up there?" Leigh asked.

"Jake says I have a way of overwhelming people when I'm emotional. Mary-Esther and I have only begun to know each other. I'll find her when I go into town to the grocery store." Hattie snapped her fingers. "I'll work in the flowerbeds today. That'll keep me from blasting off."

Bobby blew out a breath and ran his fingers through his hair.

Hattie noted the way his temples pulsed. Guess he was pretty excited too. Been a while since she'd seen him clench his teeth like that.

Chapter Twenty-eight

Jake Witherspoon slowed the Dragonfly Florist's delivery truck. He inched past the Herring residence. A large transport truck hunkered in the driveway with its back hatch open. He fumbled for the cell phone and jabbed a speed dial entry.

"Elvina?" he asked.

"What are you up to, this late in the evening?"

"Had to deliver flowers to a memorial service in Sneads. How are you?"

"On the upswing," Elvina said. "Can't talk as much as I'd like yet without coughing, but my fever broke yesterday and my throat no longer feels like it's been scoured with steel wool. Reckon I'm going to live."

"That's good, because I have something to tell you. There's a moving van pulled up beside the Herrings'. Bet you good money those charlatans from Chipley are back. I wonder if Mary-Esther knows about it."

"Where are you now?"

"On the way back to the shop. Why?"

"Come get me. I need you to take me to the Herrings'. I don't have time to explain. Step on it!"

By the time Jake pulled to Elvina's side door, the old woman had made her way down the wooden ramp, a manila envelope clasped in her free hand. Jake shoved the shift lever into park and jumped out to hold the door open for her.

"You sure you should be out? You'll relapse, 'Vina. Tell me what you need and I'll take care of it."

"You can't do this, but you can stand behind me when *I* do." Elvina motioned frantically. "Now put this damn thing in gear and get me to that house!"

When they reached the Herrings', they met a burly man hauling a chest of drawers out the side door.

"Save yourself the trouble of putting that on your truck, buddy. Take it right back to where you got it from," Elvina ordered. "You're not taking anything from this property."

"Not what I've been told, lady." He steadied the loaded dolly.

"I'll take this cane and beat you to within an inch of your life if you defy me."

Jake stared at Elvina, his mouth agape.

The mover set the chest down with a thud. "I don't get paid enough to put up with any crap. Take it up with Mrs. Watson."

Elvina and Jake entered through the back door. Sue Ellen Watson stood at the kitchen counter, swaddling crystal goblets in bubble wrap. Her husband crouched beside a large cardboard box, packing the protected glassware in careful rows.

"Sure didn't take the circling vultures long to land, now did it?" Elvina asked.

Jake hesitated in the doorway behind her, watching the delicious drama unfold.

Jonathan rose. "Now, that's not a very Christian-like way to speak."

"I wouldn't bring the Lord into this," Elvina fired back. "He wouldn't touch this with a ten-foot angel wing."

Sue Ellen stepped forward. "We simply don't have time for whatever it is you seem to be upset about, old woman. Leave. Now."

Elvina's eyes narrowed. "I don't think I will. But *you* will."

"My, my . . . Gloves off," Jake said in a low voice. "No pound cake and niceties *this* time around."

"Oh really? By whose authority?" Sue Ellen spat out the words. "We have every right to be here. My husband and I own this house and everything in it." Sue Ellen spread her arms, then hugged them to her chest.

An evil smile spread across Elvina's lips. "Where is Mary-Esther?"

"That white trash?" Sue Ellen snorted. "We told her to move along. She left out of here like a scalded dog. And I'm certain she took dear Rose's dolls with her. As soon as we finish packing, we plan to stop by the police department and report the theft."

"You threw her *out*?" Elvina asked. "Where did she go?"

"How should I know?" Sue Ellen curled her upper lip. "Good riddance to bad rubbish. Jonathan and I have to clean out that apartment, and she would've been in our way. She probably carted off the furniture too."

Jonathan kept mute, but his porcine eyes watched the action as if it was a prizefight.

Elvina stepped forward. Jake edged behind.

"I'm the one who's going to call the law if you don't leave here immediately." Elvina shook the brown envelope in Sue Ellen and Jonathan's direction. "I do so love to be the bearer of *your* bad news. Rose changed her will and the trust right after your last little visit. You are no longer the trustees. You get nothing. Nada. Big zippy-dee-doo-dah-day, *nothing!*"

Sue Ellen snatched the envelope from Elvina's hand and ripped the seal. Her painted lips moved as she read the enclosed paper. "This can't be." Her gaze shifted from Elvina to her husband. "Jonathan?" Her screechy soprano upped the tension. Jake jiggled his cane, *tap! tap!* on the linoleum.

Jonathan took the document. He read. He looked up. "This has to be some kind of hoax. My cousin Eustis set up that trust."

"As I told you once before," Elvina said, "Rose was her husband's sole heir. It was within her legal rights to write a will and set up a new trust and trustee. Which is exactly what she did. She called me, and I drove her to Tallahassee to a lawyer Hattie recommended."

Sue Ellen stomped one heel. "Jonathan?"

"I want a copy of this." Jonathan shoved the papers back toward Elvina. "I plan to pursue this. Believe you, me."

"I will be happy to have Rose's attorney speak with you," Elvina said with the same sugary sarcasm Jake had heard her use with phone tele-marketers and rude salespeople. "Matter of fact, I picked up an extra one of these." She pulled a business card from her purse and held it out. "Told her you might be calling. Phone her now if you wish. She's a very nice lady."

Sue Ellen snatched the card. "What do you expect us to do? We've already packed all of this!"

"I'll call the police before that van moves even two feet from the driveway if you try to leave with so much as a piece of toilet paper. Have your men put everything back."

Sue Ellen's pencil-thin eyebrows shot up. "That will cost us a fortune."

Elvina crossed her arms in front of her chest. "You'd best get them started, and pull out your checkbook. I'm not leaving here until I'm satis-fied nothing is missing and you hand me the keys you obviously removed from beneath Rose's hidey hole on the porch."

Jake and Elvina stepped outside.

"You can go on to the shop, Jake. I'll be all right here. As soon as they talk to Claire, they'll know they've been kicked to the curb. I can have those men unpack an easy chair so I can prop my foot up while I watch over things."

"And miss this? I'm not going anywhere. This scene will go down in the annals of Chattahoochee history." Jake tapped his phone. "I'll call Jolene. She can take care of things at the shop."

"Suit yourself." Elvina turned to step back inside.

Jake waved both hands. "Wait, 'Vina. You can't keep me in suspense. Who's the heir? You?"

Elvina frowned. "Don't be absurd. Why would Rose Herring leave everything to me? I don't have need of another house, and I'm beyond wanting a pot load of possessions at my age."

"Who then? Tell, tell, tell!"

Elvina grinned and winked. "Mary-Esther. That's who. And we must find that gal, pronto."

Chapter Twenty-nine

Jake pulled the delivery van in front of the farmhouse on The Hill and shut off the engine. He took a moment to sit, watching the cardinals and wrens visit the birdfeeders beside the porch. Could set a watch by those creatures, nine a.m. and six p.m. He knew that fact from when he had lived on The Hill with Hattie, before both of them were happily connected to their respective life partners.

He got out, walked to the front door, and girded the strength and words to tell his best friend that her sister had disappeared from her life, again. He knocked in their code—*shave and a haircut, two bits*—five staccato raps, a pause, two short taps. No real need to knock, since he was family by love. He did it to make her smile.

"C'mon in!" Hattie's voice called from within.

Jake entered. His best friend in the whole wide world, heck the universe, stood by the sink, sipping from a tall mug. And wearing a tiny smile. Bingo. How he hated to take away that smile. He stopped by the playpen and kissed Sarah Chuntian on the cheek.

The nature of friendship baffled Jake Witherspoon. Few of his New York buddies had kept in touch over the years since his move back to the Deep South. Many had shared the deaths of friends and lovers whose bodies suffered the ravages of impaired immune systems. The bonds forged in the fires of intense emotion should've survived distance and time. But they had not.

Only one person remained a constant in Jake's life: Hattie. Since childhood, the two clung together like soul twins, sharing secrets, weaving dreams, and healing wounds. Jake substituted for the sister Hattie never had. Sex and maleness had nothing to do with it. The two friends—one button-down collar straight, and one, feather-boa gay—had so much tangled karma, they could never separate.

"Sister-girl, you really should join some kind of Java-junkie support group. I'm surprised you don't mainline the stuff."

"It's only my second cup, and this one's decaf. Don't act like I'm stealing from my grandmother to support a crack habit." She took a loud slurp. "To what do I owe the pleasure? Oh, don't tell me, someone ordered flowers for me."

"Like I need a reason to visit?" Jake toddled past, rummaged in the refrigerator, and pulled out a diet soda. "I can't pop by and see my best love? Since your shoulder has been on the fritz, I haven't seen your smiling puss at the shop as much as usual."

"I could easily turn into a hermit. Hopefully, if my shoulder continues to improve, I can start back a little bit in a couple of weeks." Hattie regarded him with narrowed eyes. "You're always welcome out here on The Hill. You know that. You don't usually come out this early in the day." She topped off her mug. "Glad you stopped by, whatever the reason. I was going to come find you before Sarah and I went to the grocery store. I have huge news. And it's way too big for telling over the silly phone."

Jake settled onto one of the bar stools next to the kitchen counter. "I'm all ears." His report could wait, and maybe, be cushioned by whatever Hattie had to share.

Hattie rummaged in a basket of opened mail and handed him a torn envelope.

"What? Your letter from the IRS stating you overlooked a huge allowable deduction and they're sending you a check? When can we go shopping?"

She pointed. "Read."

Jake pulled out the folded sheet. He looked up. "It's official then."

"Yes!" Hattie clasped her hands together. "Mary-Esther is my sister. Can you believe it? I'm going to stop by the Homeplace soon as I get to town. Tell her this gurr-reat news."

Jake closed his eyes. The second before spoken truths drew blood seemed worse than the aftermath. "Sister-girl, I have something to tell you. Mary-Esther is gone."

"What do you mean, gone?" Her brows crimped together. "I just saw her. She came out and we had the most wonderful afternoon."

Jake related the scene at the Herrings'.

"They ran her *off*?"

Jake nodded. "Seems that way. She wasn't at her apartment, and it looked like she'd left in a hurry."

Hattie sank onto the barstool next to his. "No, Jakey. That can't be so. She told me she liked it here."

"I rode up to the lake to make sure she wasn't camping like she did when she first came. One guy said he had seen a van pull in, but he heard it crank up before dawn."

"I refuse to believe she would just up and *leave*."

"Do you know her well enough to say for sure, Sister-girl? Or is it wishful thinking?"

Hattie jumped up, riffled in a drawer, and pulled out a thin local phonebook. "I bet she's with that deputy guy from Quincy. Has to be it. Where else would she go?"

Jake considered. "A possibility. Know his name?"

"Jerry Blount. She talked about him. Sounds like it was getting serious, maybe."

"It's a good place to start. If he doesn't know, at least he has the resources to locate her. It's important in more ways than one."

Hattie followed a fine line of print with a finger and punched a set of numbers into the handset.

"Mary-Esther is the sole heir for the Herring estate, Hattie."

Hattie's mouth hung open. "You're kidding me."

"Sister-girl, I'm serious as a drag queen in Army fatigues."

Sergeant Jerry Blount stepped into the Homeplace Restaurant, scanned the room, and walked to a booth where Hattie, Jake, and Elvina waited. The expressions on their faces pumped his heartrate higher.

"I came as soon as I could." Jerry sat down. "Any ideas on where she might have gone?"

Hattie twisted a paper napkin in her hands. "We hoped *you* knew."

"She gave no indication of leaving town last time I saw her." Jerry's thoughts skipped to the instant his lips had touched Mary-Esther's.

"We have the Watsons to thank for this mess," Elvina said. "The gall of those people! Coming over here and marching in like they owned the place. What kind of decent people would pitch someone into the street without proper warning?"

Jake patted Elvina's wrinkled hand. "Water under the bridge, 'Vina. We need to brainstorm here."

"Jake's right," Jerry said. "Has anyone asked Mr. Bill if he's heard from Mary-Esther?"

"We didn't even think of that." Elvina tapped her temple. "Goes to show you how a person's mind shuts down when it's rattled."

Julie appeared beside the table carrying a coffee carafe. "Hi Jerry. Coffee?"

"I could use a cup. Thank you."

Jerry emptied a sugar and a little cream into the steaming cup and asked, "Julie, have you talked to Mary-Esther?"

"Why do you think I look like a semi ran over me?" Julie topped off the other coffee mugs. "More hot water, Elvina?"

Elvina shook her head.

"She called me early yesterday morning," Julie continued, "said she was leaving town. We're short two people. One of the other servers is out with the flu."

"At least we know she bothered to contact someone," Elvina commented.

"What did she say, exactly?" Jerry asked.

Julie hesitated. "Let's see . . . something about her grandma's house and having to take care of things."

"So she's coming back, then?" Hattie leaned forward.

"I kind of assumed that." Julie tapped her pencil on her chin. "Come to think of it, she didn't commit one way or the other."

"You haven't heard about what happened?" Elvina asked.

"Hang on a sec." Julie checked on her other diner, refilled his mug, then returned and pulled up a chair at the end of their booth.

Elvina said, "Those carpet-baggers from Chipley threw her out."

Julie held one arm akimbo. "Get outta here!"

"Sure enough. Guess she felt she had no place to go." Elvina snorted. "Little does she know, but she has plenty of people in this town who gladly would've taken her in. I can't fathom why she didn't ask."

Julie held her hand to her chest. "Mary-Esther could've camped out on my couch for a couple of days."

"Bobby and I both have extra bedrooms," Hattie said. "No sister of ours would have to sleep on the streets."

Julie, Jerry, and Elvina stared at Hattie.

"Sister?" Elvina asked.

Hattie bobbed her head up and down. "I got the DNA report. Mary-Esther Sloat is our biological sister."

Elvina cut her eyes at Jake. "Did *you* know this?"

"Sorry, 'Vina. Hattie told me. Didn't think it was my news to share, not until Hattie had a chance to tell Mary-Esther."

"Suppose I can forgive you." Elvina pursed her lips.

Jerry shook his head. "Mary-Esther has no idea?"

173

"I had planned on telling her in person." Hattie's eyes watered. "Now I don't know if I'll ever see her again."

Jerry's chest constricted. Too bad men couldn't openly emote in public, especially those in uniform. "We have to focus." Jerry pulled out a pad of paper and pen. "If we can piece together details from Mary-Esther's life in New Orleans, it might provide a lead."

Hattie curled her shoulders forward. "New Orleans is such a big city."

"Not to mention, half of it has been wiped off the map," Jake said.

"If Mary-Esther is there, I *will* find her." Jerry's voice echoed resolve.

Hattie dabbed her eyes with the ragged napkin. "You'd go looking for her?"

"Soon as I can get off my shift," Jerry stated. "I'll call in some favors, get another officer to cover my zone for a few days or however long it takes. Now, think people. Names of little clubs she might have mentioned, street names, anything."

Julie stood. "I'll go grab a fresh pot of coffee. And yes, Miz Elvina, I have some decaf teabags for you."

Chapter Thirty

Hattie stared at the television, her face as motionless as the rest of her. Sadness, a sucking black hole of it.

"You're watching *Jeopardy*." Holston picked up the remote then frowned. "And you didn't even *try* to wrestle me for the control. I'm worried."

"I don't care what's on."

"You despise *Jeopardy*. It makes you feel dense and uneducated." Holston sprawled on the couch beside her. "Sarah's out like a light. Want to talk."

"Talk?"

Holston toggled the volume control and the game show proceeded sans noise. "Ever since you found out about Mary-Esther leaving town, you've barely said a word."

She shifted her gaze to meet his eyes. "I'm sorry."

He slipped his arm across her shoulders. "What's going on with you?"

"I don't know how to put it into words." Hattie inhaled, then let the air out slowly. "I feel like I did after I lost Daddy, then Mama. I barely have the energy to breathe."

"I was concerned you might be getting too attached."

Hattie closed her eyes. "I knew about the baby Mama lost when I was a kid, but not a lot of details. Mama didn't talk about her death. What I know, I learned from Aunt Piddie when I was in college."

Her eyes watered. "When I was little, I had this fantasy about my big sister. How she'd be my protector. My best friend. Someone I could confide my deepest secrets to. Someone who would love me no matter what."

"You had Bobby."

Hattie pinched her lips together. "That's different. He tormented and kidded me mercilessly, like a brother will do, I guess. Then he got married and moved out. I went my own way too. After he started drinking heavily and divorced, our relationship got downright nasty. My friends hated to come home with me if there was any possibility of bumping into him."

Holston gave her shoulder a squeeze. "You and Bobby have put the past behind you, now."

"True. Losing Mom, Jake's assault . . . brought us together again. Yet there's always been distance between Bobby and me. It *is* better, much better, since he sobered up and married Leigh. Still, I think twice before I say certain things to him. Lately, I get the sense his mean part is still there, waiting."

Hattie pushed a stray hank of hair over her left ear. "Thanksgiving's coming up. I had this whole scenario in my mind. I would pull out Mama's china. Her good linen tablecloth, the one with the gold embroidered edges. I'd make Jake help me polish the silver. He loves that.

"We would all sit around the big table: you, me, Sarah, Mary-Esther, Bobby and Leigh and Josh. And Joe and Evelyn. Jake and Shug. Elvina always comes. Maybe Margie and John if they don't go to one of their kids' houses." Hattie gestured with her hands as if she placed people around a long table. "You would be here, at the head. Carving the turkey."

Holston listened.

"I'd make Mama's dressing. The giblet gravy, nice and thick, without the lumps I usually get. Mashed potatoes, or maybe scalloped potatoes. Leigh would bring the green beans and turnips. She's a wiz with vegetables. And desserts, yes desserts! Jake's hummingbird cake and my pecan pie. Shug would bake a pumpkin pie. That's his favorite." She touched his hand. "You could make one of those deep dish apple pies, your mom's recipe."

She jabbed one finger upward. "And rolls. Shug makes those delectable homemade yeast rolls. Elvina would bring one of Aunt Piddie's casseroles. No matter which one. They're all great."

"My mouth's watering."

Hattie gave a little chuckle. "I'll have to pull Joe aside and plot with him so Evelyn doesn't try to cook. Every time she brings food, I find globs of it secreted in every potted plant within close range.

"Mary-Esther would ring the bell." Hattie looked toward the door. "She would be carrying a pot of something. I don't know what. Doesn't matter. She would be wearing this brilliant smile, the kind that stretches from one side of her face to the other, the way Mama's did. Maybe Jerry would be with her. That would be nice."

Hattie slouched back into the couch cushion, deflated.

Holston cupped Hattie's chin and turned her face to his. "You can count on me. I know I can't take the place of a sister."

Hattie brushed his lips with hers. "The way I think of you, Holston Lewis, that would be weird and sort of incestuous."

"Good point." The skin around his eyes crinkled when he smiled.

Hattie snuggled into his arms.

"Anything I can do to help cheer you up?" He nuzzled her neck.

Hattie's lips slid into a weak smile. "Maybe."

Holston stood and pulled her to her feet. He led her to the bedroom. For the next hour, she let him love away some of the sadness.

Elvina, Wanda, and Mandy turned to see Evelyn dashing into the stylist salon, her cheeks flushed.

"Has anyone seen my pinking shears?" Evelyn said between gasps for air.

Mandy gave Elvina a conspiratorial wink. "Sure, Ev. I decided to try them out to do those fringe bangs that are all the rage."

"Oh, thank goodness." Evelyn rested her hand over her heart. "I can't seem to keep up with anything, here lately."

Mandy spritzed cleaner on the counter and herded stray hairs into a soft cloth. "I was kidding. I haven't seen your pinking shears."

"Oh great." Evelyn frowned.

"Try the front desk," Wanda suggested. "Everything seems to end up there."

Evelyn snorted and speared Elvina with the stink-eye. "I hope you haven't been using them for one of your projects, Elvina. Cutting paper with my good shears makes them so dull, they wouldn't even slice warm butter." She twirled around and sped off in the direction of the reception desk.

"That'll be a fight," Mandy said to Wanda. "Way to go, hon."

"What'd I do?" Wanda hosed hot water over a stack of cleaned combs and brushes. "She wanted to know. And everything *does* end up there."

"No worries," Elvina said in a whisper. "I hid them in the bottom drawer. I'll slip them back into her room later."

"I swannee, Elvina, you two go at each other like Evelyn and Piddie used to," Mandy said, then to Wanda, "You don't need to provide them with any ammunition, Wanda-loo."

Wanda's eyebrows rippled. "I don't get it."

"You must learn how to steer around the rocks, hon." Mandy pushed aside the tall arrangement of autumn leaves and flowers blocking her mirror.

The Halloween specters and fake spider webs had disappeared, replaced by pumpkins, wreaths of fall leaves, and pots of yellow and rust-colored mums.

Wanda stood with her arms akimbo. "If I live down here until I'm a hundred and two, I will never understand Southern women's ways."

"And we do have our ways . . ." Mandy sashayed a few steps.

Wanda motioned in the direction of the reception room. "What's up with this collage thing?" she asked Elvina.

"I'm making a big wall hanging of the Davis family for Mary-Esther, from pictures I've gathered."

"I thought Mary-Esther skipped town." Wanda scraped her red hair into a short ponytail and secured it with a strip of bright cloth.

"She'll be back," Elvina said with a head nod.

"Elvina's been out talking to Piddie in the memorial garden," Mandy said. "Says Piddie is working her other-worldly juju magic to bring Mary-Esther home."

Wanda pointed toward the ceiling. "Sure wish I had someone on the other side who would help me out with issues."

Mandy straightened a row of hair products and moved the pot of foliage again, this time to the floor. "Piddie and Elvina had this thing, like they knew what the other was thinking. Kind of eerie. But cool."

Wanda waved in the general direction of the reception desk. "One thing I've come to know about you, Elvina. Once you decide you like someone, you'll do whatever it takes to help that person."

"Piddie was the same way," Elvina said.

"Only, with bigger hair." Mandy smiled.

"Wish I could've known her," Wanda said. "Some people are memorable like that. Larger than life. Hope I'll be that way."

Elvina regarded the impish red-haired woman with the New Jersey accent. "I don't think you have anything to worry about, dear."

Wanda lowered her voice. "I heard the DNA test proved for sure that Mary-Esther is Hattie and Bobby's sister."

Elvina moved closer. "That's what makes it so tragic. Hattie was so excited. Now, with Mary-Esther just up and leaving . . . Leigh came in yesterday morning, and she's really worried about Hattie."

"What about Bobby?" Wanda asked. "He's never struck me as the warm and fuzzy type."

"Seriously," Mandy said. "Those silent types will surprise you."

Chapter Thirty-one

The closer Mary-Esther drew to New Orleans, the more she lingered at rest stops and any kind of roadside tourist trap advertised on the interstate billboards. A road trip that normally would have taken Mary-Esther ten hours stretched to three days. Plus two tanks of expensive gas.

Over a year had passed since Katrina had blown ashore and erased her life in the Big Easy. Seemed like ten.

The van had held little when she fled the city in August of 2005: a minimum of clothing and canned food, the urn containing Loretta Boudreau's ashes, the rock collection, and five jugs of water. Certainly, the storm couldn't last forever. After a few days' inconvenience, she would return and tidy the small yard. Life would return to its dismal sameness.

When the first aerial photos appeared on national television, any hope of an immediate return withered. Her neighborhood floated in several feet of filth-strewn water. Basic utilities and services ground to a halt. Looters ran amok.

Days passed. Then, months. Mary-Esther moved from shelter to shelter, relying on the kindness of strangers and picking up odd jobs to supplement the cash culled from her meager savings account. Time pushed forward, and the aftermath of the devastating storm dulled in the American consciousness. Relief stalled. Tempers and resentment festered. Mary-Esther found excuses to delay her return. No way could she bear witness to a colorful city pounded to its knees. Too much had happened before the storm, and she simply had nothing left to bolster either herself or her neighbors. When she finally shucked the inertia, she headed in the opposite direction toward the Panhandle of Florida.

Now, she picked her way toward Louisiana with Rose's dolls and a road-weary cat. Otherwise, she returned with the same amount of next-to-nothing. And her heart ached in fresh ways.

Mary-Esther fought sleep at the end of each day; the nocturnal vision of her grandmother's house haunted her. As she neared New Orleans, the dream became more detailed. Sections of a cabinet appeared. A board in a wall. Mary-Esther grappled to understand.

A distinct line separated her Louisiana life and the one she thought she had created in Chattahoochee. Emotions warred: her love for the city where she had spent the majority of her life and the growing affection for the small town that had recently enfolded her.

Mary-Esther pulled into a gas station a half-hour out of the city. On a dinged-up pay phone smeared with strangers' sweat and spit, she dialed Jerry Blount's number. The tang of urine wafted from the cracked concrete.

The line rang three times before his deep voice interrupted and asked her to leave a brief message. Her eyes burned with tears. "Jerry. This is Mary-Esther. Sorry I haven't called. Maybe I can explain so you'll understand . . . some day."

Mary-Esther swallowed. Her mouth tasted of dust and sorrow. "I don't know when, or if, I'll be back. A lot depends on what I find. I . . . Be good to yourself."

She returned the headset to its cradle then leaned against the edge of the booth and wept.

Jerry shifted a packed duffle bag from one shoulder to the other and waited at the car rental counter in New Orleans's Louis Armstrong airport. Even this long after the storm, its effects stood out around him. The terminal held a handful of people, not anywhere near the level he would have expected.

"How many days, Mr. Blount?" the sweet-faced car rental woman asked. Her accent, so much like Mary-Esther's.

"Make it a week. I really don't have a firm departure date, yet."

She entered his credit card information into the computer then handed him a stack of papers and a tagged keychain. "Do you need a map, sir?"

"Yes, ma'am. That'd be good."

Who knew where he might be going? Following the breadcrumb clues Mary-Esther had left of her life in New Orleans, he had a general idea of where to start. But it was a sprawling, damaged city. Time to rely on his law enforcement training and the gut-intuition that had served him well during his years in the field. An eerie connection stretched between him and Mary-Esther, solid as a steel-link chain.

He turned on his cell phone.

Bobby slumped into a porch rocker. His wife and son wouldn't be home until the end of the weekend. Hours stretched out before him, a fact that usually pleased him. Woodworking projects waited in the small shop behind the log home. Christmas loomed, and he had barely started. Normally, he would be up to his armpits in a quagmire of pine and oak shavings. Guilt niggled him like wasps hovering over rotten fruit.

Once, at an AA meeting, Bobby had overheard a fellow abuser joke: *Know what* sober *stands for? Son Of a Bitch, Everything's Real!*

So true. Without the cloak of drunkenness, reality stood out, ugly and neon-studded. The hell with taking on reality without something to help.

"You've really screwed the pooch this time, Davis," he slurred. He slung back his head and downed his tenth beer in less than an hour. The alcohol wasn't working. The pain of his betrayal seeped in around the fuzzy edges.

He imagined Hattie's face, disappointment smudged across her features. She'd know what he did. Eventually.

Bobby stood up and stumbled. Before his alcohol-pickled brain could tell his body how to upright itself, he fell. The rocker arm gashed his forehead. He roused long enough to feel the pounding pain.

He vomited and blacked out.

When Bobby awakened, the headache rivaled any hangover in his history. Filtered light from a blind-slatted window pierced his eyes like a meat hook into sirloin. Leigh and Hattie's worried faces swam in and out of focus.

"Bobby?" His wife's voice struggled through tears.

He squeezed his eyes shut and reached up to touch his forehead.

"You're in the hospital." Leigh grasped his hand. "You have a pressure bandage, babe. And stitches. When you fell, you cut your head pretty bad."

"Passed out." Hattie spat out the words. "Call a dog a dog. What in the blue blazes were you thinking, Bobby?"

The back of his throat felt like packing peanuts mixed with plaster of Paris. He tried to swallow and held one hand to his neck. "Could I have something . . . ?"

Leigh poured water from a small bedside pitcher into a Styrofoam cup and held it to her husband's lips.

He rested his head on the pillow and blinked to focus. "I let you down. I never thought . . ." Dear God. He'd take five cases of pneumonia over this. At least that was a sickness he could beat in a few days.

The muscles at Hattie's temples pulsed. "You never thought it would hurt you to *just* drink a beer, did you?"

When Bobby looked directly at her, Hattie gasped. Could she see the raw ache mirrored in his eyes? "Hattie, you'll never forgive me."

Hattie sank onto the edge of the gurney. "Does it make me mad as a wet hen to know you drank again? Yes. It brings up all the times when you came stumbling in, barely able to stand up, not to mention the times you got behind the wheel. Bobby, you cannot drink. You're a freakin' alcoholic. You can't pick it up like it never affected you and expect to handle it. God knows your liver already looks like Swiss cheese."

"I know. I know." He nodded and blanched at the sickening swirl the motion caused. The musk of metabolizing alcohol boiled in waves from his skin. "What I did was dumb."

"Why, babe?" Leigh asked. "You were fine when I left for Mama's. What could have caused you to . . . ?" She paused. "You haven't drank at all since way before we were married."

Bobby shifted to relieve a cramp in his back. The room warped, then settled. "Things snowballed on me last night. Guess it was last night—" He looked to his sister and wife for confirmation.

"Nine o'clock, to be precise." Hattie frowned. "I was coming down to make sure you were doing okay while Leigh and Josh were away. Good thing I did. You'd still be face down in a pool of blood and chunks of what you had for dinner."

Bobby's stomach lurched. "Leave it to you to provide the sordid details."

Hattie leaned in. "So, tell me. Must be a heck of reason to drive you back to the bottle."

Bobby inhaled and exhaled. "Mary-Esther left town because of me."

"What?"

"I don't know what came over me, Hattie. Well, I do, sort of. . . Think I figured it all out."

Hattie narrowed her eyes to slits. "You . . . *what* did you do?"

"I went to Mary-Esther's place." Bobby took a moment to find the words. "What everyone said was true. When she looked at me, I saw Mama." He squeezed his eyes shut. "Something in me tore loose." He opened his eyes, stared at the wall to avoid their reactions. "I told her I thought she had shown up looking for a handout. Gave her down the road. It got pretty nasty."

"Dear. How did she react?" Leigh asked.

"Denied it. Said she couldn't care less about anything you or I had. Said she was trying to find out where she belonged." He rubbed his eyes. "I cussed her out, told her I didn't much care where that was, long as it wasn't in my damn family."

"Oh, Bobby." Leigh glanced away.

Hattie studied her brother. "Cold, even for you."

He huffed. "Thing is, I believe her. She wasn't playing us."

"I can't imagine what Mary-Esther could've said to win you over." Hattie's features relayed her anger. "Nothing I said or did, nor the point-blank fact that our DNA matched, swayed you at all. You never gave her a chance."

Bobby stared down at his weathered hands. Rough. Stained. Like him. "Mary-Esther said she would never do anything to hurt me or you. Said we were so lucky. Said she had heard story after story about our folks, and how they poured love over us. Said she wished things had been different. That she would have liked to have had a brother who was so protective. Said she admired the way I stood in front of anything or anyone I perceived to be a threat to you."

Leigh's expression mirrored Bobby's anguish.

"Even after the things I said to her . . ." He pressed his temples with his thumbs. "It squirmed around in my brain. I wanted a drink, bad. I sat out on the porch and rocked for a long time. Then, I jumped in the truck and went to find her, try to make peace. I pounded on her door. No answer. The apartment was locked up, but I found a key under the mat and let myself in. Nothing left. Anywhere."

Hattie raked her fingers through her hair. "No wonder she beat it out of here so fast. First, you come at her, all full of piss and vinegar, then those freaks from Chipley show up."

Bobby dipped his head in agreement, careful this time not to move too fast. "I heard about them." He cleared his throat. "After I realized she was gone, the craving took me over. Fought it at first. Picked up the phone to call my AA sponsor. Didn't." The bitter taste of vomit lingered. "Could've found a meeting to attend. Didn't," he muttered to himself then looked at Leigh. "I had ruined everything again. I got in my truck, rode around a while. Stopped at the package store for a couple of beers."

"You had more than two," Leigh said. "Your blood alcohol concentration was really high."

Bobby frowned. "I didn't drive drunk. Why'd they run a BAC?"

"Really?" Hattie folded her arms across her chest. "You end up in a puddle of puke and blood. You don't come to. Of course they're going to check."

Bobby looked from Hattie to Leigh.

"You were close to full-on alcohol poisoning, babe."

Hearing the fear in his sister's and wife's voices, Bobby's spirit sank lower. Like that was possible. "I rode out to the lake to sit and think. Some stuff came back to me. Stuff I hadn't thought about in years."

Hattie pursed her lips.

"I'm not one to talk about all this touchy-feely junk." His eyes sought his sister's. "I prayed for Sarah to die. Can you imagine that?"

Hattie waited.

"I didn't want that baby to be born. Didn't want to share Mama, I suppose. Who knows? I sat by the lake and I remembered, clear as it was yesterday, getting down on my hands and knees, day after day, begging God to kill that baby in Mama's belly. Don't you see? I hated Sarah. I wanted her to die. And she did."

Leigh squeezed her husband's hand. "Sarah died because of bacteria she picked up in the birth canal. Back then, they didn't have the same preventive measures we have now. You were a boy, Bobby. Children can be terribly selfish. *You* didn't cause Sarah's death."

Bobby squeezed his eyes shut to ease the burn of tears. "Then, when Mama told me she was pregnant with you, Hattie, I was so happy. Mama had been sad for so long. Nothing I did helped. Her depression made me feel guiltier. This time, I prayed for the baby to be born okay. When you came fast, and Mama had to have you at home, I freaked out. I knew you would die, that God would repay me for wishing my first sister dead." He opened his eyes and wiped the moisture aside with one forearm. "I pledged to always look after you. I haven't done such a great job."

Hattie traced her finger through the tear trail on his arm. "Mary-Esther coming here . . . It brought back all of this?"

Bobby's upper lip flicked up. He took three breaths to staunch a wave of nausea. "An awful blackness smothered me every time I heard her name and especially when I finally saw her. There she was, my mama staring at me through Mary-Esther's eyes, with that same sorrowful look. Like I was a huge disappointment. Like I had crushed her heart to dust. I can't find enough bad words to tell you how sick and twisted my insides felt."

"What did you do after you left the lake?" Hattie prodded.

"I wanted to numb out completely, like I used to do. I bought a case of beer. On some level, I reckon I was thinking straight; I didn't go on driving around. I went home and sat on our porch, and knocked 'em back. But all of it kept coming at me."

Bobby looked at his sister. "I was that same little kid, murdering my sister all over again. I prayed for the first Sarah to die, then I ran the second one off. Now I'll be lucky if my baby sister ever forgives me."

Hattie leaned over and rested her head on his chest. Bobby remembered how she had done that as a child, how she said hearing the strong pound of his heartbeat made her feel safe.

"We'll find a way through this," Leigh said in a soft voice.

Hattie pushed away and looked into his eyes. "Don't ever try to hurt yourself like this again. Promise?"

Bobby wrapped one arm around his sister then reached the other to draw his wife into the circle.

Chapter Thirty-two

Cities of any size appeared gray to Mary-Esther. In the early morning mist, she couldn't tell if her gloomy mood or the abundance of pavement and buildings colored the Big Easy.

Mary-Esther's eyes stung. Other than the feelings linked to Nana, no tender emotions tied her to this place. What had she been thinking all those months spent dreaming of the triumphant return home?

None of her dreams remained in the storm-ravaged streets.

No familiar faces waited for her.

Only the past. And loss.

The battered street sign listed to one side. She slowed the van and crept down the once-familiar lane. On either side, mounds of debris stood like funeral pyres awaiting a torch. The structures still intact were deserted. Bright orange spray-painted crosshatches slashed the doors, reminders of the emergency personnel's grim search for survivors.

She parked the van in a small space clear of trash and shut off the engine. It no longer went into smoky seizures when she turned the key.

Her grandmother's house, though badly damaged, still stood. The shingles hung in tattered pieces, and only one of the visible windows contained unbroken glass. The curtains dangled in shreds, gauze ripped from a wound.

The magnolia branches that once draped over one end of the house were gone. *Her* tree. Didn't need to step into the back yard to confirm, it was probably twisted like the rest she'd seen on the block.

A police cruiser pulled beside her. Mary-Esther automatically grabbed her purse and fished for identification. The officer flipped on his strobe lights and got out.

"Morning. May I see—?" The officer stopped when she held out her driver's license. His expression revealed no emotion. Mary-Esther guessed he had little left. "You live here?" he asked.

"Was my grandmother's house. Guess it's mine now."

"We don't allow anyone except property owners to enter these neighborhoods. Most of the houses have been condemned. Looters aren't so much a problem. Not now."

"Nothing left to steal?"

He offered a wry smile and handed her license through the lowered window.

"I talked to the FEMA people. They sent me a letter." Mary-Esther glanced toward the house. "I have to get anything of personal value out of here before they level it."

"Yes, ma'am." His gaze canvassed the deserted street. "Do you need a place to stay tonight? I could direct you—"

Mary-Esther shoved her ID into her wallet. "I can't imagine I will be here long. But thanks. If I need to, I can sleep in here." She pointed to the rear of the van.

"I wouldn't suggest parking here after dark." He tipped his head, returned to the patrol car, and drove away.

Funny, at one time she would've dreaded seeing a police car. It usually meant the party had gone on too loud or long, or one of the neighbors had heard the fight. A law officer was an intrusion. Deal with the man, or woman, and coax 'em to leave. Now she appreciated the concern. At least, she wasn't totally alone, even if he got paid to care.

Her thoughts drifted to Jerry. He would be getting in from work, doing some mundane thing around the house, maybe driving over to his mother's to help her with a chore. Sleep wouldn't come until much later for him, in the hours before his evening shift. She knew his routine almost as well as her own, the one she had grown into before she left Chattahoochee. Mary-Esther missed Jerry and the life she had constructed so intensely that her chest hurt.

"Damn it," she whispered.

The van's door opened with little effort. No more banging with her shoulder, thanks to Jerry's cousin. Every well-oiled hinge on the old clunker operated without screeching complaints.

Mary-Esther approached the house tentatively, as if she expected someone to erupt from the ruined structure with a loaded shotgun. When she stepped onto the porch, a powerful longing mixed with fear swept over her. Her mouth tasted sour. She swallowed and opened the door.

The stench of decay and mold accosted her nose. She sneezed violently. An evil brown tinctured the once-white walls, with lines of mildew creeping down from the ceiling. In several places, the overhead plaster

188

drooped like soiled diapers. Ruined rugs studded the warped wooden floors.

In the narrow living room, Mary-Esther spotted one picture frame, still in place on the mantle. Thank God. She wove past the overturned furniture and picked up the black and white print. The frame had warped, but the image seemed intact. Her mother—so young, so thin—stood on the front steps of this house, her lips curled up for the camera. Beside her, Nana Boudreau cuddled a baby: Mary-Esther, several months old.

Telling. Even then, Nana was the one supporting me.

Mary-Esther held the frame to her heart, checked the rest of the room. Nothing else worth touching.

The house warranted demolition. No miracle of modern construction could exhume it from the filth.

She made her way to the kitchen. The cabinets stood ajar. Dishes and flatware littered the buckled linoleum. After placing the frame on the small table, she knelt down and rescued a cream-colored pottery bowl from the clutter. Through some miracle, the piece had remained intact—her grandmother's favorite mixing bowl.

Nana Boudreau's knotty hands appeared in her mind like a well-loved video.

Dusted with flour, moving up and down, dough pipes through those long fingers as she digs into some gooey mixture. Biscuits, cornbread, wheat bread, rolls. Never blended by an electrical or mechanical device. Instead, by dancing hands in love with their work.

Mary-Esther closed her eyes, yielded to the memory.

Those same hands wipe on an apron before reaching out to hug her. Then the hands lead her to the cabinet under the sink.

"Shh, child." Nana taps her lips with a fingertip. "Don't tell a soul."

Nana moves aside a stack of pans. Raps on one of the boards until an end sticks out a fraction. Her fingers pry the board loose. It swings aside to reveal a void between the wall and insulation.

"If I ever want to hide a treasure, I will put it here. Remember . . ." Nana touches a finger on Mary-Esther's young forehead, sealing in the secret.

Mary-Esther's eyes popped open. She gently set the bowl down and shoved away the clutter in front of the cabinet door. When she opened it, the hinges loosened and the rotten door fell onto the floor.

Inside, she found a few cleaning supplies and a pile of mildewed rags. In the dim light, she strained to see the edges of the boards. She went back outside to the van, returning with a small flashlight.

The weak beam hit the cabinet wall where waterlogged planks bowed outward like the hull of a boat. Mary-Esther dug through the spilled flatware, located a butter knife, and pried one of the boards loose. A rectangular, chipped blue tin was wedged into place by shreds of cloth.

After several unsuccessful attempts, she pried open the tin's rusty lid. A small gold cross on a delicate chain rested in a bed of blue velvet.

Mary-Esther worked the clasp and fastened the chain around her neck. She noticed a folded piece of time-yellowed paper beneath the tattered velvet. She recognized the swirling artistic script.

My little one,
No matter where you are, or where I am, I will be watching over you.
Nana

All these years, Nana's cross had been here, waiting. Her grandmother's words whispered in her ears: *Be patient. Magic is everywhere.*

Mary-Esther grabbed the tin, bowl, and frame, and returned to the van. She considered leaving. But how many items—small things of great power—would she miss if she did?

Hattie watched the gold Delta 88 float up the driveway and park in the fall-browned grass in front of the farmhouse. The car was as much a part of its driver as her signature. Many times, Hattie recalled hearing Aunt Piddie trying to convince Elvina of the wisdom of trading for a more economical automobile. No go.

The car door opened and Elvina Houston emerged, cane first, casted foot next.

"Mornin', Glory!" The old woman called out as she rounded the front of the car.

"Morning, Elvina." Hattie stood and helped guide her to a porch rocker.

"Whew!" Elvina blew out a long breath and hooked her cane on the arm of the rocker. "I surely will be proud to get this walkin' cast off. It takes all my energy to haul this blasted thing around."

"How much longer?" Hattie dragged up a stool for Elvina's foot.

190

The old woman propped up the casted leg with a grunt. "All goes well, a couple more weeks. Bones don't knit as fast on a person of my age, but I've always been pretty active, so I'm hoping that stacks the deck in my favor."

"Offer you something to drink? Coffee?"

Elvina nodded. "I could use a cup of coffee. I usually drink my green tea, but I might like the change. Not to be a botherment, now."

Hattie smiled at her Aunt Piddie's slang for *bother*. "Cream and one sugar, right?"

"That'll be fine." She nodded. "You young folks have such good memories. I can barely recall how I take my own coffee, much less anyone else's."

When Hattie returned with a refill for her cup and Elvina's coffee, Elvina said, "Suppose you're wondering to what you owe the honor of my company."

"You're welcome on The Hill any time, Elvina. You know that. I figured you were coming out to discuss Thanksgiving."

"I'd have just called. And I already told you I'm bringing a couple of Piddie's favorite casseroles. Haven't decided which ones yet. Maybe the squash and one other." She tasted from her cup. "You make good coffee, Hattie. Not like some of it—so weak you could read a newspaper through it."

"Why bother drinking it if it's not rich and strong?"

Elvina hummed agreement. "I'm getting busy on my Christmas projects. I came to get your help."

Hattie tilted her head. "Oh?"

"I need to borrow any old photos you have of your folks, you and Bobby . . . that sort."

"May I ask why?"

"I'm using my new scanner to copy them and make a framed collage."

"That's nice."

Elvina sipped and continued, "I have a few of Piddie, and Joe and Evelyn. A scattering of you and your brother when you were children, but not enough. Hoped you'd be able to fill in the blanks."

"Sure, Elvina. I have a few albums, but most of them are loose pictures in a couple of plastic bins in the back closet. Sure you're up to pouring through all of them? It will take some time."

"Time, I've got. I can do this project with my leg propped on a pillow. I can only watch so much television. When I'm not at the Triple C, I

191

nearly climb the walls with boredom. It's not like I can get out and do my walks right now."

"I'll put them in your car."

"Good, good. I'll get Jake and Shug to swing by and carry them inside for me."

They watched a cardinal squabbling with a finch at the feeder near the porch. The creak of the rockers blended with the bird chatter.

"Are you making the collage for someone in particular?" Hattie asked. "Don't want to spoil anyone's surprise by asking. Just curious."

"For Mary-Esther. Your sister needs to have a sense of history. If she can see pictures of you all, it might help her feel more settled."

Hattie's spirit sank. "Elvina, my sister is gone."

Elvina shot her a disgusted look. "I know everything that goes on in this town, Hattie. I studied at the feet of a master. And I was there with you at Bill's. Remember?"

"Silly me. What was I thinking?"

Elvina reached over and patted Hattie on the hand. "Mary-Esther will be back."

"How do you know?"

"Jerry's on the case, is how I know." The old woman pointed one finger up.

"He may find her, Elvina. There's no assurance she'll *want* to come back."

"She'll return."

Hattie sighed. "Bobby's even changed his attitude. If only Mary-Esther will let us have another chance."

"Your sister *will* be back, Hattie." Elvina's voice carried the conviction of blind faith.

"How can you be so certain?"

Elvina tapped the space over her heart. "I believe in the power of love, that's how. You best believe in it too."

Chapter Thirty-three

Boudreau and Mary-Esther heard the movement outside the van. His ears pricked forward, and his eyes grew round and alert. Mary-Esther huddled inside the sleeping bag, straining to listen. Why had she talked herself into spending the night in the van? Stupid, stupid, stupid!

She inched a hand from the warmth and groped for her purse. A fingernail file, the only thing her terrified mind could conceive as a weapon. She never had possessed a gun. The only knife lay at the bottom of the cooler, wedged beneath a stack of cardboard boxes. Even if she could reach it, the blade was only three inches long. Hardly a dagger.

When the rap sounded on the back window, Mary-Esther jerked so violently Boudreau hissed and dove beneath the blankets. What to do? If she answered, the intruder would know she was female and probably alone. Not good. If she remained silent, the van would likely fall prey to theft.

No. Who would steal it? Too embarrassing. The tires were good. They'd jack it, jerk them, and set fire to the heap.

"Mary-Esther?" a voice asked. "Mary-Esther, you in there?"

She flipped the layers of bedding off so quickly, Boudreau bolted for the passenger side floorboard. "Jerry?"

"Mary-Esther?"

She butt-crawled to the back door, flipped the lock, and opened it a crack. Jerry Blount's features were barely discernable in the dim light of the waning moon. "What are you doing here?"

Jerry's breath came out in steamy puffs. "I was in the neighborhood and decided to pop by. Took me a truck, a jet, and a rental car to get in the neighborhood, but here I am." He chuckled. More puffs.

She pushed the heavy door open wide. "C'mon inside. Too cold for you to stand around out there."

Jerry ducked inside, shut the door, and huddled in front of her. Good thing the lighting was so poor. He couldn't see the asinine grin plastered across her face.

"You came looking for me."

"I did."

"All the way to Louisiana," she stated.

"Seemed the most likely place to start." She heard amusement in his voice.

Boudreau crept up beside her and meowed. Mary-Esther nestled the cat into her lap and scratched the fur between his ears. "How'd you find the address?"

"By aimlessly wandering around this city, asking questions of complete strangers. Trouble with that approach, most of the little clubs you talked about are either gone or closed. Then, it dawned on me I should consult the obvious source. I talked to the local police. Ran your name, pulled up your driver's license—terrible picture, by the way. You look half drunk." Mary-Esther couldn't see his face clearly, but she knew from his tone he wore that lopsided grin. And she probably had been feeling no pain when the official picture was taken. Or hung over.

"I could've been here sooner if half the dang signs weren't down. Most of the streetlights don't burn, either. And the rental car didn't come with a spotlight like my squad car. A GPS would've been nice. Still, I'm part bloodhound, so I sniffed my way here."

"Resourceful."

"Didn't hurt being in law enforcement. We help each other out. I'd do the same if one of these guys showed up in my neck of the woods."

"Why'd you come?"

"Figured I'd offer to help you drive back."

Mary-Esther tilted her head. "What makes you think I plan to do that?"

Jerry leaned over, kissed her softly on the lips, and caressed her cheek with the tips of his fingers. "I don't have any false hopes, Mary-Esther. My return airfare has been paid. Maybe I won't have to use the ticket. Maybe you'll decide you'd like to have a little company on the drive home."

"Home." Mary-Esther took a deep breath, held and released it. "I don't have a clue as to where that is anymore, Jerry."

"I know about your encounter with those folks from Chipley. Hard for me to fathom the likes of them running you off."

"They didn't. Well, sort of, but not really."

"You promised to explain. Heard your message on my cell when I landed."

"I got a letter from FEMA. I registered a forwarding address when I finally had one, so I guess they found out how to contact me. I called them. Seems they're trying to reach as many former residents as possible. Most of the houses in this area have been condemned. I had one last chance to come back and see if there were any personal items worth salvaging before they level this place to the ground."

Saying that aloud, to Jerry, made the reality pop.

Boudreau shifted position and Jerry ran his fingers across the cat's fur. "You said the Chipley folks were 'sort of' the reason? Other than the FEMA letter, is there more?"

"Rose's dolls." Mary-Esther tapped on one of the plastic containers. "She made it clear I had to keep them safe. I promised her, before she died. She even helped me catalog and pack the boxes. Rose was adamant. She knew what Eustis's cousins were all about. They gave me a couple of days to clear out—generous of them—but I knew as soon as they discovered the dolls missing, that nasty, rat-haired witch would search the apartment and demand I hand them over. I couldn't allow it. I will probably face some kind of charges if I go back."

Her shoulders drooped. "I had a rather heated discussion with Bobby Davis before I left town too. He made his feelings pretty clear."

"All of this can be worked out." Jerry hesitated.

"That Sue Ellen woman practically salivated over Rose's stuff. No way she'll stand by and let me off easy. Her husband is a whipped puppy. She runs that sleazy sideshow."

"We can cover all of that later."

Mary-Esther tried to read his expression in the insufficient light. "I'm sorry I didn't let you know what I was doing. I made a decision and acted on it before I could talk myself out of it. Still, I almost turned around so many times."

"Something pulling you back?" he asked.

"Yes. No. I don't know."

Jerry glanced around. "Kind of cramped in here. Never was much room to start with. But now . . . how can you sleep?"

"After Katrina, I got used to crawling anywhere out of the weather. Boudreau and I manage." The cat trilled at the sound of his name.

"I have a hotel room about a mile from here." Jerry paused. "Two beds. Why don't you follow me back and get a decent night's sleep where there's heat and a hot bath?"

Mary-Esther considered. A shower would be heavenly. Her skin itched as if it carried as many layers of mold and filth as Nana's house. "You wouldn't mind? I could pay half."

"Wouldn't have offered if I minded. Don't worry about the money. Not like I rented a suite at the Radisson."

"Oh, why not? You lead the way." Mary-Esther shifted boxes to find her purse. "Better yet, give me the name of the hotel and the road it's on and I'll lead."

"Okay. I made it here after about half a dozen turns and a couple of backtracks. I usually have a full-on sense of direction, but this city has had me turned around from the time I landed—even with my blood-hound leanings."

"New Orleans has a way of confusing outsiders." She scrunched her brows. "Wait. What about Boudreau?"

"Slip him under your jacket and we'll smuggle him inside. No one has to be the wiser."

Mary-Esther searched in her purse and retrieved the van keys. "Never would've figured you for a rule-breaker."

"Lot of things you don't know about me." His voice came out low and sultry.

Mary-Esther's face flushed. Was it him, or did this city have that effect on people?

Cleaning out Nana's house took longer than Mary-Esther imagined. Though the water and mold had damaged most of the furnishings beyond salvaging, a few spots high in closets and in top bureau drawers had escaped harm. As she picked through the mementos, Mary-Esther shared bits and pieces of her history with Jerry. She admired the way he listened; she needed that quality more than sympathy.

By the end of the second day, they were dog-tired, covered again in a layer of dirt, and emotionally drawn.

One task remained. She'd take care of that later.

They stood in the front yard. Mary-Esther took a lingering look at the house.

"I can find a store and buy a disposable camera, if you'd like to take a picture of this place," Jerry offered. "The one on my cell phone isn't very good."

"No. I would much rather remember it as it used to be." She ran a hand through her matted hair. "It's like when they have a person's body at a viewing. That sticks in my mind and I can't remember what they looked like alive." She shook her head to dispel the recent images of Eustis and Rose. Waxen. Pasted on smiles.

"Sure you have everything you want to take?"

"The stuff that means the most to me." Four boxes—Nana's rosary, some trinkets, and a few dishes—all she salvaged from her fragmented past.

"Glad you came?" Jerry slipped one arm around her.

His concern caused emotion to rise to the top. Tears burned her eyes. She managed a nod and a shuddery breath.

"Where to now?" Jerry said.

Mary-Esther rubbed the crest of one shoulder. Everything ached or itched. "I'm almost too tired to think. What I'd really like to do is shower the filth off me, check on Boudreau, grab a bite to eat, and take you to hear some good jazz."

"I'd be up for that." He motioned for the van keys. "I can drive if you'd like. I finally feel like I can find my way back to the hotel."

Later, after they shared gumbo and a muffaletta, they parked the rental car and strolled arm in arm through the French Quarter. Used to be, she'd doll up for a night out. Nothing expensive, just a smidge flashy.

Her life didn't include a closet full of bargain-rack clothes. What was she thinking? She didn't have a closet. Again.

Small signs of the great city's resurrection coexisted with marks of the storm's destruction. They ducked into an intimate blues club, grabbed a corner table, and ordered a couple of beers.

"Kind of place I like," Jerry commented. "Not the typical tourist clap-trap."

"The best music and food in this town are in these little out-of-the-way joints. Lucky, this one's still standing. You're with a local here, and I wouldn't dare take you somewhere most out-of-towners would frequent."

Mary-Esther's gaze traveled around the murky room: a narrow elevated stage with a single wooden stool, ten round tables with mismatched chairs, a long wooden bar, and one server. She spotted a cluster of people in a far corner and gasped. "I don't believe it!"

Jerry followed the line of her vision. "What?"

"My ex, well, one of them." She glanced back to Jerry. "Mind if I go say hello?"

"Of course not."

Mary-Esther picked her way across the room and stood in front of her ex-husband's table. One of the two women who hung on him like Mardi Gras beads noticed her and whispered something into his ear.

"Mookie!" John R. Sloat jumped up so fast, he jostled the table. One glass overturned. He grabbed Mary-Esther in a suffocating hug, then held her at arm's length. "Let me look at you, girlie! You are a sight for my sore eyes. I worried you might have gotten washed away by the storm!" The brown-haired woman sopped up her spilled drink with a wad of paper napkins.

Mary-Esther ignored the blonde woman's scowl. "No. I rambled around, misplaced for some time."

"Heard about your mama. So sorry." John R. ran his hands up and down her arms. Her skin responded with a warm quiver. "Damn, but it's good to see you again. So many people are gone. No way to know if they're dead or alive."

"I suppose your place got ruined too?"

"Nothing worth saving." John R. twisted his lips.

"Where are you living now?"

John R. glanced toward the women. "I get by." The brunette winked. The blonde looked even more sour than the brunette, if that was possible.

Typical John R. Sloat. Even when the man was married to her, he often laid out with first one woman then another. John R. always managed to land on his feet. A tomcat falling from a balcony into a padded feline bed.

"You back to stay, dahlin'?"

God, he was still so sexy. Mary-Esther shook off the spell. "I came to pick over what was left in Nana's house. They're going to level it. Don't really know where I'll end up." Her eyes flicked back to the booth where Jerry waited. The heated spots where John R. held her arms cooled. As if he sensed her withdrawal, he released his grasp.

John R. followed her gaze. "That your man?"

Mary-Esther smiled. "Yes. He is."

"Ain't he the charmed one? Who knows, Mookie. Maybe you'll luck out this time. Find someone who'll stick by you."

Remorse? From John R. Sloat? Mary-Esther stared at her playboy ex-husband. "There's hope for both of us, John R."

"My next set's in a few minutes. I'll play you a song or two, for old time's sake."

"I did promise Jerry some good jazz before we left the city."

"You found it." He motioned toward the bar. "Tell Carl to put your drinks on my tab."

"I should go." Mary-Esther glanced over her shoulder.

John R. leaned over, brushed her cheek with a kiss.

The bottle-blonde woman, clearly the more possessive of the two, grabbed John R.'s hand and pulled him to the table. Mary-Esther walked to where Jerry waited. At one time, she had been the poor female trying to tether the musician in one place, a foolish futility.

When John R. Sloat picked up the saxophone a few minutes later, the scattered patrons quieted. "This song, I dedicate to a woman who deserves better." He tipped his head toward the corner booth where Mary-Esther and Jerry watched.

The saxophone sounded. The familiar melancholia rushed in.

It wasn't the man Mary-Esther longed for when she heard the lonesome wail of a sax. It was the spirit of an old city that refused to die.

Jerry allowed John R.'s music to flow around him. The spell of the Delta captured his imagination more than any costume or bauble.

He studied Mary-Esther's profile. How could he compete for the affections of a woman wooed by such a place? He glanced around the room at the rapt expressions of the women who watched the performance. And how could he measure up to a dark-featured man who oozed charisma and played an instrument so well, he could charm the underpants off females? As if she sensed his insecurity, Mary-Esther reached over and curled her hand in his.

Later, deep in the night, Jerry awakened to a stealthy movement. Mary-Esther slid into bed next to him. Fully alert now, he lay on his side with his eyes closed. She edged closer and nestled into the cocoon of his body. He mumbled and allowed her to wrap his arm around her middle. He waited, forcing his breathing to remain deep and even, ignoring his body's reaction to her heat and scent. When he heard her breath settle into a peaceful rhythm, Jerry willed himself back to sleep.

In the morning, when the first light crept through a crack in the cheap hotel curtains, Mary-Esther rolled over and opened her eyes. Jerry's features appeared almost boyish. A fine line of freckles trailed across the bridge of his nose. The hair above his temples, mostly gray, but still thick. She hadn't noticed his high cheekbones before. Perhaps, some Native American heritage?

Jerry opened one eye a crack. "Hard to sleep when you feel like someone's watching you."

"Sorry."

He pulled her into the circle of his arms. "Did you get cold last night?"

"Did it bother you I came into your territory without permission?"

Jerry grinned. "You've had my permission for a while, Mary-E."

She stretched up and kissed him. "I'd like to do much more."

"You sure?"

"Never in my life have I been so sure."

It was well past mid-morning before either spoke again.

"Mmmm." Mary-Esther gathered the sheets around her. "You redneck boys surely know how to love up a woman."

"You Cajun women know a thing or two."

She rose up on one elbow and regarded him. "Jerry, can we go home today?"

"Home, as in back to North Florida?"

Something odd glimmered inside Mary-Esther—*hope*? "I'll have to find a place to live. See if Mr. Bill will let me keep working at the Homeplace. And figure out how much trouble I'm in over Rose's dolls." Concerns bounced in her head like drunken parade revelers jostling for beads. "But yes. I'd like to go back."

"Sure I haven't pushed you to this?" He traced the outline of her face with a fingertip.

"I missed Chattahoochee as soon as I turned onto the interstate heading west."

"If you'll follow me to drop off the rental car, I'll help you drive."

"Hoped you'd say that." Mary-Esther's mood sagged. "There are a couple of things I have to do before we leave Louisiana."

Mary-Esther palmed one of three rocks she had retrieved from the yard before they pulled away for the last time. Soon, a bulldozer would reduce the ruined structure to a pile of rubble. At least the last hands to touch that front door knob were hers.

"First light, take a right. It's two blocks down," she said.

Jerry navigated the broken asphalt then parked beside a small cemetery and gave her a questioning look.

"You can come, if you'd like." She got out. Jerry joined her. They walked past several uneven rows, then Mary-Esther took the lead. Halfway down the weedy path, she stopped. "I couldn't leave without saying goodbye."

The headstone wasn't embellished, barely large enough for the name and dates. All she and Loretta could afford. Maybe one day, she could replace it with something fitting for the one person she could always count on. Mary-Esther knelt down, set a rock in front of the marker. At least Nana would have a solid remembrance of the place she had once called home. Besides, Nana didn't believe in leaving cut flowers by a grave. And for sure, plastic plants would've sent her into a tizzy.

A few minutes later, the van was eastbound on I-10. Mary-Esther pointed to an exit sign. "Turn off here."

Jerry followed her directions to a small public landing on Lake Pontchartrain, where he pulled over and parked.

She opened the door. "I won't be long."

"Want me to come with you?"

"No." Mary-Esther took a steadying breath. "I'd rather do this alone."

She walked to the water's edge. For a few minutes, she stood on the bank, staring out across the dark lake. The wind kicked up frothy white-caps. Mary-Esther unscrewed the lid from the brass urn and emptied the grainy contents into the lake.

"Hope you have a safe journey to wherever it is you're going, Loretta. Maybe you'll meet your real daughter. I wasn't always the best substitute."

Mary-Esther watched the powdery ashes and bits of ground bone swirl into the dark water until no evidence of Loretta Day remained.

That's all it amounted to, a handful of what was left of a person, then nothing.

Chapter Thirty-four

Hattie removed the slumping shells of carved pumpkins from the porch. Atop the bales of hay, she placed pots of mums and bound dried cornstalks. The colors of the surrounding woods were particularly vibrant this year, and she added culled branches from sweetgum and hickory trees. Might as well take advantage of the time since the baby was with Holston in the workshop.

Hattie didn't recall the original 1940s farmhouse, but stories wove through the family lore. The walls and floors had holes big enough for vermin to pass through, the porch listed to one side, and the roof had leaked in so many places, her mother would run out of catch pots if a summer thunderstorm lasted more than a few minutes. As money allowed, the old structure had been torn down in sections then rebuilt by her father and any hammer-handy friends who happened by. First, the country kitchen. Next, the expansive living room, master bedroom and bath. The last section of the original house fell to allow for two bedrooms, a second bath, and a sewing porch.

Hattie stepped inside and tried to look at the house through impartial eyes. The furniture, though clean and functional, wouldn't win for fashion. Books, baby toys, and magazines occupied most horizontal surfaces.

A few pieces had changed since Hattie inherited the home, but the essence of the farmhouse remained: a place welcoming family, friends, and wayward strangers. Homeless animals periodically appeared, dropped off beside the road by uncaring owners. Somehow, they found their way to The Hill to be taken in, fed, bathed, and routed to the local veterinarian.

No pedigrees necessary on The Hill.

Of the holidays, Hattie preferred Thanksgiving's slower pace. The focus fell to family gatherings and time-honored recipes. The kitchen brimmed with the blended aromas of cinnamon and spices. Dan and

Tillie Davis had been known for taking in stray people, especially during the holidays. Since moving back into the farmhouse, Hattie and Holston slipped easily into the role. Hattie couldn't recall a Thanksgiving with fewer than ten guests.

The phone rang. Intent on arranging foliage in a galvanized pail by the front door, Hattie jumped then snatched up the headset and spoke before the caller had a chance. "Really, Jake? Three times in less than two minutes? A record, even for you. I told you to ask Elvina. I don't know if she's bringing her sweet potato casserole."

A deep male voice said, "Hattie? It's Jerry Blount."

"Oops. Sorry. Jake's been driving me nuts about the dinner menu." She stopped. "Did you find my sister?"

"I have to make this quick. I'm on my way back . . . with Mary-Esther. She's in the ladies room right now. She doesn't know I'm calling."

"Did you tell her?"

"I haven't said anything. We're east of Pensacola and should be stopping by The Hill in a couple of hours. I'd rather she hear it from you."

Hattie bounced. "This is fan-freakin'-tastic! I'll call Bobby."

"Mary-Esther's been through a lot in the past few days. She's pretty wrung out. Perhaps it would be best for her to talk to you alone. The last time she tangled with your brother wasn't so easy on her."

"Well, okay. If you think—"

"Got to go."

Hattie heard the line disconnect and stared at the phone headset as if she expected it to either glow or burst into flames. She did a little dance and whooped so loud, Spackle howled in reply. Shammie opened one eye before settling back into a nap.

Elvina Houston stepped from the rear door of the Triple C Day Spa and Salon and bobbled down the slate walkway to the Piddie Longman Memorial Garden. A full sack of peanuts hung over her crooked arm.

The squirrels appeared as soon as she settled down on the bench with her cast-covered leg propped in front. She scattered a handful of the peanuts around her. The squirrels fanned out and chipped away at the papery hulls.

"A little gratitude would be nice," she said. "Fat chance."

She turned her attention to the dormant flower garden. A layer of fresh pine straw covered the turned dirt. After the final freeze of the late spring, Jake would plan the arrangement of bulbs. In the meantime, the spot mirrored nature's winter sleep. Elvina looked forward to spotting the first tentative spears of green peeking through the mulch.

"Morning, Piddie. I don't have a long time to talk today as I am needed in my legal capacity out at Hattie's. It must be good to see life from your perspective." She looked up. "You must know how things will turn out, so you don't have to fret like we do down here. I've worried myself into an absolute froth over this thing with Mary-Esther. How I longed to jump in my car and hunt for her myself. Would have too, if not for my bum leg."

She turned her attention to the squirrels, talking as much to them as to Piddie's spirit. "Hattie asked to have a little time with Mary-Esther before I came out. She wants to be the bearer of the good news. Then, I will swoop in and slap the frosting on the cake. I can't wait to see the look on that Louisiana gal's face!"

Elvina threw another handful of peanuts onto the ground and dusted her hands on her dress. "I miss you something fierce this time of year, Piddie, with Thanksgiving and then Christmas. 'Member how we used to hole up and bake until we were purely sick of it? Now, Jake is the one cooking up a storm in that little kitchen of yours. Shug's no slacker, either. I hear they might throw a party between Thanksgiving and Christmas."

Elvina laughed. "You ought to see all the stuff Shug has gathered for that yard. He's a fool for the holidays. I don't honestly know how he's going to wire it all without blowing up a power substation. All manner of light-up deer and trees. Big bubbles that look like snow globes. I heard he even bought a life-sized Grinch to sit on one of the porch rockers. Hattie'll get a kick out of that. She natural-born loves the Grinch.

"It's sad, how the other holidays get pushed around in favor of Christmas, though. Don't get me wrong. I love the hoopla, but I think most folks completely miss the reason behind it all. Seems it's a time to buy the most expensive gift you can get, even if you can't afford to pay the bills you have already. I plan to steer clear of Tallahassee until after the first of the year. Those people over there drive like sprayed cockroaches on a good day, much less with Christmas shopping on their minds.

"But here I am talking about Christmas and we've not even made it past Thanksgiving. Seems to melt together in my mind, like it's the same holiday. Time flies, Piddie. Like you said, life is like a roll of toilet paper. It spins faster and faster, the closer it gets to the end."

Crying shame squirrels couldn't laugh. That line of Piddie's was a good one. Elvina pitched the remainder of the peanuts onto the ground, then used the cane to steady herself as she stood.

"I'll have Jake bring some pots of those big pretty Poinsettias to sit here after we get past Thanksgiving. You loved the color red. Surely did. Can't plant them in the ground, on account of they don't cotton to freezing weather. We can move them inside when the temperatures drop. I'll be back later to share what all went on, out on The Hill."

She took one long look toward the heavens. "Don't you worry, Piddie. I pledged to watch over your kin, and I plan to do just that."

Mary-Esther opened her eyes and yawned. Boudreau, curled in her lap, stretched and watched her with droopy yellow eyes. "Why are we turning off here? I thought you wanted to swing by the airport in Tallahassee first and pick up your car."

Jerry turned left at the end of the interstate ramp and headed north toward Chattahoochee. "I need to make one stop."

Mary-Esther studied his profile. "Why do you have that stupid grin on your face?"

Jerry winked. "A fellow can't smile for no reason?"

That wink again. Every time he did that, her heart flip-flopped. "Liar." Mary-Esther play-punched his arm. "You don't fib well, by the way."

"I didn't fib. I promised to make a stop."

In a couple of miles, Jerry turned left onto Bonnie Lane.

"Oh, you're going by The Hill. What, to see if Bobby wants to take up where he left off? Maybe, hog-tie me and drag me behind his truck? Really, Jerry. Let's ride on into town. I'll rent a room for a couple of days then beg Mr. Bill for my job back."

Jerry didn't reply. When they pulled into the driveway in front of the farmhouse, Spackle bounded from the porch, sounding the doggie doorbell. The front door swung open and Hattie stepped outside.

He killed the engine. "Let's get out and stretch our legs. I have a couple of things to discuss with Holston. Maybe you and Hattie can find something to talk about for a few minutes."

"Don't know why this couldn't wait. But okay." She urged Boudreau into his cage with kitty treats and promises of upcoming freedom. Mary-Esther paused for a beat before opening the van door.

Jerry waved to Hattie then disappeared around the side of the house. Mary-Esther sniffed a set-up. For sure.

"Hey!" Hattie walked forward, her arms held up to hug Mary-Esther. She hesitated, lowered her arms, and stuck her hands in her jeans pockets. "How was your trip?"

"Long. Better with two people sharing the driving. Umm . . . may I use your bathroom?"

"Sure. Come on in. I have fresh coffee. We can catch up while the men talk."

Did every woman in this town have a constant pot brewing?

When Mary-Esther returned to the kitchen, Hattie had mugs, creamer and sugar, and two plates with thick slices of pound cake arranged on the table in front of the couch.

"So you don't think he tried to pull one over on you, I asked Jerry to bring you by here."

"Oh?" *Duh.* Mary-Esther helped herself to coffee. No cake.

"Don't be mad. I begged him to let me know *if* and *when* you were coming back."

"At least you don't want to string me up. Your brother certainly made his feelings clear."

"Bobby has some . . . issues. He wants to talk to you later."

Mary-Esther chewed on her bottom lip. "I'll look forward to *that.*"

"I'll get to the point, Mary-Esther." Hattie handed her an envelope. "The DNA test results arrived, right after you left town."

Mary-Esther held the letter in her hand.

"You can look at the printout for yourself, if you'd like." Hattie perched on the edge of the couch. She twirled her wedding band around and around until her finger blushed pink. "You *are* our middle sister. There's no doubt. Though, I felt all along that you were."

Mary-Esther opened the envelope and stared at the official document. A flush of warmth rose up from her middle. "Is it hot in here?"

Hattie smiled. "Not really. However, I'm not a good one to ask. I've started having midlife power surges."

"What do we do now?" Mary-Esther asked.

"Find a way to go from here, I suppose." Hattie reached over and touched Mary-Esther's hand. "I'm not expecting anything of you. Really."

Mary-Esther combed her fingers through her hair. "It's a lot . . ."

"Take all the time you want. I'm not sure how we can make this whole thing work, but I'm willing to try. So is Bobby, believe it or not." Hattie's lips drew into a thin line. "He told me about how he treated you.

And I know he's truly sorry. He's not such a bad guy. A little misdirected at times. Well, a *lot* misdirected."

Outside, Spackle sounded the doggie doorbell again.

"Busy out here," Mary-Esther commented. She sipped the strong coffee. A little caffeine might help the light-headed, out-of-body sensation.

Elvina Houston navigated through the front door.

"Look who's decided to come back home!" Elvina bent over and hugged Mary-Esther.

The day grew stranger by the second.

Elvina looked to Hattie. "Did you tell her anything?"

"Just about the DNA results. The rest, legally, is your department." Hattie swept her hand through the air as if introducing the next act.

"*Legally?*" Mary-Esther's gaze darted between the two women. "Don't tell me you hired a lawyer."

Elvina frowned. "Jumping to conclusions is unattractive. Calm yourself down."

"I have green tea, Elvina. May I fix you a cup?" Hattie offered.

"Yes. I can use all the antioxidants I can get, at my age." Elvina settled onto the couch and propped her cast foot on an ottoman. She turned her attention to Mary-Esther. "I'll not beat around the bush. Before Rose died, she had me drive her to visit an attorney. She was most upset by those horrid Watson people. She made a new will designating me as executor of her estate. And she put the house and her accounts under a trust, naming you as the trustee."

Mary-Esther's mouth dropped open.

"You are the sole heir of the Herring's house and land," Elvina stated, "as well as a small amount of money in the form of CDs. Rose was no investor, but Eustis was, apparently."

The walls closed in around her. Mary-Esther jumped up and tore from the house.

Chapter Thirty-five

Mary-Esther pulled into a space in front of Sewanee Springs Assisted Living. "The Fall Festival fairy has sure slammed this place."

Bales of hay leaned against the white entrance columns, topped with sprays of yellow, red, and orange silk leaves, gourds and pumpkins in assorted sizes, and a scarecrow wearing a plaid flannel shirt and ripped denim overalls.

When Mary-Esther stepped into the lobby, she noted that the same theme-oriented sprite had flitted inside. Like walking into a fall craft booth.

The now-familiar Southern belle at the front desk pushed a massive dried flower arrangement to one side with a slight frown. "May I help you?"

Two syllables in *help*: a true talent. "I'm meeting LaJune Stephens for lunch."

The receptionist pointed to a clipboard. "Sign in, please. The residents' dining room is to your left and down the hall to the end."

The woman watched Mary-Esther scribble her signature. "Aren't you the one from New Orleans?"

Would she ever hear the city's name without feeling her spirit droop? "Yes. Formerly."

"You poor dear. I spoke with my husband's cousin and his wife a few days back. They've given up on returning to Mississippi too. Nothing left of their house, bless their hearts, and no jobs to go back to. They've decided to settle near relatives. Griffin, Georgia. You know of it?"

"Don't believe so." Why did people believe she automatically knew every little pig-trail town because she lived below the Mason/Dixon line?

"Griffin is a lovely town not too far from Atlanta. Wouldn't give you a million dollars and my firstborn to live in Atlanta, but Griffin's a nice little place to make a home."

For some reason, the woman had become Mary-Esther's new best friend. Go figure. "I'm sure it is."

"How about you? Have you been back to New Orleans?" The city's name flowed from the receptionist's mouth with the mandated extra syllables.

"Got back a few days ago."

Miz Belle's painted eyebrows lifted. "Oh? And how did you find it? A few of us have been thinking of riding over to see the destruction. I've never been, myself. Not the kind of place *I* ever wanted to visit." One hand fluttered to her chest. "Slam full of wanton wickedness."

Just what the city needed: rubbernecking disaster-tourists. Mary-Esther glanced at the woman's gold nametag: *Patsy Pickles.*

"Well, Patsy . . ." Mary-Esther leaned over the front desk and lowered her voice. "It was a pure hotbed of iniquity. Behavior the likes I have never seen before. The newspapers don't tell the real story. No, they don't."

Patsy Pickle's horrified expression urged Mary-Esther on. She practiced her best deep-fried, Southern accent. "Even in your wildest imaginings, you could never fathom what all goes on! It will take years before it's anywhere near where an innocent person such as yourself might make it out alive." Mary-Esther flashed a grin. Nailed it; *alive* had at least three syllables. "You have a nice day, now."

She left Patsy Pickles sitting in stunned silence, probably trying her best to visualize the debauchery in Mary-Esther's home city.

"One less Disaster Debbie to worry about," Mary-Esther muttered under her breath.

The line-up of walkers along the walls—assisted living's version of valet parking—funneled her to the dining room entrance. She spotted a familiar smiling face across the room and wove through the tables toward LaJune.

"I usually dine with Martha Jean and Louise." LaJune motioned to a nearby table. "But they set us up special at this separate table. So glad you could come."

"Me too." Mary-Esther settled into an upholstered chair and scrolled utensils from her napkin.

LaJune handed her a printed slip of paper and a pencil. "These are today's lunch offerings. You circle what you want, and how big 'a portion. They come around with the drinks, then a cart of desserts later."

The old woman studied the menu. "Chicken 'n' dumplings." She glanced up. "They make some delicious dumplings. I'm here to testify.

The lima beans are fitting to eat. Or if you like ham, theirs is passable. Not dried out." She drew circles around her selections. "You can't go wrong here. The cooks make food the old-fashioned way."

Which meant, full of salt and fat, but oh so good. "I'll trust your recommendations, LaJune."

In a few minutes, an apron-clad server appeared with a glass of iced water for LaJune and took Mary-Esther's drink order.

"Tell me what you've been up to," LaJune prompted. She freed her utensils from their napkin corset.

"I had to take a trip back to New Orleans."

"Is that so? How did you find everything?" LaJune's questions sounded with genuine concern.

Mary-Esther pushed the mental image of Nana's devastated house from her mind. "Things are beginning to recover. Very slowly. My old neighborhood, pretty much, no longer exists."

"I am so sorry to hear that. I don't own my little house here in town anymore, but I take comfort in knowing it still stands." LaJune's expression grew wistful. "Houses are a lot like people. They need love and kindness, and they get lonely if they're left bereft."

The server deposited their lunch plates and Mary-Esther's tea. "Anything else for you?" She plunked down a stack of extra napkins.

"No, dear. We're fine. Thank you." LaJune flipped one napkin into her lap and fashioned a second into a bib.

Mary-Esther took a tentative bite of the dumplings. As long as she had lived in the South, she had not sampled the signature dish. "This is seriously good."

"You should've tasted mine. I was quite the cook in my day."

They ate in companionable silence before LaJune asked, "So, Mary Lou, did you work things out with your people?"

Mary-Esther caught herself before she corrected LaJune. What did a name matter, really? "There've been some interesting developments."

"I'd like to hear all the details, but could you wait until we have our coffee and dessert? I have a time chewing and listening at once."

Mary-Esther took in the old woman's attire. Must be one of LaJune's good days. Everything matched, her hair brushed and the clothing right side out. Advanced age had a way of causing some people to flicker like faulty light bulbs. One day, things clicked, memory served, and conversations flowed in a logical line. The next, you ended up discussing hothouse tomatoes.

As they finished, a second server pushed a silver, linen-draped cart next to their table. LaJune leaned over and inspected the double tier of saucers and bowls. "I'll have the egg custard."

"What's that one?" Mary-Esther pointed to a slice of cake.

"Chocolate Sin." The server held it up. "Some kind of torte, I think."

"I'll take it," Mary-Esther said. Any dessert made from chocolate, and with *sin* in the name, had to be worth every calorie.

"Bring us a couple of cups of decaf, if you please," LaJune said. Then, to Mary-Esther. "Forgive me for ordering for you, dear, but you're way too hyper for the high test coffee. And if you eat that mound of chocolate, you'll end up bouncing off the walls."

"Suppose you're right, but who cares?" She forked a piece of cake and slipped it into her mouth.

"Good choice?"

Mary-Esther moaned. "I may have to go to confession after this, it's so good."

"Confession. That's Catholic, right? Baptist myself, though I never quite understood the quibbling about how one church is better than the other. Seems we curtsy to the same boss. I always thought confession a fine idea, to be able to blather about what all you'd done wrong and get to say some stuff to ease you off the hook." LaJune flipped her hand. "We Baptists prefer to corral our guilt and wallow in it."

Mary-Esther laughed. "LaJune, you're a card."

Religion. Yet another difference between her and Hattie's group. What if they disliked Catholics? Not like she regularly attended mass since Nana died, but still . . .

LaJune winked and dabbed her mouth with the tip of one napkin-wrapped finger. "Tell me your story. Don't leave off anything. God knows, I could use the excitement."

For the next few minutes, Mary-Esther recounted the experiences of the past few days.

"So, you settled into the little house that lady left to you?" LaJune asked.

"Not yet. I moved back into the apartment over the garage."

"What are you waiting on?"

"I don't know." Mary-Esther took a sip of coffee. "I know Rose would be aggravated at me. She left me a letter."

LaJune leaned forward. "What'd it say?"

"That she and her husband thought of me as family. How she appreciated me bringing home food from the restaurant. And the times I cleaned and washed for them. How I *saved her* after Eustis died."

"Goodness is its own reward," LaJune said. "You did what you did with no thought of repayment."

"Some folks in Chattahoochee see it differently."

"There will always be people who look for something to gab about. Don't pay them a bit of mind. They'll move onto something new in no time flat." LaJune studied Mary-Esther. "Suppose that's the reason you've hesitated to move into that house?"

Mary-Esther considered. "Could be."

LaJune slapped the table. A few white-haired heads turned their way. "Then you *must* do it as soon as possible."

They savored their coffee in silence before LaJune asked, "What are you doing for Thanksgiving? I'll be at my niece Sheila's house. I know she'd be happy to set one more place at the table."

"Jerry invited me to come to his mother's house, but I don't think I'm ready for that. The Davis family wants me to join them out at Hattie's, at that big house on The Hill where my real mother and father used to live."

"Sounds fitting. You're planning on attending, I hope."

Mary-Esther polished off the last bite of chocolate torte and licked the fork. "I haven't decided."

Around them, residents vacated their assigned tables. Nap time. Bingo didn't start until two, Mary-Esther recalled.

"You beat all I've ever seen," LaJune said. "First time I met you, you were hot on the trail of your people. Now that you've found them, you've frosted up over spending time with 'em. How are you ever going to know if they are worth your while, if you don't make an effort?"

"My feelings are all mixed together. I like Hattie a lot, but Bobby . . . Who knows if we can get past our first impressions."

LaJune skewered Mary-Esther with her gaze. "You have plenty of time to sort them out, now that you're back to stay. You *are* back to stay . . . ?"

When Mary-Esther failed to reply, LaJune took a delicate spoonful of egg custard and chased it with a sip of coffee. "One of the best times to get a handle on people is during the holidays. Brings out the best and worst in folks. If I was you, I'd cook up my finest dish and show up with a smile pasted on my face."

Hattie worked with last-minute preparations. The good silverware appeared from its velvet-lined mahogany chest; the table linens were laundered, starched, and ironed; and the heirloom Limoges china and crystal had been hand-washed and dried.

Hattie wasn't certain Bobby shared the same appreciation for holiday decor. When her parents were alive, a special responsibility fell to the Davis children at Thanksgiving: the construction of the table centerpieces. Armed with a pair of scissors and a paper sack, Hattie and Bobby set out for the edge of the woods to collect branches from sweetgum, hickory, and dogwood trees, depending on which leaves had turned the deepest shades that year. They added pinecones in assorted sizes and sprigs of evergreen. Tillie supervised, but only to check for insects and to veto inappropriate items, such as the sun-dried skull of some small animal Bobby found appealing.

Some years, the weather proved mild enough to eat outside on the two long, pine picnic tables. Clean, pressed white bed sheets took the place of the fine linens, and the kitchen stoneware trumped the china and crystal.

Not this year. Hattie was determined to go full out, regardless of the temperature. Especially if her sister might show. She filled the Mr. and Mrs. Pilgrim salt and pepper shakers and set them on the table. No homemade woodsy sprigs this year. Hattie sort of missed that. Just as well. Nothing spoiled a formal dinner like a pine beetle stumbling across the lacework.

Jake Witherspoon carried one of two fall-themed low arrangements into the dining room. "I assume you will have multiple seating areas, Sister-girl?"

"Yep." Hattie wiped her hands on her mother's faded apron, an heirloom she used every day. "The big table will seat eight. There will be, let's see . . ." She pulled a quick mental tally. "Twelve of us, right? No, thirteen. Fourteen, *if* Mary-Esther comes."

"I'd think the poor woman's been a bit overwhelmed. Don't go getting yourself in a funk if she doesn't show, Sister-girl."

"I'm not, Jakey." *Liar, liar. Pants on fire.* Hattie crossed her fingers behind her back.

Jake set the floral arrangement down and dusted his hands on his pants. "I came out early on purpose. Put me to work."

Hattie walked to the stove and held up a spoon clotted with flour and turkey-drippings fat. "I could use help with the gravy. I got lumps."

By late-morning, most of the family boiled underfoot. Leigh provided several side dishes and gallon jugs of tea. Evelyn and Joe picked up Elvina and drove out from town, the trunk of the Lincoln Towncar weighted with food containers. Wanda and Pinky Green provided the rolls and a tossed green salad, and the neighbors walked up the lane carrying a coconut, layered cake and a pot of turnips. Shug bustled in with a red velvet cake and pecan and pumpkin pies. Holston's offerings, two deep-dish apple pies from his mother's recipe, cooled on the side table. Bobby appeared with a roasting pan heavy with the turkey and a pork roast he had prepared in a smoker.

In the oven, Parker house rolls browned. Hattie flitted between the kitchen and dining area with last-minute additions. Finally, everyone stood around the kitchen island, eyeing the food.

"It's high noon." Bobby tapped his watch. "Let's get this show on the road. I'm so hungry, my stomach is scratching my backbone."

Hattie glanced again from the front window.

"No use to keep checking." Bobby patted his sister on the back. "She's not coming."

Hattie's good humor crumbled, but she forced a smile. "You want to say the blessing, bro?"

They formed a circle and held hands for Bobby's Thanksgiving prayer—a hasty jumble of words tagged with an *amen* —then the group descended on the food table. Leigh and Hattie were the last to sit down after the children were strapped into their highchairs, with their plates and drop cloths.

One spot remained vacant. Hattie sighed. So much for wishful thinking.

Outside, the doggie doorbell rang. "Did you feed Spackle?" Hattie asked Holston. "He gets like this when he feels left out."

"Last time I saw him, he was lying on the front porch, contentedly chewing on the bone from the roast."

Hattie pushed away from the table. "I'll see what's up." She heard a rap at the kitchen door. When she opened it, Mary-Esther stood on the other side.

"Too late to crash the party?"

Hattie held the door open. "Absolutely not!"

"I would've been here on time, but I had a little trouble with the oyster dressing. I haven't made it in a while." Mary-Esther carried the baking dish inside and managed to find a clear spot on the island.

"Looks delicious! I'll have to make room on my plate."

214

"It's my Nana's recipe."

"Come on into the dining room after you grab a plate." Hattie's lips felt like they would split from grinning. "We saved a place at the big people's table for you."

"Never had dressing quite like that, Mary-Esther," Bobby commented after the meal. He handed her a cup of coffee and sat in the porch rocker next to hers.

"Glad you liked it. A little different from the cornbread style that's popular here."

"It's good for us to try different things." His gaze captured hers. "I'm glad to catch you alone. I want to apologize."

"Bobby, I—"

He stopped her with his upheld hand. "I'm not good at admitting when I've been a complete horse's ass. Just ask Hattie or my wife. Still, let me try."

In spite of his calm tone, Mary-Esther braced herself.

"First of all, I'm sorry for jumping you like I did. I had no right. Second, I owe you big."

"Oh?"

Bobby drank his coffee and rocked. "I've been pretty doggone pissed off for a long time. You've probably heard I used to hit the sauce . . . a lot. I quit drinking before I married Leigh, but there was always this thing waiting, ready to send me into a rage. Like I was possessed, or something, best way I can describe it."

Mary-Esther listened.

"After I found out you really were our sister, I got knee-walking drunk, stinking hammered. Ended up in the hospital."

"Hospital! What—?"

"A story I'm sure Hattie will tell on me, later. Important part is what came of it all. I remembered begging God for you—my baby sister—to die. Reckon I didn't want anyone stealing my thunder. When Sarah got sick and died, I knew it was my fault."

Mary-Esther's feelings thawed. A little. Weren't they all just hurt children wrapped in grown-up skin? "You couldn't have been that old, Bobby. Kids can have cruel thoughts."

"Leigh said the same thing, nearly word for word." He gave one short nod. "Suppose I stuffed that muck down all of these years. The guilt gnawed away at my insides. Small wonder I don't have a hole in my gut," he motioned over his shoulder, toward the house, "if you go by that mind and body connection crap Hattie carries on about."

A slight land breeze swept the aroma of evergreens across the porch. Mary-Esther took a deep breath. Not the scent of Louisiana, but growing on her.

"Hattie told me about what happened to the baby. You aren't responsible for Sarah's death." Any more than she was responsible for Loretta's death.

"I know that. Now." The corner of his lips lifted. "Better, I really believe it. The miracle in all of this, other than you being here: I don't feel pissed off anymore. It vanished."

"Brought to the surface."

"Exactly. And I owe it all to you."

"By my being alive, you mean?" Mary-Esther said.

"That and it forcing me to shake my demons loose, once and for all."

"All of us have things in our pasts, Bobby. Things we'd rather not claim." God knows, she had a boatload. And he surely wasn't the only one who'd turned more than once to alcohol.

"True enough." He rocked back and forth. "Hope you'll give me a second chance. I may not be the brother you bargained for. Shoot, Hattie had to put up with the worst I could dish out for years, and she still speaks to me."

Could she ever forget those horrible accusations he had flung at her, not that long ago? No. They would stay with her, the way harsh words do. Trust might come, in time.

Bobby turned to face her. "I'd like to get to know my other sister, if she'll have me." Spackle barreled onto the porch, licked Bobby's hand, then sniffed Mary-Esther's and shared a little slobber with her too.

Mary-Esther patted the dog's muzzle. Animals were easy.

Chapter Thirty-six

"**Wowsa.** Two days past Thanksgiving, and Christmas has shoved fall to the curb." Hattie stood next to Jon *Shug* Presley, regarding the front porch of Aunt Piddie's house.

Lighted wreathes swathed in red ribbon hung from the center of the two front windows, with a third smaller wreath centered on the door. The ivy-printed rocking chair cushions had been replaced with candy-cane striped pillows. Two animated standing figurines—Santa and his equally rotund wife—stood to one side of the door, their arms holding flickering electric candles.

Hattie looked toward the yard. A life-sized nativity scene dominated the lawn, nestled amongst a forest of white, illuminated Christmas trees. The trunks of the pines dotting the side yard wore blue lights, and white lights intertwined the moats of dormant azalea bushes. Glowing four-foot candy canes stuck from the ground at intervals. The crowning electrical exhibit occupied the driveway in front of Hattie's car: three inflated globes, each containing a different snow-littered scene.

Jake pushed through the front door with two cups of coffee and handed one to Shug and one to Hattie. The life-sized Grinch seated in one rocker regarded the three of them with a curly, evil grin. How she loved the Grinch. Hattie made a mental note: check the TV listings. They always showed *How the Grinch Stole Christmas* early in December. Heaven help she missed it. Only seen it every year of her life.

"I don't know," Shug muttered. "It still needs *some*thing."

"I can't imagine what," Jake said. "It's reached critical mass. If you add any more lights, the electric meter is going to spin off into space."

"I can't be finished," Shug fired back. "I still have three boxes of decorations left."

Hattie laughed. Nothing could compare to Jake and his partner at war over holiday décor.

Jake considered. "I know exactly where to take the excess. It will be our contribution to world peace, not to mention *my* peace."

For the first time since Elvina had handed over the keys, Mary-Esther entered the Herring house. Boudreau trailed behind her. The house still carried the scent from its former owner, a blend of rose water cologne, plug-in air fresheners, and the underlying aroma common to many older houses. She walked from room to room, surveying the furnishings. Could she really live here?

The front doorbell rang. When she opened the door, Jake Witherspoon greeted her, a furry Santa cap plopped at a jaunty angle atop his head. In one arm, he held a red plastic box. The other clutched his holiday walking cane—crimson and white striped, with jingle bells tied at the top.

"Ho, ho, hum!" he chortled. "Going to invite me in? This box is getting heavy."

She stepped aside. "Sure." Boudreau jumped onto the sofa arm and watched.

Jake set the box down on an end table, gave the cat a pat. "I see you haven't changed anything since you moved in."

"Actually, I've been coming over here only to use the kitchen. I'm still staying in the apartment."

"Heavens why, when you have such a lovely old house to call home?" He propped one arm on his hip.

Mary-Esther shoved her hands in her jeans pockets. "I don't know, Jake. It seems like . . . it still reminds me of the Herrings, especially Rose."

"Mind if I look around?" Jake asked.

"Be my guest."

With Boudreau leading the way, Jake strolled through the rooms. She heard him mumbling aloud to the cat and Boudreau's yowled replies. The bells on Jake's cane jingled with each step. Finally, he joined Mary-Esther in the kitchen. Boudreau settled back on his haunches and regarded both of them with round yellow eyes. Jake reached down and ruffled the hair around the cat's ears. "Put on a fresh pot of coffee, will you?"

Was this how a friendship started? Mary-Esther's heart warmed. He certainly had won over her cat.

"Love that old print on the mantle," Jake said. "Your family in Louisiana?"

218

"My Nana Boudreau, the woman who's holding the baby version of me. She mostly raised me." Mary-Esther dumped out a measure of roasted coffee beans, then waited to continue after the noisy grinder stopped. "The other woman was Loretta, my mother."

"I see." Jake waited her out. A good listener, obviously. Probably why Hattie and Jake were such longtime pals.

"It's the only picture I could salvage." She breathed out. "I hate the ratty frame, but I'm leery of messing with it. The whole thing might disintegrate."

"One of my friends in Tallahassee restores old photos. Could have him take a look-see. You'd be amazed how a fresh frame and glass can improve the image."

The connections between people defied her. Sure, she'd known lots of people in New Orleans, but the crowd she ran with wasn't dependable for ordinary needs.

"Now, down to business." Jake rummaged through the mandatory kitchen junk drawer and located a piece of paper and pencil. "What would you say is your decorating style?"

"Can't believe you're asking that of someone who's lived in the back of a van for over a year." Boudreau yowled. First thing she'd have to move here: his treat container.

Jake slipped a hand into one pocket, then held out his palm. "Mind?" She shook her head. Jake handed a kitty morsel down to the cat. Boudreau sniffed then dug in. Wow. A true animal person. Probably had a dog biscuit in the other pocket.

"Now, back to decorating this place. Due to your past meager accommodations, you'll be easy to please." He sniffed. "Gosh, that sounded uppity. Let me rephrase. Do you prefer modern or something with an antique feel?"

Mary-Esther started a short pot of coffee, then found two mugs and set them on the counter. "Never thought about it, really. I like oak. Old pieces with some scrollwork . . . like that." She pointed to the buffet behind the kitchen table. "And there are several others I adore. That old secretary desk in the guest bedroom. The curio in the living room."

"You could mix things up. Update a few things, add color to the walls—"

"Redecorating takes moolah, Jake. I have a little bit of what Rose left, but not the kind of money it would take for a complete overhaul."

"Won't be that much, when you do a bit at a time. I redid Hattie's house for next to nothing. We kept many of her parents' things and mixed in stuff Hattie liked. When she married Holston, I helped her add in his belongings. It's all about blending the old and new. The idea is to make it individual."

"Are you offering free assistance?"

When Jake grinned, the freckles across his cheeks crowded together. "I *live* for stuff like this, Mary-Esther."

"Does this mean you've given up on the notion I'm a carpetbagger come to plunder the Davis family fortune?"

Jake puffed up his chest. "I will be just as protective of you, Mary-Esther."

She poured two cups of coffee. "I'll take that as a *yes*."

"Cream. One sugar, please."

"Sugar, I have." Mary-Esther set a china container in front of him. She opened the refrigerator. "No such luck on the creamer."

"I'll make do."

Mary-Esther slid the mug and a spoon in front of Jake. "So, I acquire a friend by right of verified blood ties?"

Jake sipped, nodded his appreciation. "Uh-hmm."

"And a decorator to boot. What a deal."

Boudreau hopped into a vacant chair and watched.

Jake's head did a little swishy dance. "You could do worse."

Mary-Esther motioned in the direction of the front room. "What's in that box you lugged in?"

"My contribution to your happy holiday. There are three more in the truck. If you take these off my hands, I will be your friend forever. And I am *very* loyal."

"Depends on what's in them."

"Ten, or thirty, strands of lights, festive trinkets to adorn every nook and cranny, three wreaths, four angels—fully electrified—and a couple of stuffed Santas. Knock yourself out."

"Thanks, I don't have any decorations yet. Figured I'd hit the Dollar Store for anything I could buy for a few bucks."

"I could help fling them around. Or I could send Shug over." He paused, tapped on his chin with one finger. "On second thought, I'll spare you. Shug is *deathly* infected with holiday spirit."

Mary-Esther laughed. No wonder Hattie liked this man. If he was a friend by default, she would gladly accept. "As to the house makeover, I welcome any suggestions, Jake. I have a little spare cash—emphasis on *little*."

Jake clapped his hands together. Boudreau trilled. "Fantastic! Let's start right away. You'll be simply flabbergasted at what a coat of fresh paint will do. Rose had wonderful taste. Some of these things are worth a pretty penny." He flicked his fingers. "We can move things around, pitch the clutter, and it'll feel like yours in a flash." He motioned to a battered cardboard box sitting on the kitchen table. "What's up with the rocks?"

Mary-Esther picked up a hunk of quartz the size of her palm. "I've collected these for years." She flipped the rock over. "Used a marker to put the date on one side." She put down the quartz, selected a piece of sandstone. "Don't know why they fascinate me so much, but I've picked up one from each place I stayed for longer than a couple of days."

"Must run in the family. Hattie has rocks too. I corralled them into the clear glass base of a lamp when I helped her redo the living room. Miz Tillie had a few. Added those to Hattie's stash." Jake tapped his chin. "Don't think Bobby does the rock thing. He prefers mounted fish and deer heads."

The sandstone warmed in Mary-Esther's hand, collecting body heat. Why *had* she carted them from one place to the next? Something about their weight reassured her. As long as she had them, she couldn't spin off into nowhere.

"Can we find a good place for them?" she asked.

Jake picked up one stone, then the next. "I envision these displayed on a series of glass shelves across your kitchen window. They'll add a certain natural element to the room. We can pick up some of the colors, to use as accents around the house."

"I like it! Sure you have time for me? This has to be a crazy time of year for you."

"Jolene practically runs the shop. Shug is gone a lot with his hospice work. I'll welcome the diversion. Otherwise, you doom me to sitting alone in a house full of so many nauseatingly merry decorations, I'll need a bottle full of sedatives to survive."

They laughed. "For certain," Mary-Esther said. "We must find a spot for Rose's dolls. They're still packed up in one corner of the apartment."

"I'm sure I can talk your brother into building some display cases, if you'd like. Bobby does woodworking and he's quite good. When he's not being a donkey butt."

Mary-Esther threw up her hands. "It's like, no matter what you need, there's someone around who does it." It had become a bit easier to think of Hattie as a sister. Not so easy to plug Bobby into the role of helpful brother just yet.

"Networking, Big Sister-girl. Networking." He giggled. "When do you want to start? You off today?"

"Yes. I pulled double-time around Thanksgiving to cover for a couple of the other servers. That's why I was over here, trying to get a handle on things."

Jake picked up the pencil and slid the pad into place. "Big Sister-Girl, I am at your service."

Holston leaned against the extension ladder with a string of lights while Hattie tied fresh bows on the wreaths. When she lifted the first one into position on the front door, a stab of pain radiated through her shoulder and down her arm.

"Crapola!"

Holston glanced down. "You okay?"

"You know the old saying about someone being about as useful as a one-armed paper hanger?" She massaged her shoulder. "Well, I'm there. About the time I think my shoulder's well, I move wrong and it reminds me it's not."

"Don't sweat it. I'll hang the wreaths as soon as I finish this. Why don't you drape lights across the hedges? You won't have to reach up."

"I suppose." Hattie chided herself for the harsh tone. Cranky-pants attitude would bump her from Santa's Good Girl List.

Sarah Chuntian toddled around the front yard with Spackle trailing her like an overprotective nanny. Each time the child veered too close to the edge of the grass by the driveway, the dog nipped the butt of her trousers and dragged her gently back.

"Spackle, you are such a good boy," Hattie said. "Santa Paws will leave a bunch of treats in your stocking."

Shammie reclined in the front window ledge, observing with aloof interest. The activity was bound to be more entertaining than watching lizards scuttle through the boxwoods. The holiday must be a feline's wonderland, Hattie thought. Every year, an evergreen filled with dangly stuff appeared in the house and was left unattended for many hours. Boxes with crinkly paper and curly ribbons would stand on the floor beneath the scented branches. Maniac-Cat heaven.

Hattie heard the rumble of Bobby's pick-up when it turned from the main highway. He parked in the lane, far from Sarah and her four-legged bodyguard.

"Hey-ho, neighbors," Bobby called. The truck's door hinges complained when he stepped out. "We have a surprise for you." Leigh and Tank popped out from their side.

Hattie dropped the convoluted mass of wires, grateful for the interruption. "Hope it's some kind of miracle invention to help me unscramble these dang lights."

"No such luck, Sis. That's Santa's test of your character. You can snuff a whole year of good behavior in a few minutes, if you don't maintain your cool." Bobby pointed up. "He's watching you, you know."

"I stopped falling for that ploy when I was ten." *Maybe.* Hattie propped her hands on her hips, but still held two fingers crossed to counter the lie. "What's your big surprise?"

"Two surprises, actually. I brought y'all a nice Fraser fir. We were over in Quincy and they had just hauled them in. Tall, with perfect shapes. Got one for our house and one for y'all."

"Think they'll last until Christmas?" Holston climbed down the ladder.

"Oh, for sure. Fraser firs are great. They cut these weeks ago. We'll crop a couple of inches off the bottoms and stick the trunks in some buckets of water outside. As long as a tree has plenty to drink, it'll last for weeks. We probably won't put ours up until next weekend."

"Thanks. Considerate of you." Hattie narrowed her eyes. "What do you want?"

Bobby lunged for his sister and lifted her from the ground in a twirling hug. "I don't want one dadgum thing. I'm like the Grinch. Now that my heart is not so small, I'm filled to the brim with Christmas spirit."

When he set her down, Hattie grabbed her stomach. "I feel a bit nauseated."

"Get used to it. It's the new me." Bobby spread his arms wide. "Speaking of feeling a little nauseated . . ." He lifted one eyebrow and tilted his head toward his wife. "Leigh can tell you about the second surprise."

Leigh held up one hand, palm up. "Nice segue, Bobby."

Tank chased Spackle in a circle. The dog urged the boy on, stopping to bark playfully, but always a step ahead. Sarah stood and watched, clapping her chubby hands.

Hattie looked from her brother to her sister-in-law. "So, what's up?"

"Your brother is going to get his Christmas wish." Leigh slipped her arm around her husband's waist.

Hattie jabbed Bobby in the side. "What? A truck that runs without spitting smoke and waking half the county?"

"Nothing wrong with my pick-up. The old gal has character."

Leigh touched her belly, then her hand hovered protectively to a spot slightly below her waist. "We have another Davis on the way."

"Ohmygah!" Hattie squealed and hugged her sister-in-law. "That's fan-freakin'-tastic!"

Holston shook Bobby's hand, then joined them in a back-slapping group hug. Sensing the adults' excitement, both toddlers ran full-tilt and body-slammed their huddle at knee level. At times like this, Hattie imagined their parents looking down, sharing the wonder.

The trick was, figuring a way to ease Mary-Esther into the picture.

Chapter Thirty-seven

Mary-Esther spied LaJune after she pushed through the doors to the Sewanee Springs lobby. The old woman's face brightened.

Great gobs of fake greenery sparkled with miniature white lights, and oversized glass ornaments draped over the entrance and most of the inside passageway doors. A seven-foot, live Fraser fir stood in one corner of the lobby, filled with lights, wide strips of wired ribbon, and red and gold glass balls. Animated figures waved and danced on every table, and the scent of coffee, mulled cider, and hot chocolate competed with evergreen air fresheners.

"Look who's here!" LaJune pulled herself upright, using the walker for support. "Hoped you might make it by before Christmas. I have a little something for you in my room."

Mary-Esther held up a beribboned gift bag. "Looks like Santa came a bit early for you too."

She followed the old woman down the hallway, where LaJune used the key hanging from a long chain around her neck to open a door. "You've never been to my private space, have you?"

"Nope. First time."

"It's a mess. Please excuse it. I just spread up my bed quickly this morning."

The room appeared larger than the resident's quarters in most of the facilities Mary-Esther had seen. A queen-sized bed centered on one wall held a homemade quilt in shades of green and blue. An upholstered rocker stood beside the bed, an antique-styled pole lamp behind it. Two long chests of drawers opposite the bed provided the platform for a small television and a multitude of family photos. Framed pictures lined the walls, some faded with age.

"Is this your husband?" Mary-Esther pointed to one sepia photograph.

"That's my Robert. He had a full head of hair when we were first married." The old woman's sweet expression touched Mary-Esther. How would it feel to have loved someone for so many years?

Mary-Esther leaned closer to study the petite female in the picture. "And this is you!"

"I was quite a looker, back in the day." LaJune rested her chin on her cupped hands.

Mary-Esther compared the image with her friend. "You still are."

"Do we have to wait until Christmas to open our gifts?" LaJune's gaze locked onto the package in Mary-Esther's hands.

"No rule says we do. I'd like for you to enjoy this now, and I probably won't see you until after the holidays, with work and all."

The senior raised her hands and wiggled. "Oh, goodie!" LaJune walked to the chest of drawers and pulled out a manila envelope. "I didn't have a way to wrap it. Not much. Something I made for you in art class."

"I made yours too." Mary-Esther handed over the gift bag.

LaJune settled into the rocker and centered the present in her lap. "You go first."

Inside the envelope, Mary-Esther found a piece of heavy art paper painted with two penguins standing close together in the snow. At one corner, the words *with love from your friend LaJune* were scripted in shaky block letters.

"You did this?"

"I'm not an artist, but I believe it turned out passable."

Mary-Esther hugged it to her chest. "I love it! I'm going to frame it and put it in my kitchen so it's the first thing I see every morning."

LaJune beamed. "Let's see what I've got." She tore into the mounds of tissue paper like a delighted child and pulled out a large plastic zippered storage bag. "You made me chocolate cookies!"

"Not just *any* chocolate cookies, LaJune. Those are my famous double chocolate mocha chip cookies."

The old woman clutched the plastic bag. "I'll not be sharing these, mind you. If I don't get too carried away and eat them all at once, they might last me a good while."

"I can make you more, now that I have a decent stove."

LaJune slid the wrapped cookies back into the gift bag and tucked it beside her chair. "You've moved into your little house, then?"

"Not totally. But I hope to, by the first of the year. There's a lot of cleaning out to do, and I'm doing some painting and refreshing."

"Making a nest. Good for you."

"What are you doing for Christmas? I could come pick you up."

LaJune's smile transformed her face. The wrinkles shifted to joy crinkles and the sagging skin disappeared. "Mighty sweet of you, dear. I'll be at Sheila's. I won't spend the night. I'd much rather be back here in my own bed by dark, but I'll be over at her house for Christmas Eve and Day. What about you?"

"I've been invited out to The Hill with Hattie and Bobby."

"You're getting used to your family, as it should be." When Mary-Esther didn't reply, LaJune said, "I don't like the shade of that look. What's the matter?"

"I don't know, LaJune. I can't quite put my finger on it, but I feel so . . . out of place."

"Only natural, with what all you've been through. Life is wacky. We'll go along a particular way for so long that we know it's the only way to be. Then, bang and whoop-de-doo, things shift and we're in a different life altogether."

The old woman pointed to one of the black and white photos, a young version of her and her husband posing by a white house with a wrap-around porch. "I stayed in my home for over sixty-three years. Lived with a man I loved dearly, but sometimes wanted to choke senseless. Then, in the blink of an eye, he was gone and I was alone. Had to get used to that new life. Then, I started to *fall and forget*—the two old age foibles—and ended up here. I went from taking care of myself and a five-room house to this, one room and a bathroom I can barely turn around in without running into myself." LaJune swished her hands through the air to take in her space. "Some mornings, I still wake up and wonder where I am."

LaJune wagged her finger toward Mary-Esther. "What I learned is this: you only have right now. The past—all those memories of fun and love and hardship—makes you what you are. But you can't go back and crawl into your old skin. It won't fit."

"How did you get so wise?"

LaJune chuckled. "When you get past seventy or so, life stacks up."

The old woman leaned forward. "I'm not one to tell a person what she ought to do, but I'm going to make an exception. Mary Eve, you think long and hard before you go pushing those folks aside. You and I haven't been acquainted 'cept for a few months, though I feel we've known each other for a long, long time, somehow . . .

"I see folks here who don't have anyone, or the people who *should* care about them don't. They would give anything to have family come around." LaJune paused and looked up toward the left. "What was the old saying about feeling out of place? Ah yes. 'It's like being a fly in the ointment.' You ever hear that one?"

Mary-Esther shrugged. "Maybe, but I don't know what it means."

"Folks used to make medicines—back in the day before all this modern hoo-hah—tinctures and plasters and creams for any ailment. You'd be going along okay, being so careful about stirring and adding herbs and such, and a fly would settle into your mixture, making it seem like it had spoiled the whole batch you'd worked so hard to make."

Mary-Esther nestled into a chair. The moral to LaJune's stories often took a couple of detours. At least they weren't discussing tomatoes today.

"In reality, that fly didn't spoil a dang thing," LaJune said. "Just made it different. Maybe had no impact to amount to much, except to be a little unsettling."

The senior took a deep breath and continued, "Just because you came along and stirred things up in your family, don't feel like you're the fly that fell into their ointment."

Chapter Thirty-eight

Mary-Esther passed through the threshold of the Davis farmhouse. Cooking aromas filled her nose: the scent of warm sugar and vanilla, the tinge of stewing tomatoes, and the yeasty smell of fresh bread. She paused, slammed by an intense wave of bittersweet longing.

Jerry stepped in behind her, carrying the pot of her gumbo. "Don't stall in front of me, woman. These pot-holders aren't that thick!"

She mentally shook herself and stepped aside. "Sorry."

Hattie appeared, wearing a Mrs. Santa apron wrapped over a crimson T-shirt and jeans. Topping off the outfit, a furry camo-printed Santa hat. "Set it down on the stove, Jerry. I'll turn the element on low to keep it warm."

Hattie hugged her sister, then drew back. "You okay? You look a little pale."

"Fine." Mary-Esther took a shaky breath. "I'm fine." The farmhouse enveloped her like a long-lost lover home from the Great War. The feeling wasn't totally unwelcome. The sound of a piano and laughter came from another room.

Hattie waved them into the kitchen. "We're waiting on Jake and Shug. Everyone else is here. Y'all want something to drink?"

"Lite beer, if you've got one," Jerry answered. He carried the heavy stockpot to the stove.

"Maybe, a glass of red wine?" Mary-Esther shucked her raincoat. A soggy warm front had pushed aside the recent cold spell. While other parts of the country enjoyed a white Christmas, the South experienced a steady, pissy drizzle.

"Isn't this weather something? One true thing about this part of the South," Hattie said, "if you don't like the weather, wait a few hours. By morning, as much as four inches of rain could fall across the Florida Panhandle."

Bobby walked into the kitchen. "Don't mind her, Mary-Esther. She watches the Weather Channel too much. Hattie has the hots for that one dude who always shows up when there's a hurricane bearing down. What's his name—"

"Rick Santorum?" Hattie's left eyebrow shot up.

Bobby looked from Hattie to Mary-Esther. "Rest my case." He lifted the lids of the simmering pots, one by one. "Dadgum, this all smells so good."

Hattie rapped her brother's knuckles with a wooden spoon. "Quit huffing the soup."

"Hattie, I surely appreciate being included on the invitation," Jerry commented. "Beats a heavy meal. I'll have one of those at Mama's tomorrow. Seems like all I've done since Thanksgiving is eat, eat, eat."

"Glad you could come, Jerry." Hattie patted him on the arm.

"The Annual Davis Soup Competition has been going on for years," Bobby said. "Wouldn't seem like Christmas without it."

"Competition?" Mary-Esther glanced from Bobby to Hattie.

"My mom . . . *our* mom . . . came up with this as a way for us to get together on Christmas Eve without anyone slaving over a stove for hours," Hattie said. "Everyone makes some kind of soup or stew, and the hostess provides the bread and beverages. We've had as many as six or seven pots here at once. We turned it into a contest, a few years back. We vote by secret ballot after we eat to determine who wins the Soup-Wiz title for the year."

"Hattie makes this wicked-good cheesy potato soup," Bobby said. "It kept winning, so we had to switch up the rules. Now the winner can bring the same kind of soup back the next year, but not to contend for the title."

"I can still beat you all, hands down." Hattie turned her attention back to Mary-Esther. "You'll probably smoke us this year with your gumbo. Everyone who's eaten it knows how wonderful it is."

Mary-Esther offered a slight smile and nod. "Thanks. It was my Nana's recipe. I really can't take credit."

"Sure you can," Bobby said. "Hattie takes credit for Mama's old recipes."

Hattie wagged the spoon in her brother's direction. "And you pilfer recipes off the Internet and swear on a stack of Bibles you made them up, right off the top of your pointy little balding head."

Bobby sniffed. "I merely use those as a guide, my dear sister. I add secret ingredients to enhance the flavor."

"Sticks his finger in it, more than likely," Hattie fired back, with a wink toward Mary-Esther.

Was this how it went between siblings, this friendly childlike banter?

Elvina stood at the threshold of the kitchen. "Did Leigh fix her widow-maker chili?"

"Tradition calls for it," Bobby answered. "Christmas Eve wouldn't be complete without the wild fits of cover-flapping at my house when the beans take effect later on."

Hattie winced. "Thanks for sharing *that*."

"Hey, Elvina. No cast!" Mary-Esther motioned when the old woman stepped into the kitchen.

Elvina's gaze dropped to her legs. "I wondered *if* and *when* someone would notice. Been here going on half an hour and nobody has so much as commented on it."

"Does it still hurt?" Hattie said.

Elvina dismissed the question with a wave. "It swells a bit if I don't remember to prop it up every now and then. I am proud to trade that cast for this boot. I can assure you."

Hattie stirred the contents of the stockpots and lowered the heat settings. "I can't believe Jake isn't here yet. Actually, I *can* believe it."

"Joe wants you to give his tortilla soup a stir, Hattie," Evelyn yelled from the next room.

"Keeping an eye on it," Hattie called back. "Despite what my loving brother says," she gave Bobby the slit-eye, then directed attention to Mary-Esther, "I won't sabotage anyone's entry."

Leigh popped her head around the threshold. "Y'all come on into the living room. Tank really wants to sing Christmas carols."

"For that, I need a glass of wine," Mary-Esther said. "Makes me sing better, or at least I don't care."

Holston stepped into the kitchen carrying Sarah, who was resplendent in a red and green nightgown. "This little one's getting pretty sleepy. How about her little cousin?"

"Tank's still going full tilt," Leigh said. "I doubt he'll wind down for at least another hour. I have a pallet of quilts on the floor next to the tree if you want to lay her down."

Holston delivered a quick kiss to his wife as he carried the child through the kitchen. Mary-Esther hung back from the conversation, absorbing the easy banter of people who clearly cared for each other.

Had she ever experienced this? Nana would talk to her while she cooked. They might discuss a few things about what she did at school, but it wasn't a guarantee every day. The business of living got in the way of idle chit-chat. Certainly, Loretta never made the effort. When her mother talked, it was to scold Mary-Esther for some real or imagined infraction.

Not until certain death loomed over her left shoulder did Loretta Boudreau begin to open up, as if a cork had popped off and a lifetime spewed out. A lot. Too late. But at least Mary-Esther had something she could hang onto. She took a gulp of wine.

Mary-Esther surveyed the country kitchen, noting more details than she had before. Nothing fancy, but welcoming. Plain oak cabinets. Over-hanging pot rack. Lines of Fiestaware dishes in a rainbow row.

In the living room, Leigh played "Jingle Bells" for the fifth time. No problem. That was generic. Did this family sing certain Baptist hymns? Surely, the Catholics shared that part of the season in the same way, though the only tune she thought about immediately was *Ava Maria*. And she didn't know the words to that.

The wine made the edges of her vision fuzzy. How had it been when Tillie Davis ruled this room? Did she kid with her children? With every smile and gesture, did she tell them they were her most precious posses-sions, that Christmas meant family to her? Did Hattie and Bobby learn to cook by her side, tasting and stirring? The questions rose and popped in her head like champagne bubbles.

Hattie's voice broke her reverie. "Mary-Esther? Earth to Mary-Esther?"

Mary-Esther jerked. "Oh . . . what?"

"I wanted to know if you like eggnog. I make the real deal from fresh eggs. Then, I kick it up a little with the *nog*, whiskey. Old family recipe, for the adults after the kiddies trip off to dream of sugar plums."

"You *drink* raw eggs?" Funny question since she sucked the heads of boiled crawfish. And once, in Vegas with Ricky, she'd slurped down the Tequila worm.

Hattie washed her hands and dried them on a snowman-printed tow-el. "Been doing it for years. Hasn't killed us yet. Mama said the whiskey drowns any harmful bugs."

"Living dangerously takes on a new meaning," Jerry commented. "Think I'll stick to beer."

"You really think I would slaughter my guests, not to mention my only sister?" Hattie said. "No confidence in me. No confidence at all."

The yap of a small dog stopped the conversation, and they all turned toward the door. Jake Witherspoon, dapper in a red cashmere sweater, stepped inside and put Shug's Pomeranian on the floor. The little blonde fur ball twirled around in circles before dashing into the forest of human legs. Spackle pushed through the door in the Pom's wake.

"Festive little outfit, Elvis." Hattie leaned down to accept a few hand-kisses. She reached into a ceramic hound jar and handed out two treats. The dogs gobbled them down, then dashed from the room in search of more humans to enchant. "Feel kind of bad for Spackle. All he has is a strip of red and green cloth I made into a bandana."

"I thought the sequins a bit overdone," Shug said. He slid a cake carrier onto the island. "Evelyn designed it. She deserves all the glory."

"Elvis has a new chenille lounge jacket that is absolutely sweet," Jake added.

"That dog dresses better than I do," Hattie said.

"Sister-girl, not hard since your idea of high fashion is a sweatshirt, or in tonight's case, a shirt with, I'm sure, some quippy holiday saying plastered across the front." He stood back and eyed her. "And where ever did you find that attractive Santa's spare-outfit apron and Billy-Bob cap?"

"For you, I'll whip up some special salmonella eggnog. And my T-shirt is this year's official Grinch print, so there." Hattie boxed her life-long friend on the arm. She held out one hand. "This, from the man with a spiffy new cane that looks like Rudolph the Red-nosed Reindeer on crack."

Evelyn breezed into the kitchen amid the laughter. "Good! We're all here." She motioned over her shoulder. "Doesn't Elvis look smart in his little doggie ELF-wear outfit?"

"You've hit your stride, Ev." Jake unloaded a six-pack of soft drinks into the refrigerator.

"I'm planning a complete pet-lovers' line, and not just for the holidays either. Bandanas, little rainwear. The possibilities are limitless." Evelyn's hands flitted with her words.

Shug nodded. "You'll probably make as much—if not more—than you do on people clothing, Evelyn. Folks go hog wild on their animals. Excuse the obvious pig reference."

Evelyn agreed. "I wish cats would lend themselves to accessories. They positively resist any effort on that behalf." She eyed Shammie. As if the cat understood her intentions, he perked his ears and stared.

Joe Fletcher stepped up behind his wife and hugged her around the waist. He nodded greeting to the rest of the group. "If there's a way to do it, I'm sure you'll figure it out, hon." Mary-Esther noticed his appreciative glance at the stove filled with stew and soup pots. Probably thrilled his wife was so involved in sewing, even if it was for dogs.

Hattie pulled a cookie sheet filled with rolls from the oven. "Proof, once more, of the mental superiority of felines. If you tried to get Shammie into an outfit, you'd more than likely end up in the E.R." She tonged the hot rolls into a bread warmer and covered it with a linen cloth.

"Speaking of cats, how's Boudreau adapting to the new digs?" Jake directed toward Mary-Esther. Then, to the group, "We've been redoing the Herring house."

"My cat is a lot like me. He can live most anywhere."

They gathered at the long wooden kitchen table for the informal meal. Conversation flowed. People scribbled notes on score cards. Tank and Sarah wore most of their soup, but some made it inside. When the watery dregs of five kinds of soup rested in their empty bowls, Bobby tallied the results.

Bobby bowed to Mary-Esther. "Congrats to our new Soup-Wiz champion. Your gumbo takes this year's title! Don't pay any attention to Hattie. She pouts."

"Not true, Bobby Davis. I'm an extremely gracious loser!" Hattie balled up her napkin and pitched it in his direction.

"I thought your soup was excellent, Hattie," Mary-Esther said.

"Last year, when Joe's catfish chowder took top honors, she went into mourning for a week," Holston said.

Hattie slapped her hands on the edge of the table. "I did no such thing!"

Leigh laughed. "Fess up, Hattie. You gained five pounds eating every piece of chocolate in sight. If that's not depression—"

"Okay. I'll admit. I do get a bit overzealous when it comes to the soup competition." Hattie stood and stacked the dirty dishes, her lips pinched together.

"A *bit?*" Joe smiled. "She'll start tomorrow, looking over recipes for next year."

Hattie carried the bowls to the kitchen sink. "Why don't we open gifts?"

"That'll work," Bobby said. "The kids will be asleep in a few minutes. Time for some adults' playtime."

After Tank and Sarah were settled into a crib, the group moved into the living room. Bobby hustled to the tree. He read the tags and handed out wrapped presents.

"He always does that." Hattie poked out her bottom lip. "I wear the Santa hat on purpose, and every year, my loving brother gets to sort out gifts. *So* not fair."

"Just hush and open this." Bobby passed her a sparkly gift bag.

"To Hattie from Mary-Esther," she read the tag, then glanced toward Mary-Esther. "Oh, you shouldn't have!"

Bobby spoke in a loud stage whisper to Mary-Esther. "Don't let her kid you. She *lives* for this part, even more than the soup thing."

Hattie dug beneath curled tissue paper and removed a small velvet box. When she opened the clasp, she gasped. A sterling hawk pendant rested on a bed of gray satin. "This is perfect!" She clipped the chain around her neck. "How did you know?"

"Know what?" Mary-Esther asked.

"I'll tell you the whole story later. Pretty cool." Hattie rested her fingers on the hawk pendant.

Jake spoke behind his hand, "Warning, Mary-Esther. Hattie thinks everything that moves, breaths, or creeps is carrying some sign from the great beyond."

Mary-Esther threw a befuddled look toward Jerry, then said, "Glad you like it. I spotted it in a little shop off the interstate when Jerry and I were on the way back from New Orleans. I found yours there too, Bobby."

"Too strange." Hattie motioned to Bobby, who held up his gift from Mary-Esther—a silver hand-tooled belt buckle with a similar hawk etching. "Hand her that little red box, bro."

Mary-Esther peeled the paper from the present and looked inside. A garnet and diamond ring sparkled in the twinkling tree lights. "Oh . . ." She held one hand to her chest.

Bobby and Hattie exchanged meaningful glances, then Hattie said, "It was Mama's. Ruby is her birthstone. We thought you might like to have something . . ."

The moisture left Mary-Esther's mouth. She slipped the ring onto her finger. Precise fit. As if it had been sized just for her. "Thank you." Her voice came out in a hoarse whisper.

Evelyn jumped up. "Don't be shy. There're gifts for everyone."

A few minutes later, the living room floor disappeared beneath a layer of crumpled Christmas paper.

"I simply love everything I got," Hattie said. "Thank you, everyone." She wore a chenille vest hand-sewn by Evelyn, Mary-Esther's pendant, and a new watch from Bobby and Leigh. She clutched a box of vanilla latte-scented beeswax candles from Shug and Jake, and the gift certificate for an hour massage, a gift from Elvina. Her Grinch-printed T-shirt held an array of stick-on bows.

"You can never say Hattie Davis Lewis hates Christmas," Jake commented.

"And she hasn't even gotten my present yet," Holston said.

"We have to wait on our gifts to each other until the morning so we'll have something to open with the kiddo." Hattie pecked her husband on the cheek.

Elvina pulled a gift from behind a chair and handed it to Mary-Esther. "I saved this for last."

When Mary-Esther removed the paper, she gasped. Her face grew warm.

"Thought you might like to have some family pictures, so I put together this collage. Took me some time to scan them into the computer. Not that I had anything more pressing to do with my foot in a cast."

Hattie leaned over Mary-Esther's shoulder. "This is great. You have pictures from way back. I don't even remember some of these. Look, Bobby. Here's one of us at the fish pond with Daddy."

"There's the Chevy we used to have when I was a senior in high school," Bobby said. "Man, was that a sweet ride."

Jerry pointed to a copy of a faded Polaroid. "This is Miz Tillie, right?" He looked at the picture, then to Mary-Esther. "You really do look like her. A lot."

"I figured you could hang it in your new house," Elvina said. "That way, you always have pictures of your family nearby."

Hattie handed over a decorative envelope. "Hope you might like this too."

Mary-Esther's fingers trembled. She slid out a sheet of pastel paper. She read the scripted print, then looked up.

"Mama never claimed to be a writer," Hattie said, "but she often mentioned how she had been the poet for her senior class. This is a copy of one of my favorite pieces, *At Twilight*, from a little handwritten chapbook I found in her bedside table right after she died." Hattie's eyes watered. "She loved twilight. Her favorite time of the day. Said it was when sundown made things soften, calm down. I especially like the line about the whip-poor-will's call. We had the preacher read this at her funeral."

"Excuse me." Mary-Esther leaned the frame against her chair and stood so suddenly, Elvis yipped and dove behind Spackle. She rushed from the living room, the pastel paper still clutched in one hand.

The front door slammed shut behind her.

Chapter Thirty-nine

Mary-Esther dashed through the misting rain. As soon as she slid into the driver's seat and wrapped her hands around the van's steering wheel, the tightness in her chest eased. The old vehicle—her safe place for over a year—enveloped her like one of her Nana's hugs. No matter how far she went, or where, the aging Chevy had proved the one constant. She concentrated on deep breathing. Quivers rattled her center.

A few minutes passed before Jerry entered the passenger's side and closed the door against the night's dreary dampness. "Want to tell me what that was all about?"

She closed her eyes and rested her forehead on the steering wheel. "I felt . . . trapped."

"Trapped. By what?"

She lifted her head. "I don't know. It's like the walls were closing in on me."

Jerry sighed. "Mary-E, I have to be honest. You absolutely confound me. Here, you traveled hundreds of miles in the hope of finding out if you had any family to claim . . . heck, that's what you were doing when I first saw you.

"You settle in, carve out a life for yourself. You seemed content, leaving New Orleans behind. Just as things are beginning to make a turn, you act like you're being backed into a briar patch with a shotgun aimed at your head." He motioned toward the house. "These people are doing their best to fold you into their family, into *your* family. What's your deal?"

Mary-Esther glanced at the poem, smoothed the spots where her grasp had fouled the damp paper. She stared from the rain-speckled window toward the lighted farmhouse. Indistinct, shifting forms silhouetted in the glow of flickering Christmas lights. The curtains were open, like the people inside.

She turned to face Jerry. "I want so badly to be here. I go through the motions. But something inside of me won't let me."

"I took a psychology class in college. You're having what I remember them calling an approach-avoidance conflict. That's when you want something strongly, but at the same time, are busy repelling it."

She tried for an amused huff, but it came out more like a derisive snort. "Didn't know it had a name."

Jerry held up his palms. "Those psychology types. They like to label everything. Makes life into a neat package."

"Did they say how to get beyond it?"

He shook his head. "Don't recall them ever giving any answers."

"What am I going to do, Jerry?" She strained to make out his features. The mist droplets reflected red, green, and blue from the outdoor holiday lights.

"Way I see it, you have two choices, Mary-E. You can pack up this van and high tail it out of here. You can keep moving from town to town, making a handful of acquaintances—won't call them friends. Friends require work and commitment. You can ditch the house. List all the stuff inside on eBay and pocket the money. Leave Boudreau with me, though. He deserves a stable home."

Her eyes burned.

"Every now and then, you might run up on a man who will take you into his bed for a night or two. He might even start to care, if you stay too long."

Trickles of water trailed down the windshield, gathering speed until they disappeared beneath the idle wiper blades.

"Or you can get your butt off your shoulders and march right back in there and start your life again."

Mary-Esther blinked back tears. "I'm not the golden person they, and you, believe I am. I'm not Tillie Davis's sweet baby girl, all pink and innocent." A pleading edge crept into her voice. "Don't you see, Jerry? For me to turn my back on my past would be like saying Nana didn't exist . . . or Loretta, for that matter. She wasn't a great mother. Far from it. But she was what I had. All the mistakes, I would gladly leave behind. But some things, I can't, and *won't*."

Jerry's words came out so soft, Mary-Esther strained to hear. "You're not the only one who's lost someone. You're not the only one who's been hurt. Who's scared."

When she glanced over at him, Mary-Esther noticed the muscles at his temples pulsing. How his eyes glimmered the way men's eyes do when they're forcing back tears.

"I love you, Mary-E. Probably did from the first time I laid eyes on you in front of the sheriff's department, eating that white bread bologna sandwich. I've only loved two women. Lost one. And it will hurt like someone's ripping out my soul all over again if I lose this one."

He opened the door and slid out, stood for a moment. Rain droplets peppered his hair and face. "It's your choice."

She watched him huddle against the drizzling rain as he walked back to the Davis farmhouse.

Mary-Esther's hand sought the small gold chain circling her neck. Her fingertips traced the lines of the diminutive cross. What would Nana Boudreau say?

Her grandmother's words popped into her mind—the words Nana said so many times when Mary-Esther's small world closed in, too scary to face. *Find your safe place, little one. Find your safe place and go there.* She touched the ruby ring circling her finger, the same ring her real mother had once worn.

When Mary-Esther closed the front door a few minutes later, Hattie glanced up. A wide grin transformed her face. "Good. You're back in time to help me serve the eggnog."

No probing questions. No need for windy explanations or apologies. Just her sister in a tacky holiday apron covered with stick-on Christmas bows, standing there with an egg white foam-coated spatula clutched in her hand like a fairy godmother's wand.

Chapter Forty

Mary-Esther admired the modest diamond ring circling her finger, not the smallest she had ever had. Heck, Ricky had never given her anything to mark that union. Certainly not the largest. Jesus took that prize. That one, hocked long ago. She'd pitched J.R.'s plain gold band into the gutter mud.

This one held the truest intent. Good thing Tillie's ruby fit the same finger on her right hand.

"Look, I know it's not much," Jerry had said as he presented the black velvet box the night before. Valentine's Day. What a romantic. "Can't afford Tiffany's on my salary."

"Oh." She had stared at the ring in its satin cocoon, maybe a little too long.

"And I know it's kind of sudden. Folks date for years before this kind of thing. I know what I want. I want to be with *you*, Mary-E. And I don't mean spending an occasional night together. Take some time to decide, if you need."

"I don't, Jerry." Yes. She had a history of fast, bad decisions. This one would be the charm. Had to be.

Add to the deal: she had met and actually liked her future mother-in-law. A lot.

Ricky's mom had hated her from the get-go for *stealing her baby*. Jesus's mother was deceased before he met Mary-Esther. And John R.— who knows where his mother was? Probably in rehab somewhere, or dead.

Mary-Esther heard Jerry's muffled curses. He crawled from beneath the Herring house. A mask of dirt and spider webs pocked his face. "Looks like the water's spewing from a broken pipe below the bathroom. Surprised all of them aren't leaking."

"What do you suppose it will take to fix up this place?" she asked.

Jerry wiped his face and hands with a faded bandana. "Old houses like this . . ." His shoulders rose and fell. "The framework's sound enough, but the wiring's shot. Not to mention, adding central heat and air. Now the plumbing."

"I love this house, Jerry. It's the first place I have ever had that was truly mine." No use counting Nana's, a pile of worthless rubble by the time she had inherited it.

Inside, four narrow glass shelves spanning the kitchen window housed her collection: feathers, slivers of river driftwood, and her rocks. First place Jake had helped her lay claim to the old home. One of Nana's rocks rested on the top shelf, separate from the others.

Hard to fathom, in a few weeks, the weather would shift. She'd turn the dirt for a vegetable garden. Tomato plants for sure. LaJune had already put in her order for as many as Mary-Esther would bring.

She ran one hand over the back porch banister. Flakes of dead paint confettied beneath her fingers. "I thought what Jake and I did on the inside was major."

"You're talking about a huge outlay, honey. If you have your heart set on it, maybe we could live in Quincy, or in the garage apartment, while we give this old girl an overhaul."

"I'll have to pull a lot of extra shifts." Money sifted through her life, again. Already, she and Jake had made four trips to home improvement stores in Tallahassee. Add to that, the cash she'd spent having the old photo restored. Worth every cent. Seeing Nana Boudreau smiling at her from atop the mantle made the house feel like home. The Davis collage hung on a nearby wall.

Jerry regarded the structure, clicking his tongue. "I can pick up some off-duty work."

Mary-Esther hugged him hard. "I can see us living here. Like Eustis and Rose. This house kept them safe and happy for years."

"Have any clue as to where Rose might have kept the original plans for this place? It would help me when I start working on the updates."

"Only spot I can think of is the little safe in the master bedroom closet. I've cleaned out everywhere else. Rose wrote down the combination and left it with the will."

In moments, Mary-Esther dialed the five-digit entry code and the safe's door clicked open. She pulled out a ragged pile of papers, some brittle with age.

"Here," Jerry held out a hand. "I'll take half."

Boudreau sauntered into the room, meowed, and settled at her feet.

A few minutes later, Mary-Esther dropped her portion of the papers back into the safe. "A lot of paid-off bank notes and a few sweet love letters, but no house plans. What about yours?"

"Unfortunately, no blueprints. Just this." He handed her a folded piece of parchment.

"It's some kind of bond." She read the date. "From the early nine-teen-hundreds. Where is this Gadsden County Bank?"

Jerry's brows furrowed. "SunTrust bought out the Gadsden County State Bank a few years back. Maybe that was the name back when this was issued."

"This bond was originally for a thousand dollars. Wonder if it's still good?"

"One way to find out. I'll call Kenneth Johnson, a buddy of mine who's one of their officers. He can research it for you," Jerry said.

"Even if it's worth a little more than face value by this point, it would pay for some supplies. Anything will help."

Mary-Esther poured two cups of coffee and sat down at the kitchen table across from Jerry. The new Cuisinart was getting a workout. The list for the home supply store took up two pages of a legal pad. Boudreau jumped into her lap and she scratched behind his ears. *Add cat door to the list*, she mused.

The phone rang. Jerry answered then glanced toward Mary-Esther. "Yes. Why?"

Jerry's face blanched. "Get outta here!"

Mary-Esther grabbed his arm. "What?"

"Thanks, Ken. I'm sure Mary-Esther will be in touch real soon." Jerry picked up his coffee mug and took his time taking a long drink.

"You going to share, or do I have to get rough?" Mary-Esther tickled him in the one spot on his side guaranteed to make him squirm. Boudreau gave an annoyed yowl and deserted her lap in favor of his food bowl.

"Let's say, at nine and a half percent interest compounded annually all those years, you won't have to worry about having enough to fix up this place." He winked. "Makes me glad I fell for you before you were rich. I'd hate for you to think I had been after you for your money, all along."

Chapter Forty-one

Mary-Esther curled her knit scarf around her neck. No matter how many layers she added, the late February cold seeped in.

"You want me to go with you?" Hattie asked.

"Thanks, but I'd like to do this alone if you don't mind."

Hattie pointed. "It's the third one from the end." She reached across the seat and cupped her sister's shoulder in one hand.

Mary-Esther took a deep breath. The scent from the van's new upholstery and carpet reminded her of the changes in her life. She ran her fingers across the buttery tan leather. Next week, the clunker would sport a fresh sky blue paint job. Rose's money could pay for a new ride, sure. But loyalty won out. Why would she commit the van to the junk metal pile when it had provided security for so many months? Old thing deserved a second chance too.

Same way with the job at the Homeplace. If she had to stay home every day, she'd scrape the ceiling. Perhaps Mr. Bill would consider selling the restaurant. And she'd be ready.

Mary-Esther fought the lump threatening to squeeze her airway closed. When she exited the van, the wind sliced through her coat.

Twilight, her *real* mother's favorite time of day.

She lifted her nose to the frigid air. Her eyes watered from the breeze. Tears added to the mix.

Rows of headstones extended to the edge of Highway 90, ten miles east of Chattahoochee. The same historic highway stretched beyond the horizon to cities and towns, some so small they had one sign marking the spot. Along its way west toward California, Highway 90 would meander to within half a mile of Nana's decimated neighborhood.

Soon, Nana's grave would have a new marker. Rose granite, with a simple cross etched above her name. Jerry promised a road trip as soon as the weather warmed, to honor the placement of the headstone, add in a couple of days to wander the streets in search of good food and jazz. Whitewash the dark memories. Maybe she'd talk the family into going along.

Beneath her boots, winter-dead grass complained with every step. Mary-Esther walked past the memorials for Whitaker, Jones, Adams, and Smith, then stood in front of a dark gray slab of granite surrounded by a marble-edged moat of pale gray chipped stones.

"Dan Davis and Tillie Davis," she said.

As if reading their names aloud would make it count somehow.

Her parents.

The ones she had started to know through Hattie and Bobby, through pictures, family letters, Tillie's poetry, from the stories shared by the people of Chattahoochee.

A battered black ragtop BMW convertible turned into the cemetery, trailing blue smoke. Crooked front bumper. Paint faded with dull hotspots where the clear coat finish had baked and peeled.

The car passed two rows over at a slow speed. The driver's head rotated side to side. No doubt, someone else checking addresses for their dearly departed. Dude had his hand slung over the steering wheel. Chin held up. Proud. The auto might have been a hot little ride at one time. Now, not so much. Probably didn't get it new, but at least he *got* it.

"Secondhand. Like me. A secondhand *sister*." The word still tasted strange.

Mary-Esther looked back at the van, at Hattie patiently waiting in the passenger seat.

No way could she and Hattie, or Bobby, return to their childhoods for a do-over.

"If I spend all of my time back *there*, I won't have room for right *here*." The brisk wind chipped her words. She'd had so many epiphanies lately; she might set up a booth and shower wisdom on passersby. Let them wash that wisdom all the way down Highway 90, back to the Big Easy.

She turned her attention to the second, smaller marker. Tiny etched hearts surrounded the name, and cupid-like angel figurines stood guard at its base on either side.

"Sarah Anne Davis." The instant Mary-Esther spoke the name, a wind gust raked her hair like icy fingers. She shivered and lowered herself to sit cross-legged amidst the marble chips covering the family plot.

Mary-Esther hunched her shoulders against the chill. She rubbed her numb hands together and cursed herself for not wearing gloves.

What could she say to a long-dead baby girl?

"You don't know me, Sarah, but I knew your mother and your Nana." She looked off into the purpled sky. "I'm here to tell you about them . . . and about me."

She reached in her pocket and placed the last of Nana's rocks in front of the gravestone.

White house paint lined her nails—a weird reverse French manicure—but the cuticles were intact, healed.

No need to pick them to shreds, trying to uncover the real Mary-Esther.

Not anymore.

THE END

Elvina's Pick-of-Summer Casserole

"This is my favorite summer casserole. The moisture from the tomatoes and onions ooze down onto the squash layer and keep it moist. Especially good recipe for when the garden produce starts to come in and folks drop squash, onions, and tomatoes off at the Triple C nearly every day."
  Elvina Houston

1 ½ pounds yellow squash, washed and sliced into ¼ inch cross sections (can use ½ Zucchini)
1 tsp seasoned salt
1 tsp pepper
1 tsp garlic powder
1 large Vidalia onion (or other sweet white onion), sliced into thin cross sections
3 large tomatoes, sliced (no need to peel)
8 oz. sharp cheddar cheese, shredded

Grease a large, shallow baking dish. (I use the same one I use when I make lasagna)
Place sliced squash in a layer on the bottom.
Sprinkle with the seasoned salt, pepper, and garlic powder.
Layer sliced onions over squash.
Cover onion layer with sliced tomatoes.
Cover top with shredded cheese.

Bake in a 400° oven for 15 minutes.
Reduce oven temperature to 375° and bake 40 minutes.
Makes six servings.

Hattie's Best and Easiest Spinach Salad

"Everybody who knows me will tell you I don't abide recipes that take hours or a long, picky list of ingredients. This is a light, refreshing salad. Sometimes, I substitute toasted pecans for the almonds, as we have plenty of pecans around here. I've also used raspberry vinaigrette dressing, though the bacon and honey flavors really add a kick."
Hattie Davis Lewis

1 bag fresh spinach, washed and drained
1 large red onion, thinly sliced
1, 11 ounce can of mandarin oranges, drained
8 ounce package of feta cheese, crumbled
1 cup toasted, slivered almonds
½ cup dried cranberries

Toss all ingredients together. Add Hidden Valley Honey and Bacon French dressing and toss to coat.

Serve with toasted French bread.

And a glass of wine. Before, and maybe after, you toss the salad.

Mary-Esther's "Boo-Coo" Bananas

"Nana taught me how to cook. When I have a proper kitchen, I can make gumbo, jambalaya, or a fantastic King Cake. For a while, I had no such luxury. A van in some random campsite was home, and a campfire went a long way to provide comfort. So did this simple dessert I invented one lonely evening. I suppose you could bake it in an oven—probably 400° for 15 to 20 minutes."
Mary-Esther Sloat

1 banana
1 chocolate bar
2 Tbsp. peanut butter
Heavy-duty aluminum foil

Wash outside of banana. Gently strip back one narrow section of the peel, but don't detach from the tip end.
Using a knife, split the banana's insides lengthwise and open slit slightly.
Mash peanut butter into the gap with a spoon.
Stick hunks of chocolate bar into the peanut butter.
Reseal the stuffed banana with the flap of peel.
Wrap the banana in two layers of heavy-duty aluminum foil.
Place wrapped packet directly into hot coals. Leave for 10 to 15 minutes.
Carefully remove hot packet from coals with tongs. Remove outer sooty layer of foil, then use a knife to split open the inner foil liner. Remove strip of peel.
Use the rest of the peel as a natural bowl.
Eat the gooey melted layer with a spoon.

About the Author

Rhett DeVane is a true Southerner, born and raised in the muggy, bug-infested forests of the Florida panhandle. For the past thirty-plus years, Rhett has made her home in Tallahassee, located in Florida's Big Bend area, where she splits her workdays between her two professions: dental hygienist and novelist.

Rhett is the author of five published mainstream humorous fiction novels set in her hometown of Chattahoochee, a place with "two stoplights and a mental institution on the main drag": *The Madhatter's Guide to Chocolate, Up the Devil's Belly, Mama's Comfort Food, Cathead Crazy,* and *Suicide Supper Club*. She is the coauthor of two novels: *Evenings on Dark Island* with Larry Rock and *Accidental Ambition* with Robert W. McKnight. In addition, Rhett has released two books in a series of middle grade fiction, *Elsbeth and Sim* and *Dig Within*.

Suicide Supper Club won first place in 2014 for fiction from the Florida Authors and Publishers Association. She'd wear the medal every day if it wasn't so heavy and perhaps a bit *braggity*. Plus finding earrings to match, there's that.

Rhett writes to stay balanced and reasonably happy. The way this world is today, it's a must. "Humor lifts me. As long as I am on this side of the dirt, I will find a way to laugh, and to share that with as many people as possible."

All of Rhett's titles are available on Amazon and other online vendors. To learn more about Rhett and her writing, visit her website: www.rhettdevane.com

Book Club Discussion Points

1. The idea of nature versus nurture plays into the plot in several places. How does Mary-Esther's upbringing reflect in the woman she is becoming? How would she have been different had she been raised with Hattie and Bobby on The Hill?
2. What both attracts and repels Mary-Esther about Chattahoochee, Jerry, and the Davis family?
3. In your circle of friends or community, do you have the equivalent of Elvina Houston? What role does Elvina play in the lives of the Davis family and the town?
4. What issues will Bobby face in his dealings with both Mary-Esther and Hattie?
5. Mary-Esther has close relationships with Rose Herring and LaJune Eldridge. What drives her to form such strong emotional connections with elderly women?
6. Mary-Esther carts a few belongings with her, notably her rock collection and Mother's ashes. If you had to leave your home and could take limited belongings, what would you take, and why?
7. How do you envision Mary-Esther, Hattie, and Bobby moving forward? What problems do you foresee?